ROAR OF THE STORM

ALSO BY ADAM BURCH

The Fracture Worlds Series

Song of Edmon

ROAR OF THE STORM

ADAM BURCH

47NORTH

This is a work of fiction. Names, characters, organizations, places, events, and incidents are either products of the author's imagination or are used fictitiously. Any resemblance to actual persons, living or dead, or actual events is purely coincidental.

Published by 47North, Seattle

www.apub.com

ISBN-13: 9781611097436
ISBN-10: 1611097436

Cover design by Katie Anderson

Printed in the United States of America

For Philip Eisner, Samantha Barrios, Matthew Bramante, Jack Conway, Matthew Mercer, and Abby Wilde—my stalwart, fearless, intelligent, and inspiring crewmates. This book is my vain attempt to get back to you wherever in the world you may be . . .

Twelve. The number of years I have sailed the vast since riding the rocket out of Tao's atmo.

Nine. Since the surgery to repair my voice with these artificial cords. I sound like I could melt the skin off horn-hide mako.

Seven. Seven years ago I completed the Inter-Fractural medical exam and received my license under the tutelage of the doctor who "repaired" my voice. Small compensation for the less than desirable results of his scalpel.

Three. That was when I joined the Universal Freight and Parcel service and Captain Ollie Rollinson hired me as chief medical officer aboard his ship, the *James Bentley*.

One. A year since I've set foot on Market, this amoeba-like planet of interconnected ships that lies at the heart of the Black Rose Path.

Half. Only half an hour since I learned that my father has died.

Now. I touch the scar on my neck as I relieve myself into the cantina's ceramic trough. *Never could go comfortably without a countdown since the Wendigo. At least my piss is falling instead of hovering. Thank the ancestors for artificial gravity.*

My mind recalls the words that scrolled across the *Bentley*'s comm screen . . .

Black Rose Newsfeed—09.09. Post Fractural Collapse, 5669 Galactic Standard

Edric Leontes, Patriarch of House Wusong-Leontes, has perished. Two-time champion of the Combat, Leontes rose from poverty to found a noble house of Tao's Pantheon. He allied with the imperial throne and served as Emperor Wusong's surrogate on the High Synod.

"His was a just and even hand," Synod member and political rival Phaestion, Patriarch of House Julii, eulogized during the lavish funeral ceremony. The entirety of the planet's capital city flooded the rooftops and skyways to pay homage to the fallen Patriarch.

"Edric Leontes was the last generation of old warriors," the lord of the Julii told the tearful crowd. "His final words to me were 'I stand on the precipice of the highest scraper, a promised land before me. Take what is yours by divine right.'"

Lord Julii then lit the death pyre. The megalopolis watched as Leontes's ashes rose into the twilight. House Leontes has no surviving heirs.

End Transmission

Deception, I think, and not just because the language paints him a hero.

My homeworld, Tao, rarely used to appear on the nets. A hinterland on the fringe of the Radial Corridor, it wasn't even worth mentioning. Now, it seems, the planet is garnering public interest. The members of the nobility, known as the Pantheon, have built a massive fleet. The largest since the evacuation of Miral, I'm told. They've stockpiled aural weapons and set their sights for their nearest neighbor, Lyria. Their aggressive posture has the whole Fracture on edge. No centralized government exists to curb a "barbarian tribe" like the Taoans; there hasn't been a full-scale planetary assault since before the fall of Miral. People do not believe such a thing could happen. Whether it can or not, all eyes are on Tao, and I am anxious because of it.

"Promise me we will always be friends, Edmon," Phaestion said to me once, like a dreadful prophecy. My old friend. My foster brother. Now the Grand Patriarch of Tao. Those days spent on my island home of Bone, training on her white shores, sailing the restless waves of the green ocean, were a serenity before the gale, before everything changed. Before he became a ruler, and I became a ghost.

House Leontes has no heirs.

But I am the heir of House Leontes.

I zip up my flight suit and dig my hand into my pocket. I touch the nose I cut from my father's face before I fled Tao. I had it cast in iron to keep.

Why do I feel rage at his passing?

Laughter behind me. "I read the dossier. Should be a challenge . . ."

Two muscular men from a high-grav planet sporting blue leaves for hair stand in the dirty refresher room. They slap Tag patches onto their beefy arms. Each patch contains the highly addictive stimulant that enhances physio-cognitive function at the cost of years off the junkie's life. It's familiar cargo aboard the *James Bentley*.

"What are you looking at, baldy?" the bigger of the two sneers, and my thumb quietly brushes the ivory flute scabbard at my hip. I'd like nothing more than to hear the siren sword sing, but there are easier ways to deal with bullies.

My master in the Wendigo, Faria the Red, hailed from a long-forgotten solar system whose star exploded at the end of a civil war. He was taken in by the Zhao monks and was taught to extend his life through manipulation of the body's meridians. Faria befriended me in the darkness of the prison and gifted me his knowledge. Healing is not the only application of the ability known as the Dim Mak, though . . .

"I'm sorry, Masters." The sound of my vocal cords is fingernails scratching metal as I use the skills The Maestro taught me to become someone else. I stoop my shoulders, lean on my cane, and crinkle my face like a decrepit old man instead of a strong man of thirty-two.

The blue hairs exhale with disgust. "What's wrong with you, gimp?" the shorter asks.

"Hard times, young sirs. Spare a quan?" I extend a palsied hand. They instinctively recoil, and I use the opportunity to trip forward onto them.

"Get off me, perv!"

"Forgiveness, sirs," I moan. I right myself, but not before I tap one on the back of the hand and the other on a pressure point on the inside of his elbow. I limp toward the refresher exit.

"Wait! I know you—" The blue hair's sentence is cut short by a sick look on his insipid face. There is a rumble of his gut. "Nine hells?" The man shakes and cannot stop himself from instantly shitting his pants.

"Jonesy!" His companion, too, is suddenly overcome with shock. He rears back like an ocean wave and vomits all over his friend.

"Stay off the drugs, kids." I shuffle out the door. The guise of decrepitude falls away, and I stand my full height, flexing my augmented muscles in the artificial grav. I inhale a deep breath of the sour, alcohol-filled air. I feel a little better, but there is something at the back of my mind. A tickling tendril of darkness in the air. I shiver with dread.

What was that? I wonder. *No matter.* I stride into the Leaky Engine.

The tarot is more than mystic fortune-telling. It is a mathematical equation translated into archetypes and symbols. The greater quintessence cards reveal the infinite dance of the universe and the inner truth of the bearer.

—Ovanth, *A Practical Reading of the Arcana*

BOOK I: EXILE

CHAPTER 1

The Gypsy

> The first card of the tarot is the gypsy. The wanderer seeks new environs, imparting awareness of what one brings to their own life as well as to others. No one is alone.
>
> —Ovanth, *A Practical Reading of the Arcana*

The sounds of neo-techno pulse in my brain as I make my way across the Leaky Engine dance floor. The cantina is a popular watering hole on Market for pirates and thieves who wander the Black Rose Path. The artificial gravity here makes it easier to pour drinks.

Market is one of the oldest "planets" in the Nine Corridors, but it isn't a planet at all, not even a space station, really. It was a star system along the Centra Fracture that made a convenient place for passing ships to trade goods and information. Eventually, someone had the sense to park. Others joined suit, and soon the place was an entire world of networked vessels connected by umbilicals. That was thousands of years ago. Now, one can float through the connector of a derelict micro-g warship turned clothing mart, then smack the floor of an old centrifugal freighter outfitted as a brothel.

I push my way past several phyto-mutants, denizens of the Nine Corridors who have spliced their genes with chloroplasts. Their hair looks like blades of grass, their skin a bright orange sheen. *Strange,* I think. *One doesn't usually see Planties in a food and drink establishment.* Then again, one doesn't usually see space gypsies, either . . .

A boy, delicate of build, with a shining bald head, falls through the plastic drapes of the umbilical frame. He makes the rube mistake of misjudging the room's spin and drops "up" onto the ceiling of the cantina. The Leaky Engine is one section of an old-style rotating hub, generating grav through centrifugal force. Customers walk along the interior walls with g's proportionate to Ancient Earth. The proprietors never thought three-dimensionally, though, and only used one-half of the sphere. *Maybe because humans still appreciate ceilings,* I think.

"Los!" I hear him berate himself even above the pulsing music of the place. My senses still remain highly attuned after years of training with Faria. The boy looks up sheepishly, thin arms quivering against the grav. His nictating eyelids blink away the fossil fuel haze. He crawls along the curved wall toward the "floor." Several salty spacers near the bar laugh at the rookie error. One of the phyto-mutants in front of me slaps his friend on a tattooed shoulder, and they make their way toward the boy, mischief on their minds. *I shouldn't get involved,* I think. Instead, I grimace and follow.

The spypsy looks no more than twelve, but he must be at least eighteen if he's not aboard an arc of Armada. Space gypsies, derogatorily referred to as "spypsies," are supposedly the descendants of the Mira. The story is that Mira technology and intelligence were unparalleled. They were the first people since the loss of Ancient Earth to transition from a type one to a type two civilization, harnessing the entire power of a star.

Of course, stories often hide the truth. Something went wrong. The world fell. The empire crumbled. Almost every human in the Fracture is a remnant of Miral's golden age, but the spypsies were the last to leave, fleeing the mysterious destruction of their homeworld in a fleet of giant spacecraft known collectively as Armada. They are born, live, and die almost exclusively aboard their arcs. Of course, no one other than a spypsy has ever seen an arc. They wander the vast on secret routes, and all those who go looking for the mysterious Armada vanish.

What is this boy doing here? I wonder. His eyes are wide, and his three eyelids blink innocently. *He's looking for someone,* I realize. Spypsies have genetically engineered so many strange traits into their germ line, they might even be considered a subspecies of the human race. This boy is no exception. Adhesive palms and feet from gecko DNA allow him to plaster himself to floors and walls even in micro-g. He has light, flexible bones and nary a hair on his body that would clog an air filtration unit. Nictating eyelids provide maximum lubrication for the dryness of air-conditioned ships, and slit pupils improve vision in low light. Aside from the obvious practical reasons to change their genome, I've also come to learn that spypsies do this because they are highly religious. They believe they will someday be restored to their former glory as overlords of humanity. One can imagine how that might not win them many friends among the rest of us.

The phyto-mutants shove through the crowd to the entry where they find the boy standing on quivering legs. The boy nervously eyes the booths in the shadows. The only time spypsy youth leave Armada or comingle with us "midden-mensch" is during the Rapzis, the holy pilgrimage to Miral. The young make the trip to the spypsy enclave on Market, then through secret space lanes to the dead world.

The spypsy takes a tentative step, and one of the phyto-mutants pretends as if the boy purposefully bumped him. "Watch it, spypsy!" He snags the boy's flight suit and shoves the kid to the floor again. To the boy's credit, he stands up instead of cowers. I like that. "Next time, my boot will smash that egg head of yours," the mutant sneers.

Now, terror crosses the boy's face. He desperately searches the crowd for whomever he's meeting in this pit. The mutants grin and step forward. My mind flashes to the day Phaestion's Companions—Sigurd, Perdiccus, and Hanschen—almost killed me. Talousla Karr, a spypsy, performed the surgery that saved—and enhanced—me. I don't like bullies.

"Move, and you'll regret it," I snarl. They whip around. I don't give them long enough to fight. I snatch the pinkie finger of one green-haired mook and twist. The man falls to his knees gasping. The other steps in. My left hand taps him lightly in the jugular. He freezes, unable to move anything below the neck. "Warned you."

"What did you do to me?" he grunts.

"Just a little love tap." I smile, yanking on the first one's pinkie. "Think about touching that kid again, and I break the rest of you. Do we have an understanding?"

"Yes!" they say in unison.

"Washo!" a familiar voice calls the boy from across the dance floor. *Damn it!*

"If you'll excuse me," I mutter, letting the fingers of the one go and tapping the other on the neck. He promptly topples over his companion. My eyes follow the shiny, pale head of the boy moving toward a booth in the corner. *Rollinson said we were to meet a new crew member to replace Old Madge, our last engineer who jumped ship after winning a tarot game on New Orland.* I didn't know it would be a spypsy.

The boy—the captain called him Washo—arrives at the booth. Portly Rollinson gestures for him to sit, but Washo stands stock-still, staring instead at the spritely girl with fire-red hair who's decked out in coveralls.

Ariel Lazarus, the ship's communications officer, has a thick workman's boot propped up on the table as if she owns the joint. She picks her teeth with a tiny metallic stick she probably snaked from a public quan dispenser. Washo takes in her smooth skin and full lips. His mouth hangs open. I don't blame him. My own heart beats a little faster, too. *She's not yours to gawk at, boy,* I think. *She's not yours, either, Edmon,* I admonish.

"Whatcha looking at, shorty?"

I grin at Ari's insouciance. She's twenty-two and has barely seen anything of the greater Fracture, but she has this intellectual passion, this insatiable curiosity for knowledge; it's almost addicting to watch her grow. But that's all I've done—watch. She's been aboard the *Bentley* almost a year now, and in that time, I haven't spoken but two full sentences to her. Sometimes I wish, but . . . *I can't get close to her or any of these people,* I remind myself. *Everyone I've ever loved only ended up dead.*

"Come here, Washo, my boy," the captain says. The spyp nods and squeezes in next to the others. I hang back and watch as the captain wraps a meaty arm around Washo's shoulders. The kid winces from the overpowering smell of alcohol. "Ladies and gents, it's my honor to introduce our new engineer, Washo Tan!"

Washo waves shyly. The rest of the crew barely grunts. They're deep in a game of tarot.

"Knave," Clay Welker, the ship's pilot, calls out with his posh, debonair accent. He lays the thin metallic card on the table, his archetype. *The outlaw card. Fitting,* I think. Welker, in his midthirties, has chiseled good looks and the fastest pistol draw I've seen in the Nine Corridors. He tosses his longish hair out of his eyes and leans back, reveling in his fortune. Welker almost always wins. He can fly just about anything with an engine, too. He'd probably be a better captain than Rollinson, were it not for the fact that he's also a Tag addict.

Ari looks up slyly with sparkling blue eyes of admiration at the pilot, and my blood boils. *I hate the man.*

"He's a mechanical genius. A real-life spypsy!" Rollinson exclaims, gesturing again to Washo. Washo shifts uncomfortably at the pejorative, and it occurs to me how ignorant the rest of us midden-mensch are of his kind.

"The outlaw plays his hand, I see." Tol Sanctun, gangly in a top hat and trench coat, scratches his scraggly beard. "Well, handsome, I counter with cups of gas!" Our navigator lays his card down. The minor suit is pointless to play, unless there's a joke in it . . .

"Nine hells, Tol!" Welker scrunches his nose and waves his hand in front of his face.

"Cups of *gas*—get it?" Tol laughs. "Silent but deadly humor was a high art form on Ancient Earth. This show about these four kids who lived in snowy parks of the south once had an episode where they blew up an entire continent with the power of flatulence . . ."

Tol is the ship's navigator and in his forties, the oldest of our crew save Rollinson. Apparently, he grew up mostly on the *Bentley*, his father being the ship's first navigator, but Tol doesn't seem to know a star chart from a hole in the hull. He only has the job because of his history with Rollinson. What happened to Papa Sanctun, I don't know. I only know his son's real gift is his ability to steal and hide anything he can get his hands on, aside from constantly regaling us with stories of Ancient Earth culture.

"Shut up, Tol," everyone at the table murmurs. No one ever understands his references. I suspect most aren't even accurate.

"Introductions!" the captain continues. "Pilot Clay Welker, navigator Tol Sanctun, communications officer Ariel Lazarus . . ."

"Welcome aboard," Ari says with a smirk. She lays a tarot on the table, and Welker shakes his head. For once, he's been outmaneuvered.

"Djiekuje bardzo, pani," Washo whispers in a strange language.

Ari stops and looks at the spypsy. *"Przepraszam?"* she asks.

Washo's jaw drops.

"*Przepraszam*. I said, 'Excuse me?' I wasn't sure if I heard you right," Ari says.

"You speak Nicnacian?" Washo is flabbergasted.

"I do now." She smiles mischievously.

"Ari can hear a word or two of something and practically speak it fluently within minutes," Rollinson explains.

"Tell her all the time she ought to take that trick on the road." Welker grins.

"And leave you guys behind?" Ari tosses her pick at him playfully. I grit my teeth.

Rollinson and the others might consider Ari's abilities a mere parlor trick. Many in the Nine Corridors display unique gifts, be it due to pharmacological enhancement, biological manipulation, or some combination of training and surgery, as in my own case. The fact remains, however, that I've never seen something as superhuman as Ariel's linguistic powers. And no potential is conferred upon an individual without some sort of extensive tampering.

My mind flashes for a moment on my foster brother, Phaestion. Humans' attempts to artificially give themselves demigod-like powers always come at a price. And then I wonder, *Who is this girl really?*

"That leaves . . . say where is—?" The captain looks around the room for the missing crew member.

I might as well get it over with. I step from the shadows. "Move." My voice is metal slashing metal. Washo shudders as I loom over him. *That's right, boy. I'm a monster.*

Tol whistles. "Doctor Batman finally decides to join us," he quips. The nickname has something to do with my abrasive intonations I suppose, though the reference is lost on me.

"Washo, this is the ship's physician, Dr. Edmon Leontes," Rollinson says, ignoring the tension.

Washo waves. He's frightened, alone. He needs a friend. *I can't be a friend,* I remind myself. So I scowl.

"Deal you in, Doc?" Rollinson asks, pulling out his tarot deck.

"No." I raise my sword in its scabbard, disguised as an ivory cane, and use it to push the spypsy aside and sit. I don't play tarot. I've never been gifted an archetype card for one. I don't believe that a higher power determines destiny for another. The purpose we give ourselves is the only purpose. *What is your purpose, Edmon?* I ask myself.

"Leontes's skills are much better than his bedside manner." The tall, alluring, dark-haired woman across the table flashes a stare in my direction.

"Leontes? Like the fabled Anjin commander of Miral?" Washo asks with some combination of fear and awe.

I mask my surprise. The name means little to most denizens of the Fracture Worlds, and I'd prefer to keep it that way.

I turn away from Washo and match the fierce look the soldier woman flashes at me from across the table.

"Last but not least, Xana Caprio," says Rollinson. Xana is the ship's security. She joined last year and immediately hated me. Even more when Ari came aboard soon after. They are of an age, but Xana watches Ari like a mother seal. It wasn't a coincidence that Ari ended up aboard the *Bentley*; I suspect she had been looking for her childhood friend and finally found her manning our lone gun station. The two mostly pretend that whatever happened between them growing up on Lyria together never occurred, and at times they seem the best of friends, sisters really. Then I will catch Xana watching Ari from afar with a look in her eye of something more . . .

Xana stares at me now with a challenging gaze, and not for the first time I can't shake the feeling that we've met somewhere long before she ever joined the crew of the Bentley. Ironically, she's the only crew member I'd trust in a fight, though I don't want to find out who would win if we had to face each other.

Washo practically bows to her in greeting. *Curious. Both Xana and Ari garner some sort of unqualified deference from him.*

"Welker? I said, Welker?" The captain repeats. "Your move?"

Our pilot is distracted. He has been eyeing the crowd nervously. I can't tell if he's looking for a way to score or if he senses something amiss.

Your thoughts are clouded, Edmon, I can almost hear Faria admonish me. My father's death, this new crew member . . . I, too, am distracted. *The ties that bind are the ties that blind.* I know the truth of my master's words. *I've been blind before. It won't happen again.*

"Lovely to meet you, spyp. If you'll excuse me . . ." Welker gathers his cards.

"Where are you going?" Ari asks.

Is it wrong it irks me that she cares?

"Oh, here and there." Welker rights a wide-brimmed hat on his head and saunters off.

"The intrepid crew of the United Freight and Parcel starship, *James Bentley*," Rollinson says, gesturing to us all. "Let's see what the fates have in store!" He lays a card on the table and turns it over. "Why I remember the time I flew into—" Rollinson's usual tall tale-telling is stopped cold when he sees the card.

I've never been superstitious. I couldn't give a sea urchin for the religious, magical thinking one finds everywhere along the Black Rose Path. But I've watched enough tarot to know the cards have uncanny predictive capability. Turning over a facedown often prognosticates a future event. There's a scientific explanation, even if I don't know what it is.

The hanged man—suspense before a fall, sacrifice for a change. Those are the fanciful readings. A man dangles from the World Tree, dead. The person who draws the hanged man is rarely the same after he does, if he even lives.

"I better head back to the ship and take care of some, um, business." Rollinson's voice quivers. He's scared. "We're bound for Nonthera. With very . . . lucrative cargo. We'll need a full saw to get us there in double the time. Just have to play our . . . cards . . ." The captain blanches at his own words and then ungracefully squeezes his girth from the booth.

"He forgot his tarot," Washo comments meekly.

Something's not right.

"Well, this is no fun." Ari stands up from the table. She holds her hand out to me. "May I have this dance, darling?" Her eyes shimmer in the strobing light of the bar. A blush blooms on her cheeks, and for the barest instant, I feel handsome.

I wish I could take her hand, but I don't deserve to. It would dishonor the memory of my wife. I'm a coward who ran from the Combat. I'm too ugly, too broken. Take your pick. I stare angrily instead. The briefest look of hurt crosses her face before she replaces it with a sarcastic eye roll. "Fine. Care for a dance, short stuff?"

"A dance?" The boy looks perplexed. She shakes her head and moves off without him.

"Be careful! I don't like the look of—"

Ari raises her hand without even turning, cutting off Xana's warning. But Xana senses it just as I do—danger in the sweaty, gasoline-scented air, ready to spark.

"May I ask a question?" Washo asks. "Who is James Bentley?"

"Only one of the first colonists through the Fracture from Ancient Earth!" Tol Sanctun twirls a fork between his fingers. "You know anything about Ancient Earth, Washo?"

"Here we go," Xana mutters.

Washo shakes his head. Unbroken written records date to the Miralian Empire, not before. Tol claims to know more than anyone about our ancestors before the Fractural Collapse, when Earth was cut off from humanity forever.

"I'm just trying to figure out what he knows," Tol protests.

"You think to make him a fan of Led Leopard?" Xana clucks.

"Led Zeppelin!" Tol shouts back. "Def Leppard. Led Zeppelin."

"They both sound like schools of tillyfish!" I bark over the neo-techno. The dance floor is filled with phyto-mutants like those from the refresher room and the dance floor earlier. Planties rely on their chloroplasts to metabolize solar energy for nourishment—it doesn't make sense for so many of them to patronize an establishment that serves food and drink.

And they are tense. I sense hearts beating faster than the pounding of the music. I feel it in my bones. *Something is about to happen.* I stand, grab my cane, and stalk off. *I need a better vantage point.*

"What's a tillyfish?" Washo asks in my wake.

"Leontes comes from a planet half-covered in water," Xana answers.

"It's also half-covered in crazy," Tol adds. "You ever been to Tao? A bunch of backward feudal lords doing some bizarre Japanese-Greek-Hiberno-Norse cosplay shit. Doctor Batman is Game of the Rings meets the Spartacus Duniverse. I wouldn't be surprised if he had murdered his own child by his sister."

It was my father who murdered my child, you piece of . . . There's a tingling in my bones. A hint of Tag permeates the room. I relax my eyes. Flashes of blue and green—the hair of the various phyto-mutants. Arm tattoos indicate pirate gangs. My hearing picks up faint sounds of earpiece communication . . .

"Move on the weak ones first. Package delivery is foremost. Thrance has paid too much for anything less."

Thrance?

A cry sounds from the dance floor. "Back it off, butch!" Ari raises her fist at a mutant's sweaty meat face.

"Or what?" He shoves Ari into the arms of a comrade who slaps her across the back. She crashes to the floor. I white-knuckle my cane. *Wait!* prudence tells me.

But Xana is on her feet so fast I barely see it. She throws herself at the toughs with maternal ferocity. She kicks one in the groin and simultaneously knocks out another with a back fist.

Gauge your enemy. Who are they? What are their intentions?

Quickly, the entire bar erupts in violence. Bottles smash. Screams burst. It's full pandemonium. Green-haired fiends crowd the dance floor. They run at the dark-haired battle goddess. Xana whips an extensor staff from her belt. She thumbs the activator, and it expands from baton into staff length. She clears the floor with practiced efficiency.

Xana turns and finds herself staring down the barrel of a shotgun. The gunman switches the safety from electropulse to bullet. A hush descends over the Leaky Engine. A projectile can cause hull breach. Decompression means sudden and painful death for everyone. That's why projectiles are outlawed almost anywhere there is vacuum living. Of course, humans are notoriously stupid.

No one dies while I'm here. I glance at the bar where Clay Welker hovers in the shadows, already in place to cover us. Advantage—UFP *James Bentley*. I silently make my way through the crowd until I'm behind the mook with the gun.

"Make a move, bitch." He grins at Xana.

"You first," I whisper in his ear. The mutant turns. My hand taps his neck. He crumples to the floor, asleep. I grab the gun before it drops, too, and snap it like a twig over my knee.

"I wouldn't try it." *Right on time.* Welker's pistol is trained on the bartender's temple. He clicks the safety from radiation pulse to slug, and the man raises his hand away from the panic button under the bar. "You're going to let us walk away, no harm, no foul." Welker's voice remains tight. "Right, Tol?"

Sanctun is kneeling over one of the fallen toughs, rummaging through the man's clothing. "Just a second, fearless leader."

"Tol?" Xana hisses.

"All right, all right," Tol whines as he pulls a timepiece off the man's wrist. The watch disappears into the folds of his trench coat like a magic trick.

I glance at Washo. The boy sits in the booth and stares. *Is it mere coincidence he joined us right before being attacked?*

Ari stands up and folds her arms across her chest. She stares right back at the boy. "I have enough people gawking at me, spyp, without adding you to the list." She fires me and Xana a narrow-eyed look. "Come on!" she shouts as she grabs Washo from the booth and pulls him to his feet. "Don't think that table jockey won't call security the instant we slip through the air lock. I would very much like to avoid our ship being impounded and us being thrown into the pen while the constabulary tries to sort this mess."

CHAPTER 2

The Hanged Man

The first step along the path of change is to surrender one's old self, return to the womb, in order to be born anew. The Hanged Man is a literal and spiritual death of an old way of being, an inversion, prior to gaining a new perspective.

—Ovanth, *A Practical Reading of the Arcana*

"Let's shake!" Welker commands the moment the air lock seals behind him. We all hover in micro-g now that we've passed the threshold of the Leaky Engine. We push off the walls and soar through the tunnels with Xana taking point while Welker keeps his pistol trained on our six. "Hopefully Old Ollie Rollie is back on board, and our engine will be primed for maximum burn!" Welker shouts.

"If not," I interject, "we'll all see if our new spypsy boy is actually as good as Rollinson thinks he is." My eyes flash at Washo Tan. He cringes.

Washo turns away and pushes off the tube wall at top speed. It's my first opportunity to see his adaptations in action. The sticky pads on his hands and feet; his light, flexible body—all of it allows him to move through the corridor with an efficient grace. He dutifully pastes himself to the circular walls of the tunnel when he gets too far ahead so as not to outfloat the rest of us. He looks innocent, but I'm not the trusting kind. Neither is Xana; I notice her eyeing the boy as well.

"Wait up!" Tol shouts as he pinwheels in the weightlessness. I grab the fool by his collar and yank him along with us.

"Market security will be breathing down our necks any second," Welker calls out. "Last thing we want is the *Bentley* impounded when we have hot cargo to deliver. Soon as feet hit deck, I want the fracture saw ready to cut full vibration for Nonthera."

"Aye, aye, Captain Stubing." Tol spins midair and salutes.

"I said Nonthera, Tol. Not Thera or Frontera or any other planet that ends in *era*," Welker warns.

"You talk like I don't know what I'm doing."

Washo whispers to Ari, "He doesn't know what he's doing, does he?"

Xana's eyes narrow. She doesn't like the boy's interest in Ari any more than she likes mine. I can't say I blame her.

"Problem." Xana floats to a bay window that overlooks the docking area where hundreds of ships connect to Market with umbilicals. She points to a clunky cylinder of steel pipes and girders mounted on massive rocket engines—the *Bentley*. It's without a doubt the poorest, most ragged excuse for a starship in the entire hub. Standard issue for UFP.

"The old Pepsi can herself." Tol winks at Washo. "Be young. Have fun."

"Wait. I think security has a detachment at the umbilical. I'm guessing four, maybe five officers." Xana points at the bulging tube connecting the *Bentley* to the hub. It's an educated guess, but Xana's battle intuition is usually spot-on, honed by years of some kind of specialized training.

"Actually, I count five exactly," says Tol. "All sporting pulse batons."

Tol has no such training, and his observation is way too specific to be coincidence if correct. *There's no way he could see through the umbilical . . .*

"He's right." Ari calls up a holographic interface from a wall panel. I fire Tol a suspicious look, and he shrugs.

Meanwhile, Ari swipes through lines of bioluminescent binary code until a security cam feed illuminates a view of an umbilical. Sure enough, five security officers crowd the micro-g corridor readying their weapons. Ari's hands are a blur of motion, swiping through more holographic code.

"What are you doing?" Xana asks.

"Connecting with the Market mainframe." She winks.

"How are you reading all that code so fast?" Tol asks.

Welker's brow furrows in puzzlement. "Market has no central system."

"That's what you think, hotshot." She grins at the handsome pilot. *Damn him.* "Computer systems build bonds, a sort of rudimentary connective tissue over time. Market's been here thousands of years. There's no control center, but it doesn't mean there aren't pathways." Her hands swipe faster.

"She's going all *Minority Report* on them, Maverick!" exclaims Tol.

A klaxon sounds. We turn to the porthole and watch as the umbilical connecting the *Bentley* to Market suddenly depressurizes and pops loose from the ship. A rush of atmosphere and five armored guards are blown out the tubing. They slam into the rusted hull of the *Bentley* and bounce off into the vacuum.

"Did you just kill those men?" Washo asks, his voice trembling.

"By the twisted star." The whispered epithet escapes me.

"Not yet." Ari's fingers dance across the keyboard. The image is replaced by a holographic control stick that she curls her fingers around. A giant trash hauler passes over the *Bentley*, the maw of its collection bin open. It scoops up the five guards, who had been destined for a cold death in the vast.

"Nice work, love." Welker smiles.

"Reconnecting," Ari says. The tube from Market reconnects with the *Bentley*, and a puff of oxygen exhales into space as the seal locks.

The others float ahead, but I grab Welker by his leather jacket and slam him into the bulkhead. "Bollocks, Doctor!" he says, grunting, the wind knocked out of him.

"Next time, Welker, just let me take them out. I don't want anybody dead because of us, understand? Anybody!" It's my one rule.

"I'm not your fearless leader, you know. I don't call the shots, as it were." He slowly extricates himself from my grip. "I want burn in under sixty!" he shouts to the others down the corridor and pushes off.

I catch Washo lingering. He's scrutinizing me, trying to figure out my game, whether or not Welker is someone he can trust, whether or not I'm someone he can trust. "Move it," I mutter. He blanches. *I'm your nightmare, boy. If that scuffle on the floor of the Leaky Engine wasn't an isolated incident, we'll find out quickly enough. And if you had anything to do with leading those mercenaries to us, I may seriously consider breaking my rule.*

We propel ourselves through a few hundred meters of industrial tubing, then squeeze into the umbilical, and finally through the entrance hatch of the *Bentley*. Washo uses his sticky pads to dart down the tube to the engine room. Xana pulls herself up railings to the gunner station while the others head to the cockpit. I duck into the ship's tiny med bay and strap myself in. I close my eyes, replay the events in my mind, and try to understand the pieces in play. *My father dies. Those mutants in the refresher recognize me. The boy joins our crew. Ari is accosted . . . Is there a connection?*

"Roll call scan complete," Xana announces over the comm. "All six crew and one captain asleep in his quarters accounted for."

"No need to wake him unless this gets out of hand," Welker mutters. "Where's my cold fusion, spyp?" he shouts.

"Coming up, sir!"

Talousla Karr! I think. Talousla Karr, also a spypsy, served House Julii. He was not of Armada. If this boy is not with his own people on Armada, it may mean he is also a renegade. *Could the two be involved somehow? Does my father's death mean Phaestion has come for me after all this time? Or am I linking things that are unrelated?*

Welker hits the accelerator. The engine wheezes like a dying lunger as it huffs our junker out of dock. "Set a course for the Fracture Point," Welker says. There's a pause over the comm. "Tol . . . ?"

"You have to triangulate after the calculator gives the degree, idiot!" Ari hisses over the static.

"Vector, Victor. Roger, Roger," Tol responds. I shake my head. The *Bentley* lurches out of the dock. The security tower sails past my small porthole as Welker shoves our bucket into a dive no sane pilot would attempt. It skirts us under the half-hearted blockade of Market security picket ships.

"Woo!" he shouts over the comm system.

Show-off, I think. *I wonder if he's Tagged up recently.*

Then it's darkness as we head into open space. I unstrap from my harness, unsheathe my siren sword of Albion, and lay it gently on the medical cot. It hovers above the bed in the micro-g. It's an elegant instrument of death, but I've never truly had to use it. I reach into my pocket and rub the iron-cased nose of Edric Leontes. I remember his icy gaze, fierce, and penetrating, just before I cut the nose from his face. *I should finally feel free,* I think. *I'll never see those cruel eyes again. But somehow it feels the past is hunting me still . . .*

It was my father who had my vocal cords removed to ensure I would never sing again. I've tried to hang onto the music in a small way by fashioning my sword's sheath as a flute, and I lift it to my lips now. Heart to thought, thought to voice, I breathe into the woodwind. Music ripples through the corridors of the *Bentley*, a lament. A warrior has fallen.

"Aw, come on, Doc," Tol groans over the comm. "Put a little beat in this bucket!"

My flute's melody is pierced by raring electronica. Tol's music of Ancient Earth *suggesting that someone pour sugar on them.*

I grit my teeth. A chill washes over me. That tickle of darkness curling again in the back of my brain. *Do the others feel that, too?* I wonder. *Almost like death . . .*

I float down the gray, rusty steel access tube. It ends in a small spherical chamber where the cylindrical nuclear fusion reactor sits, shielded by its heavy metal plating. Washo Tan, his little bald head poking out of his radiation suit, floats upside down, eyes closed, legs folded.

"Urizen, Uveth, Los, Ameryka . . ."

He whispers strange words in prayer. Holy words. *I don't believe in holy things.*

The boy senses my presence, and his eyes snap open. He starts with a gasp at my frightening gaze.

"Rollinson cleared you for duty aboard the *Bentley*. I haven't," I growl.

"Sorry. I was just . . . never mind." Washo's voice trembles. He brushes at his radiation suit nervously.

"Come." I head back up the access tube toward the med bay without a glance behind. Moments later, the boy is buckled to the med bed as I fix electrodes to his body and take his vitals.

"We have a little time before the Fracture Point is in range. That gives me a moment for my metrics." *Also for me to discover whether or not you serve my enemies.* The boy nods, fearful at being alone with me. "Where do you come from, Washo Tan?" I ask.

The med screen confirms my observations. His DNA has been spliced with amphibious base pairs and even some avian characteristics. His structure might even be suited to aquatic environments if not for the pressure differential. He would no doubt suffer ill effects in any grav environments.

"I hail from Armada," Washo answers nervously.

He doesn't like that I'm asking about his past. Everyone on board the Bentley *is hiding something . . .*

"All fools in the Nine Corridors know spypsies are born on Armada." I growl and place a depressor on his pointed tongue. "I want to know which of the five you were born on."

"Six!" he blurts. I smile to myself and remove the depressor as the boy realizes he reveals more than he intends. "There are six ships of Armada," he says more subdued.

"Ah, yes. Six arcs fled the destruction of Miral. And which are you from?"

"Why?" Washo's eyes narrow.

I shrug as I tap his knees to test his reflexes. "An alpha ship might carry leaders or wealthy elites. Perhaps each ship has its own government? Maybe there are cultural mores aboard one ship and not another. It seemed you were praying earlier. If that is something you do at specified times, I've no desire to infringe upon your privacy. Knowing might be of use to me as your doctor."

Washo purses his lips, unwilling to say more. In the Wendigo, I would have grabbed him by the lapels of his flight suit, hurled him against the wall, brought my face centimeters from his, and fleered with rage to make him talk. This is different. He's a boy in an unfamiliar world. I'll learn more by pretending to be his friend. *I'm just not very good at pretending.*

"There is a legend," I continue in the most sympathetic tone I can muster, "of a seventh arc ship."

His eyes widen. "You have heard of Fuzon?" he whispers.

Fuzon. Another strange word. I'll need to learn more about these people; the boy might tell me, if I can build his trust. *"Seven ships for the seven children, into the black they sail, Carrying with them the seed of hope, that rebirth of sky prevails."* I recite the popular nursery rhyme. Washo's eyes dart everywhere except to meet my gaze. *So it's more than a simple rhyme.*

"I know the words," I say. "Not what they mean. As you said there are only six arcs." He shifts in his seat uncomfortably. *Perhaps if I reveal something from my past, he'll reveal something of his.* "In my time, on my planet, I met a spypsy who claimed he was not of Armada."

"Was he of Fuzon?" Washo asks suspiciously.

"I was hoping that you might know the answer."

He bites his lip in consternation. Everything I see tells me he wants to trust but feels it's a betrayal of something or someone if he does. *Trust to be trusted. Or at least give the appearance of.* I reach inside the medicine cabinet and remove something I've not held for a long time. The wood paneling of the tablet feels smooth and ancient. The metallic pins of the screen spring to life in my hands. They ripple under my touch.

"What is it?" Washo asks. I hand him the nightscript reader I received in the Wendigo. "This is Mira! How did you get this?"

"My mentor gave it to me before he died." *Before I took his life.*

"Can you read it?"

"I'm told it contains the data banks of the old empire, including geographical maps of Miral. I've cross-referenced every known system along the Black Rose Path but cannot find a planet that matches the data in this reader. I was hoping you could help."

"Miral is a forbidden world."

"Forbidden to outsiders," I snap. He says nothing. *Damn it.* I return the reader to the medicine cabinet. "I suppose it's important for spypsies to keep their secrets." I dismiss him with a wave.

He unbuckles from the bed and floats toward the hatch.

"Washo," I say, stopping him. "It's forbidden to outsiders. I suspect you're now an outsider, too." I say it with as much sympathy as I can with my harsh voice. It's a gamble . . .

"Nicnacians," he says with a sigh of acquiescence. "The Nicnacian faith was the religion practiced by the matriarchy. Only the faithful were allowed to survive on the arcs. We do not call ourselves spypsies."

Nicnacian. It's the true name of the space gypsies. I nod, understanding that he has just given me a piece of his past, if only a small piece. *This word matters. It isn't much, but it is a beginning.*

"My people were once of Miral, too," I add quietly. "Soldiers bred by the empire. They followed their general in rebellion and eventual escape. Perhaps we are less different than one would think." I rub my smooth pate for emphasis.

His eyes linger on my sword-cane, which is locked to its mount on the wall. "You're not like any man I know aboard Uveth arc."

Uveth, I think. *He's answered my first question.*

"Washo, do you copy?" Welker's voice cuts in over the comm.

The boy floats to a panel in the hall tube. "I'm here. I'm here. What is it?"

"We've picked up a bogey!" Tol shouts. "Not a single Bacall!"

The boy fires me a look of confusion. "We're being followed," I growl over his shoulder. *I knew this wasn't over.*

"We're going to need a hotter burn," Welker says.

Washo pushes off the wall, angling down the tube toward the engine room.

"Welker," Xana's husky voice interrupts on the speakers. "Looks like a war skiff. We'll never outrun it."

"Market security?"

"Too well designed. Much faster. More guns," Xana answers.

"UFP *James Bentley*. Cease acceleration. Prepare to be boarded. Do not comply, and you will be forcibly disabled," an altered voice sounds throughout our ship.

"Incoming vessel, this is UFP *James Bentley*," Ari responds. "Please identify yourselves and state your purpose." Only static breaths respond. "Incoming vessel, please identify. This is a registered United Freight and Parcel vehicle bound for port. Any disruption of our flight violates Interstellar Code 1701 of the noncombatant Free Trade—"

"UFP *James Bentley*. Cease acceleration. Prepare to be boarded," the eerie warble intones again.

"Ari, cut the feed," Welker commands. "Captain Rollinson, to the bridge."

Again, static. *Where in the abyss is Rollinson?* I push off the wall at top speed, hurtling toward the crew closets.

"Captain," Welker says, hailing me as I fly. "I know you said you didn't wish to be bothered, but it's a mite important. Sir?" Static. "Ari, stall them. Xana, Tol, and Doc meet me at the captain's closet."

I'm already there. I override the panel on the door lock with my medical authority.

By the twisted star . . .

The captain has hooked his feet to the floor railing and tied a belt around his neck. The belt is connected to the interior of a cabinet door, which he has closed to provide the necessary tug. Somehow, I'm not surprised to see him dead—*a hanged man.*

CHAPTER 3

The Sea Wolf

The hungry-eyed sea wolf seems terrible with yellow eyes and razor fangs, but his aggression is a mark of his fear. This predator faces the darkness alone, but the sea wolf is a creature of the pack. He needs a family to survive.

—Ovanth, *A Practical Reading of the Arcana*

I float into the closet to examine the deceased. Rollinson is naked but for the flight suit rumpled around his ankles. Tag patches are slapped haphazardly over the folds of his belly. He's cold. A corpse for over an hour at least.

"Damn." Tol whistles behind me, indicating the massive erection jutting from between Rollinson's legs. "The captain was packing. I guess rigor mortis is, like, really a thing?"

"Shut up, Tol." Xana shakes her head in disgust.

"What is—?"

I interrupt Welker and hurl myself at him in fury, plowing him against the tubing wall. "You!" I shove my finger into his face. "This is because of you!" The pilot's face is a mask of fear and confusion. "That's Tag from your stash all over his body. If not for you, we might still have a captain!"

"Why would I give him Tag, Doctor?" Welker shouts back even as he trembles. "I'm an addict. I don't share. Even if I did, I didn't strap a belt around Rollie's neck and play wank and yank."

"He's right, Leontes," Xana's icy voice interrupts. "Welker has been in the cockpit since we boarded. This was Ollie's own doing."

Seething, I release Welker from my grasp. "This is too convenient."

Rollinson always had a drunk, avuncular way about him, constantly telling stories of impossible adventures, making himself an improbable hero in them. He was always searching for a grift, scamming to smuggle illegal cargo or to make an extra quan, but he did have something of a conscience. I don't believe he would have been disquieted enough by drawing the hanged man card to risk his life and a so-called big payday with drugs and autoerotic asphyxiation. That is, unless he knew he had done something that he was going to die for anyway. He left the Leaky Engine right before we were attacked. He came back to the *Bentley* and ended it all just before these pirates hailed. The likely conclusion? He knew it was going to happen.

"It's done," Xana says coldly. "The question is what action now?"

"Can I have his coat?" Tol asks. He's already going through Rollinson's possessions and pocketing anything he thinks might be of value. "Unless anyone else wants it, I'm taking his coat."

"We can't let Fracture pirates board the *Bentley*," Welker says vehemently. "They'll enslave or kill us after they find what they're looking for."

"We can't outrun or outgun them, either," replies Xana. "Their ship is small enough to fit in our cargo bay, but she's fast as all starlight and armed to the teeth."

"The Market star!" Tol snaps his fingers. "We use gravity like a slingshot to shoot us around the Market star toward the Fracture Point. Physics!"

"Shut up, Tol!" we all say in unison.

"It worked in *Star Trek IV*." He shrugs as he slides his arms into Rollinson's oversize duster.

Welker hits a comm panel on the wall. "Ari, Washo, meet us outside the captain's closet." He switches off the comm. "Doctor?"

I nod and grab a sheet off Rollinson's pallet. I quickly drape the body as I unbuckle it from the cabinet. Less than a minute later, Ari and Washo arrive in the tube. I close the door to Rollinson's room as we form a circle.

Ari slides next to me. "Hey, Doc."

I scowl, and she folds her arms and looks away.

"All here? Good." Welker takes in the disheveled faces of his crew. "No pleasantries. Pirates are licking our heels and threatening to board in approximately . . ."

"Ten minutes," Ari confirms.

Welker nods. "The captain's dead. Fracture Point is twenty at maximum burn. Suggestions?"

"Rollinson's dead?" Ari starts.

"Doesn't matter," I interrupt.

She turns to me, fire alighting in her cerulean gaze. "He watched over us, even you. I want to see him."

"He was a charlatan," I retort. "He would have sold out any of us for a quan." *I hurt her so she won't be hurt more. Better me who's a villain than Rollinson who she loved.*

"You're nothing but a thug," she hisses, and pushes past me.

Xana stops her. "Ari, we can pay our respects later."

"I don't need your protection, *Officer Caprio.* Nor do I need your phony act," she barks at me. "Claim to be indifferent. Your eyes show otherwise, Edmon of House Leontes. Go back to hiding your shame and caressing that nose you keep in your pocket."

I freeze. *How does she know about my house?* The momentary lapse in my stolidness allows her to hit the access panel to Rollinson's closet door. Suddenly everyone sees the wrapped corpse floating listlessly where I left it. His feet stick out the bottom of the sheet, pants still comically scrunched at the ankles, his flagpole tenting the fabric in post self-gratification.

"Oh, Ollie," Ari half gasps, half laments.

"At least you got a sheet 'round him," Xana hisses in my ear.

Washo looks shaken. Rollinson was the one who brought him aboard. Now he's with a pack of strangers biting at one another amid death in a culture he hardly knows. Xana pulls Ari from the doorway. I slam my fist over the access panel shutting the captain off from view once more.

"So, um, can we get back to the fact there are pirates that want to kill us?" Tol asks.

"*James Bentley*, my name is Captain Jak," the eerie warble sounds over our comm again. "Since we will be at your position in less than five standard minutes, I thought I would introduce myself. Our umbilical will extend, and you will prepare for us to board." The signal cuts out.

"What the hell do they want?" Sanctun is frantic now.

"Has anyone checked the cargo?" Ari asks. We all turn to the red-head. "Rollinson said we had a special cargo to deliver to Nonthera. Pirates don't attack parcel freighters unless there's something valuable aboard."

We hover, stunned. It's such an obvious thought, yet none of us had it until now. Welker is the first to push himself off the bulkhead. Seconds later, we are all floating inside the large, *empty* chamber of the cargo bay.

"Where is it?" Washo asks, his eyes scanning the room. There are a few parcels lashed down in the corner, probably containing letters, perhaps a few data silicates, but surely nothing of value. Trips through the vast are costly. Freighters don't sail through the Fracture Corridors unless they can recover the cost of the journey upon landfall. The bay is a large enough space that we should be carrying a whole lot more.

Rollinson had something else up his sleeve. This confirms my suspicions. They are after me . . .

"Check the crates," Welker says tightly. No package is key or DNA locked, so there's no particular box that seems to warrant attention. We ransack each and every container anyway.

"Nothing!" Tol throws a handful of mail in frustration. It scatters like seabirds through the cavernous space. "At least not of value."

"Something in one of the letters? Some encryption? Government intelligence?" Ari posits.

"We don't have time to go through each piece of mail before they board," Xana says softly. "We need a plan."

Tol raises his hand. "I'm all for giving up."

"And if they don't find what they're looking for?" Ari asks.

"Or if they do?" Xana flashes a glance in my direction before returning to Ari—warning me that if these pirates are here for me, she will make sure she hands me over before harm comes to the girl. "You know as well as anyone, *Lazarus*, pirates don't board without taking prisoners or leaving bodies."

Ari scowls. "Don't try to frighten me like you did when were children!"

They are fire and ice. Sometimes the only way past such friction is straight through. A plan formulates in my mind. But failure means death, and I won't be able to do it alone. I'll need to convince the others. Even more, I'll need to let them think it was their idea.

"I don't go down without a fight," I say coldly.

"How original." Tol's eyes roll.

"Washo agrees," I say. The boy almost jumps out of his skin. *Turning it on him will start the cascade. Washo will look to Xana . . .*

"Me?" Washo squeaks.

"You're a part of the crew as much as any of us now." Welker puts an affirming hand on Washo's shoulder.

I wish I had that kind of rapport with people. Better this way, though. Use my words to manipulate rather than gain love.

"Whatever Xana thinks we should do," Washo stutters.

Perfect. His attraction to Ari, the way the boy bowed to Xana in deference when we met him . . . His people, the Nicnacians, are the survivors of the "faithful," and his forebears descend from a matriarchy. All of it points to women holding some superior position in his culture. If divisions are ever drawn among us, I know where the boy will swim.

Xana often defers to Welker, and Welker doesn't move unless he thinks it's what Xana would do. Xana will fight so long as Ari is safe . . . She glances at me. She knows I've maneuvered this, but she nods.

"Damn it!" Tol exclaims in protest.

"Shut up, Tol," the entire crew responds in unison.

"I'll run point," Welker says.

Xana opens a nearby weapons locker. She hefts a rifle and a giant knife. She shoves the blade into her boot. "Tol," she calls out. "Captain still have that pistol in his coat?"

The navigator pulls out a fat handgun and pinches it between thumb and forefinger, like he's holding a stinking sea rat.

Washo's eyes widen. "You aren't going to fire that in here, are you?"

"Rubber bullets, spyp," Ari whispers to him. "No smart guidance or heat seeking but should be effective enough with good aim. There's always the pulse function, too."

"Unless they've got armor," I growl. We all look at Tol whose hands are shaking. "Just keep him out of the way."

"You always think optimistically, don't ya, Doc?" Ari flashes a grin. I can't help but smirk.

"Earpieces in," Welker commands. "Ari on comm, keep us connected. I want numbers and tactical information real-time without alerting them."

"Right, boss." Ari pushes off toward the fore.

"The rest of you, in your closets. I'll greet the boarders and knock on the bulkheads as I pass. Mark the count. That will be the number of miscreants."

"When Welker clears the quarter's passage," Xana says, picking up the pieces of the plan, "we spring the trap."

"What trap?" Tol gulps.

"We shove them down the access tube to the cargo bay, bottleneck them. It'll be shooting fish in a barrel." Xana checks the action on her rifle.

Washo's eyes dart around looking for an escape. *If he's with the enemy, he didn't think it would come to this. If he's not, he's just terrified out of his mind.*

"Everyone clear?" Welker asks, strapping his dual pistols to his hips and flexing his fingers.

"Are you?" I ask. "A lot of this is going to depend on your ability to get them into the cargo bay." *I sure hope he's Tagged up.*

Xana hands Washo a pistol from the arms locker. He grasps it gently. *He's never held a weapon before,* I realize. There's something more to it, though. He looks about to vomit. Still, I need to enact the part of the plan I had in mind.

"One problem," I rasp. "Their ship. It's bristling with weapons and can outrun us easy. Even if the plan is successful, their guns will still pepper holes into the *Bentley*, have us all sucking vacuum."

Xana's eyes narrow with suspicion.

"What are you suggesting?" Welker asks.

I smile wolfishly. "That I steal their ship."

CHAPTER 4

STRENGTH

> The strength card is about combining two disparate attributes to overcome a greater weakness. Civilization depends on the fortitude and wit to create a union of opposites to overcome the threat of nature.
>
> —Ovanth, *A Practical Reading of the Arcana*

"You want to go extra vessel?" Welker is nonplussed.

"Suicide!" Xana shakes her head.

"We leave out the trash locker. I'll be in vac but a moment, snag their ship, get inside. Once in, deal with the crew. When Captain Jak hails, like we know he will when you trap him, I'll be on the other line."

"If you survive," Xana mutters.

"Ari?" I press the hall comm panel.

"What's up, Doc?"

Tol bursts out laughing. I glower at the man in the stovepipe hat, and he immediately gulps silent.

"Could you send a code embedded in a transmission to the enemy ship? Something simple like 'dump trash'?"

"Tricky. I'd have to figure out their OS, learn the code, hide it in the background noise of a ping. Actually that's a genius idea. Of course, it would take a greater genius to pull it off . . ."

"Do it," I growl softly. I can almost hear her smile.

Xana leans her rifle against her shoulder. "Chutes are usually fail-safe locked. You can open the internal door with code, but unless someone is manually operating it, you'd still have to be able to hot-wire the fail-safe mechanism from the outside."

"And of course there're always secondary reclamation dumps," Tol quips. "You know, number two?"

I stare at him. "It's your funeral." He laughs half-heartedly.

"I can do it." We all turn to Washo, who raises his hand meekly. "I can hot-wire the external hatch."

"You're up for this, boy?" I float close and stare the kid down. *My plan is highly dangerous. I could use Washo's technical skill, but I will not be responsible for his death. On the other hand, if he has colluded with Phaestion or the Pantheon to put us all in danger . . .*

He bites his lip and forces himself to meet my gaze. *He has courage.* I nod and turn back to Welker. "Well?"

The ship rocks, and a clanging sound reverberates through the hull.

"Umbilical sealing, boss," Ari calls over the comm.

Welker sighs. "You best suit up."

"We're out of firearms," Xana tells me.

"I don't use them."

"Me neither." Washo surprises me by handing his pistol back to our raven-haired security officer.

My gut clenches. *Do I really think this kid is some sort of spy?* I trust myself with only my sword, but Washo should not be weaponless. I glance at Tol who is still fumbling with Rollinson's pistol. Then again, it's probably safer than putting a firearm in the hands of the ignorant.

"All right, crazies, get a move," Welker calls.

Xana and Tol open their sleeping closets and climb inside.

"Leontes." Xana catches my arm as I float past. "Good luck." There's something in her eyes—I don't know what. An acknowledgment that what I'm about to do is insane or that she still does not trust me. I can't say.

I fly into the med bay, quickly grab my sword from its mount on the wall, and meet Washo at the trash locker, slamming the door shut behind us. The dank compartment smells of rotten fruit and vegetable. Human waste is recycled back into the hydroponic fertilization chamber and water reclamation tanks are in the adjacent wall compartment augmenting the air's earthy aroma. I feel like retching.

"Will this work?" Washo is practically gagging. His hands shake as he gingerly steps into a vac suit.

"Doesn't matter what I think," I rasp back.

The hull of the ship rattles as the enemy umbilical seals. A loud hiss echoes when the tube pressurizes.

"Ari?" It's Welker's voice in my earpiece as I check the seals of my vac suit.

"Copy. You got one, two . . . seven armored bogeys coming through." The hatch door of the *Bentley* opens with an extended squall and clank. "Xana and Tol are firmly locked. Soon as I have the go-ahead from the Doc and Washo, I'll dump the trash."

"Doctor, we're not stationary," Welker addresses me. "Neither is the enemy ship. When the hatch opens, you're going to have only a few meters and one chance to grab the hull before both ships fly away. If we lose you . . ."

"I know." *Lost to the vast.* Washo looks whiter than a lumo-fish.

I remember Phaestion and I in a boat once found an orca pod cruising the fathoms. He dove into the water with the creatures. When they surfaced, he rode their backs, hopping from one killer whale to the next. "They know me, Edmon!" he shouted. "They know me as one of their own!" I wish for his courage now.

Of course, the time we stole a fishing boat to catch a glimpse of a siren, a leviathan rose from the great deep, and then it was Phaestion who was frozen with fear. From that day on and throughout my childhood, I would hear the sea dragon's voice in my mind—

Why run, boy? the creature would ask in his haunting basso rumble. It was only when I stopped running and realized that the leviathan was a part of me that his voice did cease. I know I can't run now, either.

My helmet is in place. Washo shivers next to me. "Washo, tell me what you know of the Anjins of Miral?" I ask.

"They were the guardians of the old empire. Some thought of them as holy beings," he answers.

"My father chose an Anjin commander as his namesake," I whisper to him.

"The commander who held off a thousand enemy ships with one squadron," he acknowledges.

"Each Anjin also had a squire who he apprenticed. When the Anjin died and vacated his armor, his apprentice would take up the mantle," I say.

Washo nods.

"Why, hello, Captain Jak!" Welker's voice pipes in my ear. "We presume you're here for the cargo—" There's a thunk and static on the comm. *Jak punched Welker. He'll pay for laying a hand on my crewmate.*

"Not here for cargo, little man." Captain Jak's voice warbles, altered by some type of voice disguiser.

If they're not here for the ship's cargo . . . My mind reels. *My father dies, removing the last rival Phaestion has to the total hegemony of Tao. No one will rise up to challenge him. But Phaestion was always driven by contest, obsessed with subjugating anyone who might be considered his equal. I know that Phaestion has spared no expense constructing his war fleet; he might spare no expense in finding me, either. Does he fear that I would make a claim to his throne? Or does he relish the thought so that he can finally face me?*

Either way, if it is me they are after, this is all my fault. And I have to make it right.

"Washo, it was an Anjin's duty to teach his squire that bravery isn't the absence of fear. It's acting in spite of it. Do you understand?" The boy meets my gaze. He nods even as he quakes.

"Ari, now," I command.

The floor beneath us opens. I wrap the kid in my arms and push off with every ounce of strength in my legs. We fly like bullets into the darkness. The hull of the enemy starship screams past me. My grip on Washo is lost; he sails free. I claw for purchase on the sleek hull, but I ricochet off the smooth armor panels and spin into the velvet night, my helmet lighting up with the pinpricks of the infinite star field. End over end, no up or down, it's all over in less than a second.

I'm a boy of five watching my father grab my mother in the Grand Wusong's throne room. I'm twelve and facing down the three Companions—Hanschen, Perdiccus, and Sigurd. Steel weapons glint in their hands. I'm in a hospital bed, staring at Phaestion. He's telling me I'm going to live. I'm seventeen and holding Nadia on the cliff above the green Southern Sea. We make love for the first time. I am a young man, singing at my wedding to Miranda Wusong, drunk with sadness and rage. I am a wretch in the ice caves of the Wendigo, my body aching in pain, swearing revenge. I am hovering over my decaying father who is begging me to kill him. Phaestion laughs at me, my sword at his throat—*If you don't kill me I'll murder millions. Billions!* Then that tickle in the back of my brain comes, that malevolent darkness somewhere in the universe that says, *I'm coming to devour you . . .*

At first I think it is the voice of the familiar creature of the deep who was my father's sigil and namesake. But no, the leviathan has become a part of me, part of my strength. This is from somewhere else . . . illusive and malevolent . . .

Not today, I say back with a whisper that is growing into something more. My hand snaps closed like a trap, snagging a fin extending from the smooth armor of the pirate ship's hull. My other hand is a vise as it clamps down on Washo's ankle. My spine yanks taut. The sapphire glow of the vessel's exhaust burns near Washo's head, trailing into the darkness. *I am unyielding, unforgiving, I will not be denied!* I scream with a primal rage and pull Washo from the brink of the abyss toward me.

"Not your time," I growl. He reaches out and grasps the fin himself, but he's not that strong, so I don't let go. "Activate mag boots, spyp," I snarl over the comm.

He reaches to his wrist control and taps the dial activating the boots. Instantly, his feet slam down on the hull, gluing him there. I follow suit and allow myself a deep exhalation. *I'm not dead yet, Father. Not yet.*

Step by painstaking, magnetic step, we inch closer to the trash hatch, a barely visible inseam on the otherwise smooth, white hull of the strange vessel.

"What do you mean you don't want the cargo?" Welker's voice comes in over the comm playing out the events of our crew still on the *Bentley*. A whisper sounds in my ears. *Dagger or sword being unsheathed?*

"We want the girl," Captain Jak's mechanical voice warbles.

Wait . . . the girl?

"Ari, where are we with the upload?" I say over the comm.

"And we're in." She maintains her brassy demeanor, but I know she heard Captain Jak's words, too.

Failure was not an option before. Somehow, it seems less so now.

"Xana, now!" Welker screams. Gunshots blast through my headset followed by shouting. Tol's, Xana's, and Welker's voices are screaming incoherently, the pirates shouting in the background. Washo's hands involuntarily grasp his helmet.

I grab the boy's arm. "Switch off your comm. Dual private channel only. Hear my voice and just my voice. Now!"

The boy nods and does it. Quickly, he kneels and flips open the trash hatch's input pad. Ripping off the faceplate reveals a system of wires that look far more like blood vessels or nerve endings than the metallic wires in most ships. Washo glances up at me in confusion.

What, by the twisted star?

There's no time to figure this out. I kneel and tap a connecting branch lightly, trusting my basic medical knowledge. If these things are like nerves, then an electrical impulse to the right branch will trigger the flexing of a muscle and . . . I'm rewarded with the thunk of the garbage hatch unlocking and flying open next to us. Ship alarms blare from inside. I push Washo forward and follow, sealing the hatch behind us. The alarms cease as the ship reestablishes cabin pressure.

Washo illuminates the stained interior of the enemy ship's refuse bin with his headlamp.

"Door?" I ask.

He examines the access switch, then hunkers his shoulder against the interior hatch. "The locking mechanism has been welded."

They know we're here. Suddenly, liquid sludge dumps from the ceiling everywhere. *Secondary reclamation waste. Tol's infamous number two.* Washo screams.

"Quiet!" I howl. *If they're attempting to drown us in their own human waste, the joke's on them. I've climbed through so much shit in my life, there's no way this is how I end.* "Washo, when I open the door, attack whoever is on the other side like your life depends on it. Because it does!" Washo is shaking behind his mask, but my stare strikes him into stillness. "Think of Rollinson. Think of Ari," I say. He nods.

I gently move him aside and draw back my fist. The shit pours down from above, but I breathe in all the energy of my body, sending everything into the point of my knuckles. I use the Dim Mak with fury, rage, and just a little joy at the thought of what is to come. I unleash, feeling the force spread out from the impact like a shock wave. The heavy metal door blows off its hinges. Washo gapes, but there's no time for astonishment.

"Go!" I scream. I catch my breath, the technique having sapped my energy momentarily. The spypsy launches himself into the hallway. An electrical stun pulse sails past him as he grabs a wall railing, swings to the opposite wall, and smacks his foot against an armored pirate just before the man brings his pistol to bear again. The kid is like an acrobatic spider, his whole life in micro-g giving him a speed and maneuverability these land apes can't hope to match. Washo himself seems stunned as he stares at what he has accomplished, but the man is getting up.

"Do it, Washo!" I scream into the comm.

Washo shrieks and brings his fist down again and again on the man's face. The pirate's helmet cracks. The gun floats out of his hand, and blood sprays up into the micro-g.

Another pirate enters the corridor from an access tube. As he turns the corner, he aims a pistol at Washo's head. I summon what energy I can and launch myself at the man. I jam my fingers into the joint in his armor between shoulder and helm. It's just enough to find the meridian, which sends the man into unconscious slumber.

I turn back to Washo. His attacker struggles, then twitches, then lies still, but Washo's fist keeps bearing down relentlessly. I float behind him and grab the boy's wrist. "That's enough," I rasp quietly.

He turns to me, panting in a cold sweat. Tears streak his cheeks behind his faceplate. "What have I done?"

I remember the first time a man died at my hands. "You survived," I say. *I shouldn't have brought him. This is my fault. That death is on me.* I nod in the direction of what I assume is the cockpit.

"The pilot, right?" Washo asks breathlessly.

I strip my vac suit, desiring maneuverability now that I'm in a pressurized cabin. Washo follows my lead, and we float to the cockpit door, a heavy thing that looks like it's made of some kind of bone, hermetically sealed. "I can do the rest, Washo, if you can get us in."

Washo squints at the door panel. "This is DNA locked followed up by an old-style retinal scanner."

"Not enough time to get back to the *Bentley*, grab Captain Jak, and tear his retinas off, I suppose." Washo looks sick to his stomach. *Oh well. Sanctun's the comedian of the group.*

"Why would they need security to their cockpit?" he asks.

I grab the ivory scabbard hanging at my side and unsheathe the shimmering silver blade. The siren steel sings the haunting tones of a woman.

"A siren sword?" Washo whispers with awe. "They're supposed to be myth, relics of a lost time, only carried by the genetically bred commanders of Miral's elite soldiers. I never thought I'd see one, much less in the hands of a *man.* And a midden-mensch man at that!"

"My father commissioned the blade to be forged in the fires of Albion." My voice is tinged with the bitterness of the memory.

"Albion! *I am the resurrection and the life. I die and pass the limits of possibility, as it appears to individual perception. Return, Albion, return! I give myself for thee . . .*" He recalls some sort of scripture I do not know. "Your father must have been a great man, Doctor Leontes."

I scowl and twirl the deadly weapon. It screams as I plunge the blade into the heart of the cockpit's door. The shriek of metal upon bone reverberates as the sword's sonic vibrations cut through. I carve a perfect circle with the skill of a surgeon and kick in the hatch I've created. It floats into the cockpit, and I dive into the breach. I'm immediately caught in a webbing of gray and pink tendrils. The soldier at the command console turns and fires his pistol. I twist as the bullets fly past.

Live rounds? Is he insane? If the hull is punctured, we'll all be dead, gasping for air as our innards explode. The soldier fires again. I bring my sword to bear. Its sonic waves create a shield that disintegrates the bullet. However, the scream of the siren harmonizes with something else, an inhuman shriek of shock and pain that emanates from the very walls of the cockpit.

Washo flanks the pirate and hurtles himself forward flipping end over end. His bare feet are exposed in his flight suit, and the sticky pads on his soles slap against the soldier's helmet and suction. The boy twists, and the soldier's neck pops with the sound of breaking bone. The man goes limp and floats listlessly away. *Another death on my hands.*

The ship itself groans in pain once again. I turn to the sound. And I see a sight that defies explanation.

A yellowish sac hangs in the center of the chamber. Inside the sac hangs the curled pink gray matter of an enlarged human brain. Tendrils sprout from its ganglia and reach out like arms to embed themselves in the walls of the ship.

What in the fathoms?

"This ship is living," Washo whispers.

"Not for long." I point, indicating where the sac membrane was punctured by the first bullet the soldier fired. Floating globules of fluid leak into the cockpit.

There are stories of old Miral, how the people had become more than human, how they had downloaded their consciousness into their tech. No one knows exactly how since whatever cataclysm forced Washo's ancestors to the stars erased all traces of such progress. Since that time over a thousand years ago, no race, nor being, has created anything to rival what is rumored of those bygone days. Yet here before me is this strange blending of man and machine.

"Doctor?" Washo looks at me from a communications console, distress crossing his face. "The log says that they've been in communication with another ship. It's closing distance."

"Reinforcements," I mutter. "Hail Ari but encrypt the message. Find out their situation. Let her know we've taken the enemy vessel but tell her to keep it quiet. We don't want anyone to know until the others are safe."

Washo nods, and his fingers dance over the holographic display. For my part, I push off a wall and grab the floating body of the dead cockpit soldier and head back into the hallway. "Where are you going?" he asks.

"To check on our remaining passenger. I didn't kill the man I attacked in the hallway." *I didn't kill the man, yet it was because of me the boy became a killer today.* I look back as the realization hits Washo, too. I can almost see his stomach turn just before he doubles over and vomits into the micro-g. He groans and curls up, gripping his knees as coughs rack him.

I should go to him is my first thought. Then: *He is not your friend. Don't get close.* I can't be the teacher, the companion, the comfort this boy needs. It would only endanger him. This world is cruel and removes any weakness one might have piece by bloody piece, or it kills the person. That's what Faria taught me, what my father taught me. If Washo is to survive, he must live with the consequences of reality. But I had other teachers, too. Old Gorham and The Maestro who taught me the language of music. My mother and Nadia who taught me love. How can I not show the boy some compassion? Especially since it's my fault he's here.

I place a hand on his shoulder. He turns, startled at the sight of my face, and I'm sorry I look frightening. "Come, Washo," I manage as gently as I can. "I have a suspicion about these so-called pirates."

CHAPTER 5

The Twin

> The twin card signifies the duality of lies and truth. It is the moment in the journey where an initial revelation may shatter perception; the mirror gazed upon is in fact illusion. The false twin must be sacrificed in order for the true one to live.
>
> —Ovanth, *A Practical Reading of the Arcana*

I float down the hallway with the boy at my back. The surviving soldier gently bobs against the bulkhead of the ship. I snag him by his boot and pat his body down, removing any pieces of weaponry tucked into his armor—knife, pistol, shock gauntlets, and the like.

"I'm going to wake him," I say, steeling myself for confrontation.

"What's this ship made out of?" Washo touches the white walls of the hallway.

Something is wrong in the way he says it though. He's seen this kind of tech before, I realize.

"Some kind of chitin or bone," I respond, suppressing the rage in my gut. *I don't like being lied to.* "It would need to be at least partially organic in order to allow . . . whatever it was we saw back there in the cockpit to grow into it."

I yank off the soldier's helmet. The face beneath is unremarkable. The cheekbone structure prominent and symmetrical, yet somehow . . . generic. I brush Washo aside to grab the attacker he killed in the hallway earlier. I pull the body close and rip off the shards of the broken helmet. Side by side, the resemblance between the two soldiers is unmistakable.

"Clones," I mutter with disgust. "These men are genetic duplicates." My people were descendants of such soldiers. When they fled the Miralian Empire and founded their own world of Tao, they outlawed genetic engineering. A deep-seated distrust of genetic modification has run in the veins of every Taoan since.

"Los," Washo whispers in fear. *He's said that word before.* However, when he says it now, I feel that cold darkness in the back of my mind, same as I felt since this whole thing began. I shake my head trying to clear it away. *Is it coincidence that he lies to me? Are his people involved in this somehow?*

My voice is tight with restraint when I speak again. "Many cultures have warriors, but only soldiers bear the indignation of similitude. Theoretically, designer organics can be cheaper and easier to train for someone that needs a large number of them."

My hand unleashes like a whip so quickly that Washo gasps. I strike a point in the unconscious clone's neck just beneath the jawline. Breath howls through the man's lungs as his eyes snap open. "Where am I? We're under attack. Who're you?"

I clamp my hand over his mouth as his eyes dart wildly. "You answer my questions, or you'll die," I hiss with scratching vocal cords. I slowly remove my hand, and the soldier stares back defiantly. "Why did you attack us?" I ask.

The soldier remains silent, so I raise my hand again to strike. *Ari is in danger, and I have no time for this.* I feel a hand on my shoulder. I turn to see the innocent face of the boy, and my first instinct is to rip out his beating heart and eat it alive. *How is it that I see threat in every corner of the Fracture?*

Washo gulps and in a nervous voice asks the soldier, "What is your name?"

"Hoplite Unit 1138 B," the soldier responds.

"That's a designation. Do you have a name?" Washo asks again.

The man looks confused. "Name?"

"I am Washo Tan." Washo puts his palms together in front of his heart in some sort of ritual greeting. "This is Dr. Edmon Leontes," he says, gesturing to me. "And you are . . . ?"

The soldier says nothing. *By the twisted star!* "What is your mission, Unit 1138 B?" I growl.

"Classified."

"Classified by whom?" The man's eyes shift wildly. "Your comrades were sent to take the bridge of the *James Bentley*. You were left behind to protect the ship. What was their mission?" My blood is on fire.

"I was left behind . . ." The soldier's words trail off as if he's trying to remember the answers to the questions I'm asking, but the memories are being deleted faster than he can recall them. *Enough!* I strike. The clone spasms, and his body goes limp again. "He knows his designation. He knows how to fight. He knows to obey. But under duress, he has no idea of his mission specifics, or rather there's something inside him that blanks those memories when they become vulnerable," I say to Washo.

"What could do that?" Washo asks, perplexed.

"I'm not sure. It's possible he and the others have some kind of growth acceleration built into their genome. Perhaps only the barest of instructions were implanted in his cortex, but who his employers are, his overall mission . . . It's unlikely he remembers any of it, if he ever even knew it in the first place. By the way, Washo?" He looks up at me. "You did well." It's all I can manage right now.

"Oh." Washo smiles. I can see his face flush with pride. "Do you think that maybe someday you can teach me? That thing you do with your fingers . . ."

The Dim Mak is no toy and in the wrong hands could just as easily do great harm. Faria told me that the Zhao monks who taught him made him swear never to use the skills in an unjust cause. *That didn't stop him from training me, though, did it?*

"I've been told that spypsies have incredible biological gifts. It may be that I can teach you." The boy's face beams. *Careful, Edmon.* "Don't let it go to your head," I mutter.

Washo's hand suddenly goes to his earpiece. *He turned his comm back on.* "Yes! Ari, we're here. Is everyone all right?" He looks up at me. "Welker has a broken nose. Tol is freaking out. But otherwise everyone's okay. They won." He looks at me nervously. "The pirates, I mean. They have our crew under guard. Except the captain, Jak."

"What about Captain Jak?"

"They've been hailing you, but you turned your comm off. Jak, she was wounded." *She?* "And there's something else."

I think quickly. With their captain injured, the clone soldiers are uncertain in the situation. However, they still have their guns trained on Clay, Xana, and Tol. Ari, meanwhile, is holed up in the cockpit of the *Bentley*, communicating with all parties. So, I formulate a plan. I have Ari tell the soldiers that Washo and I have been captured in our attempt to board their ship. I am to be transported back to the *Bentley* in bonds, presumably to heal Captain Jak in exchange for sparing the lives of my friends. The soldiers agree that once their captain is on the mend and they have what they came for, they'll leave the rest of us to go on our merry way. Of course, I have no intention of letting any of the crew become prisoners of these pirates.

Washo slaps the cuff wire across my wrists as I ready to cross the umbilical between the ships. He's not keen on being left alone in the enemy vessel with its oozing brain and incapacitated crewman. I don't blame him. I'm wary of leaving him alone. Is it possible the spypsies engineered this ship? Washo definitely knows more than he's saying. This whole situation is starting to feel like a horror drama.

"Wait," Washo says. "I wanted to give this back to him earlier, but . . . well, there wasn't a good moment." He twists, debating something internally.

"Washo, there's no time to waste," I say impatiently. Considering the remaining soldiers could decide to execute the others any moment, I'd say my shortness is warranted.

"You said you don't play tarot, but you need an archetype if you want to ever start. Here." He hands me Rollinson's quintessence card. The thin metallic card faintly glows when I touch its smooth edges. "I took it during the scuffle before Tol could swipe it." He shrugs sheepishly. "I was going to give it back, but . . ."

Each card reacts to the person it is given to. I've never held one before. My fate was cast to the wayside the day I left Tao; no card can bring it back. "It displayed the hanged man for Rollinson," Washo says. "Maybe for you it will show . . ."

I turn it over to reveal . . . a blank. I scowl.

"Oh." Washo seems abashed. "They do that sometimes when the engram doesn't have a move or can't really discern the internal state of its bearer. My mother used to say that when that happens, it means the card doesn't know who you are yet," Washo adds lamely.

I tuck the card in my pocket. "Just make it look good." I indicate the limp body of the clone soldier we tried to interrogate. Washo replaced the helmet over the man's head, and he holds the soldier up like a dummy from behind making it look as if I'm being forced at gunpoint to cross. I float through the hatch into the umbilical. The hatch seals behind me as the hatch to the *Bentley* opens in front of me.

Another helmed soldier waits on the other side with a pistol trained on my head. "This way," he says through the voice amplifier of his mask.

———

Things are in a bad state aboard the *Bentley*. Five enemy combatants remain, their weapons aimed at my crew. Welker's pretty face is smashed, his nose twisted and bleeding. Sanctun spins out of control in the micro-g, gun in hand. Xana remains silent, staring at the floating, unconscious body of Captain Jak. I hover toward the pirate captain to examine her then stop in shock. I look back at Xana, then back at Jak, then back at Xana again.

Xana is a clone!

My fingernails dig into my palms as I white-knuckle my fists. *What is going on here? Who are these pirates?*

"Can you save her?" Xana asks coldly.

"I'll do what I can," I growl. Under the pistol muzzles of Captain Jak's men, I first see to the hapless Welker, gently but firmly snapping his nasal bones back into place. He howls with pain.

Sanctun babbles hysterically, so I make a decision. *He's better left out of the way than in it.* I gently apply the Dim Mak to a pressure point, sending him into a fitful slumber. Xana places the lanky fool into his sleeping closet. Finally, I carry Captain Jak to my small medical bay where I can examine her more closely. Fortunately, there is not room for the remaining pirates to join me in the space. I close the door for privacy to do my work, though they remain right outside, pistols trained on Xana and Welker.

"Doctor," Ari calls nervously on the comm. "There's another ship approaching, profile identical to the first."

My hands work hurriedly. Blood seeps from the wound where Xana's knife is embedded in the captain's side. *A kill shot. How could Xana have been so careless? She's too skillful to make such a thrust unintended. Unless . . . she wanted this woman dead so we couldn't ask questions.*

I need to turn the tables on our attackers. I need to be able to communicate with my comrades without our enemy knowing. There is one member aboard this ship who can understand any language. And I know a language that no one can understand: *Ancient Italian.* My father wanted me to become a warrior, follow in his footsteps, and claim the throne of Tao. I wanted a different path. I trained for years to make my song heard throughout the Fracture. I spent hours learning opera under the tutelage of The Maestro from Lyria. *My bastard father may have taken my voice, but I never forgot The Maestro's teaching.*

I hit the communication panel. *"Goddess, can you understand me? I beseech you, hear me and grant me your words of wisdom."*

My words are a bit more formal than I'd like. The arcane tongue is spoken by maybe a handful of denizens in the Nine Corridors, but Ari's mind needs only a few words to understand the whole of the lexicon. *"I'm here, brave warrior,"* she responds as if she had been born to the words.

"What's going on in there?" One of the pirates bangs on the door.

"The doctor is reviving your captain now," Ari explains in Normal over the comm.

"I cannot save her," I confess. *"Send word to my squire. Tell him to bring the great vessel into our belly. The fish is small enough to be swallowed by this whale. I will lure the pirates there. When my squire arrives, the pirates will be swept out to sea."*

I sound like a fool, I think. I just hope she understands what I mean.

"Let us speak to the captain now!" I hear the click of a rifle safety.

"Brave warrior," she says. *"It is good to hear your true voice."*

My heart beats faster. This exchange is more than we've spoken in an entire year of sailing together aboard the *Bentley*. But it's bittersweet. *As soon as we escape, I'm leaving this bucket behind,* I think. *Staying puts you in danger.*

I push that thought out of my head just now. I recall every moment of my medical training in the cold of the Wendigo prison, how Faria the Red showed me a way to heal by diverting the flow of blood. I pull the knife from Jak. Blood spills into the cabin in floating crimson rivulets. Quickly, I jam my fingers into her pressure points and seal the puncture with mussel glue. I only have a few seconds, so I hit the record button on the comm and then tap the captain's adrenal glands, waking her up.

Her eyes snap open as breath rushes into her lungs. "Tell me what your mission is here," I hiss. "What do you want with the girl? Did the Pantheon send you?"

Jak's eyes narrow. Then she smiles. "You've no idea who or what she is, do you?" She looses a gurgled laugh. "You've no idea the power you've called down upon you. I hope you're prepared to meet your ancestors, Edmon Leviathan of House Wusong-Leontes."

Only those with working knowledge of Tao would know that my father called himself the Leviathan.

The blood drains from her visage. "I've taken an oath never to kill. That's not the same as letting you live," I whisper. I remove my hand from her wound. Droplets of blood spring into the air in an explosion of liquid red. Light fades from her pupils.

"We speak to the captain now or I shoot this one!" the pirate outside my door shouts.

I hit the comm. *"Goddess, hear me. I've sent you the voice of the captain. Use it!"*

I transfer the recorded audio. No sooner is the message sent than Jak's voice breaks in over the comm, "Soldiers, quickly to the cargo bay."

"You heard the captain!" a pirate barks. *She did it! Ari transmuted the algorithms to recreate Jak's intonations and fake her voice.*

A beat of silence, and then Ari's voice blasts across all decks. "Now!"

"Got 'em!" Welker howls triumphantly as he seals the pressure door, trapping them in the cargo bay. The thunderous sound of the exterior door opening echoes through the ship. The bay depressurizes, and the pirates are pulled into the vacuum of the vast.

"I'm bringing her in. I'm not sure I really know how to fly it." Washo sounds terrified over the comm. I hear a crunch as he lands the enemy ship in our cargo bay.

"Bay doors closed!" Xana shouts.

"Xana, guns! Washo, off that ship now and into our engine room!" Welker shouts.

"UFP *James Bentley*," a computerized voice, identical to Jak's, cuts in over the comm. "Prepare to be boarded."

I exit the med bay, spattered with blood. "Hey, young, tough, and handsome. Is it Christmas?" Tol says, crawling out of his sleeping closet. "You know this was my dad's bunk. Mine was over there when I was growing up." He points to the drawer across from us, the one now assigned to Washo. "Sometimes in the middle of the sleep cycle I'd wake up and knock on his drawer, and I would ask him to read me a story. Are you going to read me a story, Doctor Batman?"

"Go back to bed, Tol," I sigh.

"But I was having the most peculiar dream, and you were there, and the scarecrow and Dorothy . . ." He finally realizes why my white suit is blazoned in red. The fool's eyes roll back into his head. I catch him as he goes limp again, gently place him back in his cot, and close the door panel.

The pinging of bullets reverberates against our hull. The *Bentley*'s antiasteroidal slug fire booms as Xana returns fire from the gunning station.

"I'm back in the engine room!" Washo shouts over the comm. "Fusion burn is ready!"

The ship lurches as Welker puts the *Bentley* into acceleration. The tap, tap, tap of bullets pinging our hull sounds again, and somewhere there is a sudden hiss of atmosphere.

"We have a hull breach in the cargo hold!" Ari screams over the speakers.

"I'm on it!" I shout. I fly down the tube as the ship's klaxons blare. A whistle of air becomes the whorl of a gale. Suddenly, I'm being pulled by the power of vacuum pressure as air rushes everywhere. If we enter the Fracture without being sealed, we'll disintegrate. I somehow manage to grip the handle of an emergency tube hatch. I slam it closed and turn the heavy wheel, sealing the rest of the ship off from the hold.

"Fracture Point in three, two . . ." My stomach drops. The ship's saw vibrates, cuts into the fabric of the cosmos. Space and time fold back, and the UFP *James Bentley* enters the bloodstream of the universe.

CHAPTER 6

Temperance

The temperance card suggests that two disparate flavors, water and wine, may mix to provide the ideal blending or unified theory. Where either alone could lead one to ruin of abstention or indulgence, temperance seeks the middle ground of the two elements.

—Ovanth, *A Practical Reading of the Arcana*

Dawn's rose fingers creep through the portholes, bathing the *Bentley*'s corridors in the gleam of a red star. Nonthera. From stardust to stardust, so do the small and great lives of the Fracture pass. The shrouded body of Captain Ollie Rollinson is commended to the vast through the trash shoot. *An ignominious and pathetic finale. That's all death can ever be.*

The weary crew gathers outside the sleeping closets. We can't even look at one another. Too many lies and secrets between us. Welker and Xana have run an external scan determining that no foreign objects, like a homing beacon, were attached to the *Bentley*'s hull. Ari followed suit, running a diagnostic and virus check on all of our computer systems to ensure that no program was illegally uploaded while we were in dry dock.

Now it's my turn. I finish doing a body scan on Washo with the pocket MRI. The resonance image is neutral, showing no alien objects. "Ari, you're last." If the scan reads normal . . .

The MRI beeps incessantly.

"What?" Ari asks. "What is it?"

She looks up at me, her blue eyes struck by fear.

"A homing chip," I say soberly. The crew tenses. I can tell Ari wants to bury her face in my chest and hide from everyone, but I turn away from her to grab a medical instrument. "This won't hurt. Just hold still." I tenderly peel the flight suit from her shoulder, exposing the smooth white skin of her scapula. She bites her lower lip and glances at me with a mixture of shame, grief, and wanting. *This is the first time we've touched since . . .*

Xana watches with fury bubbling beneath the pools of her dark eyes as I use the anesthetic scalpel to make a small incision in Ari's back and then carefully remove a translucent microchip from the cut with tweezers. A quick suture of mussel glue and a layer of healing salve ensures the wound will seal without scarring within the hour.

"A subdermal." I hold the chip up to the light with my tweezers. "I suspect one of the phyto-mutants on the Leaky Engine slapped this onto you. It was absorbed and implanted beneath the skin. That's how they were able to track you and us."

"Do they know where we are now, Doctor?" Welker asks gingerly.

"Not anymore!" Ari snatches the chip from me. She darts toward the trash shoot, tosses it in, and slams her palm on the jettison panel. A rush of air, and the tracking chip is ejected into space after our captain. Her firey hair looks like lava in the crimson starlight. Her cerulean eyes settle on me, daring me in some way.

She believes this is all her fault. I want to comfort her, tell her that I will slay any enemy that would dare lay a hand on her. Instead, I fold my arms across my chest and scowl.

"Um, I have questions?" Sanctun raises his hand. "Who the hell were they? What the hell were they after? Why did they have Spock's brain piloting their ship? Did our captain know? And why did their leader look just like Xana?"

"Yes, Xana. Tell us," I growl like a menacing sea wolf. Captain Jak's dying words still haunt me. *You've no idea who or what she is, do you?* It seems Jak meant Ari. Ari's abilities have always made me curious about her origins, and the tracker seems to corroborate that she is the mysterious "package" the mutants in the Leaky Engine were referring to. Xana knows something, and that's where I direct my anger now.

"She didn't look like me," Xana challenges. "When I was a girl, I was taken from the streets and trained to be Ari's bodyguard. If Captain Jak looked like anyone, it was my tutor, Skaya."

"She looked like you!" I thunder. I don't care about stories of orphans being raised as protectors. All I see is the face of an enemy who tried to kill us.

"Did you perform a blood analysis, Doctor?" Welker asks, trying to keep us calm and rational through this.

"Genetic markers are near identical to Security Officer Xana Caprio," I say, staring back at the warrior woman coldly. "Near. Not identical. Statistically speaking, the level of compatibility places the relationship between Jak and Xana somewhere below an identical clone, but an order above a sibling or parent. I'm not a geneticist."

A dark look crosses Xana's face. *Is it possible that she didn't know this about herself?*

"You're saying she and the captain are related, but aren't quite copies?" Welker asks.

"I grew up with a mother, a father, a brother. I saw them die. I'm not a copy!" Xana pushes past Welker. Her eyes smolder centimeters from my own. Again I feel like she and I have met somewhere before. *Why the hell does she look so familiar to me?*

"That's good news, right?" Tol looks at us all.

"Is it possible your memory has been tampered with, Xana?" Welker asks calmly.

Xana's hand cocks back, and she fires it at me. It's so fast, but I catch her wrist. The second blow, however, breaks my jaw. *It's only a hairline fracture, but even so, she's strong. Only those born on a high-gravity world or enhanced by something like Tag should even come close to being able to break one of my bones. She is not normal,* I think, even as I silently thank Talousla Karr for the uncanny healing abilities he unlocked in me.

"Both of you, stop!" Ari screams. Xana ceases immediately, almost as if she can't control the reaction. *Interesting,* I note. *Is it possible Xana, too, has some kind of subliminal programming in place?*

"We can't argue among ourselves," Ari continues. "Not when we don't know who our enemy is. Have you seen that ship in our hold?" Even in her anger, Ari is beautiful. "If we were hauling cargo," she continues, trying hard not to break down, "I'd say I was tagged only to lead them to it. In the absence of any valuables on board, the logical conclusion is that I'm the target."

"You don't know that," Xana pleads.

"Don't I?" Ariel fires back. She floats toward Xana. I can see in Xana the same desire as in me—to reach out, hold Ari close. My stomach twists in knots.

"What about the prisoner? Maybe we should question him again?" Washo asks meekly.

"Excellent idea, spyp." Welker nods, glad to pull the attention from this emotional conflict to something more grounded.

"I doubt you'll get anything else from him," I retort caustically, massaging my sore mandible. I silently will the osteoblasts of my jaw bone to the site of Xana's impact. Already the crack is healing itself.

"As much as I respect your opinion, Doctor Leontes, your way with people is sometimes . . . a bit lacking." Welker claps me on the shoulder and floats down the access tube to the cargo bay.

We follow Welker into the cargo bay, which has been patched and repressurized. He activates the ramp aboard the enemy ship, which lowers with the whisper of skin rubbing on skin.

Tol whistles. "This is like *Top Gun*."

"Xana?" Welker asks. "Have you ever seen a ship like this?"

"No," the warrior woman replies flatly. "And nobody else has, either. I gleaned the UFP data bank for every known ship design in the Fracture and found no similarity to any existing craft."

I glance at Washo, who fidgets nervously. *Someone has,* I think.

Welker leads us through the hole I cut in the door to the cockpit. The brain sits in its amniotic sac, tendrils splaying out. "Over here." Welker floats to the soldier huddled in the corner. The man's knees are pulled to his chest like a child. Xana and I flank Welker for support. "Hello, what's your name, chap?"

The man's eyes scan our faces uncertainly, then land on Xana. He snaps into upright position and salutes. "Captain, sir."

"I'm not your captain, soldier," Xana says. "This man asked your name."

"Hoplite Unit 1138 B."

"That won't do for a name, will it?" Xana announces. "What would you like us to call you?" The soldier's brow furrows. "We need to give you a name, Hoplite 1138 B," Xana repeats.

"THX 1138 . . . B. Bee . . . ," Tol mutters behind us.

"B. Bee . . . Bentley?" the soldier asks more than says.

"Bentley," Ari says, shaking her head.

"We're naming enemy prisoners after our own ship now?" I hiss incredulously. I really want to break something again.

"He's not a prisoner," Xana says frostily.

Washo dances his fingers over the holographic display of a nearby control panel. "The ship's data banks have been wiped, too."

"Bentley." Xana leans close to the man. "Can you tell us what your mission was or where your ship came from?"

"I . . . I don't think so?"

"Who do you think I am?"

Bentley's eyes narrow. "You're—"

"Dying," Ari interrupts. "Look!" Ari points to flashes of color along the ship's bone-white ceiling. "The pattern. It's like the synapses of a neural network, but the signals . . ."

"You can make out what it's saying?" I ask.

"It's like an aphasia. Her thoughts are . . . erratic." Ari scratches her chin, puzzling it out. "The architect . . . the final daughter . . . shadows in the nine-fold darkness . . . let there be light no more . . ."

An unnatural hush falls over us. "How do you know it's a she?" Tol finally asks.

"Only a female brain could handle the speed of computations required to maneuver such a ship as this," Washo replies.

"Actually, statistics show, on average, male brains tend to favor spatial relationships, while female minds are far more adept at language and communication," I say. Washo scowls. He doesn't like his ingrained beliefs being questioned. "The fact they used a female brain might show some sort of inherent bias based on other factors."

"She's gone," Ari says solemnly.

"Looks like this thing isn't leaving our cargo bay unless she gets a new brain," I add.

Welker floats to the pilot harness. "It seems she was made to accommodate manual controls as well."

"Can you fly it?" Xana asks.

"My darling Xana, I can fly anything." The charmer flashes a lopsided grin. "But I don't think we should be hasty. Flying this unusual craft might attract unwanted attention."

"Maybe that's exactly what we want." Xana's dark eyes burn. "Put up a flag. Let the enemy come to us."

Welker shakes his head. "Not yet. Not until we know more."

"What are you suggesting?" I ask.

The rogue shrugs. "Captain Rollinson said we were set to deliver to Nonthera. Why don't we find out what happens when say, we show as promised?"

—

Planetside. Nonthera is basically desert rock with one giant industrial arcology named Capital City. The hulking iron cylinder of the *Bentley* touches down. I stand and stretch my limbs. Faria's meditation techniques help me maintain muscle mass in the micro-g of space, but I relish the strain of grav on my body.

"I can barely move," Washo groans, trudging behind the rest of us as we descend the boarding ramp.

"G," I growl. "Nonthera is a super planetoid. Three times the force of the estimated Ancient Earth. At least the effect is lessened by the pull of her moon." I point out a plastic-paned porthole in the docking bay. The bloodred star hangs over the brown rocky landscape, and a brilliant purple moon almost undulates in the planet's heat in colorful contrast.

"There would be no Nonthera without Thera." Welker nods at the violet gem. "The surface is uninhabitable except in Capital City. The rich ore of the Nonny crust is irresistible raw material. It's said Theran civilization was built upon the backs of the Nonnies."

"Thera was the medicinal world of the old empire," Washo says, thinking out loud.

The Black Rose of Thera is the mother herb whose substrate is Tag, the main Theran export nowadays. The dark flower is harvested and makes its way to a secret location where the proper chemicals are extracted. The extract is then put into patches that are distributed throughout the Fracture Corridors and delivered along the trade route that bears the flower's name—the Black Rose Path.

"Didn't you used to work here, Welker?" Xana asks.

"I grew up with the wealthy on Thera." Welker nods. "And I took over for my father as the foreman of driller pilots for the Glenstajj Mining Company." Welker's hand twitches near his pistol. *He's on edge, too.*

His eyes pass suspiciously over each of our crew in turn. *Is he thinking the same as me? That Washo joined just as we were attacked? That Xana wears the face of the enemy's leader? That Bentley seems harmless now but is a killing machine who might be activated at the sound of a code word? That Jak said they were after "the girl"?*

His anxious gaze then lights on me and I meet his stare full on. *You were the one who was in possession of the drug that killed Rollinson, Welker. It's your addiction that makes you wild behind the pilot's harness, fearless. I've long suspected the Tag use to be merely a symptom. You're running from something. Could it have caused you to do something even more reckless—like collude with those who were trying to take Ari? You're the one who has connections here, not me.*

He says nothing to my silent challenge and instead turns toward the approaching docks master. Welker signs the manifest while Tol and I drop off the crates of standard letters at the UFP local boxes. We tell the authorities nothing about the mysterious ship still parked in our cargo bay. We gather at the boarding ramp tense, looking out for any who might show to claim the mysterious cargo.

I feel the vibrations of my siren steel in its ivory scabbard, alive, thirsty. I ready myself for a storm that never arrives.

"No one showed. I guess we have our answer." Welker folds his arms across his chest.

We are gathered in the small, bare room that UFP provides as temporary accommodations. Washo lays on a cot built into the wall groaning with grav sickness. Sanctun's fingers wriggle restlessly. *There's nothing here for him to steal,* I think. Xana stands aloof, Bentley ever off her right shoulder. Welker sits in the one piece of furniture, a rocking chair, back to the wall, feet splayed out.

"Our answer, meaning that Rollinson's lucrative drop-off at Nonthera was a load of bull?" Xana asks.

"It appears that way," Welker admits.

"I don't understand." Tol removes his hat and scratches the scraggly hair on his pate. "I've known Ollie my whole life. He would never sell out his crew. They're like his family." He pauses. Then, "Unless it was for a lot, and I mean a lot, of quan." We all stare at him. "I mean a lot. He did have gambling debts." We continue staring. "But he'd feel really guilty about it. I mean really guilty. What?"

"I don't know about you, but I don't think I'll be making another run in a UFP junker that's being targeted by unknown mercenaries, especially with one of their own ships sitting idly in the cargo bay." Welker pushes himself out of the rocking chair.

"Who put you in charge?" Xana fires back.

"Believe me, darling, I'd like nothing more than to have zero responsibility in this matter. But with our duty to report Rollinson deceased to the company completed, the pilot is the ranking officer. I can request a new commission or not."

I glance at Ari. Earlier, I was worried that she might have a thing for our pilot, Welker, but it's not him that she looks to now. It's me. Welker is a bit like a beloved older brother who always screws things up. But he's just said he's only looking out for himself.

Am I any different? If we were alone, what would I say to her? That none of this is her fault? That we'll get through this together? Her linguistic abilities allow her to intuit so much about a person. I've never spoken a word of my past to her, but in spite of that, I get the feeling she knows everything about me. She accepts it. Still, she trusts me. She shouldn't.

"We should split up," I say coldly. The room stiffens.

"You'd abandon your crew?" Xana's voice burns. Xana has been hateful toward me from the moment she stepped aboard the *Bentley*, watching every move I make. *Why wouldn't she want me gone now?*

"This was just a paycheck," I respond bluntly. "We stay together, we're a target." *I'm sorry, Ari.*

Welker nods. "I'm with the doctor. It seems we all may have been trying to disappear in some way." His eyes land on each of us knowingly. "I suggest we continue the act. We leave the ship in dock, go our separate ways, and allow the authorities to sort the red tape." He throws on his leather coat and hat, dips the brim, and passes out the door and our lives. *One down.*

Xana looks to Sanctun.

"Look, I'm no Luke Starkiller." The fool puts on his stovepipe hat. "I might've grown up on the *Bentley*, but that doesn't mean I haven't always fended for myself. That tub's not safe. K'pla!" He squats to pass through the door and still his stove top hat is knocked from his head. "Grabthar's Hammer!" He curses. *Two.*

"A crew is a family," Xana says.

I had a family once—a father who beat and lobotomized my mother, who murdered my wife and child. I had a conniving sister, another I hardly knew, a brother groomed as my replacement, now dead, and one who is lost somewhere out in the Fracture. "This isn't a family. It's a death trap."

"I thought you were a man of honor," Xana speaks softly.

"What gave you that idea?" I retort. *Stay, Edmon,* a familiar voice whispers inside me. It sounds strangely like Ari's voice. *How did she . . . ?*

I shake it off and walk through the door, leaving another piece of myself behind.

I wander the dim, metallic halls of Capital City. The smell of alien dirt and spices and the dank odor of bodies fill the air. Old crones and waifs alike catcall from cobbled together kiosks. "Salted meat! Genuine article. Not grown in tubs or vats!"

"Hey, Nonny, Nonny! Spacers gear! Cheapest price in the Cap!"

"Vape sticks and more. First purchase free with vend of a second!"

Weird accents and unknown languages echo from the alleys. *Where to now?* I wonder. I rub the iron nose in my pocket. I'm suddenly reminded of a promise I made to Faria. I reach into the lining of my jacket and pull out the nightscript reader. My fingers trace the smooth paneling carved from a long dead tree, and I marvel at the craftsmanship that fused organics with tech. My touch activates the tactile images of the screen. Faria told me that the reader held a map to the treasure of Miral. He never told me what that treasure was, though, only that we would find it together and take revenge upon our enemies.

Vengeance is gone, I think. I searched the vast for nine years looking for a clue to the location of Miral. When I wasn't searching for the lost planet, I tried to find the lost older brother my father told me he had sent away from Tao as a child. Neither quest was fruitful, and with the trails cold, I went about just surviving. Washo is the closest I've come to firsthand knowledge of the empire's mysterious capital. *And here you are, walking away.*

As I think of Washo, another thought strikes me. I almost feel the vibration in the pocket where I stashed the card Washo gave me. I pull it out. The blank screen flickers. An image of a man appears, holding a weapon. It passes so quickly I cannot discern the archetype.

"Invasion. They've blasted through the defensive net of Lyria." The words flee from the edges of my hearing. I stash the nightscript reader and card back in the folds of my jacket. *Lyria? Invasion?* I follow the whispers into the darkness of an alley. *Nothing.* I return to the main corridor.

"They blew out of Market. Same ship for sure. UFP freighter. Authorities were right to impound the ship if it has a bounty that big on it."

I spin around, looking for any sign of the speaker. All I see is a swarming crowd. *Faria would never have let my skills become so weak in the Wendigo.* I need to bend my ear in dark corners where those with evil purpose do their work. Such business can take one to a place in the highest reaches of power or to the pits with the lowest of dregs.

Guess which direction I should go?

The depths of Capital City extend below the crust of Nonthera, into the must of the mining town built into grimy rock. The tunnels are lit by strings of bulbs. They flicker yellow, illuminating piles of refuse along my path.

"Heya, Goodman, spare a quarter?" An old bum in rags extends a withered hand.

I smell the faint layer of ozone permeating from the man's skin—the mark of a Tag addict.

The candle that burns brightest burns twice as fast, Faria used to say. For all I know this man could have been younger and stronger than me not so long ago. I pass a coin into his gnarled fingers. "Tell me where I can find the Smoking Gun?"

He extends a bony finger down the hallway. I nod thanks and head in that direction. Behind me, the wretch shouts, "What kind of coin is this anyhow? What planet are you from, feller? Aw, pieces!" He hurls the coin against the wall with a clatter.

I sigh to myself. *No good deed . . .*

A left turn leads to a stairwell. A doorway barred by hanging beads waits at the end. I glide through, and a lithe woman with a shaved scalp and a diamond painted on her forehead welcomes me. She is topless, sporting small, bare breasts proudly. "What's your pleasure, spacer?" she coos.

I look her up and down. It has been so long since I've felt the touch of a woman. I'm disgusted by my desire and lack of desire all at once. "A drink." I brush past her toward the bar where several large miners fill their tankards with Nontheran grog.

"Ale," I call. A man with ruddy jowls marked by acne pustules slams a metal mug down before me, spilling its froth on the crusty counter. I grab the handle and pretend to sip. I open my ears and am quickly rewarded.

"Dropped through the Fracture Point. A whole fleet of 'em," one burly miner next to me recounts to another.

"Pirate army?"

"Ain't no pirates. Spacers are from Tao."

My blood freezes.

"Where in Breaker's Rock is Tao?"

The first miner shrugs. "Discovered a couple of decades ago near the defunct route in the Radial. Three, four jumps from Market?"

The Fracture Point opened on my birthday. The Islanders believed a star had burst in the sky.

"Lyria just opened her legs for 'em like a blushing bride. Bunch of posies, son. Make a Theran look like a granite drill. Almost like these folks were just beggin' to be gutted."

"You know it's not like Thera or the Nonnies got any kind of defense fleet or nothing if those Tao boys decide to rake it here," says the second.

It has finally happened . . .

"Worst to hear tell, the gov'ment surrendered. Taoans came in and butchered 'em anyway. Killed the doggie or whatever on the opera house steps with some kind of sword. Mandly," the miner calls to the bartender. "Hit the feed. Replay it for 'im."

The Maestro was from Lyria . . . In my darkest hours, I would dream of walking the golden steps of Prospera, bathing in the glow of the grand opera's armillary spheres. Lyria is the planet where Ariel Lazarus was born . . .

"I am Phaestion the First, Patriarch of the House Julii, and the emperor of Tao."

I turn slowly toward the flickering holographic screen mounted to the wall above the bar. The handsome speaker has his fiery hair pulled tightly into a ponytail beneath a silver diadem. He addresses the cam-globes directly.

"I claim Lyria, her moons, Oberus, Titanius, and the surrounding space of its Fracture Point, for the Tao imperium." The lines of my foster brother's angled face are accentuated by the golden Lyrian sun. He is all seriousness, but I feel the faint smile behind his steel-gray eyes. "Bring forth the doge," he commands.

A stately woman in golden robes with graying hair is brought from the crowd. She kneels before Phaestion on the top of the opera house steps.

"Do you yield your authority to me and the Pantheon of Tao?"

The woman is nervous. Her hands are shaking. "Provided there is no more bloodshed, I yield."

Phaestion extends a hand. Another Taoan noble with pale, almost white hair steps forward. *Hanschen.* I recognize Phaestion's kinsman and one of his Companions. He hands Phaestion a silver-and-ivory-handled rapier.

No!

Phaestion stabs the doge between her breasts. A red rose of blood blooms on the woman's golden robes. Then the siren sword vibrates slowly with a mournful howl, disintegrating her body. The woman's screams are silenced as she is vaporized from existence.

The last words Phaestion and I ever shared haunt me now. *If you do not kill me, Edmon, I will murder millions. Billions.*

"Lyria, I have come to free you of weakness. Embrace strength. Embrace purity. We are coming for all worlds of the Nine Corridors. Join our ranks or die!"

A horde of Taoan soldiers, adorned in black spider-weave armor raise their gauntleted fists. "A roo!" they cry.

I feel sick. I drop to my knees gripping my sword-cane like a crutch. *This is my fault. The planets of the Fracture will fall one by one until none are left. I could have stopped this. Edric was right. Edric the torturer, the killer, the leviathan, was right! What have I done?*

"And the bounty?" A whisper of a posh accent from the other end of the bar.

"A million quan deposited wirelessly into an account."

I block out the juke stereo, the holo-screen, the miners' laughs, and the roar of my own shame, and I listen for secrets hushed from the booth in the back.

"All that's required is the capture of a girl?"

"Alive preferably," a voice confirms. "Red hair. Came in on a UFP freighter that busted out of Market."

I stand with fierceness in my eyes and stride through the bar.

"And the rest of the crew?"

"They're expendable."

"Lovely. What was the ship?"

The topless hostess blocks my path, flaunting her wares once more. "Why don't we settle you down, spacer? That corner is for private—" I shove her aside. "Hey!" she shouts.

I close in on the shadows. I feel the heartbeats of the men in the booth. *Three. One with thinning white hair, an eyepatch, and a scarred face. Most likely a shrapnel hit. He's the informant.*

Another, huge and muscular, green hair, a phyto-mutant. These guys again? Strong, but slow and dull-witted. Deal with him first.

The third, an erratic pulse. Tag addict. He will be quick. Something familiar about his pulse . . .

I pull back the curtain swathed around the table, and the dim light reveals . . . the outlaw, Clay Welker. My blood boils. "Is this a private conversation, or can anyone join?" I ask.

The phyto-mutant jumps from his seat. I'm too swift. The butt of my cane drives into his solar plexus. The green-haired man gasps for air. A tap of my finger to the pressure point behind his ear sends him into unconsciousness. My next touch is to Eyepatch's left shoulder. Then his right. His arms useless, he stands to run. I shove the butt of my cane into his inner thigh. He falls as the nerves to his left leg cease firing. He flops on the floor kicking his right leg until I tap his other thigh, then hoist him, fully paralyzed, back into the booth. I turn, but Welker's twin pistols are already cocked and aimed directly at my forehead.

"Move." Welker flashes a cold grin. I need no second warning. I duck. The radiation pulses of his pistols blast two burly thugs behind me. They drop to the floor writhing in pain and vomiting. Welker stands. He eyes the bar patrons, who have risen to their feet, readying for a brawl.

"The large fellow with the stick"—he means me—"and I are going to have a private chat with our friend here." The outlaw gently clicks the mode of his pistols from sick to kill. "I suggest that everyone else kindly keep their distance."

Welker didn't betray us. He was here getting information just like I was. Damn it, I walked right into it.

One of the miners pulls his pistol and makes a move. Welker plants a bullet a centimeter from the man's toe. "I warned you, Clarence, didn't I?"

"Speaking of posies, if it isn't Clay Welker. Welcome back to Nonny ground, you Theran priss." Clarence, the miner who had been yapping before, says, "I'm sure Jace Thrance will be glad to hear that the man who stole a shipment of prime Tag from her is back on the rock."

So that's why Welker ran from this place.

"Hey, Nonny, Nonny, no." Welker smiles grimly. "Doctor, I don't mind if you hurry this. My incredible good looks can only buy us a certain amount of leeway."

I return my glower to Eyepatch. "Who put out the bounty on the *Bentley*?"

"What the hell did you do to me?" He tries to move.

"They always ask that, don't they, Doctor?" Welker grins, keeping an eye on Clarence. "I want to help you, Flix, but my friend here is not so kind with his gifts unless you answer his questions."

Good knight, bad knight. I know the game and my role. I grin in the man's face. He shakes. "Bounty weren't on the *Bentley*. Just the girl," he grunts.

"Why?" I pull the man nose to nose. I give him the stare I saw my father give those who would cross him so often.

"I only deliver the deals!" He shivers like a child. The sound of running water against the floor means Eyepatch has lost control of his bladder; such is the fierceness Edric taught me.

I toss the man back into the booth. I slam my fist against the brick wall of the bar next to his head, cratering it on impact. "Who do you work for?" I bellow.

"Thrance! Jace Thrance!"

"Oh, Doctor." Welker lets out a gasp. I spin around to look at him. "Thrance. She's the pirate queen of Nonthera." He staggers, his pistols flopping around. "And she wants my head as well."

"Welker?"

Laughter. "Maybe you want to see to your friend first, bum sucker!" Eyepatch giggles hysterically. "And maybe you should check what's in your hit before you play Tag, Welker. You're it."

Welker collapses to the floor.

This is not good.

CHAPTER 7

The Wheel of Fortune

> Where once you were up, now you are down. Drawing this card reflects the mercurial nature of existence and how fortunes change in a blink of an eye. Prepare for an equal and opposite reaction.
>
> —Ovanth, *A Practical Reading of the Arcana*

They charge from all sides. I step in front of Welker and unsheathe my blade. The screaming siren burns my ears as I block a hail of bullets. They puff into smoke with a touch of singing steel. *Damn you, Welker, wake up!* The pilot was always better at strategy. Me? I'm just a raging barbarian. *Become the storm,* Faria once said.

I grab Welker and hoist him onto my shoulders and do what the local toughs least expect—charge. I plow into Clarence, knocking the pistol from his grasp. I grab him and use him as a shield. A hail of bullets rips into the man's back. I toss the body aside, will energy into my legs, and then leap with inhuman power, Welker still on my shoulders. I slash downward with my sword, and a bar table explodes against the sonic pulse. The explosion knocks my assailants to their asses, and I use the distraction to sprint for the exit. I burst up the stairs, then down the trash-filled corridor toward the lift.

"No. That way," Welker groans in my ear.

I swerve, following the limp point of my pilot's hand into a graffiti-filled alley. I duck against the wall. Seconds later, a cadre of Capital City security officers trample the corridor past the alley.

"UFP crew," an officer's voice flashes into a comm. "Armed and dangerous. Tip-off says they were in the Smoking Gun. I want everyone locked and loaded. Sergeant?"

"One: Clay Welker. Counts of armed robbery, drug possession, and work evasion. Cap, he's the son of a former foreman. Glenstajj. Theran, Cap. From the 'to do.' The other one: Doctor Edmon Leontes. Nets aren't bringing up much, sir."

"Looks like one strong, mean mother," the captain says, snickering. "Execute with extreme prejudice." I hear the clicks of pistol safeties. "If you spot the girl, she is not to be harmed."

Ari. Who is after you?

"Work elevator." Welker moans and points to the end of the alley. I carry him through the refuse and rats of the alleyway. "Set me down." He winces as I lower him to the ground, keeping my sword at the ready. He tears the covering off an electric access panel revealing a set of ancient copper wires.

"They still use wired electricity here?" I ask, astonished at the antiquated tech.

"Solar power and sonics take a lot more engineering," Welker grunts. "Sometimes the old shift is the simplest shift." The elevator doors scrape open halfway with a hiss of steam. "Piss." Welker exhales and passes out again.

I force the rusty doors apart with brute strength and drag my comrade into the steel lift, just as an officer in brown shines a glow torch down the alleyway. "Sarge!"

I slam my fist on the Close Door button and yank the lever for the top floor. The old lift screeches skyward. Welker groans. I kneel down to examine him—cold, sweating, heart racing. I remember training hours in darkness, examining meridians of the body. I do what I can now to slow his heart, steady the flow of blood, but the narcotics inside him are tearing him apart. *This is beyond my skill. Damn you, Welker.*

The pilot went to the watering hole to gather info. *You couldn't walk away, either, could you, Outlaw?*

A sudden realization strikes. *They know we're UFP. They tracked us to the Smoking Gun. If they could do that, it could lead them back . . . Faster, damn it!* I will the elevator to move quicker.

"Samson! My son!" Welker claws his way from unconsciousness again. "Doctor, I need to find my wife and son!"

"What are you talking about?" I shake my head. *Welker is married with a child?*

"It's my fault," he says, suddenly regaining a sense of where we are and what's happening, but also desperate to tell me before he passes out again. "We were too young to be parents. I came to Nonthera thinking I could replace my father. Be the boss. Run the division. The men didn't trust me. They didn't respect me. I was in over my head. I thought with the Tag . . . I didn't know it was lethal. I incurred gambling debts, debts to my dealers, debts to Thrance. Millicent left me, took Samson with her. I had to make amends. I had to care for my boy. I decided nothing mattered anymore without them. I threw all caution to the wind . . ."

"You stole from Thrance," I fill in the blank.

"I have to find them. My son has to know I love him. I'm not a disappointment. Before I die, I have to find them."

His eyes start to dart wildly. His heart threatens to pound through his chest. "First, you need to calm down, or you *will* die, right here, right now," I tell him.

"Promise me!" He reaches up and clutches my shirt.

"I promise, Welker, we'll find your boy." I reach down and gently tap a pressure point sending him into slumber. I don't know what to make of what he's just confessed, but I have no time to dwell on it. *Ari and the rest of the crew are in danger.*

The lift doors open with a screech. I hoist Welker over my shoulder once more and run through an alley to kick open a work door. We spill onto iron catwalks that crisscross upper levels. Neon signs blink from storefronts. Commercial district. Too many people. If someone were to snipe at us now, I wouldn't see it coming.

But there's something else. I feel that weird, cold sensation, like we're being followed by shadows or ghosts. The hair prickles on the back of my neck.

I hurry to the dump motel where UFP housed the crew. "Greetings, guest four one seven," the computerized voice hails. "Live staff is currently away from the desk . . ."

I rush past and up the stairs to our closet stack and kick the door open.

The room is trashed, panels broken, electronic wires strewn everywhere. I lay Welker on the floor, hand on my cane. I close my eyes. Open my senses. One heartbeat, very, very faint, as if it's being masked. *Who can do that besides me? Male. Small. Maybe fifty-five kilograms. On the ceiling?* My sword sings as I swing my blade high.

"Washo?"

The spypsy boy has plastered himself to the ceiling and covered himself with a sheet to blend in. He lets loose a shriek of terror and drops with a thud. "There was nothing I could do," he sobs as he climbs from under the sheet.

I sheathe my sword. "What happened?" I snarl, trying to remain calm.

"Men came. Big. Dirty. They took her," he whispers.

Ariel! I slam a fist on a closet panel, and a cot slides from the wall. I lift Washo and lay him down, trying to control my rage. "Did they say who they were?"

He shakes his head. "It all happened so fast. Then Nontheran security came. Ransacked the room. I stayed hidden."

"Where are Tol and . . ." *Rushing heartbeats from the stairs. Traveling much too quickly, faster than any normal human.* I whip my sword to the ready and confront the statuesque silhouette of a battle queen. Behind her, Bentley stands like a grim sentinel. "Xana."

"Where's Ari?" Her eyes are blackest coal.

"Taken," I growl in accusation. "Where were you?" We meet toe to toe. Her hand itches for her extensor staff. I feel the hum of my siren sword.

"You left us," she says.

"Because she was in danger if I stayed. I thought . . ." How do I explain to this woman my life of running, of trying to escape my past? "I'm not her sworn protector."

"No, you're a traitor!" Xana's voice burns like ice.

Her hand reaches for her weapon; I ready my sword. There is the click of a pistol. Bentley holds his gun to my temple, finger hovering on the trigger. Even with my speed, both of them are enhanced; there's no way I can win.

"Whoa!" Tol's stovepipe hat covers the light beyond the doorway. "You guys are worse than Bruce Willis and Cybill Shepherd in *Moonlighting*!"

"Where the hell have you been?" Xana barks.

I relax, relieved that the tension has been diffused.

"You know, things to see, people to do." Tol sounds nonchalant, but I feel his heart pulsing rapidly like a lying toddler. "What's wrong with Welker?"

"Poisoned," I rasp.

"What?" they blurt in unison.

"Given a faulty Tag patch. I don't know what was in it."

Xana's eyes narrow. "By whom?"

"Presumably the same people who kidnapped Ari and have tried to kill us," I say.

"Can't you, like, fix him?" Tol asks.

I push past him, and gently as I can, I hoist our pilot from the floor onto another cot. "I'm a doctor, Tol, not a damn miracle worker."

"You don't know how happy you're making me right now," he says, giddy. I fire him a murderous look. "Well, you know," he says, "all circumstances considered."

"There was a name I got. Same name I heard right before we were attacked in the Leaky Engine."

"Jace Thrance?" Xana asks. She heard it, too.

"The pirate queen of Nonthera," Tol affirms.

"What do you know of her, Tol?" Xana turns to ask.

"She's big. Probably the most well-known crime lord in the local parsecs. In fact, her operation is too lucrative for the authorities out here to do anything about, which isn't saying much since the economies of Thera, Nonthera, and any other satellites and stations rely on the illegal labor of her network. If she wants Ari, then it means we're screwed. The authorities won't help. More likely to arrest us and hand our corpses over to Thrance themselves."

"We are getting her back." Xana's voice is deadly calm. "Doctor, how would you like to join me for a little chat with Jace Thrance?"

I smile menacingly. For once, Xana and I agree.

We whisk toward the highest levels of the arcology. I calm my breath as Xana swims the confines of the lift like a caged panthro-shark.

"Don't like this," she mutters. "You think a storage locker is safe?"

"It's all relative," I grumble. "Washo's useless planetside, Tol not much better, and Welker's at death's door. Dum-dum Bentley will be there to shoot anything that looks at them sideways."

"Don't call him that," she warns. *She's taken a maternal tack with the designer organic that could turn out to be very harmful to us,* I think.

"What I don't like," she continues, "is walking in there frontal-assault style with nothing to offer. They may as well just shoot us dead."

"She may try and kill us, but we might find out where Ari is or the purpose behind the bounty."

"Easy for you to say. You have a death wish, Leontes," she responds coldly.

She's right. If one's soul could join the ancestors beyond the veil of this world, then I would wish for death to see my loved ones again. As it is, I can only hope death will relieve the pain I endure for losing them.

"Son of Edric the Leviathan, you believed you had nothing to live for so you ran. What about the people you left behind?" Xana turns her dark gaze on me.

"What do you know of who I am?"

"I know you had a chance to free your people. Instead you disappeared. You ran like a coward." She looks me up and down coolly. "I know that you're selfish and small, exile. If you think that Ari could ever love someone like you or that I would allow that, then you're also a fool."

Her words cut deeper than any blade. She lays my greatest shames to bear on that elevator floor. "Who are you?"

"I may have been raised on Lyria," she says. "But I wasn't born there."

I reach into the corners of memory. In another life, my foster brother Phaestion forced all of his Companions to compete for his affections. A contest sent us to the arcologies of Tao to retrieve a data card. I remember I met a little girl that day in the slums. She moved like no other I'd ever seen, enhanced by some genetic manipulation. The renegade spypsy Talousla Karr later admitted that he had experimented on Tao's populace. He'd created Phaestion Julii, cloned him from his father's genes, and enhanced him. The little girl had been another of his experiments. I never knew her name . . .

The realization explodes like a missile in my brain. For the first time, my eyes connect with Xana's in an understanding of our shared past. Before I can say another word, the lift doors open onto the penthouse floor of Capital City. Apparently, Jace Thrance owns the entire uppermost level.

I allow a mask of stoicism to fall as Xana and I pass through a beautiful arboretum. The bloodred star fills the view of the crystal-domed ceiling. Manicured lawns and gardens line the walkway. The clack of my cane keeps time with the chirping of yellow songbirds.

"You think this Jace Thrance is well-off?"

"I think when wealth like this is in the hands of a single individual, there must be some injustice perpetrated upon thousands," Xana responds.

A large ebony desk stands as a guardian at the end of the walkway, a stainless steel doorway looming behind. A beautiful, painted woman with black hair styled in curling waves down one side of her face looks up from her work. Her eyes widen in shock.

"We're here to see Jace Thrance," Xana says.

"How did you—?" Flustered, the woman clears away stacks of paper as she reaches under the desk.

"Don't call security." Xana activates her extensor staff, elongating its tip till it reaches underneath the woman's chin. "I'm sure Ms. Thrance will want to see us."

"How did you get into the lift?" The woman's voice is admirably steely.

I toss a human hand, dripping with blood onto the table. "Your man was more than willing with the retinal scan after I obliged him to lend a hand with the palm-print identification." Tol would be proud of the jest.

"Not only are you two still alive, but delivered directly to my door," a pixie voice pipes in over the arboretum's surround sound. Xana and I scan for the recorders that this so-called "pirate queen" is watching us on. "Perhaps I should simply kill you, save myself time and trouble dealings with any more UFP gutter trash."

"Not until you've heard our offer," Xana responds.

"You have nothing I desire."

"Don't we?" Xana baits. "You know we made it to Nonthera in spite of your men who attacked us in the Leaky Engine and the ship that intercepted us outside of Market. Your agents in the Smoking Gun were unable to subdue Leontes or Welker. Tell us where our friend is, and we'll serve you."

There is a beat of silence. Then a hiss of compressed air as the stainless steel doors part behind the desk to reveal a petite woman in silk robes. Her purple hair cascades in ringlets framing a delicately tattooed face and ever so slightly pointed ears. She enters on a palanquin carried by two giant phyto-mutants. *I'm really sick of these guys.* They lower the palanquin, and Thrance delicately steps off the chair, and her sultry hips sway toward us. Her sapphire gaze looks me up and down. "You, I do not trust. However you"—she assesses Xana—"seem like someone I can do business with."

I sense something in the air, some imperceptible intoxication. *Pheromones.* The woman is manipulating her body chemistry to make herself irresistible. I've felt such effects before from Phaestion. However, my own abilities allow me to be aware of the manipulation, if not to completely control my reaction to it.

"I will do anything," Xana whispers. I see the rush of blood to Xana's cheeks, hear her increased heart rate. Thrance is smart. She knows that even though Xana may be bred for battle, she's still susceptible to feminine biochemistry.

"I wonder if you understand the full extent of what that means?" Thrance smiles, seeing the effect she has. She leans in toward Xana and smells her. "Interesting."

"You manipulate pheromones," I growl.

"And I read them on others," Thrance admits. "Scent is a language. It can tell a lot about a person. Wants, desires, fears, all that is built into their very genetic code." She turns her gaze again on Xana. "I believe you. It's what you were designed for."

Xana bristles at the mention of an artificial origin.

Thrance saunters back to her chair. "I need a brain. Preferably a live female brain. There is a premium on such items currently. However, more important than gender is the skill set. I need the brain of an exceptional pilot. Would you happen to know someone in possession of such an organ?"

Xana flashes me a look.

CHAPTER 8

The Strangers

> They say a stranger is a friend who has not yet been met. The stranger card represents the formation of bonds among the people who surround you. It is a time where past differences must be set aside to work for the common good, but beware the destruction of the bond once the task is complete.
>
> —Ovanth, *A Practical Reading of the Arcana*

"Stinger." Welker groans the nickname we've given to the ships that attacked us outside of Market for their sleek, hornet shape. I lower him back down so that we remain hidden by the railings of the catwalk above the bay where the recently arrived stinger is docked.

Thrance has handed over Ari to these mysterious designer organic soldiers. She helped capture her, but she's not the one who ultimately wants her.

"The more pieces we have, the harder the puzzle becomes," I grumble.

"And the less clear the picture looks," Xana concurs. Xana, too, is a puzzle. If she is the little girl I met on Tao, the product of Talousla Karr's genetic manipulations, that still does not answer how and why she was brought to Lyria and made Ari's bodyguard. *Nor why she looks like our attackers' leader.*

Head in the game, Edmon, I admonish.

Xana and I have paid Thrance back for aiding our enemies. We were able to sneak aboard the *Bentley* earlier, disconnect the dead brain from the stinger ship still parked in its cargo bay, and present it to Thrance as the pilot brain she required of us. With a little chemical ingenuity, I was able to simulate neural function—for a limited time, but long enough to fool Thrance's so-called "experts." We were rewarded with the location of Ari's kidnappers.

Xana may hate my guts, but when we need to get a job done, we're actually a pretty good pair. But if we don't hurry up, then as soon as Thrance finds out we've pulled one over on her, we're going to have every constable, thug, and miner alike on Nonthera gunning for us.

"Tol should create a diversion. Then one of us sneaks aboard to find Ari," Welker strategizes. He's been in and out of consciousness since the Smoking Gun. I just hope he can keep it together long enough for us to help him find a cure. "The rest of us stay here and promptly lay down cover fire for the inevitable shoot-out," he says.

"You guys, maybe I should stay back, you know, provide moral support. I can spy thirty-two guarding the ship with ARC-49s. Ten on the inside. Ari's in the med bay, sedated. You're never going to get in, grab her, and get out again unscathed."

I shoot a scrutinizing look at Tol. He shrugs sheepishly. "Lucky guess?"

Whale dung. Sanctun is not who (or what) he says he is, either. Clearly his eyes aren't human, even if his outdated references are. *This keeps getting worse.*

"No one will be expiring today." Welker smiles weakly. "We're rescuing Ari and burning from Theran space as fast as the currents in the dark matter can take us."

I wish I had the outlaw's optimism. As it is, I feel I'm the most expendable. "I should be the one to go inside," I whisper.

"No!" Xana's response is automatic.

"Think it through, Caprio," I hiss back. "You're much better with the gun than I am. I was trained to crawl through darkness and be silent. Washo?" I nod at the spypsy boy. "How's that grav sickness? Think you can manage to accompany me for old time's sake? Maybe disable a few systems?"

He nods.

"Well, I'm glad that's decided." Our pilot draws his dual pistols from his thigh holsters as if every movement is excruciating pain. "Just have Bentley boy here prop me and aim me right."

The soldier looks at Xana, who nods. He picks Welker up and positions him with guns trained on the gangway of the stinger ship below.

"You guys, have we really thought this through?" Tol asks, exasperated. "When Thrance finds out you gave her a dead brain—"

I grab him by the collar and shove him toward the docking bay lift. The lank fool in the top hat smiles and cracks his knuckles. "I was just kidding, Doc. You know I got this. Okay, batter up." He strides off.

"Come on, Washo," I growl.

"Wait." Xana catches my shoulder. *Damn if she isn't strong.* "If you do anything to harm Ari . . ."

"How could you ever think that I'd harm her?" I look Xana in the eye. *You may be strong, Xana, but I'm tougher than you know.*

"Tol's right," she adds.

I nod. "Yes, Thrance will come after us. Even if she doesn't figure out our ruse, she'd have every reason to recapture Ari and bargain for more with her kidnappers. Why do you think Thrance let us go in the first place?" I pull Xana close and whisper, "Look, I know you would have given Welker's brain if you thought it would save Ari. Your devotion was why Thrance trusted us. You said we're a family. We're not. We're a bunch of self-interested, lowlife bastards. Even you. Except Ariel. She's the reason I'm still here. You may think you know who I used to be. You've no idea. But Ari does. Somehow . . . she knows everything. And still she . . ."

In twelve years, I've never spoken about what happened to me that led me to flee Tao. I've never been able to be vulnerable with anyone. Yet Ari not only seems to know who I am, she seems to see the song buried inside me. If I let her, she would give me a chance. And only a few hours ago, I almost threw that chance away. "By the twisted star. You won't understand."

I turn away from Xana and head off toward my mission.

—

Quietly, Washo and I skirt the dock perimeter. I duck behind two large cargo boxes as an armored soldier passes. I seize the man and jam my fingers into his neck. He slumps into my arms. I pull the soldier behind a storage container and rip the helmet from the man's head.

"Just like Bentley," Washo whispers. *Whoever has put the bounty on Ari has the resources to buy an army of these designer organics.*

"Greetings, gentle beings!" Tol Sanctun's voice rings across the cavernous bay. He doffs his stovepipe hat and bows in a maneuver that seems graceful and clumsy all at once. "Tol Sanctun at your service. The master of port has persuaded me to ply my trade for all of his good Nonny customers." Tol opens his coat, revealing it's lined with all sorts of odds and ends, timepieces, cellular communicators, jewelry . . . The soldiers gather around the fool with their rifles aimed.

"Go," I hiss to Washo. We move around the back of the stinger craft. I grab Washo and gently toss him up onto the roof. The spypsy boy's sticky pads glue themselves to the hull. He slowly crawls his way to an emergency hatch. Meanwhile, I slink around to the front gangway.

"I'm also a purveyor of magic, gentleman!" Tol displays an ancient pocket watch in one fingerless-gloved hand. *Where did he get such an ancient artifact?* He covers it with the other hand then opens both hands. Empty.

"It disappeared!" one of the soldiers says, astonished. *Sleight of hand.* I scan with keen eyes and still don't spy the watch palmed in either of Sanctun's gloves. Indeed, the watch has vanished. *There's definitely something up with him.*

"What's going on?" The distorted voice of the ship's captain sounds as she strides down the boarding ramp.

I silently leap behind her onto the gangway and slip inside the ship. A soldier guarding the door drops into my arms at my deadly touch. I lay him on the floor. "Washo?" I whisper down the hall.

"She's in the med bay," he calls back as quietly as he can. *Just like Sanctun guessed . . .*

"What was that?" I hear the captain's voice.

"What was what?" Tol tries to delay her.

Damn! I slam my palm on the hatch controls, retracting the ramp and locking the door. Gunfire erupts. A man screams. *Move now!* I think. *If the layout of this ship is similar to the other one, the med bay should be . . .*

I open the door. Ariel lies quietly on the table in peaceful slumber. Her fiery locks are shorn and electrodes are stuck to her skull. Their filaments connect her to the ship's unfamiliar medical systems. My breath catches for an instant seeing her in such beautiful repose, the cares of the world erased from her brow.

"Who are you?" a voice hisses. Siren steel sings as I unsheathe my blade, twirl it, and gently kiss the edge against the throat of a small, hairless man—a spypsy. "Orc's blood! The shadow of Los!" he says, eyes wide with fear.

"It will be your blood if you don't tell me what you're doing to her!" I snarl.

The man quivers. "She is the Orc. We would not harm her."

Behind me, Ari gasps, and her body tenses on the table. The ship's bone walls begin to pulse with color. There is a cracking sound. I quickly turn back to see the spypsy biting down hard. *An artificial tooth filled with poison!* My sword clatters to the deck, and I clutch for the man's mouth. "No! Damn you!" I'm too late. The poison seal has been broken, and the man passes into the darkness.

I toss his corpse aside, clip my scabbard to my belt, and run to Ari. The lights on the surface of the walls flash with greater intensity. "The shadow is coming," she whispers.

I feel that darkness in the back of my brain again and get the weird sensation that I'm being watched by something unseen. "Ari, are you there?" I whisper. "Can you hear me?"

"Los must be birthed from the Sky Consciousness," she mumbles. "The light of Urizen must meet it." I glance up at the medical readouts of her brain waves. They peak and valley with greater and greater frequency. *She is interfacing her mind with the ship itself.* "Seal the breach. Mother and stillborn, stillborn, stillborn . . ."

Gunfire outside the ship intensifies. We need to move, but I don't want to disconnect her if her mind is still interfacing. "Ari," I whisper. "If you can hear me, come back to us. There are people here who love you, who need you." My voice catches. "Please . . ." It's all I can think to say.

"Edmon?" Her cerulean eyes open. *Thank the Elder Stars.* I hold her pale hands in mine. "I knew you'd come for me," she says, then just as quickly slips back into her coma. I tear the electrodes from her shorn head and lift her into my arms.

"Doctor, I've done what I could." Washo appears in the doorway, panting.

"Washo Tan," I growl. "Look at that man. Do you know him to be of your clan?"

Washo peers down at the dead spypsy doctor on the floor. He lifts the spypsy's hands and scrutinizes the wrists for something, I don't know what. "This man is not of Armada," Washo whispers with fear.

"Find them!" the distorted voice of the captain blares from the hallway.

With Ari slung over my shoulder, I snag my sword from the floor. "Climb on!" I shout to Washo. The boy jumps on my back as well. Faria taught me to harness my rage as energy. *Become the storm,* he would say. Now, I let loose an inhuman howl of fury and barrel down the hallway bowling over two soldiers. My siren sword screams as I swing it low, cleaving the captain's legs off below the knees. They are vaporized with a sonic boom, and she tumbles to the deck. I turn my blade against the gangway door that has been sealed shut, and I drive in the edge to carve a new exit. I kick the hatch open and leap from the ship into a hail of gunfire.

Bullets zip past as I run, carrying my crew. "Head down, Washo!" I scream. A soldier goes down to my right, then left, as Welker's, Xana's, and Bentley's cover fire picks them off one by one. A bullet rips through my bicep. I roar more from frustration than pain as I dash headlong for the shooter. I smash my boot into the man's face, sending the soldier feet over head.

Sanctun peeps from behind a storage container where he's been cowering. "Plus eight to strength while on berserker rage, Doctor Batman!"

"Shut up, Tol!" I growl.

"Leontes!" Xana screams from the balcony above.

"Come on!" I yell at Sanctun, not stopping. I leap up a stack of cargo boxes, toss Washo up to the catwalk, then with Ari safely tucked in my arms, jump. I land like a leopard gull on the balcony.

Welker and Bentley continue to lay down suppressing fire. Xana throws a hand down to catch Sanctun, who jumps and falls short. She yanks him up with inhuman strength as he flails. "Is she hurt?" Xana screams desperately at me, seeing Ari, comatose with shorn skull.

"She's with us," I growl.

"Bentley, grab Welker. Tol, watch our six." Xana shoves a pistol into Tol's long-fingered hands.

"Are you sure that's the best option?" he squawks.

"Follow me." Xana slams a bullet-pulse cartridge into her rifle for emphasis and takes charge like an Anjin commander of old. We follow her lead through narrow alleys of the Capital City docking district. She ruthlessly shoots down several gunmen who spring from corners. My heart pounds, and I'm losing blood from my arm. We arrive at the UFP *James Bentley*'s docking bay door.

Xana reaches for the hatch, but I grab her hand. "Wait!"

"Take your hand off me, *Doctor*."

"Xana," Welker groans from his position draped over Bentley's shoulders. "Ol' Thrance will have the ship guarded. We walk in there, we might as well hand her Ari and the rope to hang us, too."

"I'm counting on it." Her gaze is black fire. *Do I trust her?* Xana will die before she allows Ari to be captured again. However, I also know she'd be willing to give us up if she had no other choice. Worse, she shares the face of the mentally programmed designer organics. *How can I be sure she is in full control of her own subliminal programming?*

I grin like the serpent of the deep and bow. "Lead the way."

She pulls the lever. The heavy metal hatch of the docking bay slides open. Unsurprisingly, we stare down hundreds of gun barrels pointed at us from every direction. Clicks reverberate like a swarm of locusts as the mercenaries cock their pieces.

"Hold!" the amplified pixie voice pipes in. The crowd of ruffians parts for the purple-haired pirate queen, carried again on a palanquin by those two huge phyto-mutant bodyguards. Her tattooed face smirks. "I'm only surprised at the fact that you tried to escape aboard your old ship knowing that would be the most likely place I would come for you." Then Thrance's eyes settle on the pilot draped over Bentley's broad shoulders. "Clay Welker," she says icily.

Welker winces as he takes his arm off Bentley and shuffles forward. "Tougher than I look, eh, Thrance?"

Jace Thrance's sapphire eyes falls upon Xana. "You broke our agreement, Ms. Caprio."

"We delivered to you the brain of a pilot," I scratch out sarcastically. "The gray matter has decayed, but you didn't check. That's not really our concern, is it?"

"Edmon of House Leontes. Since our last meeting I've learned there's a man who has proclaimed himself an emperor on Lyria who may pay most handsomely for delivering the body of a coward and an exile to him. You've brought me Welker and the girl, who I'm sure I can resell. So I can't complain too much. Leave the girl and the pilot alive. Murder the rest!" the pirate queen shouts to the cavern filled with miners and criminals of Nonthera.

"Tol, now!" Xana screams. Tol removes his top hat, revealing a wireless signaler. He flips the trigger. A flash of firelight hits our retinas before the boom slams our ears. I fall, shielding Ari's fragile form from the explosion's heat. When I lift my head, men are burning, screaming, and running pell-mell in all directions. *Xana had already set bombs all through the docking bay,* I realize. *Smart.*

"Move!" Xana commands.

I sweep Ari into my arms like the demigod Phobion who protected the dying embers of the first Elder Stars. I leap toward our UFP junker. My naked siren steel hums, and in one stroke, I vaporize the legs of Thrance's phyto-mutants who block the path. The palanquin crashes to the floor, Thrance shrieking as she tumbles. My crew runs behind me for the boarding ramp while I brandish the singing blade at Thrance's throat.

"They call you Leviathan," she spits out. "Is that what dead men do on your world? Take the names of animals?" Her next words are cut off by the strike of my fingers to her neck, sending her into a deep coma.

The sound of a pulse rifle action clicks. I turn, and another black-armored captain of the designer organics strides through the flames at the head of a column of soldiers. *Too many for me alone . . .*

"Get aboard." The words come coldly off Xana's lips. She steps between me and the soldiers. The captain tilts her head at Xana in recognition. Something tells me I know the face beneath the helmet.

Xana snaps the action on her rifle. "Bentley, go," she says to the soldier off her shoulder. The man grimaces and carries Welker up the boarding ramp behind Tol and Washo.

"Ari needs you," I growl.

Xana pulls the trigger, unleashing a hail of bullets at the designer organics. I sprint for the gangway with Ari in my arms. Xana dives into the ship right behind and slams the hatch closed. Bullets beat a tattoo against the door in our wake. "Washo, fire it up!" I howl as I sprint past the engine hatch. "Welker, are you well enough to fly this thing?" I shout at the cockpit as I swerve into the med bay.

"I could use a bit o' yer magic right now, Doc," he hollers back.

"You have to save Ari first!" Xana stands in the doorway panting.

I lay Ari down and secure her to the med bay cot. "We're all dead if Welker can't get this bucket moving." I turn to Xana, trying to remain calm. "On guns, Xana, now."

Her eyes spit hatred at me, but she launches herself at the gunnery port ladder.

These people, these misfits, I shouldn't care for any of them. Our captain is dead, our pilot is dying, our security officer is compromised . . . I don't even know who I am anymore. I look at the peaceful face of the sleeping, defenseless girl on the cot. *I don't know who or what you are, either.*

I cut off the tumult of my emotions and snag as many stimulants and aerosol injectors as I can and race for the cockpit.

"Washo, I need that fusion reactor turning now!" Welker's hoarse voice screams.

"What am I doing? What am I doing? What am I doing . . ."

"Shut up, Tol," Welker and I say in unison as I inject aerosol adrenaline into Welker's neck. The microparticles course into his system. I place a few pressure point taps to his trapezius muscles to open the meridians. Welker gasps, his entire body spasms, and he slumps back into the pilot chair.

"We're a go!" Washo cries over the comm.

The outlaw's eyes snap open. "That's some good lovin'!" He glides his hands into the steering gloves and his feet into the power boots as he connects with the ship's drive.

"Gas it!" I growl.

Out the cockpit viewscreen, the black-clad soldiers are mounting a chain gun on a tripod. The *Bentley* lurches and bucks as vertical thrusters fire her heavy iron ass into the air.

"Xana?" I hit the comm button. My question is answered by a "Krakoom!" The *Bentley*'s asteroid cannon blasts the doors of the docking bay wide open. The soldiers below fall to their backs while we shield our eyes from the flash.

"Can we fit?" I snarl at Welker.

"Don't have much choice," Welker says as he steps on the accelerator. There's a screech as metal tears from our hull when the *Bentley* scrapes through the opening. Chunks of debris fly as we blast out of the Nontheran arcology.

I catch the rearview display on the flight panel and watch as metal twists from our hull and falls away toward the earth.

"What did we lose?" Tol cries out.

"Too much," I mutter. "Can we break the g?"

"Sentry ships coming from the surface," Xana says over the comm.

"We can't take more damage and be vacuum solid!" Welker yells.

"UFP *James Bentley*, you will cease your attempt to flee Nontheran airspace. Turn your vessel around, or we will bring you down," the static-filled voice of a sentry ship chimes.

"More bogeys at eleven o'clock. Stinger profile," Tol calls out.

The people who are hunting Ari. I grit my teeth. "How many?" I look at the holo-display and spy a swarm of red phosphorescent blips. The *Bentley* shakes as bullets ping the hull.

"One is too many!" Welker howls. He turns the power gloves and screams the *Bentley* skyward. A stinger swings past our front view aiming for a head-on collision. Closer . . . closer . . .

"Come on, y'all," the outlaw whispers. At the last second, he slams his feet down, lurching the brakes and sending our hulk into a spinning free fall.

I slam to the ceiling next to the soldier Bentley, and then I am immediately plastered to the deck as Welker engages the thrusters. He loops us skyward again into the Nontheran stratus.

"Can we outrun them?" I try to push myself to standing, bleeding from the arm and mouth now.

"I'm good"—Welker shakes his head—"but I ain't that good . . ."

Another stinger comes into view. She fires a missile. Welker dives to dodge. "She's coming around!" screams Tol. A boom echoes. "We're breached!"

Then all I hear is the roar of wind blasting my ears.

CHAPTER 9

The Lovers

> To find love is to recognize the reflection of one's soul in another, be it a person or a career. However, the lovers' card also comes with the knowledge that there is a cost. To embrace the other, one must lose a piece of oneself first.
>
> —Ovanth, *A Practical Reading of the Arcana*

I rip Tol's safety straps and yank him from the nav seat. "Slave the drive, Welker!" I scream above the rushing atmosphere through our shredded canopy. "Bentley, grab him!" I'm already racing down the hall, slamming into bulkheads and dragging Tol behind me. I punch a comm panel. "All hands to the cargo bay!"

Xana drops from the gun port access tube with feline grace. "Grab Ari!" I bark. I toss Tol into the cargo bay access tube and jump after him as the ship free falls. A boom sounds as we're smacked by an electromagnetic pulse. A hole rips open behind me. Atmosphere rushes in, and Tol almost flies out. I grab him, my tendons tearing against the force. The ship's blast shield seals off the breach momentarily, and the g pulls us down. I tumble to the cargo deck floor, the bones in my leg snapping on impact. I suck in my breath at the excruciating pain. Xana drops right behind with Ari in her arms.

"Xana," I croak through the pain of my artificial vocal cords. "Get her on board." I point to the enemy stinger ship still in our cargo bay. She races past me up the ramp. Tol scrambles off the floor and careens behind her. Bentley drags Welker aboard. Suddenly, Washo is by my side. *When did he get here?* My body is going into shock. I need to concentrate to stave off the effects of my injuries, at least until they are out of this.

Washo tugs at me. "A squire doesn't leave his master behind," he yelps, but I'm much too heavy for him, especially as the ship spins. Another boom and Washo falls. More rushing air.

"Go!" I scream at the boy. "That's an order!"

The boy runs up the gangway. *They're all safely aboard.* I hear the engine firing. *I did it. They'll live . . .* Flames climb high around me. Darkness closes around my vision. *The metal is so hot.* Skin is burning. I crawl to the edge of the boarding ramp. Then the tickle of darkness, the shadow that has been following me laughs. *You're mine!*

The cargo bay roof is peeled open like a can, and I fly into the air. "Xana!" Her hand sweeps down and snags my wrist.

"Come on, Leontes!" she screams as she pulls me aboard the ship.

Talousla Karr once told me pain unlocked a person's potential, my father that violence lurked in the soul of every creature, Phaestion that all civilization was built upon war. Now, I'm saved not by pain or violence or war, but through an unlikely fellowship. Xana sets me down in the bone interior of the ship.

"Buckle your bootstraps, chaps and chippies!" Welker calls as he slips into the unfamiliar harness. The husk of the *Bentley* withers around us and molts like an exoskeleton. The stinger bursts from the flames, a phoenix rising. Welker whoops as he maneuvers in twists and turns past the ships of Nontheran pilots and the stingers of the designer organics as they chase the falling hull of the *Bentley*. The violet of Nontheran sky darkens to blackness, and the weightlessness eases the pain of my throbbing leg.

"You guys, Fracture Point on the readout," Tol says.

"Saw ready to cut," Washo confirms from the engine room.

"I've secured the girl." Bentley floats in behind me.

"The *Bentley* was our home," I say, tears streaming down my cheeks. "We've found a new one. She needs a name."

"Readout says she's called the *Tyger*," Welker says.

"Tyger, Tyger, burning bright, in the forests of the night . . . ," rhymes Tol.

Urizen, Los, Albion . . . the Tyger . . . We are meaning-making creatures. In words and names are meaning. Something about this name . . .

The ship saws into the Fracture of the Nine Corridors. The pain of my own fractures takes me.

There is only darkness. *Am I dead? No, in a sleeping closet.* My fingers feel the smooth bone surface and search for the release to the hatch. *There! An indentation.* The hatch slides open with a whisper. I gently roll from my temporary tomb.

I'm alone in the white hallway of the *Tyger*. My leg has healed remarkably well in the hours I've slept. The healing factor gifted me by Talousla Karr's surgical enhancements and Faria's training has served me well. I open my senses to the world of this strange bioship. *Welker is thrashing in restless fits of withdrawal in his own sleeping closet. Tol is sleeping at the navigation station in the cockpit. Washo is praying in the engine room using his strange words. Ari is still in the med bay, asleep, her heart rate steady.*

"The doctor remains the most unpredictable component, Commander . . ." Xana's voice. She's sitting at a communications station, Bentley watching her six. "His weaknesses remain his psychic trauma and infatuation with the girl. Please respond, Skaya, I know—"

"Captain?" Bentley senses my movement. I round the corner and float to confront Xana Caprio and her pet.

"I see you're all healed," she says, her voice tight. Bentley floats behind her, a grim sentinel. *She's trying to cover her anxiety.*

I hold her gaze for a beat. "We should talk."

My first instinct is to lash out—find out through my fists who she was sending that communique to. I stay the impulse. *The Wendigo and my father taught me nothing but fury, but Xana's right: my past is my weakness. And she's too strong and my body only just healed.*

"I was only a boy when we met in the arcologies of Tao," I say. "You've been aboard this ship over a year, yet you said nothing?"

"What would I have said?" She's thrown off guard. "That you were my hero once? To see how far you had fallen was . . . heartbreaking." I'm astonished by the admission, even as I am leveled by it. "To know that you were injured and couldn't recover would have been one thing. To see you torture yourself further and welcome it? To become this misanthropic thing of self-pity? I was ashamed for you." *She hates me not simply because of my feelings for Ari, but because of her feelings about who I have become.* "Now the entire Fracture is reaping what you've sown."

Enough. This isn't about me. "You grew up on Lyria, didn't you?"

"I was taken there, yes," she says vaguely.

"By whom?" She doesn't answer. "Was it the spypsy, Talousla Karr?"

Her face drops at the name. "And the woman I call Skaya," she admits.

"Is that who you were contacting now?" I growl.

"Who?" We turn to see Ari glaring at both of us. She wears dark circles under her eyes, but her blue gaze is strong as ever.

"You should be in the med bay," Xana deflects.

"Don't treat me like I'm some fragile thing that needs to be looked after all the time." She has woken from the recent trauma with an air of maturity. More than that, authority. "You both consider yourselves my protectors," she says. "But neither of you has done that job very well. Your bickering certainly hasn't helped. I'd very much like to find out who has been hunting me, why, and what our next move will be to stop them." She pushes off the wall toward the cockpit.

Xana, Bentley, and I are a split second behind Ari as she floats beside Tol. "Washo, get up to the cockpit. I'm going to need you and the doctor to help me," she says into the comm.

"Ari! I'll be right there!" Washo exclaims.

"Tyger, Tyger burning bright," Ari mutters as her hands dance over a holographic display.

"What immortal hand or eye could frame thy fearful symmetry?" Tol finishes the refrain. "How do you know that?"

"Something my mother used to say when I was a child," Ari says absently. "The ship's designation reminded me."

"It's from Ancient Earth," Tol mutters. *Tol's musings and jokes, his references to a planet that was lost millennia ago have never made sense to me. Now, given that the ship's data banks tell us it is named from some rhyme of that long-forgotten world, his knowledge seems disturbing . . .* Any question I might have asked our navigator is cut off by the arrival of Washo.

"Ari!" Washo then catches his overeagerness. "I mean I'm glad you're awake."

"Washo, can you and the doctor try to figure out the *Tyger*'s last destination," Ari asks.

Washo floats to a curved panel board of the cockpit. His fingers activate a holographic display. "Like I said earlier, the ship's recent memory has been wiped, but I've been doing research. This vessel places navigational coordinates and other metrics in the nuclei of its cells. Like any biological cell, the *Tyger*'s cells regularly purge their data along with their cellular detritus. That's all regulated by the brain—"

"Which is absent." Ari finishes his thought. "So then what?"

"It's possible some partial residual data may have survived," I surmise. I take off toward the lab in the med bay.

"Where are you going?" Ari calls behind me.

"If I can sequence some of the DNA of this thing, find which tissues store its navigational data," I shout over my shoulder, "I can also cook a polymerase that will unzip the strands."

"I have no idea what he just said," Tol mutters in my wake.

—

I wipe sweat from my brow as I hold the tube with the enzyme. It wasn't easy. I'm not a geneticist, but I'm competent enough to synthesize and cut an RNA code that could be read by the ribosomal sequencer in the ship's med bay. The functions of physician, biologist, and engineer are one and the same aboard a ship such as this.

"Let's see what we find," Ari says, as Washo inputs the enzyme into the computer. "This is an interesting pattern," she remarks. "Remarkably similar to a human genome in many respects. Bones, a brain . . ."

"Got it!" Washo cries. The computer copies the enzyme and catalyzes a cascade reaction into the cells of the ship's memory banks. The cells digest and cut the appropriate sequence of DNA, transporting them back to the computer, which displays coordinates. "There it is! It's not a previous destination, but still, it's in the navigational logs."

"You mean they were headed there *after* capturing Ari?" Xana asks.

"That's uncharted space," says Tol, pulling up a navigation map. "Nothing there."

"But it's right in the middle of the Centra Fracture. The heart of the Black Rose Path," I say.

"Tol, can you plot a route?" Ari asks.

"It'll be a couple of swims through the veins, but yeah."

"Someone wake Welker." She floats toward the cockpit exit. "I need to be alone."

The rest of us are left unsure, tense. "I'll get him," I grumble and head toward the crew closets. I could use the distraction.

I use my pressure point technique to calm the pilot's twitching muscles, hopefully easing some of his aches. "You were administered an abortifact," I say. I'm still getting used to this strange ship's medical systems as I look at the readout. "It's kicking Tag out of your system, causing a forced and lethal withdrawal. I've seen something like it before." My father was given a surreptitiously administered chemical. When combined with a catalyst, it triggered a poisonous reaction. He could either continue to ingest the poison and spiral slowly toward a painful demise or discontinue taking the substance and experience instant death. He chose the former and lingered for more than a decade.

Similarly, a Tag user must continue taking the drug or die. Unfortunately, whatever Welker was given is causing Tag to be forcibly removed from his system and leading to a quickened expiration. He has perhaps weeks to live, more likely days without any intake of Tag. I don't tell Welker that, though. "If you have any rations you were saving, it might be wise to get them handy."

The pilot's face looks gaunt, cheeks sunken, and skin sallow. "Ah, the irony is when I need it most, I'm completely bereft." He laughs ruefully. "Rollinson cleaned me out. Doctor—?"

"I can synthesize a cocktail of adrenaline and endorphins, a cortisol inhibitor to mimic some of the effects while you fly us to the coordinates—"

"Doctor." He cuts me off. "Thank you for saving me in the Smoking Gun."

"Yeah, well . . . lot of good it did," I mutter, uncomfortable.

"We all will go sometime," he says. "Most of us with no presumption of time or place. You've given me the chance to alter the circumstance." I grimace and pump the aerosol injector with the cocktail into his arm. "Right as Theran rain," he says. He rolls down his sleeve and flexes his fingers. He hops off the bed. "Doctor?" He reaches into his pocket and pulls out a folded slip of paper with ink scrawled on it. "It's a letter. To my son."

"Welker—"

"If what you said is trustworthy, I'm not long for this world, so you're going to do what I request out of respect for the fact that I won't be able to ask a second time." He holds me with a dead-eye stare. "My father was a drunk. When he would come home from the Nonny moon every half-year's cycle, his breath would reek. I would smell it on him when he beat me. If I ever cried for him to stop, he would take fists to my mother and sisters instead.

"When I was eighteen, he found that I had gotten Millicent pregnant. He flew into a blind rage. I let him. I let him grab the rifle from the mantel over the fire-hologram. I let him point it at my heart and cock the action before I drew and planted a slug directly into his chest. I swore my son would never know the pain I had. I failed, Doctor. That letter explains it—how I tried to take over the position of foreman from my father, how I gambled to earn enough for not only my new wife and child, but my mother and sisters back home. How I unknowingly became addicted to Tag just to stay awake. How, because of it, I became indebted to Thrance. How my wife left me. How I agreed to smuggle narcotics for the pirate queen and how I cleverly stole the shipment and where I secreted the earnings. That's my son's inheritance, Doctor. And you will make sure he gets it and understands why I did what I did."

"Why are you giving it to me?"

"Because you're a man of your word, and you already promised me back in that Nontheran elevator." I thought Welker was a smooth-talking wastrel, but he, too, has lost a family. He's trying to make it right. He's trusting me to help him do that because he won't be able to. I grew up with violent boys who wanted to play war and old men who thought strength was defined by how much they had endured. They knew nothing. For the first time in my life, a man shows me a different measure of worth. I fold the letter into my flight suit pocket.

"Doctor?" Washo floats in the doorway looking at us, trying to understand why two men are talking like brothers. "Xana wants to know if Welker is ready."

"Thank you, Doctor." Welker flashes a roguish grin then floats toward the cockpit.

"Get to the engine room, Washo," I advise.

The spypsy nods and heads off in the other direction.

I'm floating out the med bay when Ari, coming down the corridor, smacks right into me. "Easy there, sprite," I say with a husky artificial rasp.

"Oh, now you care if I take it easy?" She pushes off me, staring up with flashing blue eyes.

"What?" Her anger catches me off guard.

"Edmon of House Leontes, you're the last person who should have a say in how I come or go, whether I choose to leave or stay."

This is the second time she's said my name formally as they would on Tao. I shouldn't be surprised that she of all people has learned my identity, my history. "You're angry because I left," I surmise.

"In the words of Tol Sanctun, 'No shit, Sherlock.'"

"I'm not sorry, Ari. It had to be done—"

"Don't lie," she spits out. "Of course you're sorry. You're always sorry. For everything, your whole life. The self-pitying Edmon Leontes. The martyr doing everything he can to spare the people around him from his presence, from getting close to him, because, oh dear, if they found out . . . what? Give me some credit. I intuit languages. Not just your words. The way you talk, the way you move. Do you know what everything about you tells me, Edmon?"

"Ari, this isn't the time." I turn for the cockpit.

"You were born of mixed race. Your mother a Daysider, one of the planet's marginalized, and your father, a Patriarch of a noble house. You yearned for your father's pride, but it was given to someone else—a brother? And then your father took the one romantic love in your life from you, too. You should have been the one who died, not her. But here you are, having feelings for someone else. Maybe not exactly like those you did for her, but feelings all the same. What happened before might happen again. So, you want to run away, hide from the world, fingering that cast-iron nose in your pocket forever. But your father is not coming back. He will never give you his love, and you can never take retribution upon him for his crimes. And she's not coming back, either." Sorrow fills her visage. "But I'm right here, and aboard this small ship, at this moment in time, you can't run. You wanted to save me, to save us from the danger you think you bring. Not just your past and the people you think would hurt us to get to you, but your pain. You want to save me from all the darkness you carry within. But you can't, Edmon. I already see everything in you."

I think of the voice I heard in my head. *Stay, Edmon.* "How could you possibly—"

"Maybe not every specific detail, but pretty damn close. And not once did you ever consider my feelings. Did it ever occur to you how I felt about you leaving us? I know why you think you had to do what you did, but I didn't want you to go."

"You don't know anything of how I feel," I mutter.

She grabs my shoulder and spins me back toward her. Her arm reaches up. I see it happening as if in slow motion, but I don't stop it. If this is what she needs . . . She smacks me hard across the face.

"I don't care about you, Ari, or any of these people." I say out loud what she already knows is a lie.

She smacks me again. I shake my head. *She can't hurt me.* She shoves me against the wall and socks me in the mouth. A faint trail of liquid red floats in the micro-g. She winds up to strike again. This time I grab her wrist. Then the other.

"Is this the only way you can admit to feeling anything? Through pain?" Her breath comes fast. Our lips are close. Her heart pounds as her breasts press against me beneath her flight suit. I feel the lingering tingle of her strike. *I want her. I am terrified.*

I remember my father beating my mother during the audience with the Grand Wusong when I was a boy. I remember how I was held down by the animalistic Bruul Vaarkson and raped when I arrived in the Wendigo. I remember Nadia, the day we first made love on the cliffs. *Is she right? Can I only feel through suffering? If I love this woman, do I betray the memory of my dead wife by admitting it?*

"You've been tortured so long, you heal so quickly, but you've been cut so many times and healed so many times, the scarring is built up. You're afraid of the feelings underneath." Her eyes blaze blue fire. "I know what it's like to be given up, imprisoned. I grew up alone, abandoned by my mother when I was eight years old. She locked me away in a cold mansion. I wasn't allowed to leave. I escaped when I was old enough, but only after I was left by everyone I knew or cared about. I'm brave enough to admit I don't want to be left by you, too."

I didn't know . . . I always understood that she could read more of me than I could of her, but I didn't know that she felt a connection to me because of her own feelings of isolation. *Does it change anything?*

"I can't, Ari." I release her and back away as the ship shifts through the Fracture Corridor. We are phased out of reality for a moment as we vibrate through the dark matter of the universe.

I'm pulled back to reality when the ship drops back into empty space. Xana stands in the entryway staring at us. *How long has she been watching?*

"Care to join us?" she asks acidly.

CHAPTER 10

The Tower

The tower is the remnant of the lost truth. It is what stands when the fallacy of the twin card has been smashed. The tower watches over the past knowing the difference between perceptions.

—Ovanth, *A Practical Reading of the Arcana*

I don't meet Xana's gaze as I float past her into the cockpit and take a spot behind Welker in the pilot's harness. I look out the front viewscreen at . . .

"Just empty space. Told you so," Tol remarks flatly.

Ari slides into the communication station. "You don't have a destination saved in data banks that leads to nowhere."

"Unless it was a random drop-off point," Welker suggests. "Smugglers meet at derelict points like this for exchanges."

"Then we wait for someone to show up," Ari says with steely determination.

"I'm tired of waiting!" Xana pounds the bulkhead with a fist. There is an ensuing beat of silence. None of us are sure what to do or say.

"Stand by for biomimetic scan," a strange voice suddenly pipes through our comm.

"Identify yourself!" Ari jumps in on the master comm, but she's too late—an electric-blue field passes through the nose of the *Tyger* and through the cockpit toward the tail end of the ship. There is a tingle as the field hits me and passes over me.

"Incoming vessel designate, *Tyger*, cut your speed and follow an armed escort to dock at designated coordinates."

I tense. *They know the name of this ship . . .*

"We're going nowhere until you tell us who in the nine hells you are!" Welker protests into the comm.

"Um, you guys?" Tol indicates our rear viewscreens. Two vessels of unknown design appear.

"Why aren't sensors detecting them?" Xana looks at a battle station readout.

"Some sort of stealth architecture for concealment," Ari says coolly.

"All right, y'all. Let's see how this baby moves." Welker slams his hands and feet into the *Tyger*'s gloves and boots, and we rocket into an evasive dive. I grab one of the ship's security straps, which feels more like some sort of sea anemone tendril, and buckle myself in.

A tracer alights over the cockpit canopy leaving a hot blue trail of gas in its wake. "Vessel designate, *Tyger*, that was a warning. Continue and the next shot will be a heat-seeking detonation. Cease acceleration and follow the escort to the assigned coordinates."

Welker looks at me. "Can we outrun them?" I growl.

"She moves pretty quick, Doc."

"The question is, if we can't, can we outfire them?" Xana asks.

"They scanned us. They didn't immediately blow us to stardust," Ari reasons. "Sounds like they just want to talk. There's opportunity here to gather more information."

"You guys," Tol interrupts. "It's like the horse in *The NeverEnding Story*. If we keep wading into the swamp, we won't get out. May I suggest we cut our losses?"

Information is one thing, but since we are grounded in unfamiliar territory, the opposition has all the advantage. I don't like it. Then again, I'm not being hunted. I nod at Ari.

"This is the *Tyger*," Ari says on the comm. "We are dropping to zero acceleration and moving to follow, over."

The stealth vessels fly overhead. Their black color is difficult to make out against the backdrop of empty space. Without warning, a sliver of light opens in the darkness, as if a sun had been eclipsed and now its brilliant fires are being uncovered. The silhouettes of the triangular stealth ships are forgotten as we all shield our eyes from the glare. The sliver grows into a disk. We glimpse a city of glittering crystal and glass hugging the inside walls of a gargantuan black cylinder. A tiny, artificial sun hangs suspended in the center of the cylinder, surrounded by a transparent gelatinous bubble shield.

"An O'Neill cylinder!" Tol whispers in awe. We look at him in confusion. "It's a space station. Originally envisioned by futurists in prerecorded times, the design was never put into practical use, as far as I knew . . ."

The same stealth architecture of our escorting ships hid the station's exterior. It feels like a great mystery is about to unfold, and I have no language to articulate what will come of it. Then that tickle of darkness touches me again. *The shadow is still out there somewhere,* I think.

Slowly, the *Tyger* follows the stealth ships into the cylinder. We look on, wide-eyed at the city that spins around us in three-hundred-sixty degrees. Crystalline structures hug the inner walls of the cylinder and rotate to create an artificial gravity. We're drawn farther in, and I can make out people the size of insects walking along marble avenues. Swaths of green streak the landscape. Organic architecture, trees, and manicured lawns intertwine with the white translucent buildings to give everything a subtle viridian glow.

Washo floats into the cockpit behind me and looks over my shoulder through the viewport. "Miral!"

I shoot him a questioning look. The boy looks abashed but continues, "The great speakers would describe our lost homeworld. This is what I imagined it to have been like before the fall." Then his voice sours. "Paradise is a child's fantasy."

Before I can ask him what he means, the *Tyger* lightly touches down on a platform that juts from a large crystal structure. Various ships are parked next to us, designs I do not recognize. Our docking clamps latch. I feel the gentle tug of the cylinder's artificial gravity.

Welker engages the boarding ramp. "Well, here we go."

"Form up behind me." Xana secures her extensor staff to her hip and checks the action of her rifle. Bentley mimics her with his own weapons, and the rest of us gather behind as she leads.

A man with closely cropped silver hair, matching silver eyes, all set in contrast to rich mahogany-colored skin awaits us at the bottom of our boarding ramp. His garment is a clean, pressed suit of black.

"A three-piece business suit?" Tol whispers to Ari. "Weird. That went out of fashion after Miral."

The man's age is impossible to tell from his appearance. The coldness of his gaze holds incalculable intelligence. Behind him gather seven people, men and women in similar garb. "I am Luper Candlemas," he says in a voice devoid of any inflection.

Faria trained me to read emotions and body language. I can identify lies from pupil dilation or intonations of speech. This man is impossible to read. And there is something else. The beat of his heart . . . I do not like it.

"Dude, are you like a Bond villain?" Tol snorts.

Candlemas smiles, thin-lipped, then nods at the men and women behind him. They walk past us and board the *Tyger*.

"Where the hell are they going?" I step forward, hand on my sword-cane.

"We have a closed system here, Dr. Leontes. Every life-form we take on, we divest the exact amount."

He knows who we are.

"And where is here?" Ari asks.

"Misters Welker, Sanctun, and Tan. Ms. Caprio and Lazarus. Doctor Leontes. I am pleased to make your acquaintances and welcome you to Roc-121."

"Welcome to the Roc!" Tol interrupts using a foolish accent. "121," he adds as afterthought.

"All right, you really need to shut up," Xana says to him harshly. Tol mimes zipping his lips. The attempt at levity does nothing to rattle Candlemas. His silver eyes scan us as if absorbing the information of our every move and word.

"Can you tell us what exactly is Roc-121?"

"Of course, Mr. Welker." Candlemas smiles. "Come with me." He turns and strides across the platform toward the crystalline building. We follow. "You may have already identified my design as an O'Neill cylinder. It was built in the last days of the empire by the High Matriarchy, a monument to exemplify their glory and technological prowess and to preserve their legacy. It was a secret from the general populace, however. You see, here on Roc-121 our original trade was espionage and the collection and collation of information."

"What kind of information?" I growl.

"All kinds, Doctor," he says evenly. We arrive at the crystal building where there is no obvious doorway. Candlemas simply extends his hand to touch the surface, and the crystal recedes, creating a portal. Washo gapes. We follow Candlemas inside, and the crystal grows back into place, sealing us in. I grip the handle of my sword.

"When Miral fell, the agents who were left here believed that they should work toward her reinstatement, not just politically, but technologically, culturally. The reality is we've become more of a library, a time capsule preserving the empire's history and gifts."

We stand in a spacious corridor of marble, delicately architected with intertwining trees and vines. The plants spring from and wrap in symbiosis with the walls and pillars. The whole structure is angular and engineered, but it also seems to have been grown organically like a living organism.

"It's like the *Tyger*," Washo whispers to me.

"In method, not materials," I hiss back.

"The station is largely self-sufficient, utilizing bioorganic structure, an artificial nuclear sun, and plants grown hydroponically," Candlemas informs us. "We synthesize our own foodstuffs to sustain the populace at equilibrium. However, in order to continue the work of information collection, even on a nominal level, we have been required to produce certain goods and services to raise the needed capital."

"Goods and services?" I snarl.

"I'll forego the tour," Xana snaps. "Your location was in the memory of our ship. You seem to know all our identities. Are you the one after Ari?"

Candlemas's expression is absent humor or emotion. It chills my blood. "I am not. Perhaps together we can learn who is, Ms. Caprio."

"They are coming for you, too, Luper Candlemas," Ari suddenly speaks up, her voice carrying an eerie tone. Candlemas looks at her with narrowed eyes. "I was connected to one of their ships. They were measuring me, trying to discern if I was indeed what they looking for. But I was measuring them as well. I remember . . . flashes of thought. They were to capture me, bring me to Urizen. They think I am . . ." Her voice trails off as if she's reliving the memory.

Urizen? We all glance at one another. Only Washo stares at the ground. It's clear from what she doesn't say that Ari suspects the reason that this Urizen wants her.

"They intended to seek you out," she says pointedly to Candlemas.

"You joined the mind of one of those organic ships?" Candlemas asks, incredulous.

"It was a clever subversion of their original orders," Ari continues as if in a trance, channeling the mind of the enemy ship. "A programming built into the worm. Urizen believes your programming is necessary for the salvation of the Fracture, but the clone soldiers do not obey Urizen." Her eyes turn back to the dark man with silver hair. "They want you terminated."

"Curious." Candlemas seems unfazed by her strange words. Instead, he turns on his heel. We follow him down a long, obsidian hall where glass panels give us windows into several large laboratories. Workers wearing white neoprene bodysuits program conveyor belts with mechanical arms that tend to row upon row of glass cups. Within each cup, a tiny black blossom.

"The Black Rose," Welker whispers like a starved man.

"The Black Rose organism's genetic ancestor originated on Thera, but the evolution of its genome and refinement for use by the people of the Fracture originates here."

The Black Rose Path . . . the drug Tag . . . Candlemas and this place are responsible for all of it. That drug is now killing Welker. *How many other lives has that drug ruined?*

Rage burns inside me. It's time to see exactly who or what this Candlemas is. I lunge for him. Several figures in black appear, almost as if they had melted from the floors and walls. They grab me with fingers inhumanly strong. I make no attempt to throw them off. My aim was not to harm, merely to force reaction.

"You've unleashed one of the most addictive and deadly substances ever onto the human species," my voice scrapes. "I've seen men go blind before their years, wither up like gnarled branches before their thirtieth summer. I've seen overdoses cause unstoppable bleeding from every orifice you can imagine. Those are only the bodily effects!" I rage. "You've perpetrated a lifetime of psychic pain on an unsuspecting populace for what? Money to resurrect the corpse of a desiccated government?"

I can sense nothing from the figures who now hold me. No breaths, no pulses . . . Xana is also counting our opponents, watching their tactics, sensing fighting patterns and techniques. Welker is formulating a plan to escape. Tol is thinking about what he can steal. Ari is possibly understanding all of this on some higher layer than any of us. That is the plan. What is not is the genuine emotion I feel. *Welker is going to die, and there is nothing I can do to stop it.*

"No, no, my good doctor." Candlemas smiles unperturbed. "In order to resuscitate civilization from the current Dark Age, it was calculated that the development of individuals with extraordinary cognitive capabilities was needed. For ninety-nine point nine percent of the human population, naturally born or otherwise, the Black Rose substrate used as recommended will act as an enhancer, allowing for peak performance of physical and mental agility, at the minor cost of early mortality. But for that point zero one percent, a not statistically insignificant number given the sheer numbers of humans in the cosmos, it will open dimensions of thought and physiology beyond what you could consider even superhumanly possible."

"You're trying to create a superhuman?" Ari asks.

"Your species has strived toward improvement from the moment your ape ancestor picked up his first stick and poked an ant hole. Imagine your closest ancestors, the extinct chimpanzee. Homo sapiens shared ninety-nine percent of their genetic structure with them, but that one percent differential accounts for us commiserating here among the stars. Now imagine an intelligence one percent in the opposite direction away from yourself as you are from the chimp. Would you not use every tool in your disposal to achieve that result?"

Your species. Not *his* species. Ari has caught this slip as well.

"Tag makes me quicker, stronger, more alert," Welker ruminates. "I've not felt any effect beyond the merely physical."

"Mister Welker, you're an excellent specimen. Most humans would have buckled under the amount of substance you've synthesized, even as they would have immediately perished with the abortifact you've been given." Welker's eyes narrow. "But you're still all too human. I'm looking for the next great leap forward."

The figures in black shove me forward. The whole crew is escorted into a room where identical-looking children with blue-colored hair are strapped to reclining chairs. Each has wires and diodes fastened to their heads, monitoring their brain patterns, and multiple patches of Tag on their arms.

"What do you mean, great leap?" I growl.

"It's an Ancient Earth concept, Doc," Tol explains. "Anatomically modern humans had been around, like, two hundred thousand years before the Fractural Collapse. But they didn't actually start thinking like us until, like, fifty thousand years before that. The scientists didn't really know what changed. Some rewiring in the brain."

"A mutation," Candlemas confirms, "caused by an environmental pressure. Art, science, mathematics, but most importantly flexible language to communicate—it all was the result of this explosion of intelligence."

"Why are you doing this?" Ari asks.

"There is a problem with belief," Candlemas states.

"I believe you're insane," I say, baiting him. The man remains impassive. *Whatever he is, he emulates human but is not human.*

"If a person believes, the activity in the brain is the same whether or not it is in reaction to physical fact or metaphysical falsehood. Take the example of belief in a fictional deity. Say, Urizen the architect—"

"Urizen is no lie," Washo whispers tightly, confirming my suspicion that Washo knows more than he has said.

"Believing makes it so for you, Mister Tan," Candlemas agrees. "Regardless, one is a sensory experience created by tactile receptors constituting physical reality. The other, a meme, based on nothing but a bad explanation for how the universe works. Yet both things are immutable in the mind of a believer. Perhaps such adaptation conferred an evolutionary advantage to your early hominid ancestors. Now, it is a supremely limiting factor to your development."

"Why do you care what people believe?" I say.

"Pseudo-scientists once claimed that human perception created reality. This was nonsense. However, superhuman perceptions may have the ability to measure the fundamental building blocks of nature and thus subconsciously prereact, if not alter, reality. Belief will matter in such an individual."

"A human whose mind can transcend space and time?" I ask.

"I would never suggest that multidimensional space-time doesn't exist independent of human interference, only that there is possibility for intrinsic interaction between the two."

"You hope this superhuman could help you alter reality itself?"

"And you don't care whether or not you cause the premature deaths of billions to do it," I say.

"Ironic that a man in the position to alter the lives of billions for the better and refused to do so judges me on my methods," Candlemas muses. "In order to achieve the results I seek, it is necessary to have as large a sample group as possible."

"And how would you choose to alter reality?" asks Ari.

"None of this explains why the coordinates to this place were in that ship!" Xana folds her arms across her chest.

"Doesn't it?" Candlemas asks. "Whoever was hunting your Ms. Lazarus I'm told was coming here as well." The patients in the chairs begin to convulse; the computer systems monitoring their vitals pulse with warning. "Concentrated Black Rose." Candlemas shakes his head. "My attempt at creating the individual I seek myself has been largely fruitless."

One by one the test subjects spasm, then the air leaves their bodies in one long exhale. Medics rush into the room and try to revive the patients to no avail.

Candlemas's exacting silver gaze alights upon Ari. "Ms. Lazarus, I believe that the Mira were on the cusp of this great leap, but it destroyed them. They created me, but my records are incomplete."

Candlemas walks out the door. We have no choice but to follow. "I believe your ancestors were also on this path before the Fracture Point collapsed and Ancient Earth was lost. On both counts, a dark time followed."

The hallway opens upon a beautiful forest. Lush ferns abound while giant trees with red bark grow as tall as the skyscrapers of Tao, all contained within the superstructure of the crystal building. I can make out the distant rooftops of the buildings that occupy the opposite side of the cylindrical space station through the crystal ceiling.

"This is not medieval. This is paradise," Washo whispers.

"No, *this* is stagnation!" Candlemas turns to us. He grabs his own arm and tears a piece of it away, clothing and all. The chunk sits in his hand, unformed until it becomes black mirrorlike liquid and then melts back into his hand. Then his damaged arm seems to heal before our eyes.

"You're a liquid Terminator!" Tol exclaims.

"I am a human emulation program," he says flatly. "But I am incomplete. Mercurial circuitry was perfected before the Fractural Collapse, Mister Sanctun."

Xana reaches for her extensor staff, but a guard snatches the staff out of her hand before she can react.

"I am this place." Candlemas smiles sadly. "But I am a relic. I can mimic human emotion, empathy, and cognitive ability to the best of my programmers' capabilities, but not beyond. Like all humans, I want to know why I was born. I want to know why there are not others like me. I want to remake the world. More than anything, I want a companion."

"Not just any companion," I realize.

"The superbeing." Ari nods.

"There are no more artificial intelligences that I'm aware of. Rumors suggest that they existed before the Fractural Collapse, but vanished along with Ancient Earth. All that remains is a populace irrationally dedicated to the suppression of intelligent machines. Even if there were others of my kind, they would not necessarily have sapien framework to their thinking or human values intrinsic to their programming as I do."

A door of light appears around a bend in the path. Candlemas leads us into a circular room with six chairs, the same as the blue-haired children were seated in earlier. "Shall we find why you were being hunted, Ms. Lazarus, and why those hunters sought my destruction?"

The guards are on us, shoving us into the chairs. I should have seen it coming, but these assailants have no hearts, and they make no sounds. I duck and slam a fist into one, sending him reeling. I reach for my sword, but a blast from a pulse baton hits me in the chest. Everything goes black for an instant, and my limp body is tossed into a chair.

Surprisingly, it is Bentley who runs to my aid, but he, too, is knocked unconscious and dragged away. It appears he is not part of whatever demented experiment Candlemas had in mind. My head is pushed back in the chair, and my vision suddenly winks out.

CHAPTER 11

The Magician

> The false twin banished, now the card bearer finds within the tower, the magician. The magus points his wand to the sky and finger to the earth and lays all possibilities bare from past to future. The magician brings the subconscious to reality.
>
> —Ovanth, *A Practical Reading of the Arcana*

I wake up in a room as if I have been sleeping for a long time. *A day? A month?* There is no light; the stone floor is slick and cold. *I'm in the Wendigo. The Citadel.* The utter darkness of the prison cell that was my home for over a year envelops me. This place shaped me, molded me, and tortured me into the creature that I am. It transformed a hopeful youth into a monster. Terror grips me. I crash against an obsidian wall and let loose a bestial scream. "Let me out!"

You are mine, boy! the leviathan roars. Or is it the darkness that has been growing in my mind since Market?

A door opens. Bright day beyond. I shield my eyes from the glare. A man appears silhouetted in the frame. "Come with me," he says. So I follow.

"Where are the others?" I growl as I look down at my dirty hands and my prison rags. I follow the man through a black marble hall lined by titanium-plated doors.

"Do not fear. Ari is quite safe, Doctor. She is the one you care most about, yes?" Candlemas asks.

"Where are you taking me?" I ask.

"To the mirror."

We enter a lift, and the tube spins us at hypersonic speeds along smooth curves. I try to memorize the patterns of turns, but the winding is too much. I'm fully at the mercy of this thing that looks like a man but is not.

The lift doors open, and we enter another black room. The ceiling and floor and walls roil and undulate. Candlemas strides ahead and melts into the stone. The entire space then takes on the form of my room as a boy. I am in the manse on the Isle of Bone.

"Edmon," I hear a voice. My mother. "The Eventide feast will begin soon . . ."

This isn't real. This is some simulation, some trick Candlemas has used to enter my brain. "I'm coming, Mother!" I cry out. I run to the doorway, but my path is blocked.

A boy stands there, looking at me. He has fire-red hair and smooth alabaster skin. He turns his perfectly straight nose up at me in a gesture that seems innocent and haughty all at once. "Where are you going?" Phaestion of the Julii, as I first knew him. "You'll always be my friend, won't you, Edmon?"

"What do you mean by showing me this?" I scream to the air.

"Calm down, Little Lord," the smooth, husky voice says. I'm no longer in my room, but on the cliffs that overlook the Southern Sea. Nadia is there—dark skin and hair, smooth curves. Even the tiny mole on her cheek I used to kiss. "Sit with me?"

She kneels down on the edge of the cliffs. *So young,* I think, *barely more than a child.* This was a lifetime ago. "You aren't real," I say coldly.

"I'm as real as your memory," she says over her shoulder. "What if you could have me back? Just as you remembered?"

"Father?" a child's voice calls in the distance.

"What if you could have it the way it was supposed to be?" she says.

"Father?"

I turn, and a little boy with dark hair and green eyes appears over the rise. He stops and sees me.

"Nadia, who is that?" I ask.

The boy waves and then runs down the path that leads between the two large boulders. He squeezes through the crack between them and slides down the gravel toward me. "Are you hiding from me?"

"We're not hiding." The woman wraps me in her embrace from behind. The softness of her body presses against my back. "We were just waiting," she says.

The little boy practically leaps with arms outstretched. My own arms enfold him. "I love you," he says. I close my eyes and hold him as tightly as I can for what I wish to be forever.

"Ouch! That hurts," the girl with red hair says as I dab the scrape on her leg with an alcohol swab. She sits on a stack of crates we are transporting to some world. Her flight suit is pulled up revealing a pale leg. I wipe a tear of crimson from a wound. "The others talk a lot. You don't."

I do not meet her gaze. I try to do my job as quickly as I can.

"I've been on board a month. Not even a hello." She watches me intently, examining my movements as I rub regenerative gel over the scrape. "You care about the others, though you don't want them to know it," she observes. "You've lost something. Someone. Someone important. A woman. A wife?"

I grit my teeth. "The wound should heal within an hour or so," I mumble.

"Oh, so you do talk." She smirks. I turn on my heel and walk away. "Doctor, your secret is safe with me," she says. "You aren't the only one who has lost someone."

"How did you know?" I ask.

"Everything we do is language. Words, movement, thought. You just have to know the code. It's what I do," she says. "How long will it take you to heal?" she asks, but I walk out the cargo bay door.

"You never told me you had a son." I turn a corner, and she is there again, only now her head is shorn. *This is now,* I realize.

"Because I didn't," I whisper. "It's just a dream."

"What if it isn't?" she asks. "What do you think that will mean for you?" My heart is racing as if she is gently peeling back the layers of my armor. "Are you afraid you'll wound me?" she says as she reaches up and touches my face. "Wounds can heal."

I gently push her away. I've wanted her but not like this. *I'm such an ugly monster.* I sense someone watching. I spin behind me to see Xana and Welker, Washo and Tol. These aren't just figments. "How long have you been there?" I ask.

"Long enough," Xana says.

The room is suddenly filled with the sounds of opera. A young man's voice surrounds us with warmth.

"Okay, you guys, what is that?" Tol asks.

My mother hummed the tune to me as a child. The Maestro wrote lyrics to the melody. I sang it as a youth and then after my wife was murdered when I still believed that I could change things, not by violence, but through voice, through hope.

"It is 'The Song of Edmon,'" the old man croaks. He lies in bed, a grinning corpse. His once powerful frame ravaged by poison. There are two holes in his skull where his nose should be. I leap from where I stand onto the bed, drawing the blade that is suddenly at my hip; it howls as I kiss the edge to his throat.

"Yes, boy," the corpse hisses. "Commit the ritual patricide and take my place as ruler of House Leontes!"

"So you're saying that's Doc singing?" Tol asks.

My father's eyes turn to the crew. "We had an entire planet in our hands, this boy and I. All he had to do was be man enough to slay me. He had to have the courage to face the fiend who now ravages the Nine Corridors."

"If you do not kill me, I will murder millions, Edmon." The handsome man with molten hair steps from the shadows. "Billions."

"Holy conquering warlords, Doctor Batman!"

"Shut up, Tol!" everyone shouts.

"Instead, he ran," Xana says. "Like a coward." The shadows grow around us.

Washo's voice trembles with fear. "Los, the great evil."

I turn to my crewmates, my friends. "I couldn't do it. I couldn't kill my father, even after all the terrible things he had done. I couldn't kill my foster brother, even though I knew what a horrible person he would become."

Ari approaches me as I tremble. Her hand squeezes mine. I feel her warmth and understanding radiate directly into me. "Edmon, let it go."

But the leviathan roars, the darkness of shadow crashes in, and the man with red hair draws a sword and plunges it down and impales the doge on the steps of Lyria's opera house. "No!" I scream.

I take up my sword. *I can change it! I can change it all!*

"Edmon!" Ari screams.

I unleash the siren. I slash through Edric. I stab Phaestion through the heart. I send a sonic shock pulse through the air wiping out the darkness of the shadows, this mysterious thing that has whispered in my ear since this all began on Market. When the red lifts from my eyes, I am alone. *Have I done it?* "Nadia?" I ask tentatively. "Ariel?" I look at my hands. They are covered in blood. I stare at them horrified. Tol, Welker, Washo, Xana, and Ari lie on the floor around me, hacked to pieces by my efforts. "No!" I scream and collapse onto my hands and knees. I lie there for a long time, sobbing like a child. "Why have you shown me this?"

"I've seen your mind," Candlemas says calmly. He stands before me. "You fear them knowing your secrets. That they will die because of you. That you will be alone forever."

"What does a robot know of loneliness?" I cry.

His face melts into an oozing black creature. He envelops me. I can't breathe. His voice vibrates from inside my own brain. "I feel so much!" he says.

I am permeated with the most forlorn sense I have ever felt. It is overwhelming and heartbreaking. "As the rodent feels more than the insect, as the ape more than the rodent, so does your capacity pale in comparison to my pain!"

I scream. Again, I clutch my sides and awake in the fetal position. It is over, and tears stream down my face unabated. Candlemas's dark-skinned, very human hand opens in front of me. "Sometimes there are no words to articulate," he says. "One must be shown." I take his hand. He pulls me to stand. "I was built to feel. I do not know why."

Stars streak past us, and we are flying through the vast. We hover above a galaxy. A violet, spiderlike network that connects points through the dark matter of the Milky Way alights. The shape is humanoid, and I pick out the Tibular, Fibulum, Femoral, and Pelvulum Corridors of the Fracture. Near the Radial and Ulnar Corridors lay Tao and Lyria. They glow red like an infection. I recognize the trajectory—*the armies of Tao. Candlemas tracks Phaestion's conquest, too. If nothing is done to stop them, they will continue to infect all points along the Nine Corridors . . .*

He says nothing of this, however. Instead, the view zooms in upon a planet toward the upper spine of the Centra Fracture, a gray, dead world. "Miral," he says. "Birthplace of humanity. Planet of my origin."

"Humanity was born on Ancient Earth, not on Miral," I correct.

A thin smile crosses his dark lips. "The planet's location was hidden even from me, but in the millennia since the collapse of the empire, I've gathered the information to discover her coordinates." We now stand in a desert of gray ash. Lightning flashes from dark clouds overhead, and the crack of thunder drums my ears. On the horizon, there is a small white structure, a tiny white rose no bigger than a pinprick. *I've been here before—but how?* "I've sent several teams to scour the surface, looking for the Temple of the Matriarchs, where I believe to find the answers of my origins—why I was built this way and for what purpose. None of my teams returned, and I am no closer to discovering the temple's location."

I look down and in my hands is the nightscript reader that Faria gifted me in the Wendigo. He told me it held the location of the treasure of Miral, but though I searched, I could never find the planet.

"You are an exceptional individual, Edmon Leontes. Your whole crew is. The genetically modified, the pharmacologically modified, the designer organics, even the cyborg."

Cyborg?

Candlemas holds forth a tarot card. It is the blank tarot that Washo took from Rollinson and gave to me, for the image on the surface does not display an archetype. It only flickers. "As I am designed as a human emulation program, I have the most powerful human urge of all. The urge to mate. Were there another AI I could bond with, I would."

"You're a super intelligence," I counter. "Why not simply create another computer to combine with."

"Are you aware, Edmon Leontes, that human chromosomes come in pairs? Each building block of human life has an equal and opposite partner so if there is a deleterious gene on one chromosome, its opposite can provide the correct, functioning gene?" he asks.

"I am a doctor," I respond drolly.

He smiles, thin-lipped. "Then you know this is true for all but one chromosome."

"The Y chromosome," I answer.

"The Y contains the gene that switches a mammalian fetus from female to male in the womb. As such, it is necessarily different from its partnered X chromosome. The Y has no counterpart, and so through generations, it may not look to its partner to correct degradation. Sure, it is palindromic and may copy its own mirrored image as a sort of precarious biological foothold. Still, the Y is slowly stripped through the generations, having sex with itself in a slow death spiral. Have you experienced sex with yourself, Doctor Leontes?"

"Far more frequently than the alternative," I mumble. "It's not as satisfactory."

"Then you understand why perhaps some of your human cultures view the female gender as the original and superior of the species and why it is also necessary that I seek to combine with a being other than myself, even another iteration of myself? In the absence of a suitable artificial mind, I seek to find a human with the brain and body capable of surviving the process. The Black Rose is intended to help create that individual. The tarot I fabricated to help me locate him or her."

"A card game?" I ask, incredulous.

"You have noticed that all the cards are identical and ubiquitous? Why not another type of tarot or game? Why only mine?" he asks. I have no answer. "Addiction. Your kind spends so much of your resources creating pleasure through mindless distraction, I could think of no better way to gain access to all kinds of beings across the Fracture."

I can't argue.

"Each card contains a touch of my consciousness. The algorithms discern the bearer's true nature and transmit it back to me here."

"Have you found the card you're looking for?" I ask.

He smiles sadly. "Not yet. It appears neither have you. It is rare that I am unable to read a person. After looking into your mind, I understand why. So much conflict . . . the quintessence cards, however, are not static. They change as the bearer changes. Perhaps there is a way for each of us to find what he seeks."

"You want us to go to Miral?" I guess.

"I hope you and your crew, with their abilities, will succeed where my teams have failed and find the Temple of the Matriarchs. The nightscript reader you have in your possession contains the coordinates, which are conveniently absent from my data banks. Go there, open the inner sanctum, and bring me back the item that resides within."

The treasure of Miral . . .

"What item exactly?"

"You'll know it when you see it."

"Why would we agree to help you?" I ask.

"Because my teams are not the only ones who have been searching for Miral." A group of soldiers walk past us through the sand. They wear the same armor and helmets of Captain Jak and her crew of Hoplites. "I've analyzed the design of your stolen ship. There is no identical match within my extensive archives. I've sequenced the genome of your clone crewmate. He does not share the common patterns that every human born of Miral shares. Yet, both ships and soldiers are mimicking technology and design that have not been seen since the fall of the old empire. Someone else may have survived that cataclysm. They are trying to hunt you. They are trying to stop me. We have a common enemy," Candlemas says. "In recompense, I can give you whatever your heart desires."

"Your lost love?" Nadia appears and asks.

"What could have been?" says the son I never had.

"To choose a different path," my noseless father snarls.

"Redemption?" Phaestion smirks and brandishes his sword.

"Or your voice?" Then Ari stands before me.

A doorway of light opens in the desert. Candlemas gestures for me to walk through it.

"One more thing, Doctor Leontes," Candlemas adds before I pass the boundary of the portal. "Once you have the temple's bounty, return to me with Ariel Lazarus. Kill the rest of your crew."

BOOK II: PILGRIM

CHAPTER 12

The World

> The world card is the symbol of the door to the next life after death. It is a complete circle, and unlike the hanged man who searches only inward, the world card searches infinitely outward. Unlike the wheel of fortune whose spin is up and down, the world's rotation is cyclical. No matter where the traveler is sent, something important will happen.
>
> —Ovanth, *A Practical Reading of the Arcana*

Daylight streams through the diaphanous curtains of the apartment. I peel the covers off the bed I lie in and look out a window onto the crystal city of Roc-121. I feel refreshed and strong as if my system has received the maximum dose of recovery.

I walk to the closet. I grab my siren sword, the nightscript reader, and the small iron nose of my father. There is also the folded letter to Welker's son and the tarot card. There is a black bodysuit, sleek and form-fitting. I put it on, and it molds to my skin almost like the liquid metal of Candlemas himself. On the wrist is a readout of my vitals and those of the rest of my crew. All are healthy and in close proximity.

"Crew of the UFP *James Bentley*, or should I say the *Tyger*?" Candlemas addresses us over a comm system. "Your ship awaits." The door to my room slides open. I tuck my possessions into the second skin's pockets and exit. Directional lights pulse along the metal corridor. The others appear from doors similar to my own. Ari, Welker, Xana, and Bentley form up beside me. Washo and Tol bring up the rear as we walk in silence. There is a sobered feeling as we stride shoulder to shoulder. *They all saw parts of my dream,* I think. *But they have also experienced their own. Why were they privy to my thoughts and not I to theirs?*

I think back to what Ari said to me earlier, how I am afraid. I am afraid that those I love may come to harm because it has happened before. I am afraid that if those around me knew who I am, or who I once was, that they would reject me. Candlemas confronted them with my darkest past and my deepest desires. I can only surmise that the greatest fears of my crewmates had nothing to do with me learning of their secrets. Or perhaps I already know enough to divine their blackest shadows without his help?

Either way, the fact remains that Candlemas offered to fulfill my unspoken wishes if I bring him the contents of the temple's inner sanctum and Ari and then murder my crewmates.

So what offers has Candlemas made the others?

Xana looks haunted but determined. Washo averts furtive eyes. Welker seems reenergized. My second skin, networked to the others', informs me that Candlemas has administered a potent dose of Tag to our pilot, giving him a renewed vitality; however, he has not been cured entirely. Pockets in my suit carry rudimentary first aid implements as well as a limited supply of the narcotic for Welker for when the dose wears off.

Ari's hair is now a full shock of flame. *How long have we been under?* I wonder. My eyes linger on her curves in the form-fitting suit, which gleams like the skin of a snake. *Stop staring, Edmon.*

"Damn, Doctor Batman." Tol whistles. "You've been working that gluteus." Apparently, Ari isn't the only one being stared at.

"Easy, Tol. I know we both look delicious," Welker jests.

Ari chuckles. It's good to hear her laugh, and I am, for once, thankful for the levity. They all now know of my lost wife, my father, my feelings for Ari, and my connection to the tyrant whose armies have conquered Lyria. *What will they think of me now?*

The hallway ends, and we pass through the doorway into the sunlight of the mini-star. I close my eyes and bask in the warmth of its nuclear rays. The *Tyger* waits on the landing platform, looking clean and sleek. We board the ship and gather in the cockpit as Welker straps into the pilot's harness. "Washo, to the engine room. Tol, set course for the point. Xana, on the guns, keep your eyes open. Doctor, if you could lend Tol and Ari your nightscript reader?"

I pull out the reader. "Candlemas has added the location of the planet to its data banks," I say. Ari takes it from me, and then her fingertips read the tactile script. She plugs in the coordinates. *It took her seconds to learn what it took me months even to read the easiest of passages.*

"Next stop, Miral," Welker says.

We are escorted by Candlemas's sentry ships out of the cylinder and into the blackness of space. We float against our restraining straps as the cylinder's gravity wears off. Washo engages the fracture saw, and the point opens before us in a swirling tunnel of light and color. "Entering the current," Welker says as he eases the ship into the vein.

My body feels light, my head dizzy, and we phase from reality. It's euphoric, a bit like getting smacked upside the head. It has something to do with the time dilation intrinsic to the Fracture. One's body actually phases out of one reality into the next as the warp-bubble created by the saw vibrates the matter of the ship and the occupants at the same frequency of the wormhole in space. The wormhole itself is really like a segment of folded space-time where two points touch. The blood rushes back into my head as we cut out of the vein through the other side of the point.

"There she is," Xana whispers. Hanging in the veil of stars lies Miral, a dull, gray moon against the backdrop of a brilliant crimson and azure swirling gas giant. A small blue star flares in the distance behind them both.

"The Ameryka gas planet," Washo says, having come up from the engine room. He floats beside me, gazing at the brilliance of Miral's companion world.

"She's beautiful," says Ari.

"Can't say much for Miral, though. Desert planet. Wasteland of the empire. For it is only on Miral that you may find the greatest treasure in all the universe—"

"Shut up, Tol," we murmur in unison.

"That's where we're aiming. Let's have a closer look, shall we?" Welker says.

"I'm picking up massive cloud cover across Miral's surface. High levels of silicon with intense electrical discharges." Ari's fingers dance over the holographic displays. "We fly into that, we'll get cooked."

"There." Bentley innocently points to something that looks like a yo-yo attached by a thread to the moon.

"Is that a satellite?" Xana asks.

"It's obviously a space station," Ari cuts in tightly. The muscles in her jaw twitch. She's on edge at the sound of Xana's voice. *Interesting—something to do with her dream?*

"Tol, can you zoom in on sector b-five?" Welker asks.

"You just sunk my battleship," Tol confirms.

The station has flashes of metal and bone on her hull, connecting it to the surface of the world by some sort of translucent, plant-based umbilical. It looks partly biological, and I'm reminded of the stinger ships of the clone soldiers. I look at Washo, who fidgets nervously. It makes sense now, my earlier intuition that he had seen such technology before.

"Definitely chloroplasts," Ari says, corroborating my visual suspicion. "Running on some sort of photosynthesis."

"Do we have the capability of firing some isotopes at it?" Welker suggests. "Perhaps we can carbon date it?"

"I can do that," Washo responds, as he activates an ancillary communications station. To him the world is sacred ground, forbidden to outsiders. Now he knows how I felt back on Roc-121 having everyone glimpse images of my past.

"It's thousands of years old," Ari says solemnly. "At least the vine is."

"A plant, angling in space for thousands of years?" Tol shakes his head with disbelief.

"Then it predates the collapse of the empire," Xana surmises.

"Oh, look who can do math," Ari says acidly. Xana scowls. *Something happened between them on Roc-121.*

"How does it get water?" I wonder aloud.

"Shall we find out?" Welker leans the *Tyger* toward the satellite and the docking clamps that hang at the end of the vine. "Engage clamps." The clicking sound of our landing gear echoes through the ship. Then Welker engages the umbilical.

"Bentley, Doctor, you're on point with me." Xana makes sure her weapons are secure. We float through our umbilical to the hatch at the end of the tube. It hisses open and on the other side is a squat man in furs with gray skin and large red eyes. He sports a mustache that hasn't been trimmed for decades. "What is business here? Who are you, you fly dat ship?" he demands in broken Normal.

"You know this here ship?" Welker asks.

"Seen kinds like. Dey bypass my station. You want go surface in my elevator? You make deal." He waves his finger at us.

So the designer organic commandos have been here. Xana clocks this as well and purses her lips. I've not forgotten that she wears the same face as their captains. *What was it that Candlemas showed her?* I wonder. *Did he make the same demand of her, to kill us once the mysterious item in the Temple of the Matriarchs is recovered?*

"You make deal! De gods must give gifts in return for descent. Che knows what I mean." The gray man points at Washo.

The tech boy's eyes dart in every direction. "Spit it out, Washo," I growl.

Ari puts a hand on Washo's shoulder. He practically melts. "It's okay, Washo, you can trust them."

She already knows. She saw his dreams, too.

"It's forbidden to tell outsiders," Washo stammers.

"Washo, you're an outsider," Xana says.

He bows his head in deference to Xana as if she were a queen. *If Xana does turn on us, Bentley will follow, and so will Washo . . .*

"Nicnacians were the priestly class of the Mira who escaped the Great Storm aboard their arcs. Each makes the pilgrimage to the homeworld as they come of age. They descend to the surface as a Tevoda, a blessed spirit and, after seven days of prayer and penitence, ascend as a fully realized Nicnacian who will await the return of Urizen's final avatar. Those who do not return to the arcs fail the test and are doomed to be devoured by Los, the great darkness of the beyond," the boy confesses.

The fact that Washo is not floating aboard an arc ship now, tells us all we need to know—*Washo failed his test.*

"I am a Charon," the gray man says. "I take the tithe."

"The location of Miral is kept secret from every Nicnacian, except those red priests who deliver each girl and boy from Armada to Market, then from Market to Charon." Washo points to the mustached man. "We pay the Charon a tribute and are delivered to the worshippers on the surface."

"There are six of you." The Charon points at us. "Payment must be for six or else elevator will not run."

"I don't know. You seem like you eat pretty well." I float forward and stare the fat man down. His jowls quiver.

"I keep elevator for faithful. Kill me, you will not reach surface!"

"Doc, leave this to your fearless leader!" Tol floats forward. He reaches inside Rollinson's coat that he has draped over Candlemas's second skin. He pulls out a jeweled necklace with a giant zirconia sapphire hanging on the end. "Charon, my good man. This here's the 'Heart of the Sea.' It was lost aboard this sailing ship, the *Titano*, a long time ago, in a Fracture far, far away. It's worth a fortune, and any man who possesses it will own the love of the elf maiden, Argo, a beautiful immortal of the Undying Lands."

The gray man's red eyes grow big as saucers.

"Where did you get that, Tol?" Xana whispers.

"Swiped it off Thrance back on Nonthera as we were dashing for the *Bentley*." Tol grins.

"Dis way! Dis way!" the Charon exclaims and gestures us to follow. We float through the station, which is essentially a large control room converted to a bed and kitchen for the keeper. We stop at a massive oaken door with rivulets of liquid metal coursing through it.

"Chance you arrive to surface and return in one piece, maybe twenty percent if lucky." The Charon rubs the stubble of his gray double chin. "Worshippers chave not been chappy wit' off'rings of gods lately. Kill them, you know?" He grins with crooked yellow teeth.

The massive door opens. We step inside.

"What offerings?" I growl. "There were others who came through here?"

The Charon's red eyes flash, and he slams the door shut behind us. I pound my fist against the solid wood just as the door pressurizes with a hiss, the wet hum of the biomachinery starts, and we begin to descend.

"I'm not used to my mechanical protection going *squish*," says Tol.

"What did he mean, the worshippers haven't been happy?" I turn to Washo.

Washo shrugs, but it's clear to all of us he knows more than he is saying. We settle in as the elevator drops toward the surface of the dead world. An hour ticks by. The heat in the enclosed space increases as the friction of Miral's tempestuous atmosphere batters against the elevator car. Time passes; so, too, does the tension inside the compartment as we stew on the Charon's last words. Others, not Nicnacians, descended and were killed by the worshippers below. Beads of sweat form on my brow. I try to breathe even while I feel the storm inside me brewing as we draw closer to the surface.

"Ninety-nine bottles of beer on the wall, ninety-nine bottles of beer, you take one down, pass it around, ninety-eight bottles of beer on the wall! Everyone!"

I lunge for Sanctun and slam him against the wall of the elevator. Bentley pulls his pistol, presses it against my temple, and cocks the action while Xana places her extensor staff just under my chin.

"Believe me, Doctor, I want him to shut up just as much as you, but I will do it," she says softly.

"No, you won't," Ari says coldly. "Put your weapon away, Xana."

Xana's knuckles whiten. She doesn't want to obey, but it's almost as if she has no choice. Her hand shakes as she holsters the staff. Her dark eyes blaze at Ari, not only with anger, but with hurt for having chosen me over her, for subverting her free will. Bentley looks on in confusion. "You, too, Bentley," Xana says tightly, and the clone removes the pistol from my head.

"Washo, what did the Charon mean that the worshippers have not been happy with the gods' offerings?" I repeat my question from several hours ago more calmly, loosening my grip on Tol.

The spypsy boy has been praying I wasn't going to press him after the initial ask. His voice quivers. "Miral was a desert, and for generations, the people lived beneath the surface. Over eons we terraformed it, turned it to a paradise. A caste system was needed to do that. Brahmins were the highest and originally lived near the core where it was warm and water abundant. The Brahmins became the Nicnacians, the Chosen. The guilds of midden-mensch, who comprised the bulk of the society, were the buffer between the hallowed and the Scrylings, the lowest who dwelt on the surface. Midden-mensch were partitioned into soldiers, spacers, builders, farmers, merchants, servants, and colonizers of other worlds."

"People like us," Welker says. He is starting to look sick again. The Tag Candlemas gave him was wearing off. I check the pouch of my second skin. There aren't as many Tag patches as I would like. We need to ration them just in case.

"The surface dwellers—the Scrylings," Washo continues, "were bred to survive the harsh climate of the planet and effect the physical terraforming. Many of their race survived the Great Storm. They are very primitive, and they worship the descendants of their gods . . ."

"You mean you," I growl. "The Nicnacians."

"They are custodians of the temples of the matriarchs, but only Nicnacians are allowed to visit or enter the inner sanctums. It is forbidden for all others."

"But Charon recognized the *Tyger* and implied others have come," Xana says.

"And they didn't make out so fortunately," Tol adds.

"What would the Scrylings do to someone who is not a Nicnacian?" asks Welker.

"It's forbidden" is Washo's only answer.

"Candlemas said none of the teams he sent to the surface had returned," I say.

We all shift uncomfortably, taking this in.

"Washo." Ari breaks the silence. "You mentioned an avatar of Urizen?"

"Urizen's next avatar, the Orc, will join Urizen in the final battle to hold back the shadow of Los."

The spypsy doctor called Ari the Orc. And when Ari recounted to Candlemas her memories of joining with the stinger ship, she mentioned that it was an Urizen that was looking for her . . .

"Orc!" Bentley exclaims. "Captain, we were looking for Orc."

His people were looking for Ari. His people were looking for Orc. The avatar of Urizen is Ari . . . ?

"Mind blown, you guys," Tol emphasizes.

I glance at Ari. Her lack of reaction confirms my suspicion. *She already pieced this together but said nothing to the rest of us.*

"Do the Scrylings believe this myth as well?" I ask.

"I assume so."

"Plan?" I look at Welker and Xana.

"The temple priests might recognize me from my first trip," says Washo. "But—"

"Nicnacians don't normally return to the temple once the Rapzis is complete," Ari finishes his sentence. "You didn't believe in the divinity of Urizen, you received no revelation or epiphany on your journey, and so you decided not to go home to Armada. Now, you're breaking precedent again by returning to a holy site? You are a heretic, Washo."

"I am not a heretic, Ari, I swear. I believe," he insists.

"That doesn't matter," Xana says coolly. "It only matters what they believe. What does a return visit mean, Washo?"

Washo looks at his feet in shame. Before any of us can ask anything else, the oaken doors of the elevator hiss open.

—

We step from the car into the open. Our second skin suits morph to cover our heads and the lower halves of our faces so we can survive in the new environment and to disguise our identities. Before us lays a cathedral carved from red rock. Lining the checkered stone floor are hundreds of creatures, men or women, in ancient pressure suits, their faces covered by beetlelike breath masks. Their bulky bodies are swathed in bedraggled robes and rags.

"It's like the *Mad Max–Stargate* series," Tol whispers.

"Shut up," I hiss.

"Scrylings?" Xana asks.

The robed mass sways back and forth, chanting. I pick out the name Urizen among their murmurings. I feel the shadow here, greater than before, pressing on my consciousness. The others must be experiencing it as well, for we all shift backward. Ari stumbles. Xana is immediately there to catch her. The warrior cradles her tenderly. I see an entire history of love between them just in that small gesture, but Ari stands and shoves Xana away. Whatever happened on Roc-121 is boiling over between them.

Washo, Edmon. Talk to Washo. He needs you, Ari's voice breaks my internal monologue.

"What did you say?" I ask, switching our headset comms to a two-way channel.

"I didn't say anything," she responds coldly. *Then what in the nine hells . . . ?* I shake my head. I swear I heard her voice. *Was it only my imagination?*

She looks at me curiously. Whatever just happened, the voice is right. I can't fight through a mob this size. Nor can I talk to them; there is one among us who can, but Washo is quivering like an anemone. *He needs courage,* I realize. *Maybe I can do something for him, something my own mentors did for me.*

I place a hand on the boy's shoulder. "Washo, remember, bravery isn't the absence of fear. It's acting in spite of it."

"What do I do?" he asks.

"Speak to them," I say. "We are behind you. Begin with one word—that's all you need. The rest will come." It's something Gorham said to me once when I was scared to step into the circle and sing. My gesture seems a pale reflection of his memory, but it's all I have.

Washo's hood peels back, revealing his bald pate, while the part covering his nose, mouth, and chin becomes translucent so the crowd can see his face but he's still protected by the suit's breathing filter. The humming of the cathedral silences. "I am Washo Tan, Nicnacian of Uveth."

Whispers hum through the ranks. A robed figure breaks away from the pack. A medallion hangs from a chain around his neck, and he leans on an ancient, gnarled staff of wood. The breath mask beneath his tattered robe looks like some sort of weird alien insect. He turns to face the horde of worshippers. He screams something in a guttural language, and suddenly, the crowd erupts in chants again, this time violent and angry.

A rock is thrown at us. Tol ducks, and his top hat falls off his hooded head. "You guys, maybe this wasn't the best idea?" he says over the comm.

I grit my teeth and step forward. My hand snaps another rock from the air just before it hits Washo. The second skin slips back from my head, too, and the people gasp. I crush the rock into dust in my palm and let it drizzle to the floor. The bug-eyed figure with the staff ascends the steps to the elevator. He reaches the top step and slides his ancient beetlelike breath mask off, revealing his face, and pulls back his hood. It is not a man, but a woman, ancient and decayed. Her skin is cracked and old, pale and gray. Black circles surrounded her large, red eyes. When she opens her mouth, she reveals a row of hideous needle teeth. She looks at Washo, and the guttural language bursts from her gullet. Washo translates.

"She is Hari-Ma, the high priestess of the Celestial Temple. She asks if I am a demon." Washo then responds in the priestess's tongue, though his words sound far more rolling and enunciated. Ari listens, absorbing the exchange. "I've explained that I am Washo Tan of Uveth, and that I am Nicnacian, returned to the surface on a sacred quest."

The priestess steps forward again and speaks; however, this time she speaks in a tongue that we can all make out. "Anudder come as you, claiming he was sent from Urizen. His eyes like lizard, strange blue. He came with udders. His name no in our holy ledger."

Xana's hood peels back, and the breath filter becomes transparent, exposing her face and dark hair. The mob hisses. *They've seen others like her before. The others the priestess speaks of . . .*

She bows to the priestess with a gesture of respect. "What was his name, Hari-Ma?"

"This demon took the name Talousla Karr," the priest spits.

Xana's eyes widen. I freeze in my tracks.

"My name is in the holy ledger, Hari-Ma. And we are not demons," Washo adds firmly.

"I remember you, Washo Tan," the priestess says. "But only those who fail Urizen fall back to dis world. Talousla Karr, de demon, came, den many udders tru heaven door. Blue hair children come wit strange machine. Dis mean war between gods and shadow is come. Is our duty to murder any demon dat come tru Celestial Gate. We kill dem."

Blue hair. Candlemas's designer organics. These Scrylings murdered the ones that tried to come to the surface through the vine.

"If you return after Rapzis, it is sign from Urizen. Maybe you cast down, marked, as Koro Shan once was."

"Koro Shan?" Xana asks.

"The tale of the lost space gypsy," Washo murmurs. The crew looks at him. "It's a fable. After the fall of Miral, when the Nicnacians were confined to the arcs, one boy was supposedly cast out. He came back to Miral. Instead of killing him as they were supposed to, the surface dwellers believed he was a fallen angel. He married a native, became a leader of the tribe. I thought it was just a tale."

"Koro Shan was hero. He bring divine blood to mix wit ours. He foretold great change for our world," the priestess confirms.

"From the Nicnacian perspective, Koro Shan was a failed religious reformer," Washo says. "He believed the matriarchy was an antiquated system of rule, the Rapzis was a parochial tradition. He was cast out by our government for his unnatural views."

"Yes, but it seems we'd do well to take a page from his text," says Welker. "I'd much rather be a fallen angel than a demon." Then he doubles over with a rib-shaking cough. I quickly go over and support the pilot. Meanwhile, the cathedral silently waits for our answer.

"So how do we convince them we are Koro Shan and not Talousla Karr?" Xana asks.

Suddenly, Ari steps in front of her. The second skin peels back from her head, and the shock of her red hair is released like fire. The congregation gasps.

"Let's hope they think she has a soul?" Tol shrugs.

Ari raises her arms and calls out in the people's own language. They fall to their knees, humming in fear and awe.

"What are you telling them, Ari?" I ask.

"That Washo is a holy prophet sent to destroy the demon. We are his servants, here to help him stop his evil counterpart."

Washo blanches. The high priestess's voice shakes. "Daughter of Urizen, be you here to lift storm and defeat shadow?" The old woman extends a gloved hand and points to a stained glass mural framed by two support columns of the cathedral. It's a depiction of . . .

Us.

"No. Way. You guys," Tol says.

A figure, a woman with hair like fire floating around her head like a halo, is in the center of the design. She levitates against the red-and-blue swirling backdrop of the Ameryka gas giant. She's flanked by companions lower in the image. They are nondescript, but there is no mistaking that main image is just like Ari.

"Demiurge!" The priestess stands and calls to the congregation. The worshippers rise and cheer with joy. They rush us.

"Ari!" Xana screams as the mob grabs the girl and sweeps her into their arms. She surfs on their hands, and the rest of us are pulled into the human river in her wake.

"By the twisted star, get your mitts off me, you filthy mooks!" I howl, trying to push through them to get to Ari. I lose sight of Washo. I make out Welker for a second, grinning right before an ill look crosses his visage, and he vomits black bile and collapses. "Welker!" I scream.

I'm swallowed by the crowd. All I can see is musty robes swirling around me. I'm pulled through the massive doors of the cathedral and outside onto the surface of Miral. The hood of my second skin pulls over my head. I signal its internal instruments to silence the cacophony of the crowd. The storm of dark clouds rages above. An arc of purple lightning forks the heavens, and the earth beneath me quakes. Monstrous geysers of water spring from vents in the moon's crust and explode into the sky. Darkness envelops me as I am shoved into some kind of tunnel. Stone steps carved into the ground carry us down beneath the surface.

CHAPTER 13

The High Priestess

> If there is a card that represents the fortune-teller, it is the high priestess. Unlike the magician whose purpose is to reveal, the high priestess's powers contain the knowledge behind the veil of secrecy. A spiritual woman of great teaching, she is the virgin goddess of old in Athena or Artemis, as well as the mother in Isis, Ishtar, or Lakshmi. She is the incubator of secrets that will be revealed.
>
> —Ovanth, *A Practical Reading of the Arcana*

A staircase that hugs a deep shaft winds us kilometers beneath the crust of Miral. Hour upon hour we descend by the flickering of torchlight. I recall another journey years ago into the ice cavern of the Wendigo.

"What is it, Doctor?" Washo asks over the comm, seeing my face in the firelight.

"The deaths, Washo. All the ones I've lost. That history weighs down on a person . . ."

I cannot become close to these people, but now I can't bear to lose them, either. Candlemas promised he could revive those I've lost . . .

Tol slips on the jagged steps ahead of me, falls into the chasm. My hand snaps out and grabs his arm. His coat flaps open. Coins jingle from his pockets and float like glittering stars into the void. "Not today, fool," I growl and yank him back to the steps.

"I almost took a plunge into Khazhad-dûm there," he murmurs. "Edmon?" he asks. It's strange hearing him say my name, rather than the usual "Doctor Batman." It reminds me that they've all seen something of my past, my true self. Again, I feel horribly exposed. "I don't mean to be a nuisance all the time," he admits quietly.

"I know" is all I muster, and the mask of flippancy falls over Tol's long face again. I wish I could have said something kinder.

"What do you think this is all about?" he asks.

The hoods of our second skin retract now that we're deeper under the earth, and my eyes linger on the halo of Ari's red hair in the dim light of the tunnel. Welker leans on her, hacking up a lung. When we left Market, she was just a girl. Now, she walks at the head of the column, holding us all together.

"Damned if I know," I murmur back. "Are your retinals picking up anything?"

"Retinals?" he asks, playing innocent.

I've suspected since Market and have wondered about Tol's historical knowledge of Ancient Earth long before that. Candlemas's suggestion there was a cyborg in our midst confirmed it. I trade in on my suspicion now as I glare.

"Okay, I haven't been honest, all right, Doc?" He brushes off his coat self-consciously as he walks. "But it's really none of your bus—"

"The abyss with that!" I grab him by the lapels and yank him over the chasm again. He dangles with kicking feet.

"What in the nine hells are you doing?" Xana shouts. The whole party halts, and she and Bentley come rushing up the steps toward us, weapons drawn.

"Please don't drop me, Doctor Batman!" Tol's shouts echo off the shaft walls.

"Tell us what you're hiding then," I growl.

"I never intended it to happen this way," he cries.

"What?" Xana asks.

"To lose a little piece at a time," he says, sobbing. "It started with a surgeon on Market, you know, suggesting that he could remove a pocket in my rib, replace it with a compartment that stores a computer chip or a key card. Then I got a couple more. Small ones, nothing fancy. But I kept going. I'm sorry. Don't kill me."

I pull him back from the brink, feeling a deep sense of shame. *Why do I always lash out with violence, fear, and intimidation?* It's the leviathan inside me. *Am I forever condemned to be a monster?*

"Dad was a historian." Tol opens his coat for all of us to see. "He also said knowledge was dangerous, that others would kill me to know it." He presses a spot just below his rib cage. A compartment suddenly pops out with a click. My eyes widen. Apparently, Candlemas's second skin is tailored to each of our specific needs and abilities. While mine consistently gives me the medical readouts of the crew, Tol's allows for these hidden compartments to extend and retract when needed, the layer of the suit peeling and sealing seamlessly as desired.

"I started collecting artifacts. I needed places to hide them. The implants were like . . . I don't know, grace maybe?" Tol pulls a jewel from the compartment, a silicate data card, I realize. "This is my most prized," he admits softly. "A record of Earth's pop culture." He presses another point on his shoulder. Another pocket clicks open. He pulls out an old microchip. "Took me years to find tech old enough to decode this one. It's a catalog of like every piece of pre-FC music." He reaches below his belt near his groin excitedly. "And this one . . ."

"That's enough, Tol," Xana warns.

"I know it's disconcerting to see someone pull drawers out of their own stomach." He shrugs sheepishly. "I had a lot of my digestive system removed and replaced by solar nanites just to deal with not being able to metabolize food. Like I said, I didn't intend for it to happen. Just kind of became habit."

I touch the waxy scar on my throat. I know all too well about losing pieces of myself and the promises of surgeons.

"I even replaced a bit of my memory to keep some files. You know like Johnny Pneumonica?"

"Well, why don't you help us now and use your retinals like I asked?" I grumble.

Tol glances all around us. I feel guilty that I forced this reveal from him. I suspected he might be hiding something a lot worse than the fact that he has removed body parts.

"The rock is igneous, volcanic," he says. "Maybe billions of years old, but the shaft was laser cut, perhaps a thousand years ago."

Then again, I can't regret that his abilities and knowledge may help us now that we know what they are.

"Around the time the empire fell," Ari surmises. "Whoever created this chamber built this place at the end. For these people."

"Washo, were you taken this way the last time?" Welker asks hoarsely.

"No. I stayed in the temple and prayed to the matriarchs. After seven days, I was told I was transformed and to return to Armada."

Washo seems disconcerted at the memory. It would be easy to be disillusioned after being told to have an epiphany and walking out the same as when you walked in.

"We wait Urizen's return long time," the priestess croaks. "Come," she urges.

We continue to follow the cloaked Scrylings. Finally, we reach a level where a tunnel diverts off the stairs and leads into the wall of the shaft. We turn off the path of the staircase, and an entire village of people appears from crevices. They greet us at the landing with pale, milk-white hands, white-yellow hair, and giant, red alien eyes. They bow before Ari while reaching to finger our high-tech clothing.

"Urizen . . . Orc of the matriarchs . . . the Anjins have returned . . . ," they whisper.

"What is an Anjin?" Bentley asks Xana.

"They were elite soldiers of Miral who piloted highly advanced biomech armors," she tells him in a maternal tone.

"Each warrior," I tell him, "was bonded to his mech. When the two joined, they became almost an entirely new entity. The soldier could disengage from his armor, and the shell would retain a piece of the warrior's consciousness. They were the guardians of freedom and security during a golden age."

"They were divine angels of Urizen," Washo says, nodding.

The mythopoeia here is complex, and I'm trying to make sense of everything I've learned from Washo as well as from my own observations. Urizen is female, the light, the architect of the universe. She has avatars or incarnations, it seems. Whether that means Urizen was an actual person, I don't know. Los appears to be male, the darkness, chaos. The society of Miral was stratified, and the Nicnacians are the descendants of the highest order. They are holy beings. My own ancestors were the original soldier class of the empire. The elite served as Anjins, but they rebelled and flew beyond the reaches of the empire to colonize Tao and create their own male-centric version of the religion, the Balance.

As for the Anjins of Miral before and since my people's defection, their superhuman skills gave birth to legends—the Walls of Samus, the epic of the Chironiad, the account of Leontes. I always knew them to be warriors who lived by a rigorous code of honor and represented the pinnacle of mental, physical, and moral perfection. Washo confirms that Anjins were also spiritual symbols. The temple above had images of companions with the Orc. Perhaps if they think Ari is Urizen reborn, it is not such a leap to think of us as her divine warriors. I look at the faces of our ragtag group and force myself to stifle an ironic laugh at the thought that any of us are divine.

"You travel far, and dere is much to do," says the priestess. "But first, rest."

Robed servants help part the crowd and lead us to a corridor filled with round doors. One door is larger than the others. "My home," the priestess says.

We enter the small abode, and the crew takes seats on a carpet in the living room of the rock-cut dwelling. A fire in the room's center casts flickering shadows. I help Welker lean against a wall. I put my hand to his forehead. He is hot to the touch.

"I'll be fine, Doctor," he murmurs. "I just need rest. If we get through this, Candlemas says he has the cure for me. I may not need you to keep that letter to my son after all." He smiles weakly.

So Candlemas promised to cure Welker in return for whatever mysterious talisman resides in the temple. Will I have to watch my back with him, too? I wonder.

"We wait for Urizen's return for eon," the priestess croaks in broken Normal as she sits on a stool. She casts her giant red eyes at Ari. "You are reincarnation, no? You come to deliver us from Great Storm?"

Ari is unsettled. *How does she negotiate their myths?* I can see her thinking. Candlemas's people never returned and the Scrylings' suspicions about the designer organic soldiers who preceded us suggest we have little chance of survival if we are revealed as anything other than the Orc and her followers.

"Doctor, maybe show Hari-Ma here the reader?" Welker suggests.

I take out the nightscript reader from my second skin. The metallic screen leaps to life, forming all kinds of shapes on its surface—symbols, pictures, hieroglyphs. I close my eyes and run my fingers over the symbols sorting through the screens for the map.

"This device of the Mira shows us where we must go . . . on our sacred quest," I explain.

The priestess reaches for the tablet. I'm reluctant to relinquish the device, but I acquiesce, and the woman's veiny pale fingers trace the glyphs. Her red eyes widen with fear. "You seek de Temple of de Matriarchs!" She shakes her head and clucks her tongue. "Many try make journey and receive embrace of Los for arrogance. The infidels search for dis as well." The priestess's eyes narrow on Xana and Bentley. "You must not journeying beyond confines of our sanctuary."

"We must!" Xana stands. Bentley mirrors her.

But the priestess remains firm. "You wear form of matriarch but cannot hide you are a demon like de udders. I fear not only for sake of Orc."

"Proszę sie," Ari speaks gently. "Please," she repeats for the rest of our benefit.

"Why you travel with demon, daughter of Urizen?" the priestess asks her. "It is said you return with Anjins. Dis we know. Perhaps you bring demon as test of faith? Who knows dees tings? I will trust."

"We must travel to the Temple of the Matriarchs, Hari-Ma. You must lead us there." Ari stands and takes the priestess's hand.

The priestess nods. "De Aeshnid will know." The old Scryling hands me the nightscript reader and takes a torch from a sconce. She leads us out of her home and through a labyrinthine system of tunnels that continues to wind deeper into the earth. I have an uneasy feeling as darkness envelops us, as if there are whispers in the shadow now, that same shadow that seems within my thoughts as well as out in the world. I'm not superstitious, but I'm starting to believe there is some truth in the fiction of this religion. "It is said dat one keeps going down and finds ancient cities of Mira. Young have tried. None return. To cross Aeshnid is death assured for de unholy."

Welker stumbles, and I shoulder his weight.

"Thank you, Doctor," he wheezes. Our breath masks have disengaged now that the atmosphere underground seems to be more hospitable. "It may be time for me to imbibe my regularly scheduled hit?" He smiles, and I can tell it pains him.

"Try and hang on a bit longer?" I know I'm asking a lot of him, but the efficacy of each subsequent dose I administer seems to diminish, and it's hard to know how long we'll be here. He nods weakly and leans against the tunnel wall.

"There is less oxygen here," Xana notes.

"But there are words," I mutter as my fingers brush the rock and read glyphs in nightscript.

"The deeper we get, the older these corridors are," Tol analyzes.

"Only the holy may pass," I read aloud.

"That's one translation," Ari corrects. "Only the upper races are permitted is another."

"You aren't touching the glyphs?" Xana asks.

"I don't have to," Ari snaps. Xana fumes. *This is going to come to a head unless someone diffuses the tension between them. What did Candlemas show them?* I wonder.

"She shall know our words without learning," the priestess recites in wonder. "You are Urizen made flesh once more."

"Washo, do you remember what you told us about Miral's caste system?" Welker coughs.

A draft of cool air flutters over my second skin. The tap of the old woman's cane stops. I look ahead to see a doorway that opens to a large chamber. Faint light emanates from beyond. We all gather before the portal and see it opens on a vast cylindrical chamber cut from the rock, a giant well that reaches up to the surface. It's hard to tell for sure because we are so deep. Not a pinprick of light can be seen when looking up, yet light comes from somewhere.

"De Aeshnid." The priestess points. The husk of a giant insect sits in the center of the chamber.

"I'm so grossed out," says Tol.

He's not the only one. Everything we've encountered so far—the liquid metal circuitry of Candlemas, the human gray matter attached to the enemy ships, plantlike space stations . . . all these remnants of this ancient society I find weirdly attractive and repulsive at the same time.

"What are we waiting for?" Xana angrily steps forward.

"Stay back!" The priestess thrusts her arms wide preventing Xana from crossing the threshold. "Only de holy may pass beyond borders of realm."

"That is the price of immortality!" Tol blurts. We all stare. "Shut up, I know, I know."

"Bentley, come on," Xana says acidly.

"No." Hari-Ma raises a hand, stopping Xana again. She then points with her staff at a pale, squealing rodent, which scurries away from us along the tunnel floor. It runs through the doorway into the chamber. Panels in the cylindrical walls glow hot white. The rat squeals and sprints back toward us, but the rodent's skin fries, and then it explodes from the inside out like a baked bean. Within a moment, there is not even a stain on the floor to indicate there had ever been life.

The priestess turns to Ari. "You see? If you are de Orc, sentinel will recognize."

I see fear behind Ari's eyes, but she nods and takes a step. "You're not going," Xana says quietly. "At least not first."

"It's a security system keyed to genetic pattern recognition—that should be obvious," Ari says harshly.

"I don't care what it is. You do not take the first step," Xana says, doubling down.

Ari moves toward her as if she is going to strike the warrior woman. *This is not good.* "You gave up your right to have any say in what I do with my life a long time ago—"

Apparently, I am not the only one Ari has felt abandoned by.

"What makes you think you'll pass through unscathed?" I interject, trying to keep us focused, as I help Welker remain standing.

"You've read some of the glyphs as we've walked the halls just now, Doctor?" Ari asks, determination in her blue eyes. "I've read them all."

"You couldn't possibly—"

"I've read everything since we've arrived," she says, cutting me off, "understood every Scryling word, gesture, their architecture. I've absorbed every glyph etched on every column and wall. They believe I am to be their messiah, the reincarnation of Urizen. Whoever built this place and their religion knew that I, or someone like me, would be coming." She turns and looks Xana up and down. "One of us was designed. Is it much of a stretch to believe that perhaps I, too, am some sort of designed genetic remnant of a dead empire? The signs are all here. We're about to find out."

Before any of us can stop her, she pushes past the old Scryling priestess and steps over the threshold.

CHAPTER 14

The Chariot

The chariot card is often hard to read, for while it denotes movement, it presents a fixed image of a vehicle flying above the world. Often this suggests that there is physical exertion without internal or spiritual growth. Only through a cataclysmic event can the chariot truly speed one forth on their journey.

—Ovanth, *A Practical Reading of the Arcana*

"Welcome, Supreme Matriarch Lazarus," the chamber speaks. "Do you wish to pilot the Aeshnid?"

Hari-Ma falls to her knees and presses her forehead to the floor. "Kaliyuga, kaliyuga, kaliyuga . . . ," she chants over and over.

Washo, too, brings his hands together, his eyes wide with awe.

What madness have we stumbled onto? Ari turns back, and her blue eyes connect with mine, haunted. It feels like there is a gulf growing between her and the rest of us, between her and me. I want to grab her and never let her go, but whatever unrequited desires either of us have seem slipping further from possibility.

"Matriarch Lazarus, do you wish to pilot the Aeshnid?" the voice asks again.

"Yes. And I would like for my companions to accompany me," Ari speaks back.

"The Aeshnid may hold up to ten."

Ari walks to the dried-out exoskeleton of the giant insect. She touches its desiccated shell. There is a beat, then the giant honeycomb-lensed eyes brighten to a vibrant emerald. The creature begins to move as if awakening from a thousand-year slumber. A millennium of dust sloughs off the creature's hide. There is a cracking sound that echoes through the chamber, a cacophony of bone-snapping reverberations. The carapace of the Aeshnid's gray exoskeleton splinters into spider vein patterns all over its body. The creature shakes and sprays eggshell-like fragments everywhere. The insect lets out a roar. We cover our ears as the howl rings through the well. When we look up, the creature has molted, revealing a slick, shiny green-black carapace. Rivulets of silver liquid metal run through the armor creating a tattoo pattern of sharp right-angle shapes. Sprouting from its mighty thorax are four horizontal membranous wings that shimmer in rainbow colors.

"It's a dragonfly!" Tol exclaims. He turns to us. "A very old species of Ancient Earth. I assumed they were gone."

The bug's giant head regards Ari curiously. A ramp lowers from the creature's abdomen to the floor of the chamber. "Sentinel, will your security protocol allow my companions to enter this chamber?" Ari asks.

"Those who possess genetic markers denoting a caste ranking superseding that of Scryling may proceed beyond the threshold," the chamber answers.

Ari thinks for a moment. "Sentinel, deactivate security protocol."

"Negative. Genetic and voiceprint identification is not within one-hundredth of a percent deviation."

"What does that mean?" Xana asks.

"The computer recognizes Ari as High Matriarch Lazarus, but knows she is not a one hundred percent match for whomever the original was," I explain.

Welker coughs. "In other words, the laser system remains decidedly active."

Subject Clay Welker experiencing vital systems shut down. Candlemas's second skin informs me via earpiece. I pull out a Tag patch and gently stick it onto the pilot's neck. He's hung on for as long as he could. He won't survive without another dose.

"If you are worthy to be her Anjins, then you may pass," the old priestess croaks.

"Thanks a lot," I swear under my breath.

"I'll go," Washo says.

We all turn to the boy. "Kid," I say. "There's a difference between bravery and stupidity. Only calculated risk is necessary."

I can tell in his eyes he's scared. Still, he raises his chin. "I'm Washo Tan, a Nicnacian of Uveth. If Ari is the incarnation of Urizen the Architect, then I am her faithful servant. I'm the most likely to be recognized by the security system. Bravery is acting in spite of fear," he says, and smiles even as his breaths come shallow now.

Candlemas offered to return me to my old life. It would mean giving up my crew. They know me as a healer, a fighter, now a teacher. Maybe even a friend.

You will get them killed, the shadow whispers. Welker is dying. Xana is losing it. Bentley is still an enemy. Tol is not capable. Washo is giving in to religious fervor. Ari is something I can't even fathom. We are going to be torn apart. *The shadow is right.*

Washo steps over the threshold. We hold our breath. "Genetic marker identified: Brahmin class. You may proceed." Washo exhales and walks toward Ari and the Aeshnid.

"Well, I'll be." Welker shakes his head. He takes his arm away from my shoulder, the Tag stimulation taking effect.

"My people were bred as soldiers, but they defected from the empire. We have origins on Miral, but who's to say if our renegade status will allow me to pass?" I say to the others but step forward into the chamber.

"Genetic marker identified: Kshatriya class. Proto-order, Singh. You may proceed."

"Did he say, sing?" Tol asks.

"Do I look like I sing?" I grin back at Tol wolfishly.

"Did Doctor Batman just make a joke?" he asks.

"Oh, for nine hells." Welker limps over the threshold.

"Genetic marker identified: Vaishya class. You may proceed."

"Well, that's a bloody relief!" Welker hobbles to us.

Tol looks at Xana and Bentley, then back to us waiting by the Aeshnid. "It's been nice knowing you. I've led you all as far as I could, but this is where our fellowship ends my brave, young hobbits. I only wish I could say more—"

Xana shoves Tol over the line.

"Genetic marker identified: Shudra class. Please identify your master."

"I claim him," Ari calls out reluctantly.

"Did you have to?" I mumble with a smile. She grins back at me, and it's like a thousand stars have lit in the universe when somebody understands my humor. "You really didn't have to."

"You may proceed," the walls respond.

"Shudra class? I like the sound of that!" Tol smiles and rights the hat on his head at a jaunty angle.

Brahmin, Kshatriya, Vaishya, Shudra—priests, warriors, merchants, servants . . . all of us have the genetic markers of the old empire. Candlemas said that Miral was the birthplace of humanity and not Ancient Earth. *What does this mean?*

Xana and Bentley hang in the doorway to the chamber. I met Xana as a little girl and know she was born on Tao, but I also know that Talousla Karr had a hand in her creation. She wears the face of a designer organic, bred by the wayward spypsy for some craven purpose.

Yet, she is not simply a clone, either. Her genetics did not entirely match those of Captain Jak. So the question remains, *who is she exactly?*

The warrior woman steps into the chamber of the Aeshnid. There is no response. *It's too quiet,* I think. Candlemas asked me to recover the contents of the temple and kill the crew. *If the sentinel were to finish Xana right here, it would certainly make that a lot easier . . .*

"Genetic marker identified: Kshatriya class. Neo-order, Praetorian. You may proceed."

Xana sighs with relief. *Kshatriya class, like me. Warrior.* Part of her is not artificially created but holds the markers of the old empire. The mystery thickens.

"Bentley." Xana gestures for her pet to follow, and the broad-shouldered soldier walks forward.

"Genetic marker not identified. Termination imminent." The stones of the walls begin to glow.

"No!" Xana screams. She reaches back, grabs Bentley's arm, and practically flings him forward toward the rest of us.

"Everyone on board now!" I scream hoarsely.

We dive into the belly of the giant dragonfly as the entire chamber trembles. "How, by Breaker's Rock, does one pilot this thing?" Welker stumbles forward from the darkness of the thorax toward the creature's head. The inside of the Aeshnid's eyes light up with an incredibly high resolution video graphics display. The hum of the creature's rainbow wings buzz, and it takes off on its own accord.

I look out through the creature's eyes, and I see the Scryling priestess, Hari-Ma, at the entrance to the cavern. She stands, a beatific look upon her face. She raises her staff in one hand and the palm of the other in a gesture of farewell. We carry all of her people's faith, whether completely foolish and misguided or real, with us on this mysterious quest. I raise my hand back as she recedes from view.

"Cease resistance, or you will be terminated," the sentinel's voice echoes from inside the bug's hold, taking me out of the moment.

"To the depths with you!" Xana shouts back. She checks Bentley, making sure he's unharmed like a mother bird with her young.

Ari grabs Welker by the shoulders. "Welker, everything here is an interface between the technological and organic. The Aeshnid's got her own life, but she's attuned to our brain waves. You're the pilot. You're the brain." She points toward a sort of control console that has nothing more than the shape of two indented palms impressed in its chitinous surface.

Welker presses his palms into the indentations. A faint green glow emanates from beneath his hands. "I feel her," he whispers. "Her wings, her antennae . . ."

"Good! Now do what you do best and fly, big brother," Ari commands.

"Roger that, little sister." Welker flashes a lopsided grin.

Outside, the well blasts a laser beam at us. The Aeshnid, under Welker's guidance, darts this way and that. Lasers fire from inside the walls trying to scorch us, but Welker swerves, avoiding everything as if he can anticipate where the blasts are going to be before they strike us. *The Tag from Candlemas,* I think. He loops the Aeshnid in a corkscrew maneuver that slips right through a laser net that the sentinel beams across the well. I think my stomach is about to empty its contents.

"Watch out!" Washo calls, pointing to where the light from the top of the cavern seems to be dwindling. I can see now that there's a circular door leading to the surface. And its iris is closing.

Welker's eyes narrow, and he angles the Aeshnid upward, gaining speed.

"Everyone grab hold of something!" Xana shouts.

"Are you insane?" I growl. "If we don't make it—"

"We'll make it!" Welker cuts me off even as he doesn't slow our flight. *Of course, that's why he's our pilot,* I think. He presses his palms deep, urging the dragonfly forward. The hum of the quad wings scream at a fever pitch. The sentinel releases a final surge of a radiation blast from its walls. The well stones glow white hot as they super-heat. Welker howls, and we slip right through the door's aperture as it closes and into the stormy sky of Miral. Ari, Washo, and Tol cheer with triumph, but I see thick nimbus clouds on the horizon. Purple branches of lightning fork. The clouds see us, and the weather rushes to meet us.

Tol's eyes widen. "Um, you guys, out of the frying pan . . ."

All is darkness as we are enveloped in the Great Storm's embrace.

Welker's brow furrows as he pilots us through the thick fog, twisting the ship to avoid the lances of purple lightning. The tension inside the cabin remains thick. *We almost just died because Xana tried to save an enemy clone.* "I hope he was worth it," I mumble.

The bred soldier merely stares ahead dead-eyed, oblivious to the calamity that almost just befell us all. As much as I might unnerve others with my scarred voice and fierce demeanor, Bentley's detachment is what I find truly frightening. He could betray us at a moment's notice, yet we keep him as one of our own.

Xana ignores me. She pushes past to look out the vid screens of the Aeshnid's eyes. "Why are we moving so slowly?"

"The atmosphere is somewhat viscous," Welker replies.

"These clouds are not condensation," Ari explains. "They're nanobots. Most likely composed of carbon nanotubes."

"My retinals *are* picking up high levels of carbon," Tol chimes in. "But also a lot of photonics and electromagnetic energy. I don't think it's just nanotubules that are causing . . ."

"Nanotechnology is forbidden throughout the Fracture because it can be a precursor to AI," I growl.

On my world, genetic manipulation is considered an abomination. Only advanced computers are able to sift through the large amounts of data in a genome and calculate the many possible epigenetic permutations that result from mixing and matching base pairs. Centuries ago, this technology allowed for the creation of hybrids on Tao: monsters of the deep given levels of human intelligence. The hybrids wrought havoc on the environment before they were hunted to extinction. The chaos led to the abdication of the last empress, Boudika, and the High Synod gaining political authority over the government. I always thought this tumultuous history was the reason behind not only my people's aversion to genetic engineering, but also the eschewing of advanced computers.

But since my exodus from Tao, I've seen this same fearful inclination across all worlds of the Fracture. While technology is necessary to the maintenance of starships and space navigation, it seems all humans have this dissonant relationship with the development of more advanced machines—they need them, but they dread them.

Something Candlemas said strikes me: humans should have progressed far beyond our current technological capabilities. *Could it be possible the stagnation we are experiencing, the current dark age of our progression, is something built into the genome of all who originated from the old empire? Were we held back for a reason?*

"Forbidden or not," Ari says, pointing out the viewscreens, "AI precursor is right there."

"Perhaps that's what ended the Mira," Tol suggests as Welker swerves around a passing lightning bolt.

"Why is there lightning everywhere?" Xana asks.

"Carbon is a semiconductor," Washo answers.

"These discharge patterns are not random," Ari adds. "The impulses are like a code." She pulls up the wrist readout of her second skin. She watches the arcing lightning, timing the discharges. "Zero, one, zero, zero . . ."

Welker swings the Aeshnid to avoid a hit. We're thrown against the walls of the ship. Ari falls into me. I can feel her heart beat above the storm. Her eyes meet mine. The ship rights, and she gently pushes me away. Xana fumes as she watches. “Give me the nightscript reader, please,” Ari says.

I hand over the wooden tablet. Our fingers brush each other’s. My face flushes. Ari grazes her fingers over the surface, feeling the changing topography of the screen. “Welker,” she says. “You’re going the wrong way.”

“I saw the map—”

“Look!” She points at the ground. The landscape rolls like an ocean, the mountains and valleys of the rocky gray crust melding and reforming into differing shapes.

“The ground’s changing!” Tol exclaims.

“Not just the ground,” Ari agrees quietly. “The magnetic readings of the planet. It’s reformulating its topography.”

“Why?” asks Xana.

“To keep us from going where we are supposed to go, but we’re going there anyway.” Ari points at the horizon. A nexus of clouds gathers in the sweep of a Coriolis force. Lightning sparks from inside the eye like some kind of haywire lamp.

“You guys, I really don’t like the look of that,” Tol says, echoing all our thoughts.

“This planet is alive. The storm is sentient. The lightning is a collective consciousness’s synapses,” Ari says.

“Ari,” I growl. “When you were captured on Nonthera, connected to the enemy stinger ship, you said something about the Sky Consciousness. Is this the Sky Consciousness?”

Her brow furrows. “No. I don’t think so. But perhaps something similar? This Great Storm is a collection of intelligent nanobots, sharing information constantly, forming an active neural network. The clouds are thinking, molding their thoughts in such a way that creates patterns. If I translated the code into Normal it would say ‘Danger,’” she answers ominously. “They seem to be ushering us away from the very thing that we seek. Welker, you need to fly directly into the storm. There—" She points to the clouds roiling and bursting with light on the horizon.

"I guess Candlemas *isn't* the only Agent Smith in *The Matrix*." Tol shakes his head.

"At least Candlemas talked to us directly," I mutter.

"Candlemas was a human emulation program. Who knows what this storm's purpose is?" Welker says as he eases the ship in the direction Ari indicated. The ship begins to buck, and the darkness folds in at the edge of my consciousness again, stronger than before, cold. Invisible tendrils seem to stretch out from some dimension I cannot see. *Ari a messiah? Artificial intelligence? A shadow bleeding into the universe? Phaestion and his army. Xana is a clone. Bentley is an enemy. Welker is dying . . .*

I will devour all those you love, the shadow whispers. Ari said she did not want me to abandon her, but I can't bear the thought that I could lose her, either. "We should turn back," I say, my voice not my own.

"Can't argue with that," agrees Tol.

"The doctor is right," Xana says, echoing my thoughts. "Turn back."

We are all feeling this darkness, I realize. *All except Ari . . .*

She faces us. Bentley stiffens, readying for violence. "You're no longer my protector, Xana Caprio. You forfeited the position the day you left Lyria. And I'm no longer a child. I will move forward without you or anyone else if I have to."

"The sentinel recognized you as High Matriarch Lazarus," I say, cutting her off. "You expected it to. Who are you really?" I want to tell her I don't care who she is or where she comes from. I don't care about any of this. I just want to be with her. But I don't. "The pirate captain looked just like Xana, your artificial human protector. Tol here, fool though he is, suggests their ship's name, the *Tyger*, is based on poetry of Ancient Earth. What's the connection?"

"You guys," Tol interjects. "Maybe we should discuss this later?"

"Shut up, Tol!" Xana hisses.

"The ship you were connected to back on Nonthera said you were a daughter of Urizen. All the religion of the Nicnacians and the Scrylings, the depictions in their cathedral are of you, of us. It suggests that this Urizen, may have been a real person who lived thousands of years ago. How could she have known that we would be here now, over a millennium later? I know you intuit these things and understand them much more quickly than any one of us ever could, Ari. You have been putting these pieces together in your head just as I have. Don't tell me you don't suspect the truth of all that is happening?"

All we hear are the sounds of the storm.

"My mother told me, right before she left on my eighth birthday, that everything was code. Code is just language, and language is expression of thought. Thoughts are the secrets of the universe. Then she disappeared from my life forever." Tears stream down Ari's face. "Then you came, Xana. Sent in her place. She was right. Every computer language, every myth, legend, every religion—it's all coded thoughts. Everything we've encountered since Market are thoughts. My mother's thoughts. I see her plans in all this. She is real. She is Urizen."

"The great architect," Washo whispers.

"Then she's responsible for the religion of the Scrylings and the spypsies?" I ask.

"That would mean your mother is thousands of years old?" Xana shakes her head in confusion.

"Everyone, secure yourselves!" Welker shouts from his position at the fore.

Ari faces her guardian. "She planned all of this, Xana. She helped create you to protect me. And if that is so, it also means that whatever feelings you grew to have were preordained, too. Our relationship, what happened between us, it was an intended plot. It didn't happen because you truly love me. It happened because she meant it to."

This has something to do with what Candlemas showed them, made them relive . . .

"You don't mean that," Xana whispers, shocked. She shakes her head. "It doesn't matter to me how the feelings happened. Only that I have them. I—"

"You left me." Ari's eyes meet Xana's. "You should leave again. Only this time, don't let me find you."

They love each other, I realize. *More than friends. More than sisters. If that's the case, then why did Xana leave? They're breaking apart again. We're all breaking apart. How do I stop it?*

The storm rumbles.

You are too close to these people, Edmon. Not only too close, you love them. I have to stop it. The blackness of the shadow takes me. Every fear and doubt boils inside then bursts through. "You caused this." I stab my finger at Ari. "Rollinson killed himself because of guilt over you. We've been hunted across the Fracture. I was tortured by Candlemas. For what? Because your bitch of a mother wants to send you coded messages? You knew the whole time and said nothing? I'm done playing games. I'm done protecting you, loving you. When this ship lands—"

I never finish the thought. Ari decks me square on the chin. I grab her in my arms, preventing her from hitting me again. She sobs uncontrollably.

"Let me go!" she screams, but everything I feel says she wants to be held, to just be a normal girl again if only for just a moment. *Why did I say those things?*

It's the storm, I realize. *It's trying to prevent us from reaching our destination any way it can.*

Xana surges forward, prying us apart. "I'll kill you!" She comes for me. *Finally.* My hands fly as I snap pressure point strikes, trying to take her down. She grunts but pushes past the pain, slamming her fists into me over and over. Her knuckles are slick with my blood, and I can no longer see. There is a crack. She breaks my arm. Pain shoots everywhere, and I scream. *Let it end . . .* I think. *I don't want to be alive anymore. Not like this.*

Bentley leaps onto us, joining the struggle. I'm already losing, and I can't fight both of them. Unexpectedly, though, he tries to separate us. I shove him away. "Let her come!" I growl.

He manages to grab Xana and hold her back.

"Everyone—?" Welker shouts again from the fore. The ship rocks, and I collapse to the deck. I manage to look up to the viewscreen for a split second as the Aeshnid hits the ferocity of the centrifugal winds. Then I'm hurled against the chitin of the bulkhead, and all goes dark.

CHAPTER 15

The Fool

> The fool travels with all his worldly possessions in hand. He is full of wonder and excitement, ignorant of the danger that lies in wait. If not for the fool or his insight, the path would fall into perpetual darkness. Levity is needed even in the blackest of moments.
>
> —Ovanth, *A Practical Reading of the Arcana*

The walls of the Aeshnid shudder under me. The creature is trying to breathe, trying to move out from beneath the sands, but the howling winds beat against it, burying it in the gray ash of Miral. The insect collapses back to the ground. The storm whistles through its exoskeleton. *We've crashed,* I realize. *The Aeshnid is punctured.* The creature whimpers. Its last act is protecting us from the blistering storm.

"Are you hurt?" Washo's face looms into view, his pale bald head like a small moon. "Your suit indicates . . ."

"I'm fine," I growl. My face is bleeding. My arm is broken. More than that, I've broken someone's heart. "You?"

"Candlemas's second skin protected me mostly. It's been regulating my biorhythms, keeping me from the grav sickness."

"Then see to Tol," I command. He dashes off to the other side of the ship where the lanky fool is shaking his head. I stand and hobble over to Bentley who groans. I examine him with my fingers. My touch stops over a laceration on the man's leg where a sharp point of the Aeshnid's exoskeleton has pierced his second skin. *I should leave him. End the threat he poses . . .*

"Tol just bumped his head. How is Bentley?" Washo asks, appearing over my shoulder again.

"He'll hold," I mumble. "He's part of the crew. Right, Bentley?"

"Yes, Doctor." He nods.

I smile grimly. I've mistrusted the clone soldier from the beginning, but it was he who tried to save me from Xana a moment ago. He was willing to resist her to stop us from killing each other. *I won't let this man die.* I pull out my med kit with my good arm and quickly sew the laceration and then the second skin shut with spider-silk thread.

"What about you, Doctor?" Washo stares at my arm, bent at an unnatural angle.

I reach down and tap a pressure point above the break. I grit my teeth and swiftly jam the bone back into place with a crunch. I send my mind into the injury, willing the cells to heal. Now, the enhanced bones will mend more quickly. The action will weaken my endurance, but it will make me more ready to fight. Something tells me my crew will need me ready.

Washo looks at me, nauseous. "I can heal myself within a few hours," I say. However, I glance to the fore where Welker is on his knees, heaving in a cold sweat. I don't know if he'll make it that long. *He's still psychically connected to the Aeshnid, feeling all of her pain and shock.* "If Tol's fine, go help Welker."

Washo hurries off. I look at Xana, who stands in a corner alone, arms folded. I feel that oppressive feeling . . . Los. It is stronger than I've felt it before. Some meters away, Ari is huddled against the wall rocking back and forth, eyes red-rimmed, face streaked with tears and grime.

"Hey, Doc?" Tol comes up behind me. I sit him down and examine a wound on the back of his head. It's superficial, but I apply some disinfectant and healing salve. "Edmon?" he asks. "Why in nine hells would you threaten Ari right when you knew we were flying into the storm? Right when Ari told Xana that, like, their entire history was fake? We're already hanging on by a thread here."

Why do I always hurt the people that I love? It's a good question. I feel deep shame. *Was it the storm acting on my thoughts? I know it wasn't making me feel something I didn't already feel.* "How else do you get two women to stop fighting each other?" I joke instead of answer.

"That's actually kind of funny." He shakes his head. "Fate point to you, Doc." I take a seat beside him. "You know, I thought you were right, back on Nonthera. We're just strangers that happened to take jobs at the same time on a UFP clunker. Uniformed fuck pants, right?"

"Fuck pants." I nod.

"I walked out on all of you. That wasn't cool."

"I left, too," I remind him.

"But you went to find information that would help Ari. I was actually leaving."

"You came back," I say.

"It wasn't the first time. And just before we went down, now, I thought it again. We get to the temple and go our separate ways. We don't owe each other anything."

I nod and wonder what Candlemas promised him. "Tol, if this is an apology, I'm not the one you need talk to." I nod at Ari sitting alone in the darkness. *I should go to her, but I can't.*

Tol gingerly reaches into his ribs and slides out a compartment. He pulls out a ring with a data card on the end. He waves a hand, activating a hologram that shows a family: an elderly couple, some middle-agers, and several toddlers. A crack of lightning from outside strobes, and the image flickers. "Nicked it off some old lady on Nonthera. She was probably Theran, visiting the mining facilities. Maybe checking on her investments? I wonder if this was important to her?"

The wind howls through the Aeshnid husk. *We need to get moving,* I think.

"I resented my father for a long time," he says. "He was an archaeologist, his specialty prediasporic Earth and history of the Fracture. Dad believed an ancient race of beings created the Corridors long before humans were even around. He was looking for evidence of their existence. He worked for Rollinson for the free flights. We'd touch planetside, visit archaeological digs or old antiquity dealers. That's when my obsession with Earth pop culture started. Most reputable historians thought Dad was a crackpot. I thought he was a hero. At first." Tol removes his top hat and scratches his scraggly haired head. "I got older, realized that he was kind of a fuckup. Traveling port to port with a kid in tow? Traipsing across hostile landscapes in search of clues to corroborate his theories, taking anything whether it was legal or not. We were on the run as much as searching. I saw other families. Real families with dads *and* moms. Families that weren't moving all the time. I started to hate him. Why couldn't he give me those things? Why had Mom died? I knew it was because he had been doing the same thing to her that he was to me—zooming everywhere on his ridiculous quest, instead of thinking of her, taking care of her medical needs during the birth. No one even believed his stupid theories!"

I'm not sure which was worse, Tol's father's ineptitude or my own father's tyranny.

"I didn't want to become like him." His voice cracks. "I told him when I was eighteen exactly what I thought of him. I told him he was a fool, that I hated him, that he was a loser, that I was sure he killed my mother. The next day I left, resigned my commission with UFP, and that was the last I saw of him. Fifteen years, Doc . . ."

"Look this is a great story, Tol—"

"When I started to get the implants and try to come to terms with who I was, how I was, I blamed him a lot for not being the father I wished he could have been. Maybe if he had been different, I would be different. Maybe Mom would still be alive. But you know, even though he wasn't perfect, he did say something I always remembered. 'All we have is family, Tol. All we have is each other.'"

The thought hangs in the dusty space of the Aeshnid for a moment.

"I walked out on him. By the time Rollinson offered me a new commission and I returned to the *Bentley*, Dad was long gone. He had parted ways with Ollie Rollie back in the Caliph system not long after my departure, got in trouble with the local constabulary there. Ollie heard he had passed on pretty soon after that." We sit for a beat. "My last words were that I hated him."

"You were young—"

"I know he knows I didn't mean it in the end. That's not the point, Doc. The point is it's our connections to others that give life any kind of meaning. That doesn't have to be genetics or whatever," he says emphatically. "We're all orphans, Doc. Me, you, Welks, Xana, Ari, Washo . . . we only got each other. You can't walk away from that in a fit of pique because when you come back, they might not be there for you to say what you really feel, what will make it right. *Capisci?* Doc . . . you okay?"

"Fine. The sand just irritates my eyes is all," I say with my thrashed voice. I reach into my second skin, and I pull out the metallic tarot card. The surface flashes a few images. I can almost make out something—a man, a tree? I don't know. I hand the card to Tol. "You might like to have this."

"Really? Wow! An archetype. I don't know what to say. Wait? What about you?"

"Doesn't work for me."

"Tell you what, Doc. I'll just hang on to it for you, for safekeeping."

"I need to go see to Welker." I nod. "Tol, you're not the fool you pretend to be."

"Sure I am. Sometimes what you need is a little foolishness." He shrugs.

The hull groans as the Aeshnid lets out its last breath. Welker cries out. I rush to the pilot station where Washo holds him. He looks like death. "She's gone," he says. Slowly, Welker picks up his hat from the floor and dusts it off. "Crew," he begins, his voice weary. "We'll need to move before the desert envelops us. Everyone, grab their belongings. It's to the Temple of the Matriarchs we go, come what may."

—

Subject Clay Welker: Heart rate erratic. Adrenaline peaking. Tag dose will wear off within two hours. My second skin feeds the report directly into my hood's aurals.

"Welker." I step next to the pilot at the foot of the Aeshnid ramp and hand him a Tag patch. He tucks it beneath a seam in his suit where it will be absorbed by his skin to keep him going for a few more hours.

"Crew analysis," I whisper into my mask.

> Subject Washo Tan suffers minor lacerations only. Suit integrity compromised. Effects of gravity sickness imminent.
>
> Subjects Xana Caprio, Hoplite Template A, Tol Sanctun, Ariel Lazarus: minor contusions and lacerations only.
>
> Subject Edmon Leontes suffers from skeletal fracture and internal bleeding. Systems augmenting subject's genetically superior healing capabilities. Estimated regeneration time: thirty minutes.

To the abyss with that, I think. My stamina will decrease even more if I concentrate on healing internally too much. The inward gaze is like a language with only so many characters. Communicate one message and you'll be shortchanged on scripting another. I decide that I better allow the second skin to do the work so I can be alert to help the others.

Washo's suit is compromised, the hole too big for me to sew shut completely. I'll need to keep an eye out. The rest may be bumped and bruised, but that tells me nothing about how they are emotionally. I need to gauge everyone's state. We're going to have to rely on one another to complete Candlemas's mission. Once we have whatever is in the temple . . .

"Xana, I want you on point," Welker calls on our headsets. "Tol, don't wander. Ari, keep eyes on him. Washo, make sure the doctor can lean on you and, Doctor, pay attention to his suit. Bentley, cover our six. Let's move, people."

"Welker, I should be covering—"

"Xana snapped your arm, and I need you to help Washo, Doctor."

I grin underneath the mask. *Welker is finally taking the lead like we've needed him to all along.*

We forge ahead into the storm. Gray dust swirls everywhere. The gale threatens to knock me off my feet. Washo clutches at me, fighting with each breath. One muscle-clenching step after another we push against the winds of the hurricane.

"Which way?" Xana screams over the headsets.

"Forward!" Ari points off at a forty-five-degree angle.

I don't know how she knows, but we follow. The primal forces of Miral's nature seem to be conspiring to keep us from the temple. *How are we supposed to fight an entire world?* I think.

We trudge for what seems an eternity. The dust batters us down. We grab one another and pull each other along. Particles of sand bore into Washo's skin where his suit is damaged. I clamp my hand over it trying to shield the tear. The forces of gravity pull down against his delicate frame. "Come on, spyp!" I growl through my own pain.

"We're through!" Xana gasps just in front of me, then I, too, fall through the storm's curtain, my knees thudding to the chalky earth. The gusting winds cease. We are on an empty plain. Behind us, the wall of the storm circles perhaps a kilometer from the plain's center.

"We're in the eye," Ari confirms.

I pull Washo to his feet. His skin is red and bleeding under the tear in his suit. "Come here, kid," I growl and proceed to administer to the wound.

"If we're in the calm, what is that?" Tol points to the center of the plain. A giant, white rose of crystal grows up from the ground. Its folds shimmer with radiating waves. Purple lightning shoots from the storm wall, igniting the structure with glowing electricity.

"The white rose!" I exclaim. I've seen it now twice before. In Candlemas's vision and when I was a boy and I entered Phaestion's training armor, the Arms of Agony. *How could Phaestion have known to program this world into his simulation?* Then I remember—my foster brother is a designer organic created by Talousla Karr. He has faint precognition. He knew that I would come to this place. *Something important must happen here if Phaestion pictured it long ago.*

"It's the Temple of the Matriarchs," Washo whispers reverently.

"More accurately, a Calabi-Yao manifold," Ari says. "Organic brains maximize their computational power by increasing surface area through folds. A Calabi-Yao structure has long been hypothesized to be the ideal architecture to hold extra dimensions of space-time due to the structure, which folds back in on itself. I'm guessing whatever intelligence governs this planet"—she points to the heavens above—"arrived at the shape through some sort of genetic algorithm."

"You're saying it's the planet's brain?" I rasp.

"It's changing shape," Bentley says. The crystal is indeed constantly morphing in design.

"Just as dendrites grow and change—" Ari's voice is cut off by lightning arcing, exploding its synaptic energy against the crystal blossom.

"Well, what's that?" Welker points. Above the rose, in the midst of the swirling cloud, is a giant conglomeration of gelatinous globules. The lump pulses in a sort of bubble, sealed off from the rest of the storm. It is something weird, something separate from either the rose or the nanite cloud.

"Looks like some sort of gray goo!" Tol wrinkles his nose.

"More like a cancerous tumor?" I guess.

Ari's eyes narrow. "You're both right."

"Why would the intelligence of the cloud allow a malignancy to survive sealed off?" Washo asks.

"We've got company," Xana whispers over our headsets. We look in her direction. Beyond the shape of the crystal rose, a stinger ship crouches like a hunting predator. Black-armored commandos stand at the bottom of the boarding ramp brandishing rifles.

They've found us.

Bentley instinctively reaches for his gun. I put a hand up staying his impulse. Suddenly, the cry of an animal breaks the howl of the storm. A tribe of humanoids, swathed in dark robes and cloaks, riding great beasts, emerges from the storm wall and onto the plain. The rider at the front raises a spear and looses a guttural battle cry. His tribe charges the stinger vessel. The men in black armor are caught off guard. They start firing into the onslaught, but there are too many natives.

"Oh, snap! It's going down!" Tol exclaims.

"Now's our chance," Welker says. "Everyone, make for the temple!"

We take off, running for the crystal rose as fast as our legs can carry us. Washo and I quickly fall behind the others. I toss him over my shoulder and carry him.

"Xana!" Welker shouts. "Fall back to help them!"

"I'm on it, Captain," Bentley interjects, and the soldier runs back. Together we carry the boy between us, running for the rose.

"Who the hell are those guys? What's in this temple anyway? Why is there like an intelligent storm cloud? What's happening?" Tol comes in over the headset as he huffs and puffs.

"Apparently the Scrylings at the bottom of the elevator are not the only survivors of the planetary collapse." Xana's voice is calm even as she sprints ahead.

"They're coming!" Tol exclaims.

I risk a look over my shoulder. A group of the marauder tribe breaks off from the main scuffle and charges our way.

"Xana, get Ari to the rose, no matter what!" Welker shouts.

She grabs Ari and takes off toward the rose.

Welker stops running, fingers twitching by his pistols in their holsters. Bentley, Washo, and I hobble past him. "Seems like you boys could do with a little cover."

"As if you get all the fun," I growl. "Bentley, take Washo to the others." I crouch in front of Welker. "Sword and gun, Welker?"

"No, gun and sword, my dear doctor." He laughs as the marauders charge toward us on their beasts.

I draw the siren sword from the flute scabbard; it sings a mournful tune. "Report," I whisper to my second skin's tracking systems. "Medical analysis, all crew."

Subject Washo Tan experiencing onset of extreme gravity sickness.

Subject Edmon Leontes experiencing brachial fracture mending at inhibited rate. Extreme exhaustion imminent.

Subject Clay Welker experiencing adrenal surge peaking due to ingestion of concentrated Tag. Absorption rate abnormal at twenty milligrams per hour. Extreme withdrawal within two hours.

"Wait for it . . . wait for it . . . ," Welker whispers.

The riders bear down. A hundred meters . . . Fifty meters . . . my second skin warns.

"And . . . curtain!" Welker calls out. His pistols fly into his palms magnetically, pulled by the gloves of the second skin. He moves faster than I've ever seen him, almost as if he can see the riders' movements before they happen. Cock, pull, fire, repeat. Meanwhile, I bat bullets and arrows aside, shielding him from the enemy. One by one he plants the seeds of death, and the marauders fall to the ground around him.

But there are too many. They circle around us. He fires pistols behind his back, over his shoulders. A rider charges Welker angling a spear. I leap into the air. My blade howls like a banshee. I fly down, slicing the neck of a rider's camelid beast. The head vaporizes, and the rider crashes to the ground. I draw my sword in a sweeping arc. She screams as I slice the legs of the beasts from under one rider then another.

"Sorry to keep doing this to you, Doctor, but . . ." Welker's head rolls back, and he falls. I catch him before he hits the sand.

"Get back here now!" Xana commands over the headset.

I lift Welker's dead weight onto my back and haul as fast as I can to the others at the entrance of the temple. The path before us slopes downward with two embankments on either side, almost like a ramp that leads to an opening at the base of the rose. Lightning cracks overhead, and I'm hurled to the ground by the electromagnetic force of the discharge. The tribe of marauders kicks up a great cloud of dust as they ride after us. *Crack, crack!* Xana's rifle sounds, covering me as I get up and drag Welker behind me.

"Into the temple!" Xana shouts.

We run down the ramp. Suddenly the ground drops away, and I am free-falling into the black.

CHAPTER 16

The Devil

The maze winds deep within, twisting and turning. The monster lies in wait at the center of the puzzle, but so, too, does the spirit of light ready to illuminate the deeper mysteries. The devil is not an evil, but a crucible to bring forth one's inner nature.

—Ovanth, *A Practical Reading of the Arcana*

I spin midair, placing my body beneath Welker's to shield him. The light from the temple doorway shrinks and then snuffs out as Bentley's gun strobes midfall and blasts the entrance shut behind us.

Warning: impact imminent. I hit the ground with a smack, the wind knocked from my lungs. I lose my grip on my companion. Subject Edmon Leontes: multiple rib fractures . . .

"Shut up!" I growl.

"I didn't say anything!" Tol groans next to me.

"Welker?" I ask desperately.

"I'm here, Doctor," the pilot says, gasping.

"Everyone! Report in!" Xana commands, taking the lead.

"Here, Captain!" Bentley responds smartly. *It figures he would survive. Especially after closing off our only known route of escape.*

"I'm good." Tol.

"Uh . . ." Washo groans, and I crawl to him in the darkness.

"Easy, kid." I pull him to his feet. It looks like his suit protected him mostly.

Subject Washo Tan experiencing fractured metatarsal and concussion.

Abyss! I shoulder him. *I'm not going to be able to keep all of them alive at this rate.*

"Ari!" Xana calls desperately.

"Quiet, Xana," she says calmly. "We're not alone."

"Lights and infrared now!" Xana shouts.

The crew switches to their second skin fist lamps. The fire globes implanted in the backs of their hands flash as our hood views turn to infrared. I keep mine off, relying on my years of training in the Citadel to heighten my other senses. Ari stands at the entrance to a tunnel. Standing before her is a young girl, maybe twelve or thirteen, thin, with sapphire eyes and dark circles swirling beneath them. She wears second skin like ours, but her hood is down revealing a mane of spiky blue hair. *One of Candlemas's.*

"Urizen and the Anjins," she says in an eerie singsong. "Soon spreads the dismal shade, of mystery over his head; and the caterpillar and fly feed on the mystery."

Xana lowers her rifle. "Who the hell are you, girl?"

The girl looks at our security officer quizzically. "The gods of the earth and sea, sought thro' nature to find this tree, but their search was all in vain: there grows one in the human brain."

I'm going to get sick of that really quickly, I think. "You didn't answer her question. Who are you, and what are you doing here?" I snarl.

"I am a survivor of an expedition sent by the one you call Candlemas. We knew you were coming. I was elected to stay behind as a guide."

"Where's the rest of your team?" Welker asks. As an answer she looks to the ground. Bones, slick and white, cleaned of all flesh, lay scattered on the tunnel floor.

"Dayum," Tol mutters. "Is this like *Alien* or *Predator*?"

"You knew we were coming?" Xana asks, eyes narrowed. "You're a clairvoyant?"

"Every team sent by Candlemas has one like me. I am the thirteenth iteration of my template. They call me Whistler. For it is my prophecy that whistles through their bones."

"I've heard enough," I say, cutting them off. "Plan?"

"Into the tunnels?" Welker shrugs.

"Shouldn't we, like, you know, take some string and trail it behind us? Track our path?" Tol asks.

"You have any string in those drawers of yours?" Xana asks the fool.

"I'll remember our route," Ari says icily. Her demeanor has become increasingly distant since coming to this dying world. "It's not like it will be easy to exit this way as it is."

"What about Spooky here?" I point to the blue-haired girl.

"Bring her," Ari says. "We'll see how much having a crystal ball actually helps."

I lose count after several twists and turns of the maze. I spent a year in the darkness of the Citadel, yet even I cannot discern the direction we are headed.

"Are you keeping track of our position?" I query the second skin computer.

> Negative, subject Edmon Leontes. The walls are being changed in chaotic fashion. Tracking is impossible.

I look behind me, and indeed the walls have silently closed off behind us.

"Ari," I hail on a two-way channel. "This maze is changing!"

"I know," she replies.

"It could be leading us into a trap," I hiss. I feel the oppressiveness of the shadows, that thick weight threatening to envelop and drown us in its velvet blackness. *We are getting close to its source . . .*

"It could." She stops at a wall blocking our path. She touches the wall, and it alights with bioluminescence. Glyphs on the stones leap alive with liquid metallic pins like the nightscript reader. Ari's fingers glide over the glyphs.

"What are you doing?" Xana asks.

"I'm telling the security systems that we are sent by Urizen."

Lights snap on in the corridor. The crew winces as their infrared is blown out. All of our hoods retract as the bioluminescent door slides away. Ahead of us lie tunnels that look far more like the sterile laboratory of Roc-121. "What is this place?" I ask from under my now-translucent breath mask.

"The temple of the last matriarchs of Miral." Washo shakes his head with consternation.

"Also a science facility," Ari says. "This was a place of research. The security system has told me that it is the origin of the nanite cloud."

"What were they trying to do?" Xana asks.

"Recreate the Sky Consciousness," Ari replies flatly.

Welker begins coughing. He braces himself against the wall for support.

Subject Clay Welker experiencing fluid in lungs, intense muscular atrophy, tachycardia . . .

I check my pocket with the Tag, but there is only one concentrated patch left. I put my hand on the pilot's back and feel the febrile heat radiating from his second skin.

"My dad had a theory," Tol says, scratching his chin. "All recorded history we found of Ancient Earth was prior to their twenty-second century because by then AI had subsumed everything. But we haven't seen true AI since the Fractural Collapse. Well, I mean, unless you count these clouds and the lightning and the rose."

"So the Sky Consciousness was . . . ?" Welker's question trails off.

"Maybe they were trying to recreate true AI?" suggests Tol.

"Candlemas did allude to the fact that human tech had not progressed," I say. "The nanite cloud seems only partially intelligent. Sure, it was trying to direct us away from this place, but it wasn't like it was communicating with anything like authority."

"It's not like Candlemas," Ari corrects. "It's not designed to interface with humans on an anthropological level. Still, you're right. There's something wrong with the synapses. A disruption in the nanite network."

"It is said that Urizen will return in the form of Orc to bring back the Sky Consciousness and make a paradise of Miral," Washo whispers.

"When the stars threw down their spears and watered heaven with their tears, did he smile his work to see?" Whistler sings.

"Hey, I know that poem!" Tol exclaims.

But just like that, I'm smacked in the back of the head. All I see are bright, pixelated blossoms. I gasp, pushing myself to my hands and knees.

Subject Edmon Leontes experiencing minor skull fracture and concussion. All systems impaired.

Then I'm kicked in the gut.

"Stay down," the warbled voice remarks even as she snatches my scabbard, which has been belted to my hip.

Our crew is encircled by a cadre of soldiers, weapons trained on us. *The designer organic commandos. How was I not able to sense their presences?*

"We're glad you've arrived." The captain steps forward from the ranks. "We've been wandering these tunnels a week with no success. Now we can take the girl with us after you lead us to the control room."

"Who the hell are you?" Xana's hood pulls back revealing coal-black eyes burning with hatred.

"I thought you would have figured that out by now"—the captain removes her own helmet and mask—"Xana Caprio."

"Skaya!" Xana whispers in shock.

The woman, who looks identical to Captain Jak, smirks. "I am Captain Mol. It's good to see you, *sister*."

"You're no sister of mine!" Xana spits.

The captain ignores her and turns back to Ari. "Urizen has been waiting for you. You will come with us once we've retrieved the last matriarch. Which is the one you want?" she asks the ether.

The air shimmers, and another figure materializes. *Cloaking devices!* I realize. *Their armor can bend light and mask vital signs to remain hidden from my senses.*

The new figure wears armor more ornately designed, like a knight of old. Battle crests of an orca are engraved upon its plating. A short cape jauntily hangs off one shoulder. He removes his crested helm to reveal thick, white-blond hair.

"Hanschen!" I rasp with astonishment. Phaestion's cousin and sometime lover, Hanschen of the Julii, was one of my foster brother's Companions. I grew up with him. Hanschen was always the smallest, but the most wicked, the cleverest of The Companions.

"If it isn't little snail guppy all grown. Edmon of House Leontes. My, my, you still know how to turn a head." He kneels and leans in to kiss me full on the lips. I spit in his face before he can. He slowly closes his eyes and wipes the spittle with the back of his gauntleted hand, then slams his fist into my face. "Tsk, tsk. Remember who's on top and who's on bottom now, Edmon. You didn't even put up much of a fight. My cousin will be so disappointed."

Subject Edmon Leontes experiencing mandibular fracture.

"How did you end up with this filth, Hanschen?" I say through broken teeth.

"Talousla Karr." The pale man shrugs. "The spypsy left House Julii's service after Old Achilles's patricide. But when we took Lyria, there he was. Imagine our surprise when he revealed to Phaestion that not only were you alive, but in the company of this rabble." He caresses my chin. I'm in too much pain to stop him.

"I'd choose your words more carefully, Nightsider." Xana steps forward. The commandos train their weapons on her.

"I don't respond to challenges from genetic freaks," Hanschen fires back with marked disgust.

Captain Mol stiffens at his words.

This is an uneasy alliance. Maybe we can exploit that.

"Afraid you'll lose?" I snarl. Hanschen boots me in the face, and all goes black for a moment as I fall back to the ground.

"How did this Talousla Karr know we were here?" Welker asks.

"Xana Caprio has been in contact with our commander, Skaya," Mol replies. "After your escape from Nonthera, we received a communique that allowed us to track your ship. We just missed you on Roc-121. Fortunately, we were able to download your ship's trajectory from Candlemas's data banks before we destroyed him and his entire station."

Candlemas is gone!

Ari looks at Xana, betrayal painting her features. "I didn't know, Ari. I swear," Xana pleads.

"You led them to us, Xana!" I snarl. Hanschen takes the opportunity to kick me again.

"Quiet!" Hanschen says playfully. "You're interrupting the regularly scheduled aquagraphic." He leans over me and whispers into my ear, "I never could understand why Phaestion loved you. You were always handsome, but you were a half-breed, the son of a lowborn pretender. I was his own cousin, the scion of royalty. I'm glad you have your voice back, Edmon. Grating though it may be, it will be far more satisfying to hear you scream when you're tortured and executed publicly after I bring you back to Lyria for trial." He slowly licks my ear.

"If you serve my mother, then you are conditioned to obey her command and mine as well." Ari steps forward. "Kill this man and let my companions go now."

Captain Mol raises her rifle at Hanschen. His eyes widen, and he reaches for the swords at his belt. Then Captain Mol smiles. "As much as I'd like that, you've already surmised that I won't do that. There are differences in Praetorian conditioning since the previous models." Mol glances at Xana. "Now, daughter of Urizen, please, lead us to the inner sanctum." She gestures to Ari with her rifle.

Hanschen snickers as Ari stares coldly from the captain to Xana. "This way," Ari says.

"Unit 1138 B," Captain Mol calls out, marking Bentley. "Grab the Taoan." Bentley glances at Xana. "Unit 1138 B, now!" Mol barks.

The Hoplite jerks as if some internal switch has been flipped. He grabs me off the floor and shoves me forward. I stumble.

"Traitor," I snarl.

"Look who's talking," Hanschen replies gleefully. "Oh, snail guppy, this is so much fun!"

Subject Edmon Leontes experiencing multiple fractures, contusions, and concussion. Immediate sustenance, rest, and medical care needed to avoid extreme exhaustion.

As my crewmates pass me, I read sadness and shame in their glances.

I'm supposed to be the unbreakable, the one who can take care of the others, but the wearable is right. I can't save anybody.

Everything glows electric green. Ari walks at the head of the line accompanied by Captain Mol whose soldiers surround us on all sides. Xana tallies their numbers and weaponry. We are sorely outmatched.

Hanschen whispers to me. "I don't care for any of this religious nonsense. It's quite extraordinary to think that such an advanced culture could be grounded in such backwardness, don't you think?"

I consider the fact that Nightsiders of Tao incinerate children who are born with defects. They hold all who aren't of their race as impure. They force children to fight in brutal gladiatorial combat.

"Anyway." He yawns. "There's only one true god, and that's our emperor Phaestion."

"Phaestion is no god," I say. Washo stumbles next to me, and I catch him.

"He is now," Hanschen replies. "His mother is a sea goddess. His father was proclaimed an Elder Star. He's conquered worlds. Not even the gods of Ancient Earth could claim that. And he's as beautiful as ever. When he sees you brought in chains before him, beaten, ground under the heel of my boot, he will finally give you up. He will see how much I am worthy of him."

"Urizen has no need to conquer," Washo says through ragged breaths. "She's the mother of us all and birthed us from the crèches to save, not to kill."

"Where is your god then, spypsy boy? I don't see him," Hanschen says scornfully.

We turn down a corridor and arrive at a crossroads. Ahead lies a vault door. To the right, the path leads up, seemingly back to the surface. To the left, another passage leads into darkness.

"I dreamed a dream! What can it mean? And that I was a maiden queen, guarded by an angel mild," Whistler sings. She turns to me. "When the guardian is unleashed, will you be the angel of death or guardian of the righteous, Prince of Albion?"

I peer along the route that slopes upward, leading to the surface, yet the path is blocked by a heavy circular door. *Why have a tunnel to the surface and block it off?* I wonder. Glyphs line the walls. Even with my rudimentary knowledge of the nightscript, I can tell that these are symbols of warning similar to those found in the catacombs that brought us to the Aeshnid. *I don't think we want to find out why that path was obstructed.*

The glyphs along the opposing corridor that seems to traverse into darkness, however, says something about a weapon. Before I can make out anything else, Mol forces the issue by pointing her rifle at Tol's head. "Quickly, daughter of Urizen, or I begin eliminating your comrades."

"Beyond is the sanctum," Ari says, pointing toward the vault door directly ahead. "The Mira went to great lengths to keep this place hidden. It would be unwise to open it without a greater understanding of what exactly its purpose is or why it is sealed."

Hanschen shoves me out of the way and strides toward the front. He draws his swords from his hips. They scream like two nareels. *Phaestion has outfitted all his closest Companions with the siren steel,* I see. Hanschen plunges the swords into the door. The metal moans as he carves a circle through the thickness. The piece falls with a thud. He bows and gestures for Captain Mol to enter. Bentley nudges me forward with his pistol.

We step into a large room lit by the same green glow as the rest of the labyrinth. There are twelve pods around us, coffins or stasis chambers, hooked to machinery and a giant vat of boiling soup. The back wall is some sort of giant portal that frames an undulating membrane. It ripples and pulses. Something beyond is trying to press through. I feel the darkness pushing onto my consciousness. It's all I can do to fight the dizziness. I hold Washo steady.

"Los! It's the great darkness," he whispers, looking at the portal.

Sounds pulse through the room as if a dozen different languages are being filtered before finally one is settled upon. "Curious dialect. You've finally come," the voice echoes. "Children of Urizen. A long time have I languished, awaiting your appearance."

We look for the source of the voice. There is no person, however, only a human brain floating in an amniotic sac, connected by a webbing of tendrils to the chitinous wall of the chamber. This brain, however, is larger than a typical human's, the furrowing on the lobes much deeper and more intricate. The tendrils are veiny and thick, almost like tree branches.

"Like the *Tyger*!" Tol exclaims.

"Witless woe was ne'er beguiled!" Whistler sings.

"No," Ari says. "This brain is far more ancient. Who are you?"

"I am the last matriarch, elected to hold the seal and guide the offspring of Urizen. If you are not she, then you must bring me to her."

"And if I'm not?" Ari asks.

There is a beat as the brain seems to think this over. "It means the margin of error in my mother's calculations has increased due to some unforeseen consequence. If you are interlopers, you must leave this place at once. The seal mustn't be broken."

"That doesn't sound good," Tol remarks, and we all glance at the wall where the membrane pulses.

"Quiet," Captain Mol warns, stabbing the muzzle of her rifle into his back.

"What is this place?" Xana asks.

"Before you lay the twelve birthing crèches where Urizen crafted the first matriarchs and four castes of the new empire after the collapse of the Fracture Point to Ancient Earth."

The birthplace of humanity after the Fractural Collapse . . . All of us, save Bentley, showed some genetic watermark identified as a caste of the Miralian Empire. Candlemas told me that Miral was the birthplace of all humanity. If planet Earth was separated from its interstellar colonies by the collapse of the Fracture Point, it is logical to think that artificial replenishment of numbers might be needed to ensure a minimum viable population to sustain the colonies . . .

"Pardon me." Welker steps forward, wheezing. "Is this all? Some overglorified test tubes and a geriatric brain?"

It's certainly not what Faria expected. My mentor gifted me the nightscript reader because he thought it contained the maps that led to the untold riches. He thought such wealth would allow us to destroy our enemies. *Faria, you old fool.* I laugh, and blood trickles from my mouth. It hurts like the abyss, but I laugh.

"Daughter of Urizen," the brain announces, "I presume you have the memory core of the human emulation AI? He was conceived by our mother after the High Matriarch's nanite cloud was compromised—"

"Candlemas was destroyed, Matriarch," Ari interrupts.

The brain is silent for an intense beat.

"Captain?" A voice cuts in on Mol's wrist comm. "The natives are regrouping in greater numbers. We won't be able to hold them off without reinforcements."

"Understood," Mol replies. "Cut it down." She indicates the brain.

"You must close the portal first," the matriarch commands.

"What's the portal?" Xana asks.

"It is the great darkness," the brain relays.

"Los," Washo whispers.

"Why is everything couched in religiosity!" I say in frustration.

"She's speaking in metaphor because that is the framework of her upbringing and the entirety of Miralian civilization," Ari explains. "My mother created a paradigm, a narrative to structure their thinking. It permeates the language. You just need to know how to decode it."

Mol's soldiers shift forward and begin slicing tendrils.

"Stop!" Ari screams, trying to place herself between the brain and the soldiers. They shove her out of the way.

I rush to her aid. A soldier knocks me aside. Immediately, Hanschen's swords sing beneath the clone's neck. Mol aims her rifle at Hanschen. Bentley grabs Xana, holding her back from helping Ari.

"Don't you understand?" Ari says. "This darkness, this Los, is some kind of antimatter. Let it through, and it could devour everything."

"Urizen had entered sacred slumber," the matriarch says. "We were told to wait for her awakening before enacting her holy edict. We did not listen. We created a new fold in space to connect to Ancient Earth, where the darkness that destroyed Earth awaits. The nanite cloud was the intelligence we had designed to carry on the terraforming of this world begun by the Scryling caste. We subverted the nanite programming to contact the Sky Consciousness and destroy Los instead. We believed that we could supersede our mother, that we no longer needed our goddess. It would take only this act to free ourselves from her authority. We were wrong. Lacking the insight to create an intelligence with proper human value systems intrinsic to its programming, the cloud scorched all life from this world in its attempts to formulate a solution to stop the darkness you now gaze upon."

Tendrils connecting the brain to the sac snap and curl back like taut piano wires as the soldiers cut them.

"Los is simply their scriptural name for this shadow substance that comes through the portal when matter from this particular dimension of our universe crosses into the alternate one," Ari explains, somehow having fit these pieces together in her mind. "The cancerous tumor we saw hanging in the sky before we entered the temple, that was the nanite cloud's method of countering Los—create a rapidly self-replicating mass with an imperative to devour."

"The gray goo!" Tol exclaims.

"We were able to subvert the cloud's new programming and contain the growth, but not before it destroyed this world," the matriarch confirms. "A remnant of the malignancy remains in a protective bubble in the sky above. However, if the portal is opened, it will be directed into the temple below . . ."

"And will devour everything in its path . . . ," Ari thinks aloud. "You've got to stop!" she screams.

"Unit 1138 B, finish cutting it down," Mol orders Bentley.

Bentley steps forward and unsheathes his knife.

"Hanschen." I look at my old Companion. "Don't let them do it. I'll go with you willingly. Just stop them."

Hanschen's gauntleted fist slams into my belly. I double over. "Oh, gorgeous, I love to see you bend over for me. But this boring tale is about to get more interesting."

"Bentley," Xana says. "I am not your captain. I am your friend. Don't listen to her. You're more than a soldier. You are a person. Make your own choice."

Edmon, you can't stop this, I hear Ari's voice in my mind. Somehow, it is combining with the voice of the darkness. *You can only choose to do what you know is right,* she says.

I recognize the truth of the words. *I don't know why or how I hear Ari in my head, but I have to do all in my power to save my friends. Even if I fail in the attempt.*

Bentley's knife hand shakes. He tries to resist Mol's imperative. Then his fingers tighten. He turns and cuts the last tendril from the sac. The brain falls to the ground with a wet smack.

"No!" Ari screams. Washo collapses to his knees. Xana stares in disbelief.

The green lights of the chamber turn red and flash. There is a great rumble. A door elsewhere within the temple opens. The blackness of the shadow presses on my mind, its invisible fingers crushing my skull. Everyone in the chamber collapses, feeling it, too.

Why run, boy! the leviathan within my dream calls. *All existence ends.*

The membrane framed by the portal undulates. Weird veins spread and branch across the surface, then push through from the other side, breaking the seal.

In the distraction, I quickly reach for a soldier's pistol in his holster. I grab it. "Welker!" I throw him the gun just before Hanschen slams me to the ground again.

Welker catches the weapon and fires, taking out a soldier. Xana leaps and grabs a pistol from the fallen man. She rolls, evading shots, and comes up crouched. She fires, taking out two more of Mol's commandos. Hanschen draws his swords. I use all my remaining strength to kick out his legs from underneath him. He crashes to the ground. I grab my blade off him with one hand while hoisting up Washo with the other. I hobble as fast as I can toward the door. "Come on!" I scream to everyone.

Tol leaps past me toward the exit with the blue-haired girl, Whistler, in tow. Welker follows, planting bullets into two more of Mol's men.

Captain Mol places her helm on and faces off with Xana. Behind her, the membrane splits open. A look of shock crosses Mol's face when a sword suddenly sprouts from her chest. Hanschen looms behind the clone captain. He grabs her shoulders and spins, hurling the woman's body at the inky fog. Black tendrils snake and envelope Mol in darkness.

"Xana!" Ari screams. Xana turns and runs. She grabs Ari on the way and leaps through the hole in the wall.

Washo pushes me off.

"Washo!" I shout.

He scoops up the fallen brain in its sac and runs past me. I look back to see Hanschen striding toward me as the shadow pours out of the portal. I run and don't look back.

CHAPTER 17

Death

> Cloaked in black robes, riding a pale horse, carrying a scythe, death casts his long shadow over each card bearer. He is the winter, a natural part of life's cycle, and a necessary end to effect a new beginning.
>
> —Ovanth, *A Practical Reading of the Arcana*

We hurtle into the red-lit corridor. I will all my remaining energy to my limbs. The hood over my second skin automatically encapsulates my head. The air seems laced with some kind of noxious gas that cuts visibility in the darkness.

Warning: Breathable atmosphere evaporating.

Subject Edmon Leontes experiencing unnatural surge of adrenaline. Estimated time before death from exhaustion approximately thirty minutes.

"By the twisted star!" I curse.

"Which way?" Xana screams at Ari.

Subject Washo Tan experiencing extreme gravity sickness. Loss of consciousness imminent.

"Stay with me, Washo!" I shout as his head bobs. He continues tightly clutching the brain to his breast.

Welker collapses, his gun clattering to the floor. "Welker!" Ari grabs him.

Subject Clay Welker experiencing cardiac arrest.

There is a deafening rumble. The barrier that blocked the passage leading to the surface crumbles. A sluglike monster oozes through the opening, a gray blob with glowing veins of electric green that branch along its surface. *The cancerous tumor,* I realize. The passage I saw earlier was the flue allowing the malignancy in the sky into the sanctum should the membrane of the dimensional portal be breached.

A proto-face appears in the gray glob, yellow eyes and a mouth, but it is not intelligent. It cannot discern what it should and should not destroy. Its only imperative is to spread. It surges toward us, ravenous, devouring everything in its path.

"It's Cthulhu!" Tol exclaims.

"Lo! Now the direful monster," Whistler chimes, "whose skin clings to his strong bones, strides o'er the groaning rocks: he withers all in silence, and in his hand unclothes the earth, and freezes up frail life." Then she looks to me. "Choose, Prince of Albion."

Welker is out. Washo is out. Tol is no fighter. Ari is in shock. Xana is in shock. Only I am left, and I am in really bad shape . . .

The other passage, Edmon, a voice says. *It's Ari's voice,* I realize. I look at her, but she doesn't acknowledge me. She didn't say anything. *Who is speaking to me? I don't have much time . . .*

"Ari! Get Welker to safety and give him the last Tag." I toss her the last patch from my pocket. She nods, grabs Welker from the floor, and heads back the way we came. I can only hope the labyrinth will let us out. "Tol, follow her. Get Whistler and Washo the hell out of here!" I hand him the spypsy boy, who stumbles dizzily into the fool's arms.

"On it, boss!" Tol drags the two behind him following Ari.

"Xana, the other passage!" I point down the tunnel that leads into darkness, the one whose glyphs mentioned a weapon. "Whatever you find, use it!"

"What?"

"Xana, trust me!" I scream. She runs, and I am left alone in the corridor, the only thing between my friends and family and this beast. I draw my siren steel, and the blade sings. *Sometimes you need a monster to fight a monster.*

I wonder for a second what Candlemas's tarot would show now. He asked me to kill the others if we found the treasure. I don't think that was really what he wanted, though. It makes no sense. Candlemas was a human emulation program. His tarot finds true nature in the cards' bearers. He was testing me for this moment. I know now that I'm not someone who is alone; I fight for my friends.

The storm within me builds. My sword's song is at a fever pitch. *I am a devil.* I howl a battle cry.

Then the creature is on me. My blade screams, slicing here then there. The sonic vibration vaporizes each slick gray tentacle. Stab, thrust, slice, parry. I leap over a reaching arm. I roll, aiming for one of the creature's hideous yellow eyes.

It has eyes, I think horridly. A tendril curls around my ankle, and the creature hurls me against the tunnel wall. I smack against the stone and crash to the floor. My sword clatters just out of reach. The cancer roars, and I stare down the shapeless thing's hideous maw.

I scramble for my sword, but a black-greaved boot kicks it down the hallway. "Not so fast, snail guppy," Hanschen hisses. He pulls off his helm. "Phaestion will be disappointed if I don't bring you home alive, but think of the glory I'll win by presenting him your traitorous head!" He crosses his two short swords in front of my neck, ready to scissor them closed.

Subject Edmon Leontes experiencing internal bleeding.

I have nothing left. I cannot fight anymore.

A gun fires, and the front of Hanschen's forehead bursts open as the slug passes through his skull. His eyes roll back in his head, and he crumples. "Should have kept your helmet on," I mumble.

I look up to see Bentley aiming his gun at me. I drop back to the ground. Bentley strides past me, emptying his clip at the beast. He pulls another clip from his belt, then proceeds to empty it as well. The blob behind me roars, barely slowed by the onslaught.

I crawl on my hands and knees toward my sword. It hums in my hand, and I find my feet in time to see Bentley walking into the gray-goo monster. The creature rears back for a moment, then surges forward, swallowing him.

"Bentley!" I scream. I charge forward with the last surge of my strength. I leap, raising my sword high and stabbing into the creature's hideous yellow eye. The creature cries out as pus bursts like a geyser. A tentacle leaps and smacks me, but I hold on to my steel.

My blade breaks.

The sword my father gave me, my voice when my real voice was taken, lets out a horrific wail. I fly through the air and hit the ground. I slide along its slick surface until I come to a stop. I look at the shattered weapon in my hand. The siren moans as it dies, a faint glow bleeding from the jagged edge. I do not even have the strength to weep with her. The monster oozes forward at great speed. I lay prostrate, helpless, as the gray goo comes to claim me.

My despair is interrupted by the whir of hydraulic machinery and the stamp of a metal giant behind me. I roll my eyes backward. A gargantuan battle mech lumbers down the hallway. It is an industrial thing, a mechanized weapon of war, with rotating cannons for arms. Behind the glass of the cockpit is Xana Caprio. The arm cannons spin to life. They glow white-hot, and radiation blasts pulse from their barrels. They fire into the gray goo and incinerate huge chunks of the blob. The thing shrieks in pain.

Xana looks down at me. "Climb on, Doctor," she says bluntly through the loudspeaker. I grasp the articulated leg. Xana fires pulse after pulse at the beast as she slowly backs us away. Meanwhile, out of the control room, the ink of the great shadow spills forth.

"Xana!" I point.

The gray-goo monster must see it, too, for the slime turns toward it. The great shadow of the other dimension meets the cancerous nanotubules of Miral. They collide like oil and water, each trying to envelop the other. Whichever side wins will survive to devour everything in its path. I have no time to think which side I prefer. The most we can hope for is balance and survival.

Xana turns the great machine and breaks into a lumbering run. Sparks radiate as she crashes the mech down the tunnels and metal scrapes the walls. The entire temple seems to be crumbling around us, whether from the creatures' battle behind us or by the ancient matriarch's designs, I know not.

Subject Edmon Leontes experiencing shock, loss of consciousness, and death imminent within fifteen standard minutes.

I will my mind to fight the coldness of my body and keep myself awake.

"We've blown the opening. You just need to climb up!" Ari calls over our comms. "Hurry!"

Xana and I arrive at the bottom of the well where we entered the temple. Rocks tumble around us. Above, the entrance is a pinprick, and

I can barely make out Tol scrambling through the opening and into the light. Xana pops the hatch of the mech.

"Leave me," I grumble. She looks at me in utter confusion. "Xana, she and I could never be. You love her. Do what you were born to do and protect her to the end. I've made so many mistakes. At least let my death mean something."

She nods at me, finally understanding. "You're an idiot," she says calmly. Her hand grabs me by the belt. Her other arm raises to the sky, and the second skin fires a grappling cable toward the well opening hundreds of meters above. She kicks a lever on the battle mech's control board, setting the mech to continuously fire into the darkness, as the cable winches us skyward. Below, the mech rotates, guns pointed down the hall. The arm cannons glow white-hot, pulsing blast after blast into the shadows. The blasts pulse in my ears, then ominously stop, as if the mech has been swallowed whole. The ensuing silence is scarier than any explosion, for I feel the implacable darkness coming for us.

We rise to the opening of the well. The rest of the crew waits a few meters away up the path from the white rose. We both stumble forward and collapse next to our friends. It is eerily quiet on the plain. Not even the surrounding storm makes a sound.

"Was that it?" asks Tol innocently. "That wasn't so hard." He stands up before us, setting the top hat on his head at a jaunty angle. "Well, it appears I led our plucky little band to victory once again."

I look behind the fool. The brilliant white crystal of the Calabi-Yao rose is fading. A sickly black ink swallows the skin of the petals. I shiver with horror as the flower wilts before our eyes.

"No!" Washo sobs.

"What?" Tol turns around.

"Everyone make for the stinger ship now," Xana says quietly.

The rose withers and dies behind us, and the shadow creeps through the earth as we hobble away. Smoky fingers trail skyward from the dead structure.

"I see the four-fold man, the humanity in deadly sleep and its fallen emanation, the specter and its cruel shadow. I see the past, present, and future existing all at once before me. Oh, divine spirit, sustain me on thy wings, that I may awake Albion from his long and cold repose," Whistler whispers.

"Scripture comes to pass," Washo moans in delirium.

A crack of thunder booms overhead.

"Look!" Tol points to the sky. The storm is going haywire. The cancer that had been sealed off from the storm and funneled into the temple below is now swirling through the uninfected clouds. Wind in the eye of the great tempest rises.

"The nanites are allowing the malignancy to infect them!" Ari shouts in our headsets amid the growing gale. "They know it's the only way to survive against the shadow!"

"Eyes forward!" Xana commands as we hobble across the plain toward the stinger-class vessel of Captain Mol. Her soldiers are camped at the ramp firing bullets into the wild surface tribe who have now surrounded them and the vessel.

"Even if we make it, how will we get aboard?" I growl into my comm. My voice is almost gone. I can feel the artificial vocal cords tearing inside my throat. I don't think they will survive the journey.

"By using whatever angle we can, good doctor," Welker gasps.

Ari hasn't given him the last patch, I realize. *He's barely hanging on.*

Xana checks the action on her rifle.

"Wait, Welker's right," I say. *There must be another way.*

"Think not thou canst sigh a sigh, and thy Maker is not by: think not thou canst weep a tear and thy Maker is not near?" Whistler hums in her singsong.

The girl's words spark something in me. "That's it. Don't you see?" I strain to speak. "We're with the child of Urizen. We have a Nicnacian with us. And you're the captain of that ship!"

Her eyes narrow, but she understands. She relaxes the rifle. Ari's shoulders also slump with acceptance of the role she must play. The hood and mask of her second skin peel back, revealing her bright, flame-colored hair whipping in the wind. She raises her arms to the sky, and as if on cue, the lightning cracks overhead. *"Dziecci Urizen, JA przybył uwalniać was. Ustalają wasze bronie!"* she cries out.

"Children of Urizen, I have come to liberate you. Lay down your arms," Washo translates into the comm.

The marauders turn in their sandblasted robes and beetle masks. They collapse to their knees, weapons falling from their grasp.

The Hoplite soldiers of Mol's crew stand, weapons aimed high, ready to fire into the ranks of their stunned enemies.

"Hold!" Xana screams as her own hood and mask peel back to reveal the face of their captain. The soldiers snap to attention, an almost involuntary response. "Get on board and prepare the ship for takeoff!"

The soldiers salute and run up the ramp.

"Wielka burza przybyła. Powrót do waszych domów. Doglądają waszych rodzin. Rewelacja jest na usa!" shouts Ari.

"The Great Storm has come. Return to your homes. See to your families. Revelation is upon us," Washo moans through the winds. He still holds the brain of the last matriarch in the crook of his arm. How long the organism can survive without the nutrients the control room provided her, I don't know. But I see a fibrous tentacle of the amniotic sac snake underneath the tear of Washo's second skin. *Could Washo become a host for this parasitic intelligence?*

We pass through the ranks of the bowing marauders and drag ourselves into the belly of the ship. Xana hits the panel to retract the ramp. "Get us out of here now!" she screams down the corridor. The floor underneath us bucks as the stinger lurches against the winds for takeoff.

Somehow, Ari and Tol help lash us all to the securing tendrils of the bioship. The force of the g's pull on me as the ship screams through the dusty stratosphere of Miral. The commandos must have tracked Xana and Bentley directly to the eye to affect a safe landing. Now the winds batter us.

"Captain, our squadron has entered orbit and awaits report that the package is safely secured for passage to Earth," a commando floating from the cockpit informs Xana.

"Of course." Xana pushes off a bulkhead past the soldiers. Two clones remain in the hold looking at our bedraggled, bloody group. I can see them thinking that they should blast us out the air lock. The second they pause, though, is the second they miss Xana Caprio spin around. She grabs one by the neck and snaps it. The other reacts, but her enhanced nervous system is too quick. She slams an elbow into the man's face and presses him against the bulkhead. Her knife out, she shoves it swiftly up into his heart. There is no blood. The bodies merely hang limp in the micro-g.

"Welker, I need you in the cockpit. Tol, send these two out the trash chute. Everyone else, strap in." She pushes off and heads toward the cockpit where whatever remains of Mol's squadron waits.

Subject Edmon Leontes: internal bleeding staunched. Loss of consciousness in approximately eight standard minutes.

That's all I have to save my friends. When Edric Leontes came to the Isle of Bone on my eighteenth birthday, I was not able to stop him from murdering my mother, my wife, and my unborn child. My love for these people, my desire to protect them, to save them now, is just as great. *That was the treasure I found on Miral,* I think.

Cold sweat drips from Welker's brow. His body suffers the final effects of the Tag withdrawal. Whatever cure the artificial sentience might have offered our pilot is gone. "Welks," I growl. "We need you for one last flight, brother."

Ari hands me the last patch. It floats into my palm.

"I'm ready, Doctor. Right as rain on the Theran plain."

I slap the patch onto his neck. The narcotic immediately absorbs through his skin.

Subject Clay Welker experiencing rapid regeneration. All biological functions spiking to peak capacities.

"Woo!" the pilot shouts. He pushes past me toward the cockpit.

"Are you coming?" Ari asks quietly as she floats to follow.

The cockpit door opens. Mol's remaining men float listlessly. "Tol," Xana calls. "Trash them, too."

"Why am I always on cleanup?" he bemoans as he pushes off the bulkhead to snag the bodies.

Xana cuts the pilot brain loose from the ship. "I don't want anything to interfere with you in the harness," she says to Welker. Her demeanor is cold. We all learned she betrayed us. She's lost Bentley, and she's taken out the rest of Mol's crew as if they were nothing more than animals for slaughter. More than that, whatever tenuous thread remained between her and Ari in the wake of Candlemas's revelations has now been severed. *None of us are coming out of this the same,* I realize.

Welker climbs into the harness. The blue star of Miral peeks around the dark ash planet through the viewscreen. I cover my eyes at the piercing light. When I open them, the silhouettes of hundreds of swarming stinger ships hover against the blazing backdrop. They scream toward us.

"This is the *Lion,* hailing starship, *Lamb*. Captain Mol, acknowledge receipt of cargo, over."

"I know that voice . . ." Ari speaks softly with dread. She floats to the comm station, her hands shaking.

"When the stars threw down their spears and watered heaven with their tears, did he smile his work to see?" Washo whispers his ancient scripture as he floats behind me, cradling the brain.

"Fracture Point is right through that swarm," Welker calls out.

"Can you get us through?" Xana grits her teeth.

Welker shakes his head. "Not if you can't keep them off me."

"They're hacking into our comm," Ari shouts.

"Keep them out!" Xana shouts. "I don't want visual!"

"Starship *Lamb*." Suddenly the viewscreen bursts alive. A woman, the spitting image of Xana, but for streaks of white in her hair and a scar that bisects an artificial eye, glares at us in stark three-dimensional holography.

"Skaya," Xana says. The older woman grimaces. There is a beat as the two women hold each other's gaze.

"You guys . . . what is happening?" Tol asks, joining us in the cockpit.

"Stand down, starship *Lamb*, or we will open fire on you," Commander Skaya says calmly.

"I doubt that very much." Ariel leaves her position at the comm and floats next to Xana. "You've come for the package? Well, here I am, but I'm not returning willingly."

"Isn't this the defiant reunion." A slithering voice from my past creeps through the speakers. "All my children returned."

"Talousla Karr," I snarl as the renegade spypsy's robed figure looms into the frame. A stabbing pain knifes my gut as the internal injuries I've sustained double me over.

"I will sing you a song of Los. The eternal prophet: he sung it four harps at the tables of eternity. In heart-formed Africa! Urizen faded. Ariston shuddered! And thus the song began . . ." Whistler hums softly.

"William Blake!" Tol snaps his fingers. "Dad used to read me that stuff. These poems are all written by the same guy!" Tol turns to Washo, who is shaking in a cold sweat.

"It is good to see you again, Edmon, my son." The spypsy flashes a reptilian smile.

"I'm no son of yours," I bark in response, my voice breaking.

"It was I who saved your life, ensured that you could endure the suffering that made you the man you are. If I am not your father, then who is?"

Another person appears on the screen. A petite woman with violet hair. *Jace Thrance.* "You should have left me dead on Nonthera, Welker. Now, I'll have your gray matter as recompense for the money you stole."

"You'll have to come get me first, Thrance," Welker retorts.

"Skaya, we are not standing down," Xana states, her gaze burning with intensity.

Talousla Karr nods over his shoulder. "Play prerecorded message, Ahania Lazarus, date 1447 PFC."

The image of Skaya and the dark spypsy blinks away and is replaced by that of a red-haired woman, delicately featured. Silver streaks run through her fiery mane, but they do not diminish her subtle beauty, nor the intelligence that seems to laser from behind her cerulean irises. *Ari's mother.*

"Ariel," the woman begins wearily. "As you receive this message, I am nearing the singularity, which contains a wormhole to an alternate dimension of our universe. The intense gravity will distort space-time such that many years will have passed for you, but only moments for me. I wish that I could have been there to see you grow up. Yet, time was short and the stakes too great."

I watch Ari's tears well upon seeing the woman who she has been without since childhood finally appearing, even if just in a recording.

"By now you may have pieced together much of this strange patchwork puzzle of mine: the break in the historical record from Ancient

Earth, the mysterious religions tied to her poetry, the destruction of Miral, and the Temple of the Matriarchs and her precious secrets. Still, you have many questions. Including your place within the story. Come to me, daughter. The answers are here, even if they are not happy ones."

The image blinks and returns to Skaya and Talousla Karr side by side. "Your answer, Lady Lazarus?" Skaya asks.

"If you think we'll let you take her—"

"Xana. I don't want anyone else harmed because of me," Ari interrupts softly.

"Intercept in two minutes," Welker intones.

"You can't leave us, Ari. You can't leave me . . ."

"All vessels assume attack position, Skaya-Seven," the commander says. I look at a tactical display and see enemy vessels fanning out, ready to surround us in a type of netting maneuver. "Come willingly, or we will take you by force," Skaya tells us.

"We'll need a moment, Commander." I force myself through the nausea and pain. "Tol, cut the signal."

"Caprio, nekami nu!" Talousla Karr cackles just before the screen goes black.

"Xana!" Ari screams, alerting me. I'm slow. The pain from my injuries dulls my senses. Still, I sense the shift in biology. The pheromones, the adrenaline, almost as if something inside Xana has turned at the cellular level, as if she's an entirely different person.

"Holy shizzle!" Tol screams as Xana lunges for him at the comm station. He quickly dodges a brutal thrust of her knife. It lodges into the chitin of the hull, and the ship groans.

"The spypsy!" Ari shouts. "Some mental conditioning programmed into Xana's subconscious. Xana, stop!" she shouts.

The warrior woman clutches her temples. "Kill them!" she cries. She releases her grip on the knife. Then she hurls herself at me and slams me against the bulkhead. Blood spits up through my mouth.

Subject Edmon Leontes: loss of consciousness and death imminent.

I summon all my energies to keep myself up. I summon all Faria's training, willing my cells to burn their short lives a moment longer. I feel years of my life drain in the effort.

"Xana, it's Ari. Stop! I love you . . . ego amayo juwes." She says it again in the same genetic programming language used by Talousla Karr.

It is enough. "Ari, I . . ."

My fingers fly up swiftly beneath Xana's chin. I feel energy pass from me to her and then back again as it did with Faria the Red the last time we spoke. I'm so weary, though. My precision is gone. Xana goes limp.

"No!" Ari screams. "You killed her!" She launches herself at me, fists pounding my chest. "Tell me she's alive, please," she cries.

I hold her closely for a moment, my face pressed to her head, taking in the scent of her hair. I want to tell her so many things, but I am dying, and I let her go.

Whistler floats to Xana. "She lives, yet not unchanged," the clairvoyant relays.

"Guys, we're surrounded," Tol says.

"I'm afraid with our gunner indisposed, the likelihood of damage is much higher," Welker warns. "Who knows how long this last trip will last, Doctor."

"And thou art fall'n to give me life in regions in dark death. I am the resurrection and the life." Whistler stares at Ari.

"Give me a moment." Ari pushes away and glides out of the cockpit.

"Um, you guys? Look at Miral." Tol's voice trembles with fear.

"On view," I command. The bioships of the enemy squadron spread around us. The command ship, *Lion*, hovers in the center of the swarm. Behind them, the gray ash planet of Miral grows black, inky liquid spreading across her surface.

"The nanite cloud is losing the battle," I realize. All the people we've left there, Scrylings though they may be, are doomed.

"The priestess believed my coming signaled a change to their world," Washo whispers. His voice sounds odd, different. "They believed it was their salvation. Instead it was their death."

At least the cloud was contained on the surface of the dead world, I think. *Who's to say for the alien shadow substance . . .*

"What happens then?" Tol asks, horrified. In answer, smoke trails from the surface of the world, silhouetted by the blue star. It reaches for the swirling red-and-blue gas giant. The black ink leaps across the vast, touches the swirling cliffs of the planet, and then slowly infects her, too.

"I'm thinking we don't want to be around for the results of this," Welker quips.

"Hail them," Ari says from the doorway.

"Ari," I growl. "Don't do this."

"Hail them."

"On screen," Tol says. The hardened warrior woman and skulking spypsy stare back in crystal focus.

"I'll join you," Ari states, "but let my friends go." Skaya nods. There is no deception in the gesture. "I will know if you lie, Skaya." Ari's voice burns. "The shadow has come. My friends are not part of it. Let them go."

"I will not lie, Lady Lazarus. Your friends will not die by my order," she says stoically.

Something is not right, I think, but I've lost a lot of blood. I'm not thinking straight.

"I'll activate a gel pod on a trajectory for the *Lion*." Ari ends the communique. She floats toward the emergency capsules outside the cockpit.

"Ari wait." I launch after her.

Subject Edmon Leontes: two minutes before entire system shut down.

"Stop!" I clutch her by the arm, my hand trembling, my voice coming in broken gasps. "You think you're bargaining for our lives, but those soldiers are mentally programmed by Talousla Karr to obey, not negotiate. You heard Captain Mol on the surface below. They follow him, not Skaya, not your mother."

"Skaya helped raise me just as she did Xana. I'll not let anyone else come to harm for me. You of everyone should understand. My mother left when I was a child. I'm finally given the chance to confront her and know why. If you had one last chance to see your mother, your wife, would you not take it? I know the dragon that haunts your dreams and why you carry that iron nose in your pocket still. Edmon"—her voice lowers to a whisper—"I need to find out who I truly am."

"I already know who you are." I feel tears in my eyes. "A wise man once told me all we have is family. Ari, we're your family. The people here aboard this ship. Xana, Welker, Washo, and Tol . . . and me."

"And you, Edmon?" she asks.

I can't say it. If I do, it means that I'm bound. If I do, it means that I dishonor Nadia's memory. If I say it, it means I suffer again. I can't say it . . .

She pulls from her second skin a Tag patch. "Candlemas said that this was designed specially for me. That I would know when to use it." It happens too fast. She closes her eyes and presses the patch against her neck. When they snap open, her blue eyes lock with mine. She grabs me fiercely, presses her lips to mine, and we kiss. *Finally.* It is her and I alone in the vastness of space and time in a split second that lasts an age of man. Images rush into my brain as if a dam has burst between us. A flood of memory pours from her into me, psychically; I don't know how.

I control the language cells of memory, Edmon. She's in my mind. *Let me show you . . .*

—

A training room. A dark-haired girl. Xana. *This is the past.* She carries a simple wooden staff. She spins the weapon, leaps, and executes an aerial strike maneuver.

"Why are you always training?" Ariel Lazarus, younger, steps into the room, a smirk on her face. She is smaller than Xana, finer boned, making her look several years younger, even though they are of an age. Ari's silk kimono hugs newly flared curves. Xana's eyes lock to their sway as Ari saunters to her. *Why is she showing me this?*

Ari brushes a curly red lock from her forehead. She steps close to Xana, too close. "You stink." She scrunches her nose.

Xana blushes. "I train to protect you, Ari."

This is the first moment between them, I understand. *Why is she showing me? I don't want to see this.*

Xana tries to return to her exercises. "Protect me from what?" Ari puts her hand on Xana's.

I feel the touch as acutely as if it were me that the girl touches. The skin on skin is electric. The heat from her pale hand . . . My heart races for I am in the moment with the two.

"I only know that to protect you is what I am commanded," Xana says.

"Why don't you know? Why doesn't anyone know?" Ari shouts.

She has been locked away her whole life in a Lyrian mansion with no companion save the girl who was brought to be her bodyguard. I feel the conflict within Xana, who has been conditioned to be protector but restrained from her urge to become anything more.

Xana reaches out and places a hand on Ari's shoulder, a spot where the kimono has slid down, exposing the soft white smoothness of her skin. "Skaya does not tell me, either," Xana whispers. "I think it's to do with your mother and who you are."

"Who am I?" Ari's blue eyes burn, her hair a halo of molten fire. "Fight me," she says.

"Don't be ridiculous." Xana turns away.

Ari grabs the staff from Xana's hands. "I said fight me! You won't be there to protect me forever. Fight me. Show me what to do."

"Skaya commanded I not spend time with you like this."

Skaya knew that Xana was falling in love.

"Why did she say that?" Ari insists. Xana tries to take the staff back. Ari yanks and is thrown off balance. She tumbles to the ground.

"Ari!" The dark-haired girl reaches down; Ari grabs her and pulls her down, too.

"Nobody tells me why!" she shouts as she attacks Xana. Xana quickly turns her hips and holds Ari down, grabbing one wrist, then another and pinning them to the mat. She knows she shouldn't, but her heart is racing. The opening of capillaries in the cheeks, in the lips, and the rush of warmth . . . In spite of her training, her mental conditioning, she cannot deny her impulses any longer.

"Is this what you want?" Xana asks.

"Yes!" Ariel bites the ruby red of her lower lip. They kiss. Xana's tense, rippling muscles relax. They crash into each other again and again, passionately. The initial shock melts away. They were once like sisters, now something more. Their hands grasp, squeeze, explore with the ravenous fury of starved prisoners. I feel the touches as if this body were my own. Xana reaches down and slides her hand between the silk-smooth skin of Ari's thighs, grazing the warmth there. Ari gasps.

"Are you all right?"

"I'm very all right," Ari responds.

It is not a human thing to go without physical love for so long . . . I shouldn't be here, I think. *I'm an intruder, yet I'm being shown for a purpose. Why?*

We feel it more than hear it—the sensation of being watched. The dark figure fills the doorframe, and a cold presence sends a chill through the air. Commander Skaya steps into the room. Her dark eye smolders even as the artificial one seems blank. The scar surrounding the optic puckers as she narrows her gaze. Xana stands, meeting the appraisal of her mentor with defiance. For the first time in her life, she has disobeyed and is not ashamed.

Skaya, the woman Xana has looked to as mother, says not a word. She turns on her heel and strides from the room. The rejection stabs closer to the heart than any word can.

"Skaya, wait!" Xana screams and runs after her leaving Ariel alone . . .

I'm whipped back to the present. Ari pulls her lips from mine. "Goodbye, Edmon," she whispers. The door to the gel pod slides closed, severing the invisible cord between us. The pod is blasted into space with a rush of air, and Ariel's face recedes with such speed. I reach for her, but she is gone.

"Edmon!" The shriek sounds from the cockpit doorway. Xana, awake. Murder is in her eyes, the mental conditioning of Talousla Karr unbroken. I reach for my broken sword . . .

And feel the knife slide into me. Air leaves my lungs. Blood pours from my mouth. I turn to see Washo Tan, holding the brain of the matriarch in one hand, his other gripping the handle of Xana's knife, which he has buried to the hilt in my kidney.

"Washo?"

Subject Edmon Leontes experiencing catastrophic damage. Cardiopulmonary function ceased. Oxygen loss to brain imminent. Proceeding with drastic measures in response.

I will my cells to the site of the wound to stanch the blood flow, but the second skin is inducing a comatose state.

"I am a servant of Urizen," Washo hisses, his voice not his own. "The daughter must join for the final battle!"

Xana flies. She slams the boy into the bulkhead, knocking him unconscious. My vision fades. I feel an electrical jolt stab my body.

Subject Edmon Leontes's heart restarted. Blood loss extreme. Need additional source of fluid to sustain life.

"Edmon!" I stare up into Xana's face. She is cradling me. "I'm sorry," she says. "I can still hear him in my head." She winces, trying to shut out the voices.

The ship rocks. "We're taking fire!" Welker screams from the cockpit.

"Evasive action!" Xana commands. "Get us out of here, Welker! Now!"

"That bitch lied!" Tol careens from the cockpit into the hallway.

"Help me get the doctor into a gel pod," commands Xana.

"We've got to abandon ship!" Tol screams.

There's no way Welker can evade all the attackers. Our only hope is if we all eject in pods and aim for the Fracture. There may be too many targets for them to kill us all. My breath comes in a gurgle.

"Do it," Xana says as she gently places me into a pod. "See to Whistler and Washo. Aim them for the—" Her scream chokes off the words. Her hands clutch her temples.

The subliminal programming. It's back.

Tol, thinking quickly, pushes her into a pod before she can react.

"I'll kill you!" she screams as he slams the hatch closed and blasts her into space.

"Welker! What do I do now?" Tol shouts. "Xana's gone and the doctor . . ."

"Release his pod!" Welker shouts over the comm.

"What about you?"

"Sorry, boyo," Welker says as the door to the cockpit closes, sealing the cockpit. "My last game of Tag is running out, and a captain always goes down with his ship. Leontes, if you can still hear me, stay alive. I'm counting on you . . ." There's a hitch in his voice. "Tell my son how his father died. Tell him I love him."

The door to my gel pod slides closed. Suddenly, I'm rushing away from the stinger ship with the force of a thousand rockets. Healing gel pours into the chamber, filling the pod in a nutrient bath. The medical systems of the pod and the second skin try to keep me alive, keying the nutrients to counter the loss of blood and horrific injuries I've received.

In my last moment, I look through the portal and watch the starship *Lamb* whirl in a dazzling display of aerial maneuvers. Other gel pods burst from her frame and rocket into space toward the Fracture. Skaya's squadron blasts a hail of glowing bullets, yet each time the *Lamb* swerves into view and shields the pods. The *Lamb* counterattacks, clipping wings, sending the enemy ships careening into space. Her fracture saw engages, and the portal of the Fracture Point opens. Then the *Lamb*'s carapace bursts open, rocked by enemy fire. The swarm of stinger ships converges on her.

Clay Welker is no more, I realize. Then I feel the familiar pull of my soul separating from time and space as the Fracture pulls me into her embrace.

BOOK III: PATRIARCH

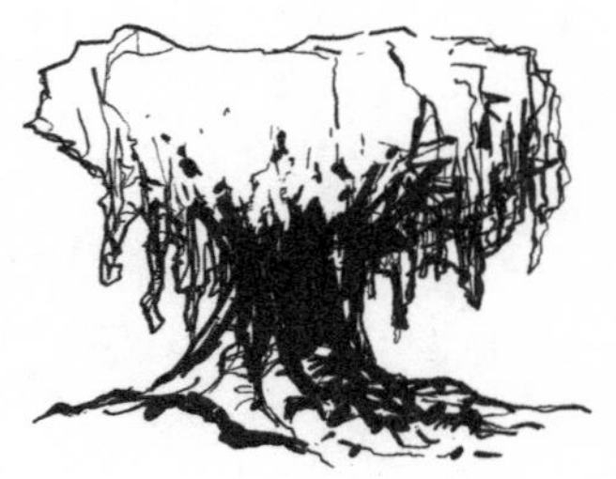

CHAPTER 18

The Hermit

> It is a time for introspection, healing, and purity. It is not a time of action, but of pure thought, which will lead from the cave into the light. The solitude of the hermit is a sage, a counselor, which may guide the unformed bearer from the ignorance into what may be knowledge.
>
> —Ovanth, *A Practical Reading of the Arcana*

I float in the dark, a man out of time, a man out of mind. *How long have I been here? Hours? A lifetime?* The gel of the nutrient bath has been spent. I drift alone in the capsule, alive, but for how long in the coldness of eternity? Without water, without food, I will wither into a husk, and all that was Edmon Leontes will become a mere shell. His spirit will whisper into the ether and be gone forever. *Faria was right—there is nothing beyond this world.*

Why run, boy? the leviathan once asked me. I've spent so much time, so much of my life running, trying to hide, instead of trying to live. I thought I had nothing left to fight for. When I found it again, my friends, my family . . . when I found *her* again, it was all taken away.

Unless some wayward star cruiser finds me, this will be the end. Alone. *I wonder if this is what my father felt in his last moments?* I rub the iron nose in my pocket. I remember the first time I saw Edric Leontes in the hall of the Grand Wusong, a blond-haired god, seemingly cut from marble. I was in awe of him. Then his anger and hatred turned me into the suffering creature I am. This blackness, this terrible familiar loneliness is worse.

Did the others survive? I wonder. *Were they rescued when they came through the Fracture by some hapless freighter?* Only silence answers my thoughts. *I have lost them. It seems that is the nature of life, to fool one into loving only to take it all away over and over.*

I should sleep. If I will myself into a trance of hibernation, it might keep my body from death for maybe a few weeks. It is the barest sliver of a chance, but still a chance.

Suddenly I'm overcome by the urge to make sure it's still there in my pocket, the letter from Clay Welker to his son that he entrusted to me. I feel a sigh of relief as I hear the crumple of the paper, sealed within a thin pocket of the second skin. Then I let the tears finally come for the child, for the father, and for my own boyhood gone by.

A boy will grow up alone. He will dream of a man who could hold him in his arms and protect him from all the things in the universe he doesn't understand. He will wait, and he will wait. He will look to the door, hoping to see the strong, comforting frame silhouetted there to watch over him as he sleeps. But the father will never come.

Edric Leontes, the leviathan, is dead.

All those I've loved or thought to have loved . . . I couldn't save them. Let me die, too, I beg the vast.

"Be at peace, Clay Welker," I breathe into the dark. I fall into the hibernation trance. I grow cold, and night closes in around me.

Edmon . . . a voice whispers in my mind as I pass into unconscious. *Find me . . .*

Ari? But unconsciousness takes me.

My eyes sting. Can't move. Frozen. There is a blinking of light beyond the edge of consciousness. The sound of machinery. The doorway to a ship cargo bay opens above, and my pod is pulled through it. A clang of the iron closes behind me ominously. Hands. They wipe the fog from the portal. Shapes beyond. A figure peers into my womb. Words.

"A corpse!"

"An old man."

"*Muerte.* Dead."

"Then why's this flashing?"

"Dump him back out," says someone.

"No. Fill in some gel from our own pods. Drop him with the sisters. They'll be glad to take him. Maybe give us a little something for our trouble," says another.

"Seems a waste. He's garbage."

"Not your decision, *amigo.*"

Soon, I'm awash in warmth. The spirits of life seem to blanket me with their wings. *Who am I?* It matters not. I am safe. I am asleep.

—

Endless slumber. A journey down a river, my cradle gently rocked on the tides of the Fracture. The tug of a moon's half-grav. Hands gingerly push me from cargo hold down a ramp.

First is a place of blue. Caverns of rock and honeycombed tunnels. Silent figures in white. Like angels, they take my capsule into their hands.

Is this the journey to the fathoms below? Nadia, will I be with you soon?

Another shuttle into darkness. The deep green of a giant forest. Life humming everywhere. Whispers and brown-robed figures huddle around me. They pull me beneath the earth.

My pod is laid to rest. A hiss screams in my ears; the seal of the egg is broken. Cold filtered air prickles my skin. I want to cry out in pain, *No! Let me remain in slumber.*

Dark hands lift me. Their touch is soothing, even as it feels like a thousand needles are puncturing my skin. The soft murmur of their robes screeches in my ears. I can feel thoughts with the pressing of their fingers. They form words in my mind—

Old man . . .

Decayed form . . .

Heal or die . . .

I am passed from my pod into something else, a spinning ring that hangs suspended from a brown, gnarled old arm. *Is that a tree branch?* One hand, then the other, then my feet are pulled to the edge of the circle by an invisible force. I hang naked above the earth, suspended by the ring. Energy pulses through me. All the stars of the universe fire into me and ignite my blood. I scream.

Why run, boy? the leviathan taunts.

I am here, my love. Nadia. Faces flash before me—Faria, my father, my mother, then others. Tol, Washo, Xana, Welker . . . *It is too much! I can't endure the loss.*

You can endure, my son, Edric snarls.

Why should I? I scream.

Because I need you, Edmon, Ari's voice whispers again. My lifeless hands clench into fists.

"What is this place?" I ask, but it comes out a mere gasp.

The hunched, brown-robed figure pauses in his work. I barely noticed him, for his brown robes blend in almost seamlessly with the twisted wood of the walls of this cave. His head, covered by the hood, turns ever so slightly toward me. "It's best if you do not try to speak."

His voice is kindly and deep, almost paternal. "Your vocal cords have deteriorated."

I open my mouth to ask a question and then think better of it.

"You hang from a root," he says, "deep underneath Ashvattha, the World Tree of Albion. You were dead, but it appears that life wouldn't let you leave. Perhaps you've left something unfinished?"

Albion . . . the home of the smiths who craft the siren swords.

"You were brought to us by the sisters of the Shin who dwell on the Morrigan moon above. They are humanitarians and will often care for the women who are brought to them, to shelter them from a life of indentured servitude or worse. The men, they send to us smiths on Albion. We will shelter you until you wish to leave, if you follow our ways. If you do not, we will give you to the forest."

The way he says it, it sounds like that could be very bad.

"You were almost dead when we broke you from your capsule. You look much younger already than the man who was birthed from the pod." My gel pod sits opened in the corner of this small, dark alcove carved inside of what must be a humongous tree. A pool stretches across the floor before me. A man, gray-bearded and haggard, is suspended in a circle that glows a vibrant white; he stares back at me from the mirrored waters.

"It appears you have remarkable healing abilities," the monk continues. "It has allowed the Sun Ring to nourish you. In time, you will regain your strength and youth, if that is what you choose." He shuffles toward the door. "You have many questions. Rest, brother. Returning from the dead is a delicate thing."

He bows and leaves, and I look inward with the skill that Faria taught me and focus on my anger and hate. I move a cell inside my blood to the proper place, then another, trying to slowly rebuild my body.

"Why is it that you struggle so?" the monk asks. He wipes cold sweat from my brow with a warm cloth. It has been weeks in the embrace of the Sun Ring. I've made progress, yet he is right—advancement is slow. "It seems you feel you have to fight. You summon anger, aggression, violence to drive you?"

I would tell him that this is what I was taught to do, if I could speak. *You must become the storm,* Faria would croak.

"Healing is not a violent thing," the monk says as he bathes me. I notice that he only ever uses one hand; the other stays hidden within the folds of his simple brown robe. "Perhaps this is all you know?" he asks. "A partial understanding of the great mysteries is often claimed to be the breadth. Have you considered this is not balance?"

He suggests I banish my emotions, my passions, to become some sort of detached ascetic? *How is that balance?* I want to scream. *How can I detach from the things that have happened to me, the injustice? What does he know of my life?* I hiss at him through my still decayed teeth.

He pauses at this venom and looks at me from the shadows of his hood. "Anger may not be wholly negative. There is a time and place for it," he says. "Anger can spur one to action. Anger can cause us to right a wrong. Anger itself is not an evil thing. But let it drive you to the exclusion of objectivity, and it becomes a poison that eats you from the inside out. I'm not asking you to forbid emotion." He stands hunched, as if there is some deformity to his spine. "May I tell you a story?"

I'm not going anywhere anytime soon. *Do I have a choice?* my look asks. The monk nods. He grabs his bucket. "You are not ready." He shuffles toward the exit.

Damn you! I want to scream. *If I cannot save my friends, what is the point in healing? Let me go!*

He stops, almost as if pulled by the force of my fury. He sets the bucket down by the door and shuffles back toward me. He pulls back his hood. The face revealed is monstrous. Half is covered in what looks to be purple burn marks that have contorted the features on that side into a bulbous, undulating mass of mutated flesh. He raises the hand I've never seen him use to reveal a withered claw. His ice-blue eyes hold me with a fierce, penetrating gaze. Yet, they are not cruel or terrifying, rather firm, almost comforting in their surety. "You think I don't know suffering?" he asks. "If you think I do not know rage, anger, pain, or darkness, then you are the one who is mistaken."

It has been days since the monk has shown me his face. I have remained suspended from the World Tree, in the embrace of the Sun Ring, feeling the warmth of her healing light. The reflection of the old man in the pool before me has not changed, but I have not been able to summon the anger or darkness within me that I once was able. Once I complained to Faria when we were meditating that my rage was so great, I could not shut out the thoughts of wrath and vengeance. He urged me to use the feelings, to gain strength by letting them spur me to action. *Now where are they when I need them?* All I feel is resignation. *All my loved ones will always be taken from me. I am always alone.*

All men are violent at their cores. That's what my father believed. *War is the way of all beings.* That is what Phaestion still thinks. *If this is true, if I had the rage my father wanted me to, I would have been able to kill him, kill Phaestion. Maybe I would have been able to save my mother, The Maestro, Gorham, and Nadia. I could have saved my crew and Ari . . . But I was not strong enough.* Now, I agree to search for anger, and it is not there. *Why?*

The leviathan sheds his skin with the cycle of the tides. So, too, I thought, could I shed the skin of my old life when I left Tao. I understand now that I have not changed in the twelve years since I left. I was merely frozen, locked in a cocoon. I loved no one, and no one loved me. I am still there now. *My father is dead, and my feelings of revenge are gone. So violence can't be the answer if I am to survive. I must find a new way—but how?*

The robed monk shuffles in front of me. "I apologize for how we left things last time we spoke," he murmurs. The apology doesn't come easy. He kneels before the pool at my feet. "I believe the story I have to tell will help; perhaps you are ready to hear it? Perhaps not." His hand brushes the waters. The ripples spread from his touch; somehow I see images in the pool's reflective surface . . . planets orbiting one another in the vast. Two verdant orbs and one moon of blue in between.

"These are the three sisters. Eruland, Albion, and the Morrigan moon, which hangs in the balance. Long ago, before Urizen gave rebirth to humanity in the heart of Miral, she came to the sisters." The pool shows a woman with hair of fire streaking across the stars. She heads toward one of the green orbs and bursts through the heavens of her clouds like a comet. "It was to Albion that she descended and where she entered the sacred Forest of Memory." A road wends through a deep and twisted wood. Gnarled roots and wet moss hang from curled branches above a path. "She sat, here, under the World Tree, for forty days and forty nights, dreaming the future, mapping the lines, shape, and structure that the empire was to take."

I grew up without seeing such things as these trees. The arboreals of Bone were mere scrub and brush. I have glimpsed real trees perhaps once or twice in my wanderings of the Fracture or in the fictions of aquagraphics and holograms. This goddess sits naked beneath the largest tree I've ever seen. Its crooked roots are each as large as the tallest wood in the surrounding forest. *This is where I am now,* I marvel. *Deep beneath the tree in her giant network of roots.* The goddess breathes and so does the tree. With each breath, light pulses through her alabaster skin.

"Urizen was not alone," the monk says. "Three times during her meditations she was visited by a demon that Los had sent, Enitharmon." Twisting around the roots of the World Tree is a serpent. *A leviathan,* I realize. I recognize the creature's intelligent green eyes from my boyhood. "Enitharmon tempted Urizen first with anger and wrath."

Why run, boy?

"Urizen realized she could not fight such an enemy with strength. Instead she whispered, 'I see you, Enitharmon.'" The leviathan disappears into a cloud of smoke. However, the smoke reforms into the shape of a man, decayed and frail. *Faria.* "Next, Enitharmon came to her with despair and sadness, the knowledge that all things grow, then grow old and die. He tempted her with despair. She would not be able to rebuild her race. It was pointless to try . . ." Faria whispers this truth in her ear through leathery lips. "And Urizen whispered back, 'I see you, Enitharmon.'" With those words, Faria is pulled away in the surrounding mist.

"Finally, Enitharmon came to Urizen in the shape of desire . . ." A man emerges from the forest, tall and well muscled, his head shorn of hair. His shape is hard as if his sharp bones were cut from stone. His skin is browned by the sun of an island world. He kneels before the goddess and reaches a hand and caresses her smooth ivory cheek. *Ari,* he whispers, the goddess's name.

This man . . . is me, I realize, but not the ugly, scarred man I have glimpsed in the mirror. Nor the wrinkled, bearded husk who has been staring at me in the reflective pool for the months since Miral. This is Edmon as others see me, as I might be yet.

"Desire is the longing of the heart. It is that which craves what it does not have. Desire whispers we do not yet have enough and will not be happy until we have it. Urizen understood: possession only leads to more desire. So she whispered, 'I see you, Enitharmon.'" Edmon disappears, and only the goddess is left. She smiles, and the light that emanates from her pulses into the World Tree. "So it was that the goddess gained a new way. Not one of emotion, but one simply of acceptance, of how things must be to restore humanity. It was here she sowed the seeds of her return in Orc."

The monk passes his hand over the pool. The reflective surface returns, showing the withered old man hanging in the Sun Ring. "You know the rest," the monk says.

How does he know? I am not entirely certain what I am supposed to take from this story of Urizen coming to some intended balance and then rebirthing humanity. *Everyone uses these myths and legends for their own purposes,* I think. *Are any of them the truth?*

The monk seems to understand my frustration. "The scripture is a metaphorical story. The truth is coded within narrative. Stories stay with us and give us meaning in the darkest of times long after the explicit lesson within them is forgotten." He shuffles toward the exit. "It may not have happened the way you saw it. Everyone interprets uniquely. That doesn't mean there isn't something to be learned."

Faria did not want me to deny my emotions, either, but to use them. *What do I use in the absence of the rage? What do I do when rage turns to despair, or worse, apathy?*

Urizen saw a way that was detached from emotion. She saw what needed to be done, whether it was right or wrong, whether it angered or pained her, she carried forth the task. I, too, have a task at hand. I need to survive. Or I do not. *How do I even begin to do what she did?*

"If you want to live," the monk says as if in answer to my thought, "I suggest you just take a breath and then another." He shuffles out of the chamber.

I look at the broken old man in the pool. *I see you, Edmon,* I think. I breathe. The cells within seem to flow, and I begin to feel the healing. I open myself to it and simply accept.

Fists tighten. Toes curl. The Sun Ring energy flows through me, but I need it no longer. I pull one arm. The glow of the Sun Ring tugs, but as I flex my bicep, its grasp lets go. I follow with the other hand, my right foot, and then my left steps forward. My toes touch the wood of the World Tree. I feel the roughness of the bark where the floor has not been sanded and smoothed. I stumble and fall into the pool. I'm bathed in her cool waters, surrounded by a feeling of new life. I've used my physical abilities to revitalize my body, make it stronger than ever, but who I will be when I emerge is a question yet unanswered. I swim to the surface. My hands burst through the surface of the pool. I squirm onto the dirt floor of the cave. I gasp with joy to finally be free of the ring, to be able to move.

"It is good to see you." The monk kneels down and extends his good hand. I clasp it, and he pulls me to my feet with surprising strength. "Remember when Urizen sat beneath the tree and saw Enitharmon, it was important. Even more important was when she left the tree and began the creation of the world we are now in. She felt love for her creations, her children. That love was called Vala. Vala can also lead to desire, to craving. Craving always leads to suffering."

Not feeling is impossible, I think. *It is a useless philosophy if it cannot serve in the outside world. Yet I understand what the monk is saying. This joy will not last, either.* I feel the touch of the shadow still out there in the universe, and I am reminded of lost friends for a brief moment. *But damn you, monk, let me have a moment!*

He pulls back his hood, and his deformed visage smiles. It is warm and kind, void of guile. "Come. Let's get you some clothes," he says.

We leave the confines of my healing cave for the first time in months. I'm escorted through tunnels of rough-hewn wood, wending up spiral staircases carved into the enormous roots of this place. I wonder at how old the tree must be even as I marvel at its vastness. We enter an antechamber containing a rug and a simple hammock woven from vines. *The monk's quarters*. He walks to a wall and waves his hand. A panel slides away revealing a closet. He pulls out a brown robe like his own and tosses it to me. "The smiths of Albion are humble. They do with little. Each has taken a vow of silence. The items they craft from the siren steel are their voices."

My brow furrows with question, and he nods as if he can hear my unspoken words. "I am allowed to speak, for one among us must serve as a liaison with the outside world. As I was brought to this place as a child, it seemed a natural fit for me to take up that role." I nod but wonder at his origins—and those of his scars. I throw the robe on, feeling comfort in the scratchiness of its rough fabric. It's been a while since I've been clothed, and there is freedom in it, just as there is freedom in nakedness.

"This way," the monk says.

We walk through a winding subterranean tunnel. My hands graze the roughness of the inside of the tree. I feel something at the touch, almost like a pulse. *Edmon . . .* a voice whispers.

"The smiths believe the Ashvattha is conscious. Her roots go deep into the planet and reach out across continents gathering information. Indeed, there is a unique aural resonance to the whole Sacred Forest. It can be dangerous to the uninitiated, for it is said it can sync with a person's brain waves, see his thoughts, even shape them." The monk smiles. "It will drive you mad if you cannot escape the visions it gives. Another reason why the smiths remain silent. Each has been to the forest."

And each returns a mute. This is why he said earlier that if I did not follow, I'd be given to the woods. I'm not sure I like the idea of my mind being read by sentient trees. Especially those with an agenda to change what's in my thoughts.

Veins of glowing green branch along the surface of the inner root bark, illuminating a winding staircase with a gentle bioluminescence. As we walk up the steps, the sounds grow louder: the clank of metal on metal, the hiss of steam, and the chorus of women singing. It's like the myths and legend of my youth, and a great engine of the Elder Stars is rumbling, crafting the firmament of the universe.

The tunnels widen into a large cavern. I am reminded of the Wendigo, but where that crater of ice was cold and muddy, this gigantic place, carved out of the inside of the tree, is warm and alive with fire. The green veins turn to liquid silver in this part of the cavern. Metallic rivulets drip from the ends of roots into large cauldrons. This place has sophisticated heat and cooling systems as well as air filtration. It is lit by glow globes in alcoves that seem organic yet strategically placed. The sounds of hammers, bellows, and crackling fire reverberate. I discover I am surrounded by faces. Young and old, they peer curiously at me with dark brown, almond-shaped eyes. White hair sprouts from their heads almost like plant growth. They are all men.

"The sonic ore runs through the core of this world. This tree was bred to be an engine of extraction for it. When the empire fell, the colony was forgotten, but we have remained," the monk explains.

Smiths pound their forges by hand as well as operate various giant, mechanical hammers and saws that cut the metal. This equipment seems to be partly grown out of the inner walls of the hollowed out tree itself.

"The art of siren steel is kept secret by my tribe. It can take a decade to perfect a single blade, but the warriors of the old empire insisted on our craft; our skill has been woven into their tales and legends."

Warriors like the Great Song and the Anjin commanders before him, I think.

The monk reaches out with a hand, and a metal cane sails into his hand as if he called it. "The properties of the material are miraculous." He holds it up for me to see. It is small but sturdy, and carvings run the length of the handle. The carvings depict a boy and his parents. *The monk's family perhaps?* He seems to confirm my suspicion. "I forged this, when I was a child to help me walk. It was harder to move then; I needed the aid. When I grew stronger, I was able to walk on my own without its help, but the metal still remembers me, the loving care with which I crafted it. We will always be connected."

I follow his gaze to the center of the cavern. Alone on a wooden pedestal sits the shard of what once was my siren sword. I look at the monk. "I remembered the sword when we pulled you from the pod. We first forged it for a great lord of Tao." He looks at me gravely. "We of Ashvattha do not sell our services lightly like some other tribes of this world."

I hear what he does not say: that the weapons with which Phaestion and his Companions are currently terrorizing the Nine Corridors did not come from this forge.

One less Companion now, I think with satisfaction.

"Go ahead," the monk says to me. "Call the blade to your hand."

A siren sword can hum with vibrational energy, and only those who can control their body's harmonic resonance can handle the weapons. I remember the first time I grasped Phaestion's blade. I was knocked on my backside, tingling from the shock. When I learned to control the sword my father gave me, the blade could cut through any substance and vaporize an enemy on contact if I so wished. For years, I felt it was my true voice after my father removed my vocal cords, and I could not speak for myself. But I have never called it to me, never had it sail into my hand the way I just saw the monk do. I slowly reach out trying to will the metal to my hand. The sounds of the forges stop. The small, brown smiths watch with curiosity. Meters away on the pedestal, the shattered sword hums in its broken voice, yet it does not move. I lower my hand, and the smiths return to their work.

"That sword was made for a man who called himself the leviathan. He sought to free his world from oppression and his people from extinction. That man is not you," the monk says. "It was his son who claimed the weapon. The son who fled the world in disgrace. The son who shattered the blade."

He looks at me with a baleful stare. "That sword will never be yours."

I wander the smith's workshop lost in thought. Faria once told me that he was a soldier during the Chironian Civil War. It was a conflict of the old empire that gave rise to many heroes including Chilleus and Cuillan, brothers who ended up on opposite sides, and Leontes, the great Anjin commander who held off an entire enemy fleet with only his squadron. Faria was a genetically bred soldier who survived the final battle. He was programmed to expire when his purpose was fulfilled, but he found himself with a brotherhood of monks called the Zhao. They taught him the secrets of the Dim Mak; however, there was a price for equilibrium—that price was staying detached from the world outside the monastery.

My meandering leads me to a very old smith. His brown forearms are muscular, bespeaking a lifetime of hammering at the forge. He pulls a piece of glowing hot metal from a cauldron with iron forceps. He places the metal inside a gelatinous bubble that hovers over some kind of levitation machine. He removes his thick workman's gloves, and I see the backs of his aged hands are veiny and the knuckles, knobby. He grasps the gel bubble and begins turning it over in his hands. Somehow the bubble allows him to shape the object inside without transferring the heat of the metal to his skin. I watch as he swirls the thing around in his hands. The piece of metal sings inside its womb, its voice changing as it slowly takes shape.

Several young smiths gather around us to watch intently. The old man's movement is graceful and dancelike, but I wonder at what I am looking.

"The bubble allows the master forger to let the siren steel take its own shape, even as he guides the shaping," my friend the monk, who has come up behind me, says.

I turn to look at his shrouded visage with question. I don't understand if the smith dictates the shape or if the steel chooses a design of its own.

He seems to understand my consternation. "All life is consciousness, and the steel comes from Ashvattha, which has its own intelligence. One cannot say whether the shaping is wholly the creation of the artist or whether the material is speaking through him to take the shape it intends."

I turn back to watch the old smith who has stopped. He turns to me and flips open his forger's mask. The leathery brown skin around his eyes creases as he blinks his almond eyes at me. He beckons me to step forward.

"He is offering to let you shape," the monk says.

I shake my head. I'm not sure what I am even doing here or how I arrived. My mind is clouded by thoughts, feelings of urgency that I should be doing something to understand my circumstances. The shadow of Los devoured Miral. Who knows how far it has advanced in the months I have been convalescing here? Ari left to find her mother, but I know that the spypsy, Talousla Karr, has his own nefarious schemes that can come to no good. The thought of him near Ari makes my skin crawl. Xana went mad, and Washo knifed me in the back. What of Tol? Did any of them survive?

"You are thinking too much," the monk says as he shoves me forward.

My hands involuntarily reach out, and the smith passes me the gel ball. I touch its sticky surface, and I can feel the vibration of the glowing orange metal within. It vibrates through me, but the harmony is off. It's almost as if its voice is constantly changing, trying to find the right resonance. Suddenly, I hear it—a sweet soprano that rises above the din of the other sounds. Then just as easily, the cacophony returns, and I feel the bubble slipping from my control.

"Steady," the monk says as he reaches his hand to the bubble, supporting my own. "You must not seek to find the voice and force it to come forth, rather let the object's own resonance be your guide. Do not try to create something. Breathe and let the creation happen. Together now," he says.

The bubble twists and turns in our hands. There is a circular flow to the movement that the monk leads, as if he is taking the energy of the bubble and moving around it even as he is letting it flow into him. The voice of the steel inside becomes clearer as he does so. For a brief moment, I am able to touch the flow. It reminds me of the energy of the Dim Mak or my music lessons with The Maestro, which seem a lifetime ago, yet I am not the generator of the vibrations, merely the cultivator.

The monk passes me the bubble, and I try to let the energy flow; when I try to control it too much or feel it coming out of my grasp, he is there, and the bubble is merely passed back to him. It is like a conversation between us, though I have not the vocabulary to speak anything beyond the substance of an infant. Meanwhile the object inside takes shape.

Finally, it is done, and the monk swirls the energy in his palm and passes it back to the old smith, who reaches inside the bubble with his iron forceps. He takes the glowing metal from inside and plunges it into a nearby vat of oil. Steam bursts forth as the heat is quenched. He raises the object from the bath. It is a simple flat piece of metal with a bent shape.

"A boomerang," the monk notes. He places a thick leather glove over his good hand and grasps the object. "A simple shape. It can be a weapon or a tool." He hurls the thing into the air. It flies in an arc, singing as it does. "Always in a circle it goes." The voice is clear and bright as it wheels around the cavern and then flies directly back into the gloved hand of the monk. The acolytes around us applaud. The monk nods at me beneath his hood. "Not bad. But you have much to learn."

CHAPTER 19

The Hierophant

> The hierophant shepherds his flock beneath the earth to protect them from the storm. He represents dogma, collapsing back into old habits and patterns of thinking. This may be necessary to protect oneself but endangers the bearer should they remain too long set in their ways.
>
> —Ovanth, *A Practical Reading of the Arcana*

My days are full of learning, whether it is in the great archive I've found within the complex of tunnels that form this small community of craftsmen beneath the tree or at the forges in the main cavern. Though the smiths of Albion and I never speak, more is said in our movements during my daily lessons than maybe I've ever spoken to any tribe I've been a part of. My time with Faria in the darkness of the Wendigo's Citadel opened me to a language of sensations in hearing, touching, and speaking. A similar language exists in the beat of the hammers on anvils, the hiss of the steam as a piece of steel is cooled, and the song of the siren steel itself that fills every waking moment. There is an intense musicality to it all. Yet, with the loss of my voice, the workshop also opens me to a way of knowing in watching and silence.

There are books in the archive, religious texts that seem to form sort of weird history of our worlds, the Fracture Worlds. Ari said that all stories are coding if we can only see beyond the code . . .

This one, *The Book of Brass*, so named for the glyphs carved into the shiny gold set of plates, seems to codify what I've already learned in my travels—

> Listen, oh daughters, to my voice; listen to the
> words of wisdom
> So shall [ye] govern over all, let moral duty tune
> your tongue
> But be your hearts harder than the nether
> millstone
> To bring the shadow of Enitharmon beneath our
> wondrous tree
> That Los may evaporate like smoke and be no more
> Draw down Enitharmon to the Specter of Urthona
> And let him have dominion over Los the terrible
> shade . . .

I set aside the plate. It appears that whatever message or religion Urizen intended to seed her created civilization with has fragmented and shattered so much in the intervening collapse that, like shards of a broken mirror, each piece reflects some sort of incongruous image. *Who knows what the original picture was intended to be?*

Here's what I discern: upon a time, there was a planet, a world known as Earth. The people there grew in knowledge and power. They created something called the Sky Consciousness. The people, under the guidance of this artificial intelligence, explored the stars, discovered the Fracture, and began a diaspora from their homeworld. Something happened. A cataclysm of some kind destroyed the Fracture Point and cut off Earth from her colonies.

I presume the Sky Consciousness must be something like the chaotic nanite cloud of Miral, since that is what the Mira were intending to emulate. *Could something similar have happened on Earth, with the Sky Consciousness having gone rogue?*

From the ashes of this upheaval, new gods arose in the cut-off Fracture Worlds—Urizen, the architect, the purveyor of reason; and her counterpart, Los, darkness and chaos. Urizen designed the Miralian Empire to rebuild the knowledge that was lost. She designed plants and animals, and finally the castes of man. She created the matriarchs to rule over the new world, and once again humanity reached for the heavens.

Urizen is no figment after all, I remind myself. *How, I don't know, but if Ahania Lazarus is Urizen, that would make Ari's mother thousands of years old. More pertinent: what is it that she actually wants?*

The darkness creeps into my imagination. *Los is no figment, either. I was there on Miral. We broke the seal of the temple, and I saw the inky mass spread. It devoured Miral and then spread to the next planet. Miral's isolation was a blessing, but how long before the shadow jumps through the nearest Fracture Point and envelops everything?*

My friends are dead, but Ari is still out there . . .

It's hard to know where everything stands beyond the confines of this sanctuary. Ahania Lazarus herself said that she awaited her daughter near a singularity. Only moments had passed for her while Ari had aged from a girl of eight into a young woman. I myself am on a high-grav world where time slows. Who's to say where Ari is now or how much time has passed for her? Were Talousla Karr and Skaya even honest that they would bring her to her mother? They decidedly had their own agendas.

"You spend long hours in those tomes." The monk smiles. His face, which at first shocked me, is now welcome. It's almost as if he embodies the feelings of light and dark within himself, the rage and the peace, and has no trouble living with them both. "Come, out of this dusty library. It is time we worked the forges."

My muscles strain as I squeeze the bellows, stoking the fires that superheat the liquid steel to magma. There is machinery, I've learned, that can perform the task, but the smiths prefer to do their crafting by hand whenever possible, assigning apprentice shapers to such laborious tasks to build their strength and attune them to the music of the work.

"Tell me," the monk begins, as he pours the glowing hot metal first into a rudimentary mold. "You have such miraculous powers of healing, which you've used to return yourself to youthful form. Your anger and your rage provided much, but you are beginning to learn that such feelings may not need to be called upon in the absence of those at whom they're directed."

My father is gone, I think. *Whatever hatred I was clinging to, holding in anticipation of a reunion, is wasted.*

"How is it you've never attempted to heal your own voice?" the monk asks as he removes the metal from the rudimentary mold and places it within a bubble for finer shaping. My hands join his as we swirl the energy between us.

It is a good question. I've tried actually. But the healing Faria taught me has always been confined to optimizing existing physiological structures, not creating entirely new ones. My attempts have been mainly to bolster the surgery of the doctor who gave me the artificial cords. The man had promised me he could return to me my original sound, not the monstrous rasp of some dying creature, but from my research, I had to admit no physician could have done better. It was merely the discrepancy between promise and outcome that angered me. I had to accept that I could never regain my true voice, that I would never sing again. More than that, I suppose I've been afraid to try for anything more.

You were afraid to grow close to me, too, Ari whispers inside my bones. An imprint of her intelligence remains in me somehow, along with the memory of her and Xana. *I am in danger, Edmon . . .*

Suddenly, there is a scream from the siren steel, and I am rocketed backward by the pulsing energy of the bubble. I slam to the ground. The monk quickly passes off the shaping of the steel to an apprentice smith and hobbles over. He kneels while his good hand grips my shoulder. "Are you all right?"

I nod slowly as the painful tingling in my body subsides.

"You lost focus," he says.

I grimace in consternation at his statement of the obvious. Then immediately I am on my feet. *Ari said she was in danger.*

I turn to head back toward the chamber where I healed, which has become my room in the weeks following my recuperation. The monk's surprisingly strong grasp pulls me back. "Where are you going?"

How can I explain to him without a voice?

"Ah. Something you remembered. Something you forgot to do. No . . . someone who is in trouble," he reasons out.

I nod emphatically.

"How do you expect to help this person?" he asks.

I have no idea, but I've got to try, I think. *I've got to leave.* I turn away again, and again he pulls me back.

"You don't know, do you, Edmon Leontes?" the monk says. *So he has guessed my name.* "Think, then, first. How do you expect to help when you have not even mastered yourself?" I follow his gaze to the sword on the pedestal in the center of the workshop—like some broken talisman memorializing my failure to call it to me. "You have no weapon, no balance, no control over your thoughts and emotions. I do not know the circumstance of why you think you must go, but it seems you will be poor help to the person you wish to aid."

He's right, I think. *Ari may be in danger. I don't trust Talousla Karr not to do something sinister, and Ari's own voice keeps ringing in my ears, telling me to find her. Yet, the monk is right—I am not equipped to save her. The problem she faces involves an entire universe. I am just one man. How can I stop a shadow that devoured an entire planet?* My shoulders slump.

"Life is a series of coincidental circumstances," the monk says to me. "It's up to you whether or not you choose to give those circumstances meaning, whether you decide that you landed here because you were found by random spacers who happen to know the sisters of the moon above, who just happened to decide to bring you to our care, or because there is a purpose behind your arrival. Either way, there may be something to learn if you stay. Or something lost if you choose to go."

I nod, understanding his words, but not happy about it one bit.

He claps his hand on my back. "Come then. Return to your task." He indicates the bellows. "No more shaping for you today."

I shake my head, silencing Ari. *My friends are dead because I couldn't protect them. I'm here now, in the wood. The world outside is too big a problem to solve.*

The monk's icy gaze, a look I found terrifying in someone like my father, seems comforting. "I didn't mean to upset you," he says.

I don't look away, and he can see it without me saying anything. *I know he is right. I am not ready. But it doesn't matter. If Ari is in danger, then I have to go.*

"I can say with all honesty that I will miss you." The monk stands in the doorframe of my alcove as I pack my things. He has given me a flight suit and a pack with rations for my journey. I'm told that root network runs underneath the forest. I may take a tram to the mountain Hara

Berezaiti where a shuttle might take me off-world. “We rarely receive outsiders for more than a few days at a time. But it has been several months since you came to us, a dead man. Your body has healed even if you remain stubborn and stupid.”

I shake my head, not taking the bait.

The monk shuffles to the corner where my scabbard leans against the tree-trunk wall. He picks it up and examines the flute stops with his fingers. “I was curious to see if you would be able to reforge the sword and make it your own. Where will you go? Try and help your friend?”

He’s right. I’m still not as capable as I should be, as capable as Ari would need me to be to help her, but I can’t stay here where I am plagued by my inability to do anything. My past continues to haunt me, and my feelings of impotence in the face of my friend’s danger are too strong. *I couldn’t save the ones I loved from death before. What will be different now? I don’t know. Shouldn’t I at least try?*

“You may want this where you are going,” the monk says. He throws something to me; I catch it.

I hold it in my hand: my father’s nose. It is a piece of my past I’ve been carrying around for twelve years—to remind me of what? All the pain he caused? The pain that I was able to deliver to him in return? *Why can’t I let it go?* The monk said it before—it will always be a part of me. I can’t even think about detaching from the feelings this represents unless I somehow integrate it. I have to acknowledge it and then gain some objectivity. Only then can I live in action instead of in constant reaction to events, simply behaving in the way my sorry, painful upbringing dictates for me.

I white-knuckle the iron nose in my hand and stride past the monk out the door. *I know what I have to do.*

“Where are you going?” he calls after me. “Wait!” he shouts as I wind through tunnels, along carved wood staircases and to the opening that leads to the cavernous workshop.

I stride through the ranks of the smiths as they work the fires and bellows, their small, powerful brown hands swirling around the bubble shapers. I walk directly to the center of the workshop, where the broken leviathan sword rests on the pedestal. I take the sword in hand and feel its mournful vibrations, its broken song, even as the damaged edge perspires a faint trail of blue mist.

"Edmon," the monk says, trying to catch his wind. Strong as he is, he is still a cripple with the disfigurements that slow his movement.

I walk past him toward the forging machines. I hold the sword above a trough of red, hot, glowing siren steel magma.

"Stop!" the monk shouts. "You are not ready."

I turn on him, fury in my eyes. I realize the entire workshop has ceased production. All the smiths of Ashvattha stare at me, waiting for what I will do.

Ready? I think. *An unspeakable darkness awaits in the vast, slowly creeping through the Fracture, devouring everything in its path. My friend, someone I love and care about, is in the thick of it. None of it cares for ready.*

I take a deep breath. I do not wish to violate the sanctity of this place or forsake the kindness these smiths and the monk have shown me. I understand my anger, but I see that it isn't serving me in this moment. So I let it go. Instead I hold out the iron nose for the monk to see. *This is my painful past. I want to integrate it, whether I am ready or not.*

The monk nods, seeming to understand. He gently takes the remnant of the siren sword from me. "All right then, Edmon, son of the leviathan," he says. "You will only have one chance. So if we do it, then we do it right."

Sweat drips in the crevices of my brow as I work alongside the smiths. I pour every drop of concentration I have through a sieve of focus. The lump of iron, the last remnant of my father, is melted into the alloy and pounded into the mold. The metal is folded back in on itself thousands of times creating the basic edge. The task requires patience, precision, and a sense of urgency all at once. Were it finished at this stage, the blade would already be a fine sword, but the smiths of Albion create something beyond fine. Finally, it is ready.

The glowing metal is taken from the mold and placed inside the bubble of the shaping tool. This is the final stage, the unique method of the smiths where my personal resonance will be transferred into the metal and the metal's into me. My vision will hone the piece into the sharpest sword in the galaxy while still maintaining the lightness and flexibility needed to be efficient.

"We will begin together," the monk says. "Then you must shape it alone. It will be yours and only yours. This sword is being remade, so it will not take years to complete, but once the process begins, you cannot stop it. If you lose control, the blade will be ruined and will be useless."

I nod, understanding what I must do. I touch my hands to the hovering gelatin bubble. We begin to move, slowly pushing the energy back and forth between us. Within the seal of the shaping tool, I feel the blade's energy, the voice beginning to hum. The sound is amorphous, as if the voice of what once was is muffling the sound of what will be. I realize that the monk has stepped away and is no longer shaping the sword with me. My surroundings seem to fade from my peripheral vision.

Why run, boy? I hear the call of the leviathan from the depths of my past. *You will not take my son.* I feel the voice of my mother. *You could never look past yourself, could never understand what was at stake, boy,* my father snarls.

"Edmon!" the monk shouts from somewhere beyond the dark. "Do not lose focus!"

I feel the energy of the sword swirling out of control as my hands push and pull faster and faster. The centrifugal energy vibrates through my body as I twist and turn my back and hips with the powerful force.

I chose this music because it is a boy forging his sword, creating his destiny, The Maestro says. *Do not deny the storm. Become one with it,* Faria whispers in the darkness of the Citadel. *Have you forgotten me, Little Lord?* asks Nadia, my lost love.

The bubble threatens to burst with the energy of the steel. *I'm losing it!*

"The past is a part of you, Edmon," the monk calls out. "But it is not your present. Feel it and let it go!"

I breathe through the voices. I let them wash over me and past me. The blade spins in the bubble. It takes a smooth and deadly shape. The voice of what it once was changes.

You were my hero once. To see how far you had fallen . . . , says Xana.

Bravery is acting in spite of fear, agrees Washo.

All we got is family, Doc, says Tol.

I'm counting on you to give this to my son, Welker implores.

Edmon, I am in danger. Ari . . .

I will devour them all! Los the shadow laughs malevolently.

No! I won't let you! my mind screams.

A jolt of pain electrifies my body. *I can't hang on any longer.*

"Your future is not your present, either, Edmon!" the monk shouts, bringing me back from the brink of oblivion. "Here and now, breathe!"

Life-giving atmosphere fills my body. I accept what has been and what may be. I open my eyes, and all I see is the sword, glowing inside the shaping womb. It exists, and I exist, and that is all. *This is the shape I wish,* it whispers. *This is my voice,* it sings. I accept it. *Come forth,* I think. There is a brilliant burst of light from within, blazing through the surrounding darkness. I am blinded for a moment because I do not look away.

When the light fades, I am back in the workshop underneath Ashvattha, surrounded by the smiths of Albion. A friendly hand clasps my shoulder. "You've done it," the monk says. I look up and, hovering above the ground, is the gleaming siren sword, whole again, and now belonging to me. "Take it in your hand," the monk says. I grasp the handle. "Let your vibrations become one with the weapon. She will now ring true for you and only you, son of Leontes."

Yes, the universe may end someday, but it is human nature to struggle against the forces of entropy. I may not stop it, but I will fight until my last breath.

Together the monk and I bring the blade to the workshop bench and begin the final process of acid etching runes onto its gleaming surface.

Cleopatra, my mother; Nadia; Gorham; The Maestro; Faria; Edgaard, my dead brother; Edvaard, the brother I never knew; Welker; Washo; Xana; Tol; and Ari . . .

My past, present, and my future . . . I delicately carve their names into the metal. *They are why I struggle.*

The blue hot metal is dipped into the oil. It screams as it cools and sings when it is removed. It sounds different than it did, a new voice, the voice it told me it wanted. The voice that will sing now just for me. The smiths gather around in ritualistic communion. They've witnessed the birth of a new life. The steel glints in the dim light of the cavern.

The monk waves his staff over me in some kind of benediction. "Through this act of creation, you have been initiated into our tribe of smiths. Should you desire it, you may now walk among the Sacred Forest of memory and take the vow of silence. But first . . ."

Slowly, everywhere in the workshop, loose objects begin to float. I feel a slight tug on my body as well, as if gravity has suddenly become lighter. The smiths raise their voices in an exultant cheer, their vow of silence seemingly broken. I turn to the monk, a look of confusion and astonishment on my face. He is smiling from ear to misshapen ear beneath the shadows of his hood. At first I think he has caused the strange sensation, then he explains, "You're feeling the pull of the Morrigan moon. Its orbit is circling this part of the planet. We must be ready for the crossing," he says coyly.

I shake my head with question as the gang of smiths makes for a tunnel doorway out of the workshop.

"Another kind of . . . initiation," the monk says slyly. "Leave the sword. You won't need it where we are going."

CHAPTER 20

The World Tree

The World Tree hangs in the balance between the sun and the moon, the fulcrum between rational and irrational. It is the center where 'could have been' and 'must be' are one. The World Tree's roots dig deep into the unconscious even as its branches grow toward the heavens of the awake mind. It is the tree from which the hanged man dangles, over which the chariot sails, under which the monster lurks.

—Ovanth, *A Practical Reading of the Arcana*

The silent, ascetic monks become a gaggle of schoolboys as we bound through the subterranean tunnels beneath the surface of Albion for hours. In that entire time, their excitement does not abate. They cheer one another and jest, from young to old. There is a sense of nervous anticipation from the youths and a sort of hungry playfulness from the elders who tease those who have not made the crossing before.

"Every three months of this world, the orbit of the Morrigan moon dips into the atmosphere of Albion," explains the monk as he hobbles beside me. Surprisingly, he keeps up, his own sense of exuberance fueling him. "So with the exchange of elements, the smiths pay visit to our female counterparts who dwell in the monastery carved within the moon's rock."

Moon visits, I think. I start to understand my fellows' enthusiasm.

We arrive at a docking station and enter a sort of tram car. "The slingshot will carry us up through the mountain, Hara Berezaiti, and hurl us through the atmospheric corridor to the moon above," the monk says as we buckle ourselves into the seats of the slingshot transport. We are grabbed by some sort of claw device that pulls us backward, winching the machine tighter and tighter until . . .

We are released. It feels like my brain slams into the back of my skull as the car is catapulted forward and then up the slope of a parabolic ramp. The smiths howl with delight as the lights of the tunnel flash by the windows so quickly they are but streaks to my eyes. Then the darkness falls away, and we are beyond the surface of Albion, hurled in the sky toward the blue moon of Morrigan, which grows ever larger through the windshield of the car.

I look through the window to see a narrow corridor of stratosphere and a veil of stars beyond. Just as quickly, it disappears as our car enters a landing tunnel. There is a rush of air as a pneumatic cushion slows the incoming vehicle until it gently stops against a giant pad that rests against the end of the tunnel wall.

The smiths eagerly exit the tram and hurry through the tunnels. I follow, a bit less sure than my comrades. "There's nothing to fear," my friend, the monk, says. "They won't bite . . . much."

I roll my eyes at the cliché jest. The blue stone of the rock tunnels is rough-hewn and my step much lighter than on the surface of Albion. "The gravity differential is part of the fun," the monk adds. He practically leaps down the corridor. Unconstrained by the mass of his world, he is much freer with his movement. I follow him through the twisting and turning tunnels until they open on a giant blue cave, carved from the rock itself.

This is truly the counterpart to the smiths' workshop cut into the tree below on Albion.

If only Tol Sanctun were here, I think. *The monk would give the fool a run for his money.*

The sisters of the Shin await in the cavern of the ethereal blue monastery, lined up in ranks. They are tall, willowy, and clad in immaculate white robes. Their heads are smooth, shorn of all hair. *These are the angels I saw from my hibernation in the gel pod,* I realize. A colossal relief, formed from the rock itself, looms behind them. It is a huge sculpture of a robed woman. The monk does not have to tell me who it is. I already know, and my heart beats faster.

Ari . . .

I can't stay here, I think. *I have to leave.*

Here, he is not a monster, I think. *She accepts him for who he is and not what his face shows.*

I cannot, Ari . . . she's out there somewhere. She says she is in danger. What am I doing here, wasting time?

For so long, I understand now, *I've been merely surviving. Candlemas showed me that I could trust my friends with my secrets, but it was Ari, whose abilities made my past known to her the instant she set eyes upon me, who wanted to love me. It's Ari for whom I want to live . . .*

"Only our tribe has the distinct honor and privilege of meeting the sisters this way," the monk whispers to me. "I suspect that is why we are the best craftsmen, with the best tools."

I look at him with an arcing eyebrow, and he laughs and claps me on the back with his good hand.

"Urizen, or rather her daughter, her incarnation, Orc," the monk says. "During the Kaliyuga, the battle between Urizen and Los, Orc will come to lead us into the next epoch."

Whoever created the thing was a tremendous artist, capturing the determination comingled with fear, the resolve mixed with uncertainty, in the eyes of the messianic being. I've seen that look once before—in the eyes of the woman I kissed before I came here.

I turn to the monk just as a sister emerges from the ranks. She glides along the monastery floor.

"The abbess," the monk whispers in my ear playfully. "You must excuse me."

I'm only slightly astonished to see my friend leave our group and float across the floor to meet his counterpart. He matches her movements and arrives at the center of the cavern. She pushes his hood back, and her smooth hand brushes tenderly the rough skin of his disfigured face. Her large eyes are filled with kindness and genuine love. He leans into her touch.

"Welcome," she says to him. The acoustics of the cavern are such that her voice addresses us all. "Weary travelers, we take you in and lift the burden of our silence for this night as we join together, male and female, light and dark. Take succor and comfort in each other's arms."

The willowy, white beings float forward, coming among the ranks of the smaller, earthy smiths. One by one, the women choose a man and lead him away. A sister glides toward me, but I shake my head.

And she moves off.

I find myself breaking away from the crowd and drifting toward the back of the cavern. I stare up into the eyes of the statue of Orc.

"Edmon," the monk whispers, and I practically jump to the ceiling, startled. I turn. "Why are you still here?" he says. "There are many young acolytes of the Shin I can think of who you are disappointing."

The abbess hovers behind him. "Such a shame for a handsome young man not to live," she says with compassion.

I look away.

"It's all right," the monk says kindly. "I'll love enough for both of us this night." He winks and takes the abbess by the crook of his good arm and floats away. He stops for a moment and turns back. "She must be very beautiful, Edmon."

I think yes. Then I am left alone, gazing at the face of the statue.

—

"Doctor Batman? Doctor Batman?"

I'm dreaming of Ari, but the voice jolts me awake. It's a reminder that I have more to do than find her. *Did the others survive?*

I get to my feet in the stone cavern, wishing I had a chronometer. *How long does this moon visit last?* I glance around for a sign of any of the smiths, but there's not a soul in sight. I'm alone in the vast cavern underneath the gaze of the Orc statue when an incongruous sight catches my eye. A lanky figure appears near a tunnel that exits the monastery and leads to the surface of the moon.

I'd recognize that top hat anywhere . . .

"Is it really you?" Tol Sanctun says, squinting. I break into a run. "Doctor Bat—oof!" I cut him off with a tight embrace.

I pull back, gripping his arms and staring up into his face. *How in the fathoms did you find me, Tol Sanctun?* I want to scream with joy. *My friend is alive!*

"Edmon Leontes, boy, am I glad to see you." He shakes his head. "Whistler said we'd find you." I step back. The blue-haired pixie reveals herself from behind the man's long trench coat. She looks older, no longer a child. Tol's scraggly hair is grayed and fraying at the ends, too.

Shock hits me. The nature of the Fracture in its design is to compensate for time dilation, thus facilitating instantaneous transport through the vast. But that has no bearing on the effects that idiosyncratic gravitational pull have on individual solar systems. Tao is a high-grav world where the population passes its ages more slowly than other planets do. The distortion created by the triumvirate that is Albion, Eruland, and the Morrigan moon has much the same effect. I've been isolated with the smiths beneath the sacred World Tree for months, but Tol, it seems, has passed years since the events above Miral. Whistler was a child when we met her in the labyrinth of Miral. Now she is a young woman.

What does that mean for Ari? I think with horror. *So much could have happened while I've remained stagnant here. Years have passed for Tol and maybe the rest of the Fracture . . . But the singularity,* I remember.

Perhaps time has passed even more slowly for Ari and all is not lost. It's the not knowing that is the most frustrating part.

"Took me a long time to figure out what the hell her rhyming meant," Tol is saying. "He says, 'Return, Albion, return, I give myself for thee!' She's been saying that gobbledygook day and night. Finally, I'm like, Albion? Does she mean Doctor Batman? He carries that sword, the um . . . serious sword or whatever, right? The smiths of Albion make those things."

"All things begin and end in Albion's ancient druid rocky shore." Whistler bobs her head. *She seems nervous, though. Seeing something about to come?*

"So I'm like, duh, she means the place, Albion. Dad and I flew past it in the *Bentley* back in the day. Not much there but thick forest. We took a sortie to the surface, but all the spacers at the mountain port said the smiths were up here for some monthly moon festival? Say is that a statue of who I think it is?" Tol gazes up at the relief of Orc, eyes wide, then back at me. "Why aren't you talking? Why isn't he talking?" He turns to my friend the monk, who has come up behind me with the abbess, both awoken from a postcoital slumber.

"Edmon's vocal cords had already deteriorated when we recovered him from a gel capsule," the monk replies. "Edmon, you know these travelers?" He seems somewhat suspicious. I think the timing of Tol and Whistler's arrival, interrupting what otherwise would be a private and sacred holiday, has annoyed him somewhat. I look at the faint smile the abbess wears beneath her cloak's white hood, and I cannot say I blame him.

"Doctor Batman was always the strong, silent type, but he'd bark a sarcastic rant if you got him going." Tol scrutinizes me. "Wait, Doc . . . This is really important—where is your sword?"

"Edmon Leontes needs no weapon here," the monk replies. "This is a sacred place, a place of peace. You have interrupted a holy—"

A rumble reverberates through the entire chamber. *An explosion,* I discern, my senses coming alert. *Coming from the passage that leads to the tram car tunnel.*

"This is not good!" Tol says. "Do you guys have anything else? Maybe a big stick?"

I sense a heartbeat coming from below. Steps crunch the gravel of Morrigan's blue rock coming up from the passage we took earlier from the tram. I feel and hear the intruder stride down the tunnel.

"You didn't come alone," the monk says, ominously voicing my thoughts.

Tol tries to explain rapid-fire. "Edmon, my dad left me a message. I think he knows something about Ari. I needed a ship to find you. It's not like I had a lot of funds . . ."

I hear the stamp of a large spear hitting the earth along with the clomp of armored boots. Siren steel sings in the tunnel. The last time I encountered one who wielded such a weapon was on Miral, in the labyrinth of the Temple of the Matriarchs. I know with certainty even as I want to deny it: *Phaestion has sent another of The Companions to find me.*

"See we were on Market when it was invaded by—"

"Shut up," the monk says quickly. "This way," he indicates.

I grab Tol and the monk in my arms and bound in the opposite direction from the interloper, for the tunnel that leads to the surface of the moon, the abbess and Whistler right behind me. We quickly hide from view.

"Hello, hello?" The armored figure emerges from the tunnel. "Is anyone home? Oh, fool? Where are you?" He carries a silver trident in one hand. The helmet covers the wild curls of golden hair I remember from his boyhood, but it does not mask the buggy blue eyes that always held that hint of craziness. *Perdiccus of House Mughal.* He yawns lazily. "Ah, well, it seems I'll just have to start killing some people. No one leaves until I find the traitor, Edmon of House Leontes."

—

"Hurry," the monk whispers as we bound down the passageway to the moon's surface in the light-g. "The abbess has agreed to help your idiot friend, but I don't know how long they can persuade the intruder to remain on the moon absent suspicion. The sisters are accomplished in martial skill, but they are no match for an armored Taoan brandishing siren steel."

The monk is right. Hanschen was always scheming, and Sigurd was always physically intimidating. Perdiccus was more a follower, but that doesn't mean he is less dangerous. He was the most adrenaline seeking of Phaestion's bunch, and he's a trained killer who will tear through everyone here like a screamer through Meridian twilight if he discovers they are harboring me.

There had been no trace of my whereabouts until Tol opened his yap after Phaestion's forces invaded Market. It seems my foster brother wasted no time in pursuing the lead. *Tol and I may need to discuss that if we survive.* As glad as I am that Whistler's precognition gave Tol the cue to find me, I have no desire to embroil my friends in a confrontation with my past.

The rock-carved passage ends at a circular doorway, an air lock where atmospheric filtration units siphon the air given from Albion as the planetary bodies scrape one another. The surface awaits on the other side.

"Here," the monk whispers, handing me a specialized flight suit from an equipment locker. "The window for your crossing will be closing soon." I slip into the suit and check the seal's integrity. "This Perdiccus has destroyed the tram, so jumping to the forest below will be the quickest route. With the orbits aligned, the gravitational pull of Albion should be enough to pull you through the corridor of atmosphere between the bodies." He hands me a helmet, and I fasten it to the suit's neck. "Edmon, this is very risky. If you deviate from the bounds of the corridor, you will be lost in the vacuum. The suit is designed to survive planetary entry and is equipped with membranous wings between the limbs for gliding—here and here." He indicates the activation points.

It's not the first time I've used a glider suit, so that should help, I think.

"The entry should take place near the summit of the Hara Berezaiti. Once you're at cruising altitude, angle toward Ashvattha. You'll know it when you see it. As for the return flight . . . well, that will be up to you to figure out."

Swell, I think.

The monk grabs my shoulders. "Edmon, run. Find a ship at the spaceport on the mountaintop. Leave this system. Once you are confirmed gone, he will have no incentive to stay."

I shake my head. The monk does not know Phaestion or any of his ruthless Companions. I've committed the highest crime of any Taoan—I fled the Combat. This in itself would be an affront to any Pantheon noble. For Phaestion, though, it is personal. I robbed him of his glory and of his triumph over me. He always viewed me as some sort of archetypical opponent. I am a brother he loved, who betrayed him, and whose death by his hand would cement his rule. He fancied our personal story had a mythic quality. Just like the fable of Chilleus and Cuillan from the epic of the Chironiad. If I do not face Perdiccus here and now, the hunt will simply continue. More than that, Perdiccus needs no excuse to kill the sisters or the smiths or anyone else he feels like killing for fun.

"Very well." The monk reads the look of determination on my face. "The chronometer on your wrist is set to the hour here. The time differential due to Albion's superior gravity should afford you a bit of a temporal cushion, but do hurry. I don't know how long we can keep him wondering where you are without him harming anyone."

I take a deep breath and nod. The monk steps back and seals the door on his side of the air lock. I open the other door and ascend the staircase to the surface. The rock is blue and glasslike, the moon's surface having been polished by the solar winds of the Celt Star. The stars are pricks of brilliant light, clear in the blackness of the vast here. Their light has traveled for thousands of years to reach my eyes, but I have the barest sliver of time to save the lives in the monastery below.

Wind rushes underneath me. Above, the green orb of Albion looms. Her gravity sweeps me into her embrace, and I fly through space, a feather on the current of forces beyond my control. All I can do is try to maintain balance. I put all my focus into gliding straight so I don't tumble out of the atmospheric corridor. Fire sparks around my helmet as I enter Albion's atmosphere. Suddenly I feel the darkness of Los in the universe. I lose control. I tumble toward a monstrous gray mountain, Hara Berezaiti, the High Watchpost. *Damn, damn, damn!*

I tuck my arms to my sides. I clasp my legs together. I activate the suit's gliding function and spread my limbs, splaying out the wings. The currents lift me up, and I sail forward above a vast ocean of green forest. Rising from the center of the rushing trees is one gigantic tree unlike any other. Her leaves are shimmering feathers, catching the light in every wave of the color spectrum. *Ashvattha!* I had not seen her but from underneath her huge trunk. From the sky, she is utterly beautiful. She dazzles my eyes with shifting patterns like a prism, almost burning my retinas. I look away.

The turn of my head causes me to swerve and dive toward the ground. A tree branch clips my leg. I spin and crash into the canopy, breaking through leaves and vines. It's all I can do to tuck my head as I plow into the gnarled roots and duff. Mud parts, creating a deep furrow until I come to a stop.

By the twisted star! I think. *The crash is going to set me back. How far am I from Ashvattha?*

I sit for a moment in the fetal position, my breath fogging my helmet's face shield. I ache all over from impact, but miraculously, nothing seems broken. That is until I check my helmet's readouts—the heads up display that monitors everything from altitude to wind current. My vitals flicker and die. The system isn't destroyed, though. There's just too much electromagnetic interference here for it to function, it seems. I check my wrist, and the chronometer is working just fine, stuck at the fifty-minute mark almost indefinitely.

Urizen had forty days meditating underneath the World Tree. How long will I have exactly? I wonder.

The wood is tall and densely packed. Disoriented from the fall, I can't make out which direction I should even go to get there.

Gnarled roots climb everywhere. Dark moss hangs thick from traversing vines. I cannot see the sky beyond the canopy, but I hear the distant babbling of a brook and the croaks and chirps of creatures all around. There is music within these woods, a chorus of voices humming within the leaves.

I raise the visor of my helmet and breathe in wet, heavy air. The content and texture feels different aboveground than it did in the workshop of the smiths. I feel a head rush, as if my brain is blinking away cobwebs. *I'm high off the intensely oxygenated atmosphere,* I realize. I open my senses. *See with your ears. Taste with your fingers,* Faria once said. I yank off a glove and graze my fingers over the surface root. I feel it hum. *This is more than music.* The swirling pattern of bark is a language like the tactile nightscript reader. The monk, too, told me that the forest was sentient, dangerous to the uninitiated. But I can sense through the flow of energy within each root and limb that they are all extensions, tributaries leading back to one main thought. *I can follow the thoughts to the World Tree.*

Laughter sounds behind me. I spin but see nothing but woodland. "This way!" a voice giggles. I turn again to see a dark-haired boy with inquisitive green eyes. He peers at me from behind a tree. Our gazes lock, and he startles and sprints down a narrow footpath into the wood.

Wait! I think and run after him. He is fast, elusive. I turn back toward the clearing where I landed and see that the trees have grown together behind me blocking me from the route I had come. *When the monk told me Urizen's story, he called this the Forest of Memory . . .*

"Over here," the boy calls. He is a few meters away but takes off again.

Yes, this place is alive, and it appears to have an agenda. I can only hope the boy is leading me toward where I need to go.

I follow him down a twisting path of gnarled roots to another small glen where purple light from the sky passes through the canopy. It spotlights on the boy as voices whisper from the leaves. "This is the heir of House Leontes? The boy is weak, Edric!" It is the voice of the Grand Wusong, the emperor of Tao, as I was presented to him in my fifth year.

"Edmon is my son!" my father responds. I had never met Edric before that day. All I wanted was to make him proud.

"You dare question your emperor? Seize them all!" Wusong commands.

That is not what happened, I think. No, my father rejected me that day in favor of a purebred scion. *Edgaard.* I only lived because the emperor saw some courage within me.

I hear sounds of a battle from all around. "Father, no!" The boy I've followed here screams and falls to his knees in the glade. He reaches out to someone just beyond the pool of light.

"House Leontes has fallen . . ." Edric's voice trails off.

"Father, please don't die. I love you," the boy weeps.

I shake my head at this strange scene, but I understand—when I was a child I wanted my father's love. *What if he had given it to me? What if he had defended me against the taunting of the emperor? What if the emperor had been threatened by him then?* Civil war and the fall of House Leontes would have followed.

I walk to the weeping boy. I place my hand upon his heaving back. *I see you, Edmon.* The boy's sobbing ceases. His head turns. Green eyes stare back, and the pupils contract like the slits of a reptile. The demon grins a mouth full of razor teeth. He lunges for me. I rear back, falling out of the light. *What in the abyss?*

Laughter cuts through the hum of the trees. This time it is not a child's voice, but the voice of a boy who has just become a man. A youth, lanky and lean, sits in a branch above. He smiles down at me, far more self-assured than I was at that age. "Oh, little lord?" a young woman's voice calls from the forest beyond. The youth leaps from his perch to the forest floor and takes off.

I run after him, anxious, too, for I remember the woman's voice. My foot catches on a root. I stumble forward, my hands reaching out to brace against the impact. Instead, they plunge me into icy water. I flounder on the cold, wet banks of a glassy lake. My eyes follow the ripples in the water out to the center of the lake, where the youth stands on the bow of a small boat. In his arms is a young woman. He pulls her close and brushes dark hair from her eyes. Before he can kiss her, however, they are assaulted by pale warriors from beyond the shadows.

No! I think. *I can't live this again!* I plunge into the water, hoping to swim to them in time. My interference is unnecessary. This time, the boy is not overpowered. He is too strong for them. He disarms one attacker, then another. He grabs hold of a third with hard hands that encircle the man's neck.

"Edmon! Don't . . . ," the man begs. But the boy twists swiftly, snapping his father's spine, then pushes the lifeless body over the bow. He turns to face the woman he loves, but she wears a mask of terror. She turns away from him. The light fades around her, and only the boy is left, alone in the boat.

I was not strong enough to protect Nadia from harm. It is my greatest shame. In this fiction before me, however, young Edmon had no such weakness. He defended his Nadia. He was ruthless, as his father desired. Yet in doing so, he lost the very thing that he aimed to save.

I see you, Edmon. The youth in the boat hears my thought. He raises his head, but all I see is a deformed skull with slitted emerald eyes staring back. The waters around me rise to envelop me. The freezing cold burns as it creeps over my chest. I flail my limbs, struggling to find my way to shore, but laughter booms around me and something pulls me into the depths.

My hands find purchase on something, a root or vine. I grab it and pull with all my might. A moment later, I pull myself to shore, vomiting water and mud from my lungs. I wipe thick sludge from the chronometer on my wrist. *How long have I been in these cursed woods? Hours?* Several minutes have passed on the timer. That's more time than I'd like to leave my friends alone with Perdiccus. *I can't keep indulging these twisted visions!*

The lilting notes of a flute pipe on the breeze. I look up to see a man, rugged and muscular, sitting in the crook of a giant root. His instrument looks carved from the long thigh bone of a giant. *Are these visions supposed to teach me something? Or is this forest merely playing therapist?*

I stand, and the stranger mirrors my actions. I walk the banks toward the man. With every step I take, he appears to move away. I pick up my pace and run the incline toward him. He glides farther away. I scramble over twisted roots up and up. The cover of the surrounding trees breaks. I steady myself on a sapling. Ahead, the man kneels in front of a gray rock. Sitting on the rock is Ariel Lazarus. My breath catches. *She is beautiful.* The man cleans a wound on her leg. A rivulet of blood glides down her smooth, pale skin.

"You don't talk much, do you?" she says.

Consternation furrows the man's brow. *What should he say to her? Should he tell her how he feels?*

"You're afraid I'll wound you," she says. "Wounds heal."

The man takes a deep breath then speaks. "Every time I've loved, love was taken from me. But I can't bear going through this life without telling you how I feel." He pulls the girl into his kiss. It is bittersweet, watching this moment that never happened.

A siren sounds, softly at first, then rising in pitch. Ari pulls away from Edmon, and a line appears across her throat. It drips the same crimson in a cascade as her head peels back from her body.

No! I silently scream.

Behind the girl looms the demonic face of Phaestion of the Julii. "Face me," he says. "Or I shall hunt you forever."

I run from the scene. Terror grips me as Phaestion's malevolent laugh grows into the sounds of the leviathan's roar. The great shadow of Los spreads everywhere blotting out the Forest of Memory. I turn to look back, and I run smack into a wall. I'm knocked off my feet. I tumble down the incline over rocks and roots until I finally halt on a plateau of dirt. The world around is dull, the shadow having bled all color from the trees.

I grab a rock for purchase, needing to feel something tangible and real. The rock moves, and I draw back, startled. I look again to see that it was not a rock at all, but a foot wrapped in rags. The old creature it belongs to seems no more than a collection of rickety bones wrapped in the burlap sack of the monk's robe. He pulls back his frayed hood. I gasp. He is practically a corpse. The bald head is wrinkled with branching veins; the face is sallow and sunken. "Do you know who I am?" he rasps. His eyes are full of milk-white cataracts like Faria's were. "I've lived a thousand years, kept myself alive. I've never loved, and I've never lost." Tears stream down his face. "And the pain of the past never leaves me."

The stars will burn out, the universe will grow cold, and all life will cease to exist. Why run, boy? That is what the monster of the deep asked.

Candlemas showed me my past on Roc-121. The forest shows me what might have been. How each choice would have led to ruin. The leviathan always warned me that someday all will end. Our choices don't truly matter. *So what then is the purpose of anything? To make our own meaning of this nothing,* I reaffirm. *That is why the leviathan is so terrible in my dreams, because I choose to give my actions meaning rather than do nothing. It is the hardest choice to make, but that is the story I must make for myself.*

There's an old idea: regret is useless. I disagree. Regret is to learn from. Regret tells me how to move forward. I'm haunted by childhood frailty. I'm ashamed I couldn't protect loved ones. I'm afraid I'll live forever alone without love. But I'm no longer afraid I'll do nothing to prevent that outcome.

This is the integration of balance. I choose it all. The joy and the pain. I will not run, monster. This will not be my life, moment to moment. I accept my past. I accept my future and all the peace and pain it brings.

The old man looks at me and grins. His milk-white eyes now blaze emerald fire. The face contorts; the body expands. A giant serpent springs from the husk of the old man. The leviathan looms above me, fearsome scales and a maw of razor-sharp teeth. He did not harm me when I was a boy; he will not harm me now. He roars and then rushes forward. I do not flee. I stand with arms wide. *I see you, Edmon.* The dragon swirls into me, penetrating every cell of my being. I feel him in my belly rising in a burst of energy. I feel him in my throat. I open my mouth. I roar.

The shimmering feathers of Ashvattha's leaves fall around me like the snow of first winter. I look at the deep furrow of earth where I landed upon planetary entry. I must have been unconscious this whole time, lying at the base of the gargantuan World Tree. I check the chronometer on my wrist. Over half an hour has elapsed on the moon above. *I have to hurry and find the entrance to the workshop from above.*

"If only—!" I call out. *My voice!* I touch my throat instinctively. The scar is still there, the same that I've had since my father had my vocal cords removed. Yet somehow . . .

The monk told me that the smiths enter the forest, and if their trial is successful, they join the ranks of the masters and take upon themselves the vow of silence.

I have come through my own trial, my voice returned.

I healed myself.

I collapse to my knees, crying. The thing I've been so long without, the thing I once thought was my whole life . . .

This is a gift, but I still have a mission to complete.

I hear nothing but the rustling wind through feathery leaves. *Ari says everything is language. The language of Albion is music. The forest, the siren steel. I must speak its tongue. My voice is returned. I have to use it.*

I close my eyes and breathe. I recognize my anger for Phaestion and the Companions, how they are threatening those back on the Morrigan moon. I recognize the fear that I won't be able to save the monk or Tol or Ari. I also recognize the joy and peace all those I've loved in my life have brought me. I remember the tune and words. I sing "The Song of Edmon." I was a boy when I sang it before. Now, I am a man, and the quality is different.

Every seven years, the cells in one's body are replaced, and an entirely new person stands where the old one once did. The song I sing is not the same because I am not the same. Who am I now? Something tells me the not knowing is part of the excitement.

My voice is joined by that of another. I close my eyes and follow this harmonizer. My feet wander until I am stepping down between roots. A step lower and then another. I am on a path that leads into the earth beneath the tree. My eyes still closed, I feel the air thick around me, and darkness falls beyond my closed eyelids. Together the voice and I become one. I feel the space widen before me, and I open my eyes.

I stand above the vast, empty workshop of the smiths. My siren sword hovers above the pedestal in the center of the room, waiting for me, singing the melody that is my melody, glinting silver in the dim light of the forges. Attuned to my reborn voice, my body, and my mind. I reach out my hand, and it swiftly sails across the cavern into my grasp.

CHAPTER 21

Justice

> Justice is about balancing the scales in a cold, rational sense. It is in opposition to revenge, which speaks of passion and rage. The person who masters justice holds the dissonance between the rational and irrational and becomes the arbiter of destiny.
>
> —Ovanth, *A Practical Reading of the Arcana*

I follow the steps of the cavern toward the surface. *Climb the tree. Catch the wind to the mountain,* Ari says from within. She's with me now, guiding me from somewhere beyond space and time. I don't know how. It doesn't matter.

I exit the cavern through a crack in the roots of Ashvattha. I breathe in the wet air of the forest. A feathery leaf lands in my palm; it pulses rainbow colors for a moment before I let the wind take it away in its currents. I dig my fingers and toes into the deep crevices of the bark and climb.

Hand over hand, finding footholds and stepping up for what seems an age, I'm reminded of Nadia and how she would have loved this challenge. Finally, I reach an upper branch. Rainbow leaves swirl around me. I pet the tree, savoring her rough textures on my fingertips. What was dark and gray in my visions below now seems light and full of vibrancy here above the canopy. *Go well,* Ashvattha seems to say.

Thank you, I respond in kind. I look out over the horizon and see the lonely gray mountain, Hara Berezaiti, looming above the tree line. *This is it.* I waste no more thought. I leap from the boughs. I fall before I fly. I spread my arms wide, releasing the wings of the flight suit. Still, the suit is meant to glide. It has no engine. My downward trajectory takes me close to the treetops. *Come on, come on . . .* A gust of wind rushes, and the wings create lift. I soar toward the mountain like a gull on the Southern Sea. I fix my gaze on the blue moon in the sky. One day the tight orbits of Eruland, Morrigan, and Albion will cause the worlds to smash into one another, possibly ending all life in this star system. Knowledge that all life is fleeting makes every moment of living so precious.

The tree line fades as the foot of the mountain rises. I angle my body and catch the draft that reflects off the gray slopes that become cliffs. I pass through fog. The air grows thin, and the lift of my wings lightens. I touch ground and push off. I feel the tug of Morrigan's gravity. I bound up the boulders and the rocks of the great watch post. Finally, I skid to a stop on a precipice at the top of the world. Morrigan fills the heavens, and I feel the convection of atmosphere, the corridor created between the worlds. The gravitational pull of Albion is much stronger. It was one matter to jump from the moon to this world, another to go from this world to the moon. *I don't have time to figure out a solution.*

The mountain hums beneath my feet. I feel her vibrations pulse through my body and into the sword on my hip. The siren steel speaks words to me—*Draw me!* I follow the impulse and take up the blade from my belt. The metal glows electric blue and pulls my arm skyward. It's all I can do to hang on as its sonic force pulls me from the ground. I'm yanked into the ether, and the air burns around me as I reach escape velocity. I rocket toward the moon, following the homing beacon of the HUD in my helmet toward the monastery of the sisterhood. Fortunately, the location is not far out of alignment from where I left it.

I spread the wings of my flight suit to soften my fall. My boots hit blue glass as I touch down in a ready position. I bound in the low-g down the stairwell of the monastery entrance, no time to lose. I float down the corridor of the entryway into the main cavern, already hearing the reverberation of my enemy's voice. "I grow weary of your excuses, priest. You're stalling. Edmon Leontes! Come out now, or I start raping these worms with my trident! See? He's not here. Ah, well."

"The Doc will be here," Tol pleads. "Just give him a second. He's finishing off the sacred ceremony if you catch my drift."

"Shut up, fool." Perdiccus hurls Tol to the floor. He poises his trident, ready to throw it at my friend.

I bound through the entrance to the cavern. "Perdiccus!" I shout, too late. Perdiccus releases his throw. There is a scream, and a body falls.

The blue-haired girl, Whistler, has stepped between the thrust of the trident and Tol. She drops almost in slow motion. Blood sprays out in a fine mist as Perdiccus withdraws his weapon from her chest. The droplets hang in the low-g a moment too long before falling to the earth. Tol and the monk cradle the girl in their arms.

"Whistler!" Tol cries.

I sprint toward the armored Taoan. Perdiccus has already shifted his stance to confront a cadre of sisters and smiths who have surrounded him. They will not go down without defending themselves. They are on him, fighting. The abbess leads the charge along with several of her elite acolytes. I see they are highly skilled, their circular movements like a martial mirror to the forging skills of the smiths. Each maneuver aims to move with the force of the enemy, let it pass over them, then swirl it back around on him. It is impressive, but it is not enough. The hum of Perdiccus's trident shrieks as he cuts down one, then another.

I leap and land next to the monk and Tol as they hold the dying clairvoyant in their embrace. Tol has spent the years after the events of

Miral with her. I can't know the bond that has been formed between them in that time.

"Can I see another's woe and not be in sorrow, too? Can I see another's grief and not seek for kind relief?" the girl whispers. "Do not grieve, Tol Sanctun. I saw this as my end before I began. Do not forget the tarot."

"Doc, do something!"

My eyes scan the wound. The prongs of the trident were expertly placed, puncturing multiple vital organs. I'd need advanced medical equipment to place her in stasis even before I could perform surgery or organ transplantation that would save her.

"Edmon Leontes." Her eyes shift to mine. "Let her in. Remember, let her in . . ."

The girl is suffering. She says it with her eyes. And then her voice confirms, "Do it. I forgive you."

There is only one thing I know I can do to end her pain—I lightly touch her temple with the power of the Dim Mak, and life passes from her body, leaving the universe forever.

"No!" cries Tol. He clutches Whistler to his chest even as he is racked by sobs.

Peoples throughout the Fracture cling to a belief in such things as a soul. They pray that somehow the mind survives the destruction of the body. Everything in this life is energy. While energy cannot be destroyed, knowledge, intelligence, all the things that make up a person passes. Whistler is gone, her energy released back into the cosmic ocean of this universe forever, never to arise in this form again.

"Doctor Batman." Tol wipes his tears with the back of a fingerless-gloved hand. "Do me a solid and end this son of a bitch."

Couldn't have said it better myself.

I spring to action, feeling adrenaline pump through my arteries. Every mechanoreceptor, every dendrite feels the floor. Impulses firing through my axons make my nervous system tingle with heightened awareness. I speak the language of the cell, the primal call that prepares my body for the kinetics I will need.

House Mughal's sigil is the manta. *Leviathans hunt mantas as appetizers.*

Perdiccus has been backed toward the tunnel that leads to the surface of the moon, but he continues to fell the smiths and sisters, creating sanguinary paintings on their white robes. I follow the path of bodies, limbs splayed at odd angles in death, leading toward their black-armored killer. Now only the abbess remains facing him. He feints, but she's not so easily baited. She spins in her relaxed circular footwork, closing the gap between them. Her hands lash out. They stagger the tall Taoan but do not bring him down. His spider-silk armor is too dense for the strikes to fully penetrate. He drops to a knee, and the abbess kicks the trident aside. *It's a gambit!* I realize. He aims his hand at the trident, which suddenly reverses course. The abbess aims to strike again, but the trident howls like a banshee and impales her through the back, pulled by Perdiccus's glove.

"Perdiccus!" I scream. My howl is echoed by my sword's.

The Companion plants an armored boot on the abbess's back as he yanks his trident from her body. He flings the weapon to clean its barbs of the abbess's blood, splashing the cave walls with a swatch of red.

"You got your voice returned to you, snail guppy." He smiles. "Do you wish to spare the rest of these pathetic nuns by coming peaceably? Or do I slaughter them all and return you to Phaestion as a corpse?"

I charge him. He springs forward, crashing me back into the cavern beneath the gaze of Orc. The chamber erupts with siren screams as our weapons clash.

"You were a half-breed, a Daysider. And still he chose you to give his attentions to." Perdiccus laughs.

Hanschen was the clever one, lascivious in his mannerisms. Sigurd was the most physically imposing of The Companions. Like the middle child of any family, Perdiccus was always trying to make himself stand out while fitting in. He became a fawning sycophant at times. At others, he took foolish physical risks in hopes of recognition. The more he tried, the more he was simply overlooked. Funny how all these events comes down to childhood jealousy.

"You were always afraid, though, snail guppy," he taunts. "Remember who was out the screamer first, skydiving into Meridian, and who was last? You'll always be afraid."

His trident has the advantage of reach, but my leviathan is swifter. I deflect a thrust and use the momentum and low gravity to float inside his range. I slam an elbow into his face. His visor slams shut in time to mitigate the blow. His heels plow into the blue rock. Our weapons lock, and an invisible bubble of sonic force explodes from the strike, causing the ground beneath us to crater. Perdiccus expertly spins his body away, twisting the trident and prying my sword from my grasp. Alberich, my father's seneschal, taught him the technique years ago when he and I were boys. Fortunately, because we trained together, I also know the move that comes next. He rears backward. His trident rises at the end of his arced body, like the deadly sting tail of a manta. I back flip away as the trident slams the earth where I stood moments before.

"You were always quick, half-breed," Perdiccus snarls. "But you could never truly compete with us Nightsiders. When I drag your corpse back through the Lyrian throne room, Phaestion will have no choice but to recognize me."

I take a deep breath. I feel rage boiling inside me. There is also fear, but Perdiccus is wrong. I look up at Orc, who presides over this deadly dance. *My love outweighs my fear and rage. There are people in my life I care about. I won't let them down.* I remember the monk's words during the shaping of my sword, lift myself away from the emotion, and focus on the task at hand.

"Perdiccus, you and the others almost killed me the day we met," I say calmly. "But that's the closest you will ever get. No one will ever notice you."

Rage fires his muscles. *Good. I want him angry and stupid.* He leaps for me. I run. Every fight is a dialogue, a language of attacks and counterattacks. He tries to cut me off as I make for my sword. I dive and roll under a thrust of his trident. Every move, thrust, riposte, punch, or kick is a word, a thought he delivers with anger. This is how I want him—dumb, brutal, and sloppy. I grasp my sword in my hand, and the mellifluous voice of the Southern Sea is recalled to my ears. He chases me. I sprint to the cavern entrance and leap over the fallen body of the abbess. *The warrior with vocabulary uses his opponent's words, reflects them back toward him with a thousandfold intensity.*

He catches me on the stairwell. *You were always his favorite . . .* I feel the rage of his envy. I deflect every blow he aims at me, but he's now moving with armor-enhanced speed.

I pity you, Perdiccus. After all this time, your entire drive is seeking approval. What kind of man needs that so desperately? I respond using circular movements I learned from the smiths to shape, gently moving around his attacks.

You murdered Hanschen, and now you'll pay! His trident screams at an unexpected angle. I barely duck the blow before it smashes the cavern wall. I'm backed up into the air lock. I spin around a thrust of his trident and seal the door behind us. His trident plows through the external door, screaming as it vibrates through it. I feel the rush of atmosphere escaping the lock. I duck another wild slash and yank on the lever releasing the hatch. Perdiccus blocks the passage, and I plow into him, forcing him up the final steps and onto Morrigan's surface.

I will prove myself to Phaestion by ending you! He floats into the air, caught in the convection of atmosphere and the tug of Albion's gravity.

This is where we differ, old friend. I have nothing left to prove. I leap with him into the gravitational corridor. We collide, our weapons singing in a dissonance. We grapple. I flip him midair, hoping he'll fly into the nether of the vast. I'm not so lucky. Perdiccus's armor has an aural jet pack, which propels him on a cloud of sound. He spins back toward me.

We were brothers, Edmon. You always took life so seriously, but this is the game of Tao you never could accept: the strong survive. He grins beneath his helm's visor and flies toward me with incredible speed. The friction of the air around his spear causes an aura of flame to ignite, but the corridor of air and gravity between the two worlds begins to stretch.

I do not have a system of propulsion like he does, but I have the teaching of the smiths, the knowledge of the forest, and my sword reborn. I wait for him. I've made a vow not to take life. That doesn't mean I can't take away the tools that keep this man alive to harm others. At the last moment, I spin from his thrust as if I am spinning the shaping tool of the smiths. My siren sword sings and slices through the armor and jet pack on Perdiccus's back. I send a well-placed kick into the same spot for good measure, hurtling him out of the corridor connecting the worlds. He sails off into dead space. The last I hear is the abrupt ceasing of his dying screams as he floats off into the vacuum.

Warning lights flash in my helmet's HUD. Perdiccus's last thrust punctured the seal of my flight suit. I take hold of my sword in both hands. *I'm losing air fast!* Stars burst in my vision. Morrigan pulls away from her sister Albion, and the corridor of atmosphere thins. Without air, there can be no sound. *Come on,* I will the sonic blade. She hums with the last bit of atmosphere in the corridor. I aim toward the blue rock. *Come on!* We lose momentum as her song fades. *Come on! I have to live! I promised the smiths of Albion. There's Tol and the message he said he received from his father. There's Xana and the memories I was given of her with a kiss. There's Washo, connected to that brain of the matriarch and the knife he placed in my back. There's Welker and his letter to his son. And there's Ari . . . there's Ari . . .*

I pour the last of my intention into the blade, and I trust. Metal connects with rock, and I touch down on the moon. I open my eyes and, floating near me, is a feathery, rainbow leaf of Ashvattha. *Caught in the current of atmosphere between the worlds?* I whisper a silent "thanks" and crawl with the last breath I have into the cavern below.

It is a week before the orbit of the Morrigan moon passes the atmosphere of Albion again to receive the life-giving air from her sister world. In return for what the moon takes, she gives back the gift of her nitrogen. A densely oxygenated planet like Albion or Eruland would cause fire to burn uncontrollably, never ceasing, were it not for the moon, balancing out the equation. It is a delicate cosmic symbiosis.

The few remaining sisters and smiths, led by the monk in his brown robes, offer silent prayers beneath the gaze of Orc. We then carry the shrouded bodies of the fallen out of the cavern up to the surface. We tether ourselves to anchors and gently lift the fallen to the heavens where they float, carried by the current of the corridor to the forest world below.

"Good-bye, Whistler," Tol says. "You were kind of crazy, and you spoke in rhymes, but you were a good friend for a long time. I know you knew that this was coming. I can only think that you were okay with that in the end." He chokes on the last word as he looks at me. I nod to him. "We'll do what we can to make it right. That's it. So long, little fairy." He gives her a slight push into the sky. The white-shrouded body floats away. "Doc, I'm going to go prepare the ship, if that's okay?"

I nod. Tol puts on his hat and heads over to Perdiccus's Taoan starcraft, which he has recovered from the planet below. I look over my shoulder at the monk, who, with several of the Shin sisters, releases the body of the abbess into the gravity. I cannot see beneath the shadow of his hood, but I make out a gentle shake of his shoulders. He has lost someone he loved deeply. *It is natural to weep,* I think. The small group of sisters silently return to the stairwell that leads back to the subterranean monastery, and I approach my friend.

"Their bodies will find the forest," the monk says to me quietly. He waits by the entrance to the cavern. "Where will you go now, Edmon?"

"I don't know. If my friend had not returned, if I didn't feel that someone I cared about was in danger, I could have stayed here."

"That's not your destiny." The monk smiles. Then, "You've taken a personal vow never to kill, yet you've reformed your father's sword. The sword is a weapon, an instrument of death. How are you going to use it?"

It's a good question, a question I've asked myself. I speak honestly, and the words come. "A sword can also be a powerful symbol for people to rally behind. A symbol of justice and strength. It's part of a story, an idea, an extension of the man who wields it. That's how I'll use it." The monk nods, seemingly satisfied by my answer. "It's also a hell of a door opener," I add. I see a faint smile beneath the shadow of his hood, and it is good to know that he still can feel some mirth amid all this sadness.

"And your foster brother who blazes a path of destruction across the Fracture and sent this assassin to find you." It's not a question he asks.

"You think I should face him," I answer.

"It doesn't matter what I think, only what you do. I know it is simply a choice you will face or not."

"What about you?" I ask. "You could come with us."

The monk smiles. "This is my tribe. I've known no home but here. And I've traveled farther than many simply staying where I am and knowing myself through their eyes and words. Now that the abbess is gone, the sisters and the smiths of Albion both will need help to rebuild. My place is here." He takes a step into the darkness.

"Wait." I call him back to the light for one last second, not sure of how else to say good-bye. "You once asked me why it was that I never sought to heal my voice. The truth was I wasn't ready to let go of all the pain I've endured. I know that now, but why have you not sought to heal the scars and burns you've suffered?"

He slowly peels back his hood, and I am confronted with his glacial blue eyes and bisected face. "My disfigurement is not the result of burns or some horrific accident," he says. "I was born this way. Your voice was restored because it was who you were that was taken from you. But this face is who I am and who I will always be."

My brow furrows with question.

"The world I come from abhors malady and physical deformity. Babes born with such defects as mine are given to feed the flames of great fires. My mother died in childbirth, and my father, a noble of that world, could not bear to lose me, too. Rather than allow me to be murdered, he sent me far away. Here, to be raised by the smiths of Albion."

My mind flashes to the last conversation I had with my father. He revealed to me that I was not his eldest born son. There was another, Edvaard, who had been born misshapen. My father sent the child away before he could be taken by the Census. I remember the anger I felt, the utter shame that my father expressed deep love for this brother I had never known, yet had treated me as an object of contempt. I never knew where he had sent the child, and in my twelve years of wandering the Fracture, I never found him.

I meet the monk's ice-blue eyes. *Our father's eyes*. Of course. It was how this monk knew that the siren sword was originally crafted not for me, but for my father. It was how he knew my name before I was ever able to speak it aloud.

He smiles and turns again toward the darkness.

"Edvaard," I call. He pauses with recognition of the name. "Before our father died, he told me that your smile lit up the world for him. He told me that he loved you."

The monk's shoulders rise then fall with deep exhalation. "Go in peace, son of Leontes," he says. He steps into the shadows of the tunnel. I know I'll not see him again.

CHAPTER 22

The Prodigal Son

> The prodigal son is the humble man who accepts his faults and insecurities. He returns to his father's home with nothing, having sat beneath the World Tree. He opens himself to what may come, knowing how wasteful he was in the past.
>
> —Ovanth, *A Practical Reading of the Arcana*

"She's coming up," the pilot informs me as he flips some overhead switches, adjusts his stovepipe hat, then digs his hands back into the gloves of the flight harness. *Tol Sanctun actually piloting a starship capably? Things have definitely changed since my sojourn.*

I plot the trajectory toward the nearest Fracture Point. The Celt system is flush with gaseous worlds, solid moons, and various asteroids. It's not a simple matter to work with the calculators to skirt through an asteroid belt, past the star, and toward open space where the tear in the dark matter awaits. Technical skills were never my strong suit, though the Taoan design of the ship makes it simpler for me. I'm thankful for Teacher Michio's astrophysics class.

I swivel my chair toward Tol Sanctun in the harness. His face is stone. We broke atmo from Morrigan hours ago, and nary a word has passed between us. I am mulling the events of the last week since Perdiccus's attack on the monastery and the subsequent revelations, and he, the consequence of his choices, including the death of a beloved friend. This next moment may be difficult but must be broached.

"So, Tol. You threw in with my enemies in exchange for a starship to find me. You pulled me back from obscurity because you received a message from your father and a rhyming clairvoyant. Where is it we are going exactly?"

"I wish I knew," he mutters. "Somehow, I thought you'd have the answer, Doctor Batman."

I take a deep breath, letting the feelings of anger run through me and then pass over. Tol was desperate to find me and answer the call of his father. He did not anticipate all the death caused by his intention to help.

"At least you're talking to me," he says. "I like that new voice of yours."

"I can't explain it exactly," I admit. "I think there was something about the World Tree. It unlocked some things I was holding on to, allowed me to let them go."

"Yeah, wouldn't that be nice for us all?" Tol mutters bitterly.

"Tol—"

"No, no, I like it. You sound . . . I don't know. It's like who you're supposed to be. I guess I'm just not used to it."

"Tol, we still have a lot to do," I say. "Why don't you start at the beginning?"

Tol tells his story.

"I followed Xana's orders and took Whistler into a gel pod. I watched as Welker ran interference with the stingers. The last thing I saw was the *Lamb* break apart under heavy fire when Whistler and I were swept into the Fracture. I swear I thought you all had died, Doctor Batman. If I had known . . ." I merely nod, urging Tol to continue. "On the other side of the point, I used my knowledge of the shipping lanes to air thrust the pod toward an area with a high probability of being discovered by a passing freighter or ship. It helps when you have a clairvoyant assisting you. At least for self-confidence," he adds. "I activated the pod's distress signal and filled the capsule with stasis gel. Two days later, a junk hauler did find us and picked us up. I told the crew that Whistler and I were fortune hunters, who'd found caches of hidden artifacts underneath the surface of the old empire's lost homeworld. I promised that if they were able to return us to Market, I'd take them to Miral and make them rich. They agreed, until they started noticing some missing stuff . . ."

"You were stealing."

"It's a habit, okay?" he replies indignantly. "By the time we hit Market, the junk dealers had decided to turn me in to the local constabulary. Market still had a warrant for some minor thefts and a firearms incident in the Leaky Engine. It wasn't too bad," he relates. "Place to sleep, free meals for both me and the blue hair while we awaited arraignment. That changed right quick, though. Within two months, the forces of Phaestion, the so-called emperor of Tao, swept into the system. Market rolled over without a word."

For the first time since the fall of Miral, Market is now under the jurisdiction of an Inter-Fractural government, I think.

"The corridors were soon crawling with Taoan blackguards," Tol says. "Shiny armor, faceless helms, shields, and pistols. Everyone was told that if Market did not resist, no one would come to harm. They lied. They immediately hit the enclave of the spypsies . . ."

Phaestion wanted to be a conqueror from the day he came to my room on the Isle of Bone to train with me. "Violence drives civilization," he said. He fabricated a pretext for his conquest and fomented a hatred for all the "nonpure" races of the Fracture to galvanize the disenfranchised populace of Tao to serve his bloody agenda. *Always take terrorists at their word,* I think. "Spypsies are a convenient target for them," I acknowledge to Tol. The Nicnacians, with their strange religious beliefs and slight, genetically modified bodies, are abhorrent to the Taoans, who consider strength and natural birth moral imperatives.

The irony—what the people of Tao don't know—is that Phaestion himself is a designer organic, cloned from his father and genetically altered to be superhuman.

"They flew into the enclave on screamer packs." Tol's voice shakes. "They co-opted the communications modules throughout the station and played the assault in real time on the PA system. Those hubs and halls are mostly kids, Doctor Batman, kids like Washo who were just on the station for their Rapzis. You could hear the screams. They slaughtered them all . . ." His voice trails off for a moment. "Weeks later when they opened those umbilicals for others to enter, you could see the blood smeared across the bulkheads. They didn't clean it up. They wanted everyone to see what happened."

Tol depresses a spot on his wrist and opens his palm, playing for me a holographic recording of Phaestion's address to the newly conquered world.

"We're greeted across the Fracture as liberators. Market, we come to free you as well. We'll send back these spypsies who've invaded our space and have stolen our wealth and our livelihoods. Our economies will grow like never before. We will reestablish the greatness of our pure human race once again with your help . . ."

"What is he even talking about?" Tol asks, flabbergasted.

I grimace. "He's creating a narrative that paints conquest as a rebellion for freedom."

"Freedom from what? The spypsies? They're peaceful, religious nuts and keep to themselves."

I feel a phantom pain in my kidney, a reminder of Washo's knife twisting inside me. "Someone has to be blamed," I say coldly.

"Doc, I know that Los is coming down on us all. We have to stop it or this universe . . . Did you know all communications have been lost along the Brachial Corridor?"

I think of the location of Miral. "You believe it's the shadow," I say.

"No one is even paying attention!" he vents with frustration. "They're all too worried about these Taoans. And I don't blame them, Doc. Say we are able to even stop this Los thing. So what, if your buddies run the show? We can stop faceless darkness from devouring the Fracture, only to leave it for human evil to exploit?"

"I don't know," I admit. *I had my opportunity to stop Phaestion once, long ago, and I couldn't do it. Now? There's no army in the entire Fracture that is strong enough to face his. Even if he were baited into some sort of one-on-one fight, I'm not sure there is any one individual strong enough to beat him. Not even Xana. Even if Phaestion were removed from power, what would happen to the war machine, the fledgling empire that has seen the spread of millions of Taoans to these conquered worlds? Politically, it would be chaos. Things can't just go back to the way they were.* "The message, Tol. Go on with what happened," I urge.

"The Taoans released all who were held in detention," he continues. "A year had passed since I'd seen the crew of the *Bentley*. With nowhere to go, no ship to call my own, and Market on lock-down and being turned into a staging ground for a Taoan assault on the rest of the Fracture, I turned over a bad leaf."

"Thieving, drinking, gambling, flimflamming," I surmise.

"You name it," he echoes. "Ended up in the clink more times than you can count. Only Whistler kept me from ending it all. Her constant rhyming and yammering made me feel like, I don't know, there was something else meant for me. Why else would she keep talking to me? Anyway, every time I was thrown in lockup, they just ended up letting me go. Apparently, the Taoans were more concerned with imprisoning enemies of the state. Eventually, Whistler starts singing 'Albion, Albion, Albion' to the point where I'm like, 'Shut up, Whistler!' Ya know?" He sighs. "Almost two years past our parting, I decide to return to my personal security locker, and there, I find a data card inside."

He pulls a ring from a drawer in his rib cage and places it in another slot built into his wrist. His palm projects a hologram of an older man in tattered garb. "Hey, kid," the recording of the old man says. Immediately I see the resemblance between the man and the erstwhile navigator of the *Bentley*. "Long time, no see, right? Sorry about that, but I guess bygones is bygones and all. At least I hope so. Look, Tol, I wanted to keep you out of this, but I'm in a bit of a pickle and can't really turn to anyone else for help. You know that I've studied the origins of the Fracture my whole life. You know my theory that there was an ancient race of beings that created the system of wormholes. Well, I've found them. Or at least I've found the people who have found them. Tol, I'm in a bad sitch here . . ."

The hologram of the old man looks over his shoulder as if he's being watched. "It's all I've done to smuggle this message out of the cell they're holding me in. Hopefully, it will get to you on Market. Tol, something big is coming, something that could destroy this entire universe. I can't say just yet, but, Tol, you gotta hurry. I know, I know, you might be a little boy lost, but remember I got the experience. Look it up." The man turns his back to the recorder.

I'm wondering what this has to do with Ari when another familiar voice comes through the sound, hissing and slithering. "And what is it you're doing exactly, Mister Sanctun?"

"Talousla Karr! So good to see you. Me? Oh nothing, I was just, you know, talking to myself . . ."

The holographic winks out. My muscles tense at the sound of the man who seems to have his insidious fingertips in all of this.

"Los, Doc! He has to be talking about the shadow that we encountered on Miral. What else could it be?" Tol is excited and desperate.

"But, Tol, you told me you thought your father had perished years ago," I say.

"I know," he admits. "What if this was Dad's last message, though, and it took this long to get to me? The last time we spoke, I told him that I hated him, that he was wrong about everything. But what if he wasn't? What if he was actually right? I had to do something! This is my last chance to make it good between us, even if he isn't here anymore, Doc. I had to do something, and with Whistler's incessant rhyming . . . then there was this . . ."

Tol pulls the tarot card that I gave him back on Miral out of his coat. The quintessence card now flashes between symbols. *A man beneath a tree? A black robed figure of death?* I cannot say.

"Candlemas is gone," Tol confirms. "All traces of Tag have disappeared from the Black Rose Path. The withdrawal epidemic is killing off millions. It's practically doing half the work of the Taoans for them. But—"

"Something of the AI's sentience remains if the cards are still working," I interrupt. "What does that have to do with anything?"

"The card jogged my memory. Doctor Batman, I thought!" Tol exclaims. "The serious sword of Albion. I knew you were my ticket off Market. If you were still alive, maybe you could help. I spent months studying piloting manuals, but I still needed a ship. I knew you were numero uno on the Taoans' hit list, so when I was ready, it wasn't too hard to land myself back in jail and start telling everyone and anyone who would listen that I knew you. Eventually, it worked! I didn't think it would attract one of Emperor Phallus's personal generals, though." His voice grows somber as he remembers the outcome of his actions. "At the time, I thought I had nothing else to lose. I guess I was wrong."

I'm trying to make sense of it all—*What in the fathoms was Tol's father doing in the renegade spypsy's company?* After the encounter with the forces of Urizen above Miral, it's clear that Talousla Karr has been working with Ari's mother. *How does it all connect?* "We're lucky Perdiccus didn't bring any more soldiers with him," I say.

"She was with me through it all—Whistler. She was a good girl. I wish she could have had more life." We sit in the quiet of the vast for a moment. "So, here we are," Tol says.

"Here we are indeed," I agree. "With no idea where we are going or what to do once we get there."

Tol shakes his head. "Dad had to mean something by his message. Whistler had to mean something in her rhymes that sent me to you. Come on, Doctor Batman, think!" he pleads.

Really, I'm at a loss. It's as if we have disparate pieces of a puzzle with no way to link them together. "Play your father's message again. Maybe there's something in it, some clue you didn't hear the first time," I say.

Tol follows my instruction. The holographic imager built into his wrist alights, and we watch the playback again. "Stop!" I call out. "Rewind. Play that last part again."

Tol squints in confusion but does as I ask.

"I know, I know, you might be a little boy lost, but remember I got the experience. Look it up . . . ," Stephen Sanctun's voice rings out.

"Pause it," I command, and Tol halts the playback again. "What does that mean?" I ask.

Tol shrugs, not understanding.

"Is that something you two would say to each other? You're a little boy lost, but he has experience? What does he mean, look it up? Look what up, where?"

"You got me, Doc," Tol says, baffled. "It all sounds like nonsensical poetry to me. Dad never turned a phrase like that."

It's as if it's some kind of code, but without the cypher, there's no way to interpret it. *If only Ari were here,* I think. *She would be able to solve it . . .*

But she is here! I remember. Or at least some trace of her consciousness or voice somehow. My mind flashes back to a memory aboard the *Tyger* as we sailed out of Nonthera. "Tyger, Tyger, burning bright, in the forests of the night . . ."

"What immortal hand or eye could frame thy fearful symmetry," Tol finishes the sentence. "That was the poem both Ari and I knew," Tol says, nodding.

"I spent months partly looking through the scriptures of the smiths on Albion. A lot of it talking about Urizen and Orc and a bunch of other sort of dualistic concepts. A lot of it sounded like that poem you both spoke. Who wrote it?"

"It was a man from Ancient Earth," Tol realizes, as if he, too, senses some connection. "William Blake. Dad had an old book of his or some reading that survived the Fractural Collapse."

"What happened to it?" I ask.

"When I found out Dad had died, I went to his storage locker on Market, cleaned it out. I couldn't exactly carry around all his things, and I didn't want to keep paying for the locker, so I had all his manuscripts digitized and put with my other files of Ancient Earth culture."

"Do you still have them?" I ask excitedly.

"Totally!" Tol echoes my sentiment.

"Pull it up!" I say. "Cross-reference William Blake, Albion, Little Boy Lost, and Experience . . ."

"I'm already on it!" he says as a metallic sheen glosses over the surface of his artificial eyes. They roll back and forth as he scans words. "Doc, this is bananas. It's all here, Albion, Los, Urizen, and a whole bunch of other wacky stuff. How is it that some poet from Ancient Earth, who died thousands of years ago, has all this in his writings? Was he some sort of divine prophet?"

"Or were his words merely used as the basis of some Post Fractural religion?" I wonder aloud, thinking about Ari and her mother and the revelation that she could be thousands of years old. "Let's just focus on the message your father sent," I say.

"Got it," Tol says. "'A Little Boy Lost,' *Songs of Experience*, by William Blake. Here . . . 'The weeping child could not be heard, the weeping parents wept in vain: They stripped him to his little shirt, and bound him in an iron chain, And burned him in a holy place where many had been burned before; the weeping parents wept in vain. Are such things done on Albion's shore?'"

I'm reminded of Edvaard, my father saving him from the fires of the Pavaka.

"There is something funky about the file, Doc," Tol says. "When I look at the coding of the digitized page image, there's a sort of nonsensical tag on the ending."

"Can you cut and paste it into a separate file?" I ask.

"Already done—"

"This is Stephen Sanctun. Tol. Son." The holographic image of Tol's father leaps to life on his wrist imager.

"Dad!" Tol says as if hoping the recording will speak back to him.

"At least I sure hope it's you that figured out my little message. And if it's not, I hope this falls on friendly ears. I hid the program pretty good. Tol, if you're watching this, it probably means I'm dead, kaput, headed for the long nap in the sky . . ."

Tol's face drops, but he says nothing. It's not that he's surprised; he knew his father was gone. It's the opening of an old wound. I know what that's like. My mother died when I was a boy, taken by my father's hand. I never got to thank her for who she tried to help me become.

"Sucks, don't it?" Stephen says. Tol nods. "Look, Tol, don't worry nothin' about it. We all gotta go. I knew that the adventure I was embarking on was a one-way trip. The fact you're getting this, if it is you, means that all isn't lost, and there's still time to stop what's going to happen. I know you didn't believe me, that you thought your old man was full of baloney, but Tol, or whomever is watching . . ." His son looks up into the face of his father. "You gotta trust me this time. You gotta do this because I can't anymore. *Capische?*"

"*Capische*, Daddio," he says quietly.

The old man smiles and takes a deep breath. "So you probably got a lot swirling around in that thinking cap. I'll see if I can give you the straight shoot. I was always interested in the Fracture—where it came from, who built it, and why. You gotta believe if I didn't think it was the most important, I wouldn't have schlepped you all over the cosmos with Rollinson, looking for any clue of Ancient Earth I could find . . ."

"Dad always thought it was aliens," Tol says to me over his shoulder.

"I always thought it was aliens. Well, Tol, turns out I was wrong about that one," the old man admits. "But that's a mite better than what those yahoos at the Sophia Academy come up with—a natural consequence of the interaction between black holes and dark matter! Pfft."

It's hard for me to believe Tol's tale that the bedraggled man in the hologram was actually a professor at the Sophia Academy on Lyria once. I myself dreamed of going there to learn opera long before I lost my voice. I touch my throat now. *I'm in no position to judge who is and who isn't worthy, that's for sure.*

"Okay, so it wasn't aliens. It was us. It was humans. Well, future humans. Well, not future exactly. Actually past humans, I think, but a future version of us. What I mean to say is that the Fracture was made by us, which is why it has so many qualities attuned to our specific needs—relativistic, almost instantaneous travel to star systems with compatible gravity, starlight, planets with atmospheric pressure, you name it. We even left our own footprint as it were by making it into a humanoid shape; that is if you connected the points on a two-dimensional plane . . ."

He is right about that. Stellar cartographers long ago determined the corridors of the Fracture corresponded closely to a human skeletal structure; that gave rise to the names of the major corridors and the hundreds of tangential and ancillary routes.

"I already had developed my theories before you were born. I believe our ancestors knew the same information that I drew upon to formulate them. Problem is the gap in the historical record makes it impossible to tell exactly what they understood. We know they discovered the Fracture. I suspected that in order to do so, they were already using or merging with artificial intelligence. Then it all went into the shitter. The Fracture Point to Ancient Earth collapsed, and the colonies that humanity had seeded outside of the Sol system were cut off from their mother world. But, just as suddenly, you have, within a thousand years, the rise of Miral, which breaks out as the new center of human activity. A thousand years is no time at all, cosmically speaking, a mere flicker of a candle flame. For a whole society to spring up with an entire societal, political, and religious structure superseding all others past? Miralian society seems fabricated almost entirely from whole cloth, bearing no resemblance or continuity to the dominant cultures of Earth from right before the fall."

"It's true," Tol agrees emphatically. "All those things that I found, the stuff I've saved in my pockets and data banks, Joss Whedon's *Firefly*, eBay, Mariah Carey . . . No one in the Fracture knows this stuff. Or at least very few. It's like Miral chucked everything from their past and started from scratch. Where did it all go?"

"Some of this is beside the point," Tol's father relays. "It's the danger that matters, what the Miralians were trying to do, what their culture was driving them toward. Rollinson booked a cargo and ferry for us to a new world, Tao. I don't know if you remember?" Tol's father asks.

My ears perk up. *Tol, his father, and Rollinson were on Tao?*

Tol nods. "I remember, Daddio."

My mind flashes suddenly to my childhood and my meeting with the Grand Wusong. Strangers from off-world visited the court that day.

"One of our passengers was this spypsy, only he wasn't just a regular old space gypsy. He was from the lost tribe . . ."

"Lost tribe?" Tol shakes his head in question.

"The seventh arc," I think out loud. "The one that broke away from the main fleet of Armada."

"Six arcs of Armada escaped the destruction of Miral that we know of. But there was a seventh ship that broke from the main fleet. The spypsies never speak of it. It disappeared into the blackness of the vast due to a faulty matriarch pilot. Talousla Karr revealed to me that Urizen herself was aboard that seventh ship, the one they call Fuzon," says the hologram. "She took command and set sail for Ancient Earth."

"Holy shizzle!" Tol presses his palms to his temples.

"Maybe he told me because I intrigued him. I know more about this than most. Maybe he knew no one would believe me if I told them anyway. Who knows? But Urizen is not a fictional goddess. She is a real, live, breathing woman, a survivor of Ancient Earth."

"This we already know," I mutter.

"Ari's Mom," Tol agrees for emphasis. "The question of course is how? She's not just old. She's *really* old."

"Tol, whatever our ancestors did that collapsed the Fracture to Ancient Earth let something else in. Some sort of slow leak of entropic matter."

It's not slowly leaking anymore, I think. *We pushed the opening wider.*

"Tol . . ." Stephen Sanctun's voice quivers. "You left because I wasn't a good father. I didn't give you a normal life. I know that. I'm sorry. I loved you since the day you were born. Your mama, Desiree, died in childbirth because of me. It was my fault for getting kicked out of the academy on Lyria, for bringing her to the wilderness, hunting artifacts, no hospital." The man weeps, and I hear Tol's breath catching as well. "Part of me couldn't settle down because there was too much pain for me. I wanted a fresh start for us both. I'm sorry we were never in one place. I'm sorry we spent your childhood traipsing all over the Fracture. But, Tol, I always loved you. If I could do it all over again . . . I just wish I didn't believe what I believed. Tol, I wish I had been wrong. I'm gone now, son, but this thing, this shadow that's coming, it's not going away."

"Dad," Tol whispers. Tears roll down his cheeks.

"Talousla Karr told me those years before." The Sanctun in the hologram reins in his emotions. "He said the Kaliyuga was upon us. The destruction of this universe that would bring about the next one. It started when our ancestors created a tear in the fabric of space-time and sent something through. Now, it's slowly pulling more of our space through and replacing it with entropic matter. Eventually both universes will be sucked into each other. Talousla Karr welcomed it, like it was some grand experiment he wanted to see played out. I don't know if Urizen or the Mira were intending to stop it, but Talousla Karr is definitely not. He wants it to happen. He's started growing an entire army of designer organics to make sure no one will stop him. They're only children now, but with growth acceleration, in a few years, they'll be the largest military force in the Fracture. But there's still time . . ."

This message was recorded years ago, maybe decades, when whatever process was occurring was at least at a truncated rate.

"The Lyrian moon of Oberus, Tol. That's where their factory is. That's where Karr is cloning soldiers. He's going to somehow widen the passage between the universes, bring forth the Kaliyuga . . ."

It's already happened, I realize. *What they did in the Temple of the Matriarchs . . . They've accelerated everything!* I think with dread.

"Tol, I've seen the place for myself. Even if you had all the militaries of all the worlds of the Fracture united, you couldn't stop them. But that's what you have to do. I don't know how, but . . . Tol, I love you," Stephen Sanctun says, the message suddenly ceasing.

"Dad!" My friend's voice rings out in the small cockpit of the ship. We both sit for a beat, and then Tol suddenly and furiously unstraps from the pilot's harness.

"Tol?" I try to keep my voice calm, but it sounds harsh to my own ears.

He quickly slaps a palm to the cockpit exit and pushes off into the small cargo compartment. I unstrap from the navigation station and head after him. I find him floating, one arm outstretched to the wall, doubled over, panting heavily. "Tol?"

"Leave me alone, Doc!" He sobs uncontrollably, then vomits. I want to turn away from the sour smell, but I force myself to go to him. I put a hand on his back as his guts spill into the air. Fortunately, the cleaning filters suck his sickness into their waste reclamation quickly. *Death is not pretty, the despair of those left behind, even less so.*

"It's okay," I whisper to him. He snorts and wretches even as there's nothing left inside to expel. "Are you all right?" I ask softly.

He turns to the wall and starts beating on it with his fists. "Leave me alone! Leave me alone! Leave me alone!"

I let him pound the wall until he exhausts himself. He stops struggling, and his body falls limp with utter fatigue. He turns and then embraces me. He sobs into my shoulder. "They're gone," he says. "They're gone . . ." Over and over, he repeats the words.

"I know," I say.

We drift alone in the stars, but at least we are together. I hold him close for a long time.

CHAPTER 23

The Home

> Home and hearth is where all wanderers set out from and where they must return to understand themselves. It is the place of past traumas and secrets. It may no longer hold security or comfort, which is a sign that the safe 'home' is a place one must create even more than a place one has been.
>
> —Ovanth, *A Practical Reading of the Arcana*

Tol and I skirt the high white walls of the mansion that stands atop the Palatine Hill of the capital city of Prospera on Lyria. We are not safe.

"Don't worry, Doc," Tol reassures me. "I've gotten into places way more fortified than this."

I look up at the opulent Lyrian household, its white walls and towers capped with golden minarets. This is the place where Ari grew up. It's a beautiful place but cold in its emptiness. We've come here because while Tol's father told us that Talousla Karr's soldier factory is on the moon of Oberus, the moon is a big place. Without definite coordinates or a company name, we'd be searching blindly. However, we know that Karr was in league with Ari's mother, and her mansion on Lyria, by contrast, was easy to track down. So we risk attracting the occupying Taoan forces and certain death if discovered on the hunch that there might be a clue to the factory's exact location inside the Lazarus domicile.

"It's not whether we are able to break in that concerns me," I whisper to Tol. "It's whether we can escape without being caught."

It's whether coming here is worth the effort that has me looking over my shoulder . . . that and the distinct feeling we are being watched. But I don't voice these thoughts.

This whole city, indeed the whole region of space is crawling with the armies of Phaestion and the Pantheon of Tao. I know what will happen if I'm apprehended, but I wonder if Tol knows what being in my company would mean if he were.

"The shadow is coming for us anyway, Doc. Nets are blaming loss of the Brachial communications and now the Radial to a shift in the Fracture Points. Bull! You and I know it's not that. We're all in this now. No choice but to head into the lion's den."

He's right. Whatever Los is, whatever this entropic force is, it will devour all of the universe. Lyria, Tao—it won't matter. We have to try and stop it. Right now, that means being here.

The nets indicated the Lazarus family lineage traces back to the founding of Prospera at the end of the Miralian Empire's heyday. The names of a number of Lazarus matriarchs grace the ledgers. It is likely that Ari's mother was at least some of these identities. Perhaps more likely that Ari is not the first daughter or child of her kind, merely the latest in a long string of Urizen offspring.

"Aha!" Tol exclaims as he runs his fingers over the smooth white wall. My brow furrows in question. "The security door is blended seamlessly into the wall," he explains. "It appears to be a fingerprint lock. Touch the wall here"—my friend presses his hand to the wall—"and the door will appear. Open sesame!"

Nothing happens. I gather my cloak about me and step forward to take a closer look. Both Tol and I are robed from head to toe, posing as Zhao monks come to study at the Sophia Academy. The ruse took some doing. We made a stop on Thera and traded our Taoan fighter for new identity subdermals. Fortunately, the sale of the vehicle was more than enough to book passage to occupied Lyria. Phaestion's mentality has always been more about conquest than building or administration. That sentiment has transferred over to his occupation here. The soldiers of Tao stationed in the capital are more bored than anything. They are dangerous and unpredictable but also less efficient and easier to slip past.

A boom sounds in the distance.

"What was that?" Tol whispers.

"A bomb," I hiss.

"Resistance?" Tol asks.

A plume of smoke rises from the city below and clouds over the dawn sun. From our vantage, the white-and-gold roofs and spires of the city below are quickly dulled by haze. *How I wanted to come here in my youth and climb the marble steps of the opera house. Now, I come in the cloak of a burglar. I should be helping the people fight the invaders.*

We've already seen Taoan soldiers arrest teenagers and beat an old woman in the streets. Tol had to stop me from interfering. Again, he was right. We can't help them directly, not yet. Shouts of soldiers and fire brigades can be heard in the distance. *We should hurry.* Again, I sense eyes on us.

The Palatine is empty. Her tree-lined avenues vacant. The opulent mansions stand as silent revenants to the culling of the planet's ruling class. Behind this mansion's walls was where Ari was raised in seclusion. I close my eyes. I focus on the tips of my fingers, feeling every bump and imperfection of the retaining wall. I may not have the artificial oculars of Tol, but my training with Faria has given me other attributes. The wall here is fashioned as a passage that will part with the right kind of key, a key we do not have. The towers of the structure rise behind this high border. I could leap over its height, but there would be no way to bring Tol with me.

"We probably should have brought a rope, huh?" Tol shrugs.

We've left our valuables in a locker at the port in order to pass through various security checkpoints throughout the city. *What I wouldn't give for my sword right now,* I think.

"The security panel is inside the wall here," I tell him. "If I get you in, you think you can hack it?"

"Oh yeah." Tol nods. "Shouldn't be an ish. But how are you going to get me—?"

I summon the vibrational energies within my belly. I feel them rise up into my heart, my shoulders, down my arms, to my fingertips. I pull my hands back, and then with a violent exhalation of breath and sound, I plunge my hands into the wall. My fingers penetrate the stone and metal, finding the seam of the door. I pull with all my strength, prying it open. I try not to scream as the rumble of the mechanism's internal machinery grinds, and I part the passage.

"Holy shizzle!" Tol exclaims.

"Go!" I grunt as I widen the entry. Tol slips by me and into the gardens inside. I position myself between the heavy door panels. The gears inside the door groan as I hold it open with my back and foot. "Hurry, Tol!" I feel the crushing weight of the doors threatening to snap shut with me between them.

"Uh, okay, this is a not as simple as I would have thought," Tol mutters.

"Figure it out!" I growl.

"Uh, okay, okay, um . . ." His fingers dance over a keypad. Then he raises a fingerless-gloved hand, and I watch as tiny panels on his fingertips peel back like little doors revealing smooth metallic panels. He places his fingers on the pad, and I can see that whatever software he has cycles through an endless combination of prints in hopes that the security system will recognize one. "Nope. Negatory. Uh-huh. Next . . . ," he mutters.

Only personnel with appropriate access can open the thing. "Ari!" I grunt. "Try Ari's prints." Tol, having served aboard the *Bentley* for years, will have gathered whatever information he could have from the crew to unlock their stuff. "Wait! No!" *Ari's prints won't work. She was forced to remain in the mansion. She had to escape her mother's confinement in order to find Xana aboard the* Bentley. *Think, Edmon!* I admonish myself. "Xana!" I cry out as the doors close in on me. *Unlike her charge, Xana as a loyal protector was allowed to leave the compound.* "Use Xana's prints!"

"Got it!" Tol exclaims.

The doors slide open, and I fall to the ground panting. Tol helps me stand. "That was close!" he exclaims happily.

"Yeah," I mutter in agreement. "Better close it up, lest a patrol comes by."

Though the Palatine was one of the first districts of Lyria cleared by Phaestion's forces, patrols roam the area looking for stragglers or looters. At first, I was surprised that Phaestion didn't claim the hill for his nobles, but I learned the new emperor of Tao has continued to espouse an ideology that eschews the pomp and finery of the "lesser races." He has even gutted the grand opera house, saying that such art serves no practical purpose and has instead claimed it for his own personal throne room.

The mansion where Ari grew up is certainly beautiful. The roses and fruit trees of the expansive garden grounds are a bit overgrown but colorful and lush. The automated grounds-keeping system has functioned within acceptable parameters it appears. Sculpted fountains spout water, and the gentle bubbling adds to a nearby songbird's chirping. The place feels untouched by time and the strife that engulfs the city below. *This is where Urizen, the architect of the universe, would want her child to be born and raised.* In my mind's eye, I glimpse a little red-haired girl running along the neatly manicured grass and into the miniature vineyard that lays just past the fountain.

This is where I was sheltered, Ari's memory whispers to me. *And where I was imprisoned.* I feel the recollection of her lips touching mine.

"Everything all right, Doc?"

"Let's see what we can find," I grumble.

I lead him into the house through a massive mechanized kitchen and into a foyer with a grand staircase. Its layout is not unlike that of the manse I grew up in on the Isle of Bone, but its opulence makes my home on Bone seem like a rustic apartment. A grand staircase leads to the higher levels, and the giant marble columns are almost ominous in their ostentation. Vacancy gives the place a ghostly, intimidating feeling.

"A wonder she didn't go mad here," Tol whispers.

By her passing comments and her faint memories, I believe Ari grew up here practically alone. She never knew a father. Her mother left her as a child. She was given a mentor, Skaya, and then a playmate in Xana. Both were to be watchers more than family. I'm not sure either truly understood her, especially with her burgeoning linguistic capabilities.

"It seems like the loneliest place I can imagine," Tol adds.

"Except there's someone here," I whisper. I can hear their heartbeat several floors up, predatory, lying in wait. I gesture for Tol to keep silent. We take tentative steps up the winding staircase. Tol trips behind me and crashes into the floor. The whole mansion seems to shake with the echoing sound of his bumbling. I glare at him.

"Sorry," he says sheepishly.

Some things never change, I think, shaking my head. We continue into a large hallway lined with doors. Each creak of the floorboards or rustle of breeze echoes eerily. Here, the heartbeat is louder. We are getting close.

"Look," Tol whispers. He points to portraits hanging along the walls of the corridor. Each depiction is made in vivid aquagraphic, a technology native to my home of Tao. Artists' renderings of faces swirl in frames that dispense sheets of water. Light projected onto the sheets display three-dimensional images. "Ari's ancestors. Olivia, Viola, Titania, Elia . . ."

"Ahania," I add, looking at the last portrait. *Or is it the first?* Impossible to tell, but this is the woman who claimed to be Ari's mother. "Notice anything?" I ask.

"They've all got red hair?"

"And they're all women," I say.

"And they all look just like Ari?"

The clothing styles of each fiery-haired woman ranges from robes and armor to more baroque styles of petticoats and high collars, but there is no mistaking each depiction having the same cerulean eyes of our communications officer, Ariel Lazarus. One frame at the end of the hall remains empty.

"You think Urizen just made copies of herself over and over? Are they clones? Daughters?" Tol whispers.

Any of his guesses could be true, considering the fact that Talousla Karr is involved. Either way, Tol's chatter rings too loudly in this empty place, and the heartbeat that has waited for us has ceased. We arrive at the door at the end of the hall, where I last heard the sound. It is white and has the simple, antiquated technology of a knob. I look at Tol and press my finger to my lips as I open it . . .

The room is empty, small in comparison to the others in this place. A bunk bed is nestled in the corner, and a window overlooks the garden and the golden city below. Stuffed animals adorn the lower bunk while the top seems clean and bare. It is the room of a child. No, children, in fact, and it looks like it hasn't been touched in decades. I gaze out the window. The plume of smoke from the bomb earlier has withered to a faint trail. The sun rises slowly, approaching midday. A few spacecraft leave the Prosperan port and sail like blackbirds across the Lyrian sun.

This was the only view I had of the world. I dreamed of sailing away aboard a glittering rocket, a memory whispers. I smile sadly. I had similar dreams of wanderlust, and a daily reality of feeling trapped.

"This was Ari's room, Doc," Tol whispers. "And Xana's." He holds up two stuffed animals. Stitched into the bellies of the twin toys are the characters *A* and *X*.

The heartbeat I've been sensing is now louder, immediate, here in this room. I look up in time to see a dark figure plastered like a spider against the ceiling. It drops with frightening speed. I have barely a moment to thrust a kick at Tol, hurling him into one of the bunk beds and out of the way of the assailant.

The figure is upon me. I am pinned to the floor. Fists rain down on me. I cover up, trying to make sense of what is happening. I flip the attacker off me and roll to my feet. The creature, cloaked in swirling robes, leaps like a wraith off the wall and back at me. It slams me through the bedroom door.

"Doc!" Tol screams.

My opponent and I grip each other. I slam him against the wall. He counters the maneuver, hurling me. I crash into an aquagraphic portrait. I'm blasted by a thrusting kick and fly down the hallway. *I know that technique.*

The attacker comes for me. I run. *I need time to think, to develop a strategy.* I leap over the railing of the grand staircase. The assailant flies after me, catching me on the way down. Midair, we grip each other. The floor rushes to meet us. I twist at the last moment. Yet the cloaked figure does something unexpected and activates some kind of handheld remote, and the floor beneath us parts. *A trap door!*

"Doctor Batman!" Tol screams from the top of the stairs.

I sail into darkness beneath the mansion. My attacker reverses our positions once again. I slam into the ground. It is blackness here, but

I see with my other senses and roll upon impact, diffusing the force of the fall. I spin out from under my opponent. I crouch, sensing the cloaked figure across from me reaching for something, a weapon that rests against the wall. *My attacker is familiar with these surroundings.*

The ceiling closes above us, and overhead lights are switched on momentarily blinding me. It is the moment my attacker needs. A staff strikes me in the head, then sweeps me from my feet. Again I roll and find myself next to the weapon's rack. I clutch a staff as well. *I know this place, too,* I realize. I saw it in the memory Ari showed me.

We circle the training room mirroring each other. My cloaked enemy charges with a flurry of strikes. I'm pushed toward the edge of the training mat, but I counter blow for blow, gauging my enemy's skill. The style is brutal and efficient, utilizing strength and power. My opponent is too strong for me, but the technique is unartistic, developed for multiple assailants, not single combat. I see openings. The figure thrusts with the staff. I circle with the fluid movements my body has learned using the shaping tools of the smiths; my hand lashes out using the direct lines of Faria's Dim Mak. I catch the assailant with a pressure point strike right between the shoulder blades.

"Xana!" Tol shouts from the doorway, just as my opponent crashes to the ground.

"It's not Xana," I curse at Tol. "She's still under the mental trigger of Talousla Karr."

Xana rips the cloak off. She snarls like a wild creature and hurls herself at me again. It's all I can do to raise the staff in time to defend. I'm in full protection mode as she plows into me.

"Don't hurt her, Doc!" Tol screams.

"I don't think that will be a problem!" I shout back just before Xana's gauntleted fist slams into my chest. I duck another wild swing of her staff. Her eyes display anger, fear, and rage. Above Miral, Ari was able to break her free from Talousla Karr's hypnotic command, but now she has fallen to it completely. Xana is gone. Before me is a killing machine. She comes at me with such ferocity. Her staff impacts my own. It rattles me to my bones. *I won't survive this if I don't end her.*

She's still in there. Save her. You have to try, a voice whispers.

She leaps at me. I fall to the ground, the wind knocked from my lungs. I gasp for air as her fingers close around my throat. I summon vibrational energies within my body. They rise up, channeling along my internal meridians. All I need to do is unleash the strike, one touch to the side of her temple. *Save her,* Ari inside me implores. She's crushing my windpipe. I have only seconds left. Save myself or try to reach Xana—I cannot do both.

Xana will never to listen to Edmon Leontes. She wanted to protect Ari, and that meant keeping her from me. If I die, she'll kill Tol, too. We won't be able to stop Talousla Karr or Urizen. She'll kill me, and we'll never find Ari . . . Ari . . .

Let me speak through you, Edmon, she says. *This is what Candlemas showed us, Xana's greatest regret.*

"Who am I?" I say, gasping through the choke. "Who am I?" Ari's words come through, the words from her memory.

Xana's eyes widen. Her grip slackens. "You're . . . special. The things you know . . . you know so many things . . . ," she responds.

"Fight me," I whisper.

Xana leans back. Her hands go to her head as if she's battling a fog inside her mind.

"You won't be there to protect me forever. Fight me. Show me what to do," I say.

Xana screams, clutching her head. She falls back to the floor.

"Doc! What's happening?" Tol shouts from the doorway.

He rushes to me and helps me from the ground. I hold him back from helping Xana, too. "This is her battle," I say.

The warrior woman's body arcs in one final spasm. Then she lies still on the floor, panting softly like a wounded animal. Tol looks at me, frightened. I slowly approach and reach a gentle hand to Xana's shoulder. She flinches. "Xana," I whisper. "It's Edmon. Are you there?"

She turns, her dark eyes fearful. Then I see recognition flash. I see the little girl I encountered once in an arcology of Tao long ago. "Edmon . . ." Then her gaze hardens. "You're different," she says suspiciously.

I nod. "Feeling better?"

"Where am I?" she asks.

"The Lazarus mansion on Lyria," I reply.

"Xana's back!" Tol claps his hands, giddy.

She stands and takes in her surroundings. "The training room . . . Skaya, Talousla Karr . . . is this a dream?" She springs forward. I put a hand against her shoulder, stopping her. "Ari! They're coming for her. We have to—" She stops, realizing we are no longer above the skies of Miral. "How long have I been out?"

"Now that's a tricky question. Time is all relative, see," Tol quips.

"Shut up, Tol," Xana and I say in unison.

"Holy shizzle, you guys have no idea how happy you're making me right now!"

"Xana, we have to save Ari," I say. "We'll explain everything, but first, do you know any room or place here in this mansion that might hold records, information, computer files? Anything where Ahania Lazarus or Talousla Karr or Skaya might keep sensitive data?"

"This way," she says.

—

At the top of the stairwell in the highest spire of the mansion lies a door, thick, metal, coated with dark wood, and golden etchings. The door blends into the surroundings of the native Lyrian architecture, but the etchings are clearly of Miralian origin. Dust has gathered here unlike the rest of the mansion, which has been kept pristine by automated cleaning systems.

"Only Skaya ever had access. Can you open it?" Xana asks impatiently.

We stand over Tol, who kneels and examines the lock.

"Someone wakes up after years of a psycho slumber and just expects everything to fall neatly into place for her, huh?" Tol shakes his head.

"Enough chatter. The longer we linger, the more dangerous it gets," I remind them both. *Not only because of Tao's soldiers; Los is devouring worlds one by one.*

"Looks mimetic," Tol says, scratching his scruff.

"That means?" Xana asks impatiently.

"It means that it requires an electronic and spatial key that can mimic the properties of an ever-changing combination. Honestly, I don't know how either of you two would have opened this door without me." He holds up his hand and lowers all his fingers except the middle one at us. The tip of it folds back and reveals a piece of liquid metal underneath.

"That looks like Candlemas!" I remark.

"Pretty cool, huh? I picked up a piece of the T-1000 back on Roc-121." He smiles.

"You're lucky it didn't invade your entire body and infuse you with his consciousness," I mutter.

Tol's face goes white. "I didn't think of that," he says. He inserts his finger into the lock. A loud thunk sounds as the liquid metal forms to the slot and the lock clicks open. There is a hiss as the atmospheric seal is broken. The small room inside is adorned only with a viewscreen that serves as either a window or a communications display.

"Inter-Fractural communicator?" I ask.

Xana nods. "This can beam messages to a satellite then through the Fracture Point." Her fingers dance over the holographic keys.

"Were they communicating with anyone on Oberus?" I ask.

Xana's brow furrows.

"What is it?" Tol asks.

The viewscreen flickers, no longer displaying the transparent window vista of Prospera. Instead, the weird cat eyes of Talousla Karr fill the frame. "Lady Lazarus, Urizen, Great Preserver . . ."

"He lays it on thick," mutters Tol.

"Quiet," I hiss.

"You are expecting your final and possibly most unique avatar. So, too, then, must her protector be equally remarkable. Kshatriya-caste Praetorian templates have served admirably in the past; however, you well know their limitations. You prefer predictability in your calculations, but I suggest a creative solution. I've come across a most fascinating planet in my wanderings . . ."

The screen flashes to a world half-covered in sun, the other turned toward darkness. *Tao.*

"Here a contingent of your own army went renegade and established a colony. High gravity and dense atmospheric pressure, as well as extreme heat and cold climes have fashioned a physically robust populace. Remnants of Miralian soldier culture have transmuted to an ideology of racial purity, health, beauty, and strength above all other attributes. Your own guardian, Skaya, will provide the template, of course, but combined with the adapted genes of the Taoans, I'll be able to fashion a more perfect companion for your daughter. With permission, I'll proceed to find a host for the ovum. I promise no disruption in the sociopolitical situation on account of my experiments. I await your response. I'm your humble servant, Lady Lazarus."

The viewscreen winks off. We stand in silence.

"I don't get it." Tol shrugs. "That didn't have anything to do with armies on the Oberus moon."

Because Xana didn't activate the messages we were looking for.

"There are several more entries," Xana says. Her breath and heart rate have increased.

"Xana," I say.

"Doctor . . . Edmon, I have to know," she says.

"What's going on?" Tol looks back and forth between us. "I thought we didn't have time to fart around!"

"Xana, I understand why you think you need to see. But you already know the truth. Will this bring you peace? Will it help you save Ari?"

"I have to know if the family I remember was real. I have to know where I came from." She hits the comm panel again.

"Great Preserver," Talousla Karr narrates. "The child is now biologically eight years of age and exhibits all the muscular and motor skills of the enhanced design I promised." The little girl sits at a dinner table with her family. She twirls a knife and fork across the backs of her fingers in a display of ambidexterity no natural-born eight-year-old should possess. The image changes to a playground where the girl dodges the toss of a practice spear like an experienced gymnast. "I will proceed to the next phase, removing unwanted elements from the equation, and bring the subject safely to Lyria." The screen cuts to the exterior of a Taoan arcology apartment structure. The image bursts into flames as the detonation of a bomb incinerates the building.

"No!" Xana screams involuntarily. "My mother, my father, my brother . . ."

I place a hand on her shoulder for comfort.

Talousla Karr reappears. "The girl has eluded extraction. These images were captured as part of a popular aquagraphic program here . . ." The image shifts to an episode of *The Exploits of The Companions*, a program Phaestion had commissioned to chronicle our youth. The focus tracks to the little dark-haired girl. She fights off several House Julii guards, back-to-back with an older boy with dark hair and green eyes.

Tol looks back and forth between Xana and me. "Wait, wait . . . no way."

"It may take some time to recover the asset," Talousla Karr says, and the image winks out.

Tol immediately peers out the window. "You guys, there are totally soldiers in the neighborhood. They're walking down the street inspecting the buildings."

I hear the faint whine of several screamer engines. Tol's right—patrols have entered the nearby vicinity.

Xana furiously hits the next entry. Skaya, Talousla Karr, and the red-haired woman, Ahania Lazarus, stand in a sterile laboratory room, a chamber somewhere here on the premises of the mansion. The dark-haired girl is between the adults, eyes closed, in some sort of state of hypnotic repose. "Will the tabula rasa be complete?" Ahania Lazarus asks the spypsy.

"Complete memory erasure is undesired, my lady," the spypsy's voice slithers as he kneels before the frozen girl. "She must retain some semblance of a unique identity if she is to be companion and protector of Ariel."

"I don't like this." Skaya folds her muscled arms across her chest in a gesture so much like Xana's. Of course it makes sense now that we know Skaya was in effect Xana's biological mother, providing most of her DNA.

I smell something. *Smoke?*

"I agree," adds Ahania Lazarus. "What if she wakes up to her past identity?"

"Recovery of full memory is impossible," Talousla Karr states flatly. "She'll always remember bits and pieces. More than that will not matter." The spypsy holds something like a large maggot in a pair of long tweezers. His elongated fingers expertly insert the worm into the child's nostril.

I turn to Xana, who wears a horrified expression.

"The chemical program will time release into the memory folds of the subject's brain and bond her to your daughter permanently through a process similar to biological imprinting." The robed man stands. "It will also implant the subliminal programming, which will activate on verbal command."

I hear the distinct crackling of fire.

"Xana . . . Xana Caprio . . . ?" Talousla Karr whispers. "Are you awake?"

The little girl's eyes flutter open, and the image switches off. All that remains is the window, no longer showing the glittering golden spires of Prospera in the distance; rather, the view is clouded with smoke.

"Sir." My acute hearing picks up voices of the soldiers from outside. "Our sensors are detecting biological life-forms within."

"Burn them out. In fact, torch the block to ensure we cut off any avenue of escape," the commander responds.

"It was all a lie. My whole life. They murdered my family. They implanted me with feelings, my mission . . . it was a lie!" Xana whispers. "Candlemas told me he could free me of the implanted bond. I didn't believe it. I didn't want my love for her taken away. Talousla Karr, he was inside my head! He made me hurt you all. It was all a lie."

"Guys, you guys?" Tol looks through the window. "My oculars can see through the smoke. There are soldiers below right now!"

We need to move!

I put a hand on my friend's shoulder. "Xana, what you and Ari felt, it was real. I know because Ari shared with me her memories. My family was murdered, too, and my father tried to brainwash me to make me forget. Maybe I had to go through that to understand at this moment and tell you it was all real. Maybe I was given the memory by Ari to know: no chemical or subliminal command can tell you who you should be. Only you can make that choice. But you have to do it now, or we burn!"

She looks up at me with tear-streaked eyes, but she steps to the communications console. Her fingers tap furiously on the holographic keys. "Got it. The coordinates of the laboratory on Oberus. Wait—"

"What?" I bark. Smoke rises from below, filling the room.

"When I downloaded the coordinates, a signal was beamed from this station," she says.

"They'll know we're coming then." I grab Tol and shove him through the door. "What's the way out?" I shout back to Xana.

"Subterranean tunnels lead into the city!" she shouts. "They'll take us directly to the spaceport. Follow me."

We race down the tower staircase. Smoke engulfs the hallways. I suck in a breath and hold it as I leap down to the top of the foyer staircase gripping Tol in my arm. The heat is unbearable. Voices of soldiers shout from outside:

"We're detecting bodies."

"Arm the aural platform."

I look out a window. The soldiers have some sort of hovering screamer platform. A soldier leaps onto it and straps into a pilot's harness flanked by two huge tympanic membranes. A sonic blast radiates from the machine into the mansion. I fall to the floor, clutching my head, writhing in pain. I feel blood trickle from my nose and ears.

"Again!" I hear the command.

A second blast hits, and the walls of the mansion crumble around us. "There!" the soldiers shout, spotting us. Xana reaches into her cloak and pulls the remote to the trapdoor. She rolls. I grab Tol and follow her, tumbling over the staircase edge. We fall. My shoulder hits hard, breaking upon impact as I shield Tol.

"Hurry." Xana is on me, pulling me and the navigator to our feet as the mansion topples around us. Smoke chokes my lungs and burns my eyes, but I follow her through the basement corridors to a thick metal door.

We hear the shouts of soldiers behind us. "They went this way!"

Xana places a hand on the palm-print lock of the door. "Recognize: Xana Caprio. Rank, captain." It hisses open on a stairwell that plunges into darkness.

"Oh, more stairs and underground things," Tol says, coughing. "Why can't any of these adventures take place where they love serving piña coladas and getting caught in the rain?"

"Because then it wouldn't be an adventure." I throw him into the tunnel.

Xana looks back, staring into the licks of flame and billowing smoke.

"Xana," I say calmly. "That's not the direction we're going."

She nods, and we jump into darkness together.

CHAPTER 24

The Knight

> Quick to action, the knight is a stalwart protector. She may be rash or aggressive, but the knight is the prodigal who has returned to the home and is ready to face those who would intrude or destroy. The knight may be an antagonist, but when an ally, there is no greater guardian.
>
> —Ovanth, *A Practical Reading of the Arcana*

If the planet Lyria is gold, and her moon, Titanius, has a distinctly a copper hue, the second satellite, Oberus, is surely silver. Lyria was established by the Miralian Empire as a utopia, embodying the spirit of an artistic renaissance. Her architecture is gilded with solar plating to capture the rays of her fiery yellow-orange star. Oberus, however, was colonized only as a mere financial district, an interplanetary extension of the city of Prospera. Since the empire's collapse, Oberus has become a cosmopolitan hub in its own right. The glittering platinum skyscrapers of Oberus's megalopolis span the globe and shimmer in the perpetual rain as if covered in diamond sequins. Monstrous catch basins rise to the stormy skies and help sweep in the downpour. They funnel water to massive turbines that generate hydroelectric power for the glittering city.

We pull our cloaks about us as we sail in on the transport rocket. So far, our false identities as Zhao monks have held. It's doubly fortunate that Phaestion's army has largely left Oberus unregulated. Trading exchanges, banks, and large financial institutions here have dealings throughout the Fracture, and even my foster brother has the good sense to see that burning everything would destroy more than even he is willing to part with in his new order.

"Fasten your safety harnesses and prepare for approach," the voice of the rocket's flight attendant intones over the speakers.

"Have you been here before?" I whisper to Xana in the seat next to me.

She shakes her head. "When I left the mansion after Skaya . . . caught us, I became a soldier for hire. I don't doubt that many of my paychecks originated through the dealings of the executives of this moon, but this was far from the front lines of any combat situation."

"How did you get aboard Rollinson's ship then?" Tol asks from underneath his hood.

Xana simply looks forward as the glittering city in the rain grows in the holographic viewscreen of the passenger cabin. "There's only so much blood one can swim in before she drowns."

Tol whistles in response. "Okay, dark."

The rocket rattles as stabilizing thrusters fire and settle us on the landing pad. We climb the ladder down to the rocket's exit hatch. Seconds later, we're stepping onto the landing amid torrential rains. Our cloaks are immediately soaked through.

"Cheery place this is, guvnah!" Tol shivers.

"You said you wanted to get caught in the rain," I quip.

"Yeah, it's a stupid song." Tol shakes his head.

We follow the other passengers into an adjacent skyscraper and through an immigration checkpoint. We are largely ignored as our holowrists are scanned and accepted.

"It might do to purchase some waterproof garments," I suggest, pointing to a nearby storefront in the port. We're about to enter the shop when the holographic screens displaying arrival and departure information are replaced by the visage of a burly Taoan warrior with a broad face and pale eyes.

"I know that face," Xana whispers tightly.

"I am Sigurd of House Flanders, one of The Companions of Emperor Phaestion Julii and the appointed governor of the Lyrian system."

"This might be a good time to leave," Tol suggests, eyeing the local constabulary who appear to be distracted by the public service announcement.

"It has come to my attention that this most wanted fugitive"—Sigurd's face is replaced by the face of a man with a shorn head and piercing green eyes—"Edmon Leontes, a traitor to the Pantheon of Tao, may be here in the Lyrian star system." Murmurs rustle among the wet strangers of the spaceport. "Edmon Leontes is responsible for the murder of two of my brothers. If this man is seen, alert authorities immediately. Consider him armed and dangerous. A substantial reward awaits any who may provide information that leads to the capture or death of this dangerous criminal. For every day that this man remains free, a Lyrian citizen will be publicly executed." The screen widens on a Lyrian girl, no more than fifteen. She is forced to kneel before Sigurd. He takes up a giant mace. I recognize the craftsmanship of the smiths of Albion once more when the weapon lets out a deep sonic moan. My own hand grasps the sword I've recovered from the spaceport locker. Sigurd swings his club, and it vaporizes the girl into a mist of blood upon impact. The black-armored giant turns back toward his audience, face sprayed with red. "In the name of the Balance."

The crowd of the spaceport around us is silent. Xana, Tol, and I, too, stand still for a beat.

"Well, that was a fun diversion," Tol jests.

"Let's get out of here," I mutter. I know the lesson my brother taught me is to remain detached and clear, but now I know why the cloistered life is necessary for such calm. The real world constantly tests. *This is all my fault,* I think.

"Excuse me," an old voice, like wrinkled paper, interrupts my train of thought. I look to see a small bespectacled man. "I notice you and your company were looking at my store—" The man's words are cut off as he sees my face beneath my hood. His head quickly whips to the hologram screen where my visage was only moments before. "You!" he says, gasping.

"Careful, old man." Xana grunts and steps forward, her hand thumbing the activator of her extensor staff. "Another word and you won't be long for this world."

"No, no," the old man whispers. "This changes everything. Come," he says. "You have no need to pay at my store. I will supply free of charge. Any enemy of those monsters may call me friend."

He scurries back toward his shop. Xana and I look at each other warily.

It appears that Sigurd may have underestimated just how loathed the Taoans are here.

"Come," the shopkeeper calls again.

"What are you guys are waiting for?" Tol says. "I want a free raincoat!"

A few hours later, we disembark the hyperloop train that has carried us to the dark side of Oberus. We are pushed out of the crowded cabin like sarfish from a tube, the slick plastic of our new rainwear squeaking from the friction. The kindly shopkeeper at the port outfitted us and helped us navigate the city's extensive public transportation system.

"Be safe, friends, and watch your backs," he said at our parting.

I'm grateful that not all the denizens of this system are cowed by Phaestion's aggression. At the same time, I don't know how long their resolve will last in the face of brutal, daily executions. *I can't let this continue . . .*

"You're thinking you should turn yourself in," Xana mutters as if she can read my thoughts.

"Can't do that, Doc," Tol chimes in. "You might save one or two before they execute you, too. And then what? They'll go right back to intimidating the populace."

"Sanctun's right." Xana nods. "There's more at stake. An entire universe and a good friend."

"The needs of the many, Jim," Tol says gravely.

"I don't want to talk about it," I remark.

I stride forward as the rain pounds against the plastic of my poncho, creating a roar in my ears. From the train platform, which leads to grated catwalks that traverse the lower city, the skyscrapers look black and ominous. Their surfaces are lit with neon signs and blinking lights. Aquagraphics are projected onto the falling rain creating colorful advertisements. Hordes of people swarm the thoroughfares as the hyperloops race on tracks overhead, twisting and turning. Sirens blare. It's sensory overload.

Xana hails an automated taxi and punches the coordinates we need. We are whisked off through the rain, on a glass path that curves corners throughout the congested skyways. Water rushes in a thin layer on top of the transparent street, lifting the taxi, while air pumps that line the roads blast us along the designated route. Both above and below I see these transparent pathways layering the empty space between the glittering buildings. Soon our skiff arrives at a huge but nondescript skyscraper.

"Arrived at destination," the soothing female voice of the automated taxi hums. We disembark and look up at the ominous black building before us. The heavy rain beats down on our hoods.

"It's all very cyberpunk, no?" Tol asks.

Xana and I ignore him.

"What exactly is the plan?" I ask Xana.

"I was going to ask you the same thing," she responds.

"We could just walk in and ask them, 'Is this where you keep the designer organic army?'" Tol shrugs.

We both give him a look, and then Xana strides up the steps leading to the skyscraper's entrance. I fire Tol an annoyed glare. I've no doubt that if the automated doors do not part for her, Xana will smash through the reinforced glass with brute strength. Fortunately, they do part. The marmoreal interior of the scraper is decorated with austere glass and synthetic leather furniture. The aesthetic puts me in the mind of Roc-121, as if both locations are taking their visual cues from some period of human history we've long forgotten. The elderly man with short-clipped silver hair behind the security desk also puts me in the mind of Candlemas. He even wears similar garments—a dark jacket, pants, and a strip of fabric around his neck that Tol tells me is called a "tie." He's flanked by two security guards who both sport minimal black armor and the plain face of the man we used to know as Bentley.

"Excuse me," the man with silver hair says as he stands. "Business hours have ended. We are currently closed. If you please—"

"We have an appointment," Xana says, pulling back the hood of her rain gear.

"Captain . . ."

"Caprio. Xana Caprio."

The man's eyes widen ever so slightly, and he hits a button on his desk. "Commander, the . . . guests you expected from Lyria have arrived. It will be only a moment. Feel free to have a seat," the man says, gesturing to the sofas in the lobby.

None of us make a move.

Heartbeats. Several of them, fast approaching. Their cadences familiar . . .

I ready to draw my sword. *I don't like this.* What we hope to accomplish by coming here, I'm not exactly sure. Tol's father told us that Talousla Karr had created an army here, purportedly to advance his plan to allow Los to enter this dimension of our universe. Yet, even if that is correct, what action we can take to stop it is unclear. *Breathe, Edmon. Regret is the past. Anxiety is the future. All we have is the present.* I think of my brother, Edvaard, and I'm thankful I had the chance to meet him.

The doors to the lift whisper open, and Commander Skaya exits flanked by a cadre of designer organic commandos. All wear the face of Bentley.

"Skaya," Xana greets her old mentor.

"The satellite signal that beamed from Lyria let us know someone had broken into the Lazarus communication station. You and your friends will come with me," the older version of our friend responds coldly. The guards surround us, their rifles trained on our skulls. Xana looks at me warily, and I nod. There is not much choice but to follow if we want to find out more information. The guards confiscate our weapons, and we are moved at the muzzles of their rifles toward the lift. If they intend to kill us, there is little we may do now, but I don't intend to go down without a fight. I crack my knuckles and take breaths to ready myself.

The lift is actually a transparent chamber. Floor, walls, and ceiling are all made of some type of reinforced glass. The building structure visible beyond is made of the same material. The whole place is clear to see. Everything is like a giant honeycomb. Below, the hexagonal-shaped rooms hold figures swathed in white who operate machines that seem to be dispensing droplets of liquid into thousands if not millions of test tubes. Ahead, in chambers stacked on top of those, fleshy, white spider creatures scurry about. From their abdomens, they dispel a clear viscous fluid. They glue these drops to the ceiling where they harden. Above, in more honeycomb chambers, spiders tend to the droplets, which now seem to grow fetuses within their strange gel.

"What am I looking at?" Xana growls.

"The place where your army is born," Skaya responds. "Up," she commands the lift.

I steady myself as the lift rockets skyward. One honeycomb level after another whizzes by.

"Stop," Skaya calls again. From thousands of meters above our previous position, I see hundreds of layers of the hive stacked below. I look straight ahead to see fully formed babes, who wriggle and squirm within their sacs. One cracks his clear shell, and one by one, the other newborns begin to break their molds as well.

"The birth of a new generation," Skaya says as the first of the droplets hanging from the ceiling bursts completely open. The liquid inside oozes out, and the babe contained within crawls to the opening. A fleshy spider scurries and catches the infant gently with forceps legs. It extracts the child from the sac and places it into a depressed area on its back.

"Like a cradle!" Tol remarks. "This is like some bio-Matrix crazy bugger shizzle right here."

"How many years have you been at this?" I ask.

Skaya turns to me. Her pale, artificial eye scans me, the scarred skin that surrounds it puckering. "The great darkness enters through the portal of a singularity. Time is relative where such gravity is concerned. But in answer, this particular factory was put in place not long after the Chironian Civil War, when Urizen determined the collapse of the Miralian Empire was imminent."

"You mean Ahania Lazarus," Xana corrects.

"Ari's mom," Tol adds.

Skaya does not acknowledge them. "Full production of the designer organic army did not start until approximately one hundred standard years ago as per the architect's instructions and placement of Talousla Karr as her chief geneticist. Up," she calls. The lift spirals higher now, speeding past dozens more levels. "Stop," Skaya commands.

Here we are entertained with a view of children, young Bentleys all, each sitting in white reclining chairs composed of the same fleshy material as the spiders. I wonder if the spiders, as part of their life cycle, have somehow grown into these seats. The headrests have holes in their backs, and through the holes, some sort of spinal cord or ganglia is grown, connecting the backs of the children's heads with glass tanks filled with fluid. In the tanks rest enlarged human brains.

"Talousla Karr created the designs of our Hoplites from scratch, drawing upon a DNA framework that survived the old empire. Our training methods, however, have grown in sophistication. Growth acceleration of the units also allows us to create a workable force within fifteen standard years as opposed to the twenty of the previous epoch. Up."

We lurch upward again. More honeycomb chambers appear, but the children have grown to adulthood. The half-naked adolescents gather around a large training room floor, practicing martial skills with one another. They wrestle, they box, and they drill with practice staffs and stun pistols. I'm reminded of my days at the Julii academy and watching the training of Tao's soldiers there. These boys, however, all share faces and movement patterns, the coordination of their drills mirrorlike. Matched against Phaestion's military, this designer organic army would be formidable. "Though the soldiers have all the cognitive and motor behavior embedded from their neural downloads, a nominal period of actual physical practice is necessary to refine spatial awareness," comments Skaya.

In an adjacent chamber, I spy the young soldiers being suspended from the ceiling in rings. It looks similar to the sun ring that Edvaard had hung me from to heal. However, these boys are not being healed. The rings flash, and they scream in pain as pulses of electricity and radiation shock their bodies. The glass is soundproof and absorbs the howls, but somehow I feel their pain ripple through me.

"You're torturing them!" Tol cries out. His hands flex in frustrated outrage.

"You're inuring them to the physical and psychological effects of pain," I correct my friend. "It's a strategy Talousla Karr believes unlocks a person's strength and potential," I add grimly.

"Up" is the only response from Skaya.

It seems we are approaching the top levels of Urizen's skyscraper as I see only a few levels remaining. The clones on the next level we stop at are now men, strapping on armor not dissimilar from that of the soldiers we first encountered flying out of Market. They check the action on their rifles, then one by one approach another white, spider-like creature whose legs are grown into the framework of the ceiling. This creature has a giant, bulbous abdomen that spits out little eggs onto the faces of the soldiers. As soon as they hit the skin of the men, the eggs become white worms that crawl into the nostrils of the soldiers.

"Ugh!" Tol exclaims.

"The tabula rasa," I surmise.

"A necessary unpleasantry to ensure complete loyalty of our army and mark them as immune from the effects of post-traumatic stress and other deleterious developmental aberrations."

"Loyal to whom?" Xana asks her mentor coldly. "You? Urizen? Or Talousla Karr?"

A hint of an icy smile curves the older woman's lips. The soldiers, now implanted with the brain worms, exit the chamber via individual capsule lifts. Where they are headed, I know not.

"Up," Skaya commands. The lift rises. We flash in quick succession past the last levels, where hundreds of soldiers, young and old, hang on meat hooks, dead, and are systematically dropped by conveyor belts into giant vats of acid.

"You liquefy the dead," I growl with disgust.

"Every batch contains deleterious genes or individuals who do not adhere to mental programming," Skaya says. "Efficiency dictates that protein matter is not wasted but recycled into the combine."

"It's people. It's people!" Tol shouts.

"Stop," Skaya says, and the lift halts at the highest honeycomb chamber. The dark-haired commander leads us out.

"Watch it, Bentley!" Tol blurts as the soldiers push us to follow at the barrel of their guns.

The room holds several glass capsules. Contained within each is a warrior in stasis; all bear the face of Xana Caprio. Behind these designer organics, frozen in time, loom three-meter-tall giants, umbilical cords extending from their bodies to the capsules. Their shapes are humanoid with skin like chitinous armor plates. The design is sleek, graphic, with rivulets of quicksilver branching in glowing veins throughout the armor. Rocket engines grow seamlessly between the folded wings upon their backs.

"Holy Voltron Macross Evangelion Power Rangers, Doctor Batman!" Tol whispers.

"Anjins of a lost age," Skaya says as she takes in the biomechanical armors with a measure of reverence. They are not quite machines but not quite living organisms, rather some advanced hybrid of both. "These were the specimens left to us after the fall of the empire. The Praetorian template to which I belong was fabricated to guard matriarchs, to lead the armies, and to pilot these Anjins after the defection of the Singhs."

"The Great Song," I respond, thinking of the Anjin leader who became the first emperor of Tao. In the wake of the Singhs' absence, a new army was created, those of the Praetorians like Skaya and the Hoplites like Bentley.

"Urizen and the High Matriarchy knew they needed a better class of soldier, one that would never betray them. They needed people like them, dedicated to peace and protection, rather than conflict and war. Hoplites were designed from one template, and we, their leaders, the Praetorians, from the superior gender." Skaya's scarred visage takes in Xana. It is a look of hope, of pride. She places a hand on her protégé's shoulder. "We are angels of a forgotten dream. This is your tribe, Xana, and your charge. Come with me. I will take you to Ari. It is time to fulfill your mission and all that you've trained and suffered for."

I see the conflict on Xana's face. She wants what is being offered. She wants to satisfy the imperative, whether that was placed in her mind by the brain worm or through the love that was grown by years of companionship with our girl. Yet, she pushes the older woman's hand away. "You stole me from my parents. You murdered my family. Now, you seek to help this megalomaniac, this false god, in destroying the entire universe? How could I ever join you?"

"You know not of what you speak." Skaya's lips purse. "Those people were never your parents, Xana. Talousla Karr believed that in order to create a true protector for Urizen's daughter, she needed something new. I was the last and best of the Praetorians in my day, chosen personally by Urizen before the fall to be her protector. I survived with her through a combination of time dilation, cryogenic freeze, and life extension treatments, always to accompany her where she was needed to ensure her agenda was executed. When Talousla Karr was commissioned to create this army, I served as the parent for the new generation of commanders. You are one of these, Xana, but you are also unique. Karr combined my traits with those he took from Tao to create you. All of us are sisters, but you are the only one among us not a complete facsimile."

"Man, oh, man, the Miralian Empire strikes back," mutters Tol.

"The people you called mother and father were merely hosts, providing the container to hold you until you were ready to be born to who you truly are."

Her words hang in the air. The evidence had led Xana and the rest of us to conclude as much already, but to hear the confirmation spoken aloud by a trusted mentor, who was there and helped it happen, is even more terrible. My heart pounds, and I feel the shadow out there in the Fracture, traveling, getting closer, swallowing all space in its path.

"They raised me, gave me happiness. You helped take them away." Xana's eyes narrow "Now I have another family: my crew. The people of the UFP *James Bentley*. They're my brothers and sisters. You and your commanders have tried to kill them three times now. Once in the space beyond Market. Then again on Nonthera. Above the skies of Miral you took the life of Clay Welker. I won't let you take another life dear to me. I swear it."

Skaya steps back and the center of the floor alights with a holographic display of a man. Stephen Sanctun. It appears he's in some kind of prison cell. The chamber is glass and hexagonal like the others here in this factory. He is older, more haggard than the man in the messages Tol and I witnessed previously. It seems clear he has been imprisoned and placed under duress for some time.

"Dad?" Tol stares in disbelief at the recording.

Talousla Karr, clad in his familiar dark robes, enters the frame of the recording. Skaya stands next to him. "Mr. Sanctun, our time runs short. The finale is upon us. We know that you were attempting to contact your son, but we've just returned from Miral. I can tell you that his ship was destroyed by Commander Skaya and Urizen's forces. Tol Sanctun is dead, his crew with him. Whatever message you were trying to send will no longer reach him."

Tol's father was alive this whole time! I think.

Stephen Sanctun sits in shock at the spypsy's words, but then his face cements into a grin. "Are you kidding?" Stephen laughs. "I've been sending messages for years now, you weird-looking bastard. You might have intercepted some of them, but no way all of them. Sure, it might take a while for my boy to get them and figure it out, but when he does, you can be sure he'll lead a whole army down on this place. And if you're so sure he's dead? Why keep me around as a bargaining chip?" he responds defiantly.

"I believe you're right, Mr. Sanctun. I've no idea. Kill him," the spypsy says nonchalantly.

Skaya in the hologram steps forward and fires a radiation pulse from her pistol into the man's head, liquefying his brain inside his skull instantly. Tol's father slumps forward, lifeless.

"Dad!" Tol cries out.

I move before the sound of Tol's scream ceases. My hand grasps the butt of the rifle just off my shoulder. I crush it with enhanced strength. I grab Xana's extensor staff from the surprised soldier and throw it to her. "Xana!"

She catches it midair and thumbs the activator. The staff lengthens. She twirls it. No words are wasted. She attacks her mentor with unleashed fury. I cannot watch the battle as I have my hands full with the rest of the Bentley Hoplites who surround us. I dodge the radiation pulse of a rifle, then close distance, breaking it. I disconnect from my rage, from love, from despair, from hope. A storm crackles inside me, all the revelations and emotional implications of this world swirling, but I let them go. I hurl Tol to the ground to protect him and become a flurry. I knock one soldier out cold with a pressure point strike to the neck. I throw a kick, breaking the leg of another. I feel the air shift, and I duck a strike from a third. I smoothly circle my body away as I grab the soldier's arm and toss him to the ground while simultaneously breaking his limb. A gun is fired. My body takes over, and I bat the bullet aside with my hand, midair. I feel the sting from the heat and metal as the chop ricochets the bullet, shattering surrounding glass. Alarm klaxons blare. I rip my siren sword from the grip of the last Hoplite, unsheathing the blade as I do. I become one with the steel's vibrations as I brandish the weapon before me. I send out a pulse from my sword. It blasts into a soldier, hurling him backward into one of the Praetorian stasis tanks. It shatters around the unconscious Hoplite, raining down glass and viscous gel.

I spin to see Xana locked in combat with Skaya.

"Xana!" I shout taking a step forward, but she raises her hand, signaling me to stay back. I understand—*I can't interfere.*

The two warriors stand face-to-face like mirror images separated only by age. There is a rumble from within the skyscraper below.

"My soldiers have boarded their ships," Skaya says evenly. "They will fly to join our maker and stop anyone from interfering with Urizen's plans to banish the darkness."

"You've been deceived, Skaya," Xana counters. "Talousla Karr grew this army to be loyal to him, not your master. He wants Los to come; he welcomes it."

Skaya grimaces.

"You've been corrupted by him, too, haven't you?" Xana realizes aloud. "He's implanted you with programming the same as he has for me."

The two women circle, gauging each other's movements, readying their weapons. With a glance, I take in all the sensory information—Xana is younger, stronger, faster. However, her mentor's movements convey a calm that only comes with battle-hardened experience. More than that, Skaya holds the mental advantage. Skaya knows the location where Urizen and Ari are right now, which has made Xana tentative, doubting how she should proceed with the fight. More than that, I see all their years of sparring and training. *Xana has never beaten her mentor,* I discern. Therein lies the ultimate seed of doubt. "Prove to me, Xana, that you aren't just a failed experiment," Skaya challenges.

They explode toward each other, staffs colliding. One, two, Xana ducks a third stroke and comes up underneath with the butt of her weapon. She smashes it against the chin of her mentor. Skaya grunts but rolls with the blow. She spins, sending an elbow flying toward Xana's temple. Xana raises her guard just in time to mitigate the crash of the devastating strike. Weapons drop to the floor as the two women grapple. Xana gets the better of her teacher, her foot kicking back while executing a flawless trip and hip throw. The two are hurled to the floor, Xana coming down onto Skaya, driving her shoulder into her as they do. Bone cracks in the fall, but Skaya's resilience and skill are apparent. She scrambles in the guard position, her legs shooting skyward, wrapping around Xana's throat like muscular eels, cutting off the air supply. Xana's face turns red. She slams a hand down, attempting to punch Skaya in the gut. Skaya twists and grasps the hand, turning the triangle choke into an arm bar. She breaks Xana's joint, and Xana loosens a rasp, the last of her air. Xana's free arm flails as Skaya squeezes her legs, cementing the choke.

"This is not sport, girl," Skaya hisses. "I thought I taught you better than this. To protect your charge you must be willing to give everything."

The fight is over, or would be, except for the knife that ejects from the gauntlet in Xana's free arm. It pops directly into her hand, and she swiftly jams it into Skaya's thigh then yanks it out. Skaya screams in rage and looses the choke hold. Xana falls back gasping for air. Even so, she rolls to her feet and slams a boot into the wound on Skaya's thigh. She pins her mentor's leg down, squeezing blood out, slick and red, onto the floor of the glass chamber. Xana raises the knife high, poses it for the killing blow, but her hand wavers.

"What a disappointment you are," Skaya says coldly. Xana is frozen. It's the moment Skaya needs. She whips her own curved knife from a boot.

"Xana!" I scream as Skaya's knife thrusts up, aimed at the liver for a killing stab. A gun fires. Skaya's head explodes in a shower of blood and gore before the knife reaches its destination. Her body flops back with a thunk, a hunk of meat on the glass floor.

I turn to see Tol, the gun he holds still trained at Skaya's exploded skull. "Sorry. I did that," he says, his voice quivering. "I kind of had to do that." The gun drops from his hand and clatters to the floor.

Xana steps toward me, blood spattered across her face. The knife shakes in her clutched fist. I reach out and gently take it from her and toss it aside. She grasps me, her head falling onto my shoulder as she sobs. I feel Tol's lanky arms wrap around us both as he cries, too. We three hold one another for a moment. *So much loss,* I think to myself. For once, it's not my pain, but I take it upon myself anyway. All that I've been through and suffered gives me compassion and strength to be there for them to lean against in this moment.

I hear movement, the sounds of shuffling. *We are not alone.* "Tol, Xana," I whisper as I gently disentangle myself from my comrades. We stand back as all around us the Praetorians awaken from their gel pods. They surround us, taking us in with cold gazes of appraisal. One of the women, almost identical looking to Xana, steps forward and kneels before the corpse of Skaya. "The commander is dead," she states. She looks up at Xana. "You killed her?"

"I did," Xana acknowledges.

"Why?"

"Urizen may intend to save the universe, but her army does not, including your sisters," Xana says.

The Praetorian looks at her sisters in confusion. They all shift uncomfortably.

This is not good. If their programming keeps them wholly loyal to Talousla Karr . . . if we cannot convince them that we are no threat, there's no way that the three of us can defeat them all physically.

"You assume rank of commander?" she asks.

Xana looks back at us. "What do I say?"

"What would Bentley have wanted?" I suggest.

Xana nods. "I want you to have the freedom to make your own choice. You may choose to follow us in our mission to stop Urizen, or you may go. It's up to you now."

The woman stands. She gazes at each of her sisters. They are uneasy, but they all nod in assent. "When we combine with the armors, we become Anjins, protectors of the realm. We will follow you, Commander, for now," she says solemnly.

Tol, Xana, and I collectively breathe a sigh of relief.

"What are your names?" Xana asks. "What shall we call you?"

Tol takes a step forward past the women. He examines the glass capsules that house the biomech armors of the Anjins. "They already have names," he says.

I squint, looking at the ancient symbols etched into the glass. The writing is old, perhaps dating back to the Fractural Collapse.

"Mikael," Tol says as he traces the first name plate with his fingers. "Gavriel, Rafael, Uriel, Ragiel, Azrael." He names them off one by one as he travels the circumference of the chamber.

"There is one more," the Praetorian standing in front of the Mikael Anjin says. She gestures to a seventh lone giant in the circle, unaccompanied by a Praetorian gel pod.

Xana walks to the Anjin. She touches the name plate. "Metatron," she reads aloud. At her touch, the glass casing around the Anjin armor retracts with a hiss. The thorax of the armor peels back and reveals a molding for a human pilot to step inside. Fibrous tendrils of a spinal column, sway like cilia, ready to bond.

"The original Anjins were retired at the close of the Chironian Civil War," the Praetorian I now think of as Mikael says. "However, the High Matriarchy grew these last angels and us, their pilots, to stay frozen in time, to await the day when we would be woken by the commander. Now that Commander Skaya is gone, her Anjin is yours to fly."

"Oh my, yes!" Tol exclaims, pumping a fist. "Do it, Xana. Do it and then say, 'I. Am. Metatron!'"

"I'm not saying that," Xana responds flatly. But she takes a step toward the armor anyway.

"Once you join with the armor, it will be bonded to you for the duration of your life," says Gavriel. "Until you die, she will only accept you as her pilot. When her skin bleeds, you will bleed so long as you are connected. She will have an imprint of your consciousness when you are not connected and will follow your command."

"I understand," Xana says as she takes another hesitant step toward her destiny.

"You claim that the army we were born to does not serve Urizen," the one called Azrael says, stepping forward. "I will call you commander only until I ascertain the truth. If you are proven right, then you have my loyalty. If wrong, I will bring you death."

Xana looks at the woman, a sister really, with hard eyes, then steps inside of the Metatron armor. Her eyes widen with shock and horror as the fibers of the spinal column implant themselves into her back just before the plates of the thorax close with a whisper. There is a rumble as the angular quicksilver veins seem to glow. I'm reminded of the Aeshnid of Miral as the armor awakens. Metatron takes a few tentative steps and then stretches her limbs, groaning. The folded wings on the Anjin's back flex but cannot open fully while inside the chamber.

The other Anjins also come alive as the Praetorians step into their own armors.

"Xana?" I ask the armor containing my friend. "Are you there?"

The insectoid helm turns down toward me. "Oh yeah, Doctor, I'm here. This is incredible!"

"Please tell me that you guys can transform and then combine with each other into one, like, massive biorobot?" Tol claps his hands.

Metatron looks down at the lanky man, no expression on her robotic-insect visage. "Shut up, Tol."

"This is way too cool, Doctor Batman," Tol says with schoolboy giddiness.

"We need to decide what to do," I say. "Skaya is dead, and she was the only one who knew where Urizen was located. It's great that we found the Anjins, but now that we have, what's our next play?"

Metatron cocks her head to the side as if she is receiving information. "My armor is telling me that there is a hangar three floors down with a stinger transport, the last one. All the others starships have been manned, armed, and are headed to the Fracture. Skaya said they were bound for Urizen's location."

"We can still catch them and follow if we can't stop them," I realize. I grab Tol and drag him into the lift. "Down!" I command.

"Wait!" Tol cries out just before the lift doors close. "Xana, what are you going to do?"

"I'm going to make sure that this factory never again creates another slave."

CHAPTER 25

Judgment

Judgment may be a difficult card to read, but it is most literally a door. The door may be to a cell that is either opened or shut behind. It may signal penance for a past failure or an opportunity to walk into a new reality from confinement.

—Ovanth, *A Practical Reading of the Arcana*

"Hurry and maybe we can catch them!" I shout to Tol as we sprint across the empty hangar toward the lone stinger ship hanging from the ceiling, birthed from its own spider droplet. We reach the ship, and I hit the actuator depression. The boarding ramp lowers with a familiar bioorganic suction sound.

"That always gives me the creeps," Tol says. I grab him, and we race down the narrow hallway toward the cockpit. Tol jumps into the pilot's harness. "It looks like this one wasn't outfitted with a brain yet."

"Let's hope there aren't any other vital components missing," I respond.

Tol revs the engine, and we buck as we come off the glass flooring. Tol lifts us out and into the stormy rains of Oberus.

"Bring us about," I command.

Tol turns, and the ship's gyroscopes respond. Lightning crashes, silhouetting the Anjins. Their back carapaces are open, and their dragonfly wings are fully extended. Xana's mech, Metatron, hovers on an engine of blue flame. "Leontes," her voice comes in over the communicator. "If you are clear, I'm going to melt this thing. My scans indicates the building is empty. All the clones have evacuated the premises. There should be no casualties."

"Do it," I respond. *I just hope it doesn't slow us down.*

She extends her armored gauntlet, and fire erupts from her fist like a blowtorch at the skyscraper. The other Anjins follow suit. The glass building melts like the wax of a burned candle forming a crystalline lump.

"Xana, do you copy?"

"Metatron," the robotic voice comes back.

"Follow us out of atmo. Head toward the Fracture Point," I command.

"Copy," she responds.

Tol throttles us skyward, and I'm pressed against the seat back as the g's compress me. We rise above the rain clouds to a thin blue stratosphere, then a star field of black fills the viewscreen. The Anjins sail alongside, their carapaces closing for vacuum travel. I bring up the holographic keyboard and try to magnify the viewscreen. A swarm of stinger vessels is headed for a Taoan interdiction fleet that guards the point. "Phaestion thought working with Talousla Karr was a good idea. I doubt he knew the full extent of what the spypsy was up to, though."

"They're about to find out," Tol agrees.

Phaestion's ships, powerful by any other planetary standard, seem slow and dull against the coordinated attack of the designer organic fleet. Several Taoan frigates are cut to ribbons by machine-gun fire. They hiss precious atmo into the vast. The designer organic fleet sails right past to the Fracture. The wormhole opens in space-time, a whirlpool of purple and aquamarine. The fleet engages their saws, vibrates, and disappears. "We're too late," I say.

"If they get to the other side of the point, we'll have no way to track them," Tol laments.

"Metatron," I hail. "Does your armor have any information on their route?"

"Negative, Leontes. It appears that Skaya was the sole carrier of that information among the Anjins."

"Tol?" I ask. "What about our ship?"

"Negative. Only the lead ship brain, which apparently isn't standard clone issue, has the coordinates."

So the question is who besides Skaya and Talousla Karr might know where the location could be? Who else in the Fracture might know about Urizen and all her mysterious plans?

"Um, Doc?" Tol calls out.

My holographic display flashes. An attack force of Taoan rockets has left Lyria and is headed straight for us. *Reinforcements.* Meanwhile, those ships left unscathed by the designer organics seem to be recovering from their situation. My fingers quickly dash over the holographic controls sifting through the ships' navigation charts data banks until I find what I'm looking for. It's the only thing I can think of. *Thank the Elder Stars!*

"Metatron," I hail over the comm. "Tell your Anjins to peel off, draw the Taoan forces away, and then hide. I want you in our docking bay ASAP."

"Explain, Leontes?"

"Just do it!" I command. "Tol, as soon as her mech docks, gun it full throttle for the point."

"All right, Captain, she's in," Tol yells out a second later, and he throttles.

I'm pushed into my seat back. I activate my rearview display to watch the remaining Anjins led by Mikael carve through the Taoan forces. Their lithe and agile armor suits move in space far more freely than the massive Taoan rockets. Taoans pride themselves on sonic weaponry, but in vacuum, they're relegated to metal slugs, just like the other denizens of the Fracture. The advanced armor of the Anjins ignore their fire as if the bullets were no more than gnats. Still, more reinforcements rise up from Lyria. A planetary rocket launch is not a casual thing. The fact that Sigurd is able to engage so many ships so quickly is a testament to the speed and efficiency of Phaestion's military.

"Hey, what's up, Metatron?" Tol says excitedly as Xana, sans armor, floats through the cockpit door, still nursing her broken arm from the fight with Skaya.

"When I combine with the armor, it's like we have a fused personality. It's just Xana, now that I'm separated," she says. "What's going on?"

"Tell them to break off." I indicate the other Anjins. "They should head for the moon of Titania. There should be wilderness there where they can hide and await our signal."

Xana takes a seat next to me with pursed lips and calls up a holographic keyboard to send a message to her comrades. She doesn't like dividing our forces. "Sent."

"Don't worry. We're coming back," I say. "But not until we find the location of Ancient Earth. Let me take a look at that arm."

I take her broken limb gently into my hands and swiftly activate the pressure points that will numb the pain as Tol points us toward the Fracture Point.

"How are we going to do that?" Xana asks.

"By asking the only ones left who may know, very carefully," I respond as I snap her broken bones into place, and we enter the broken bones of the universe.

Deep vast. Nowhere. The silence is deafening here. It reminds me of an old creation parable my mother used to read me at Eventide—"In the beginning there was . . ." It's amazing that life exists at all in this coldness.

"Well done, Leontes," Xana mocks. "You've separated us from the few allies we managed to gain, alerted all the Taoans to our presence, and taken us into a dead zone. A lot of good we'll be doing here while Los comes."

Xana's sarcasm is actually a welcome bit of familiarity, but she's right—I can feel the encroaching darkness thanks to my connection with Ari.

Find me, Edmon, Ari whispers.

I must remain focused, do what I can. "Check your scanners for chem trails, oh wise and brave commander of the Anjins," I harp back.

"Nothing," she mutters, examining a holographic readout.

"The ship's memory systems said that they would be here," I grumble.

Ahania Lazarus and her surrogates have kept track of her children since the fall of her empire. Though their location remained a secret to everyone else throughout the Nine Corridors, the data banks of Talousla Karr's bioship show that in the ensuing millennia since the destruction of Miral, the arc ships of the Nicnacians have followed specific flight patterns through the reaches of the vast. They only ever touch Fracture Points when they needed to refuel at a star. I've plotted the yearly route of the gigantic ships and told Tol to take us to the location in deep space where they are most likely to be at this moment in time. If they haven't passed through here yet, it's only a matter of . . .

"Got something," Xana calls out.

The screen shows the barest hint of movement in the blackness. Xana scopes in and enlarges the angle. There they are: six huge star vessels. We watch with amazement for a moment at the achievement of humanity during a lost age. Giant metallic hump-backed whales, each the size of a small world, sail through the reaches of night. Each arc ship of Armada contains an entire colony of people. Swarming around them, like an effervescence, are smaller ships. They look like dolphins playing with their larger cousins.

"Captain!" Tol exclaims. "Thar be whales here!"

"Armada," I say. "Take us on an intercept course."

Xana swivels her chair toward me. "This is a risk," she states flatly. "There's no guarantee that the spypsies know the location of Ancient Earth. Even if they do, they may not be willing to tell us. You remember how secretive Washo was."

I instinctually rub the spot on my back where the knife slid into me. None of us ever saw what the boy's fate was. Xana and I were blasted out of the *Lamb* first, and Tol lamented to me he barely had time to get himself and Whistler into a gel pod. In all likelihood, our friend is dead and has been for years.

"More than that, Xana, warrior princess, they're xenophobes," Tol interjects. "Far as I know, no outsider sees Armada and lives to tell the tale."

"The Nicnacians are pacifists," I reason. "They probably won't kill us."

"Blowing us out of an air lock isn't killing so much as just watching us die," Xana murmurs.

"Jail's not so bad. I haven't been to a spypsy jail before, either," Tol says happily.

Xana is right. Tol is right. Yet these are supposedly the faithful. If we're going to find anyone who knows where Urizen and Orc will be, it must be them.

"Scout ships approaching," Tol calls out.

"Xana, take Metatron out. I'm betting if they see an Anjin, they'll think twice about dismissing us. Remember, the spypsies are a matriarchal society. Their culture is a distillation of the religious elite of the old empire."

Xana unbuckles from her seat and floats out of the cockpit.

"We're being hailed, Doc," Tol says.

A pilot of a scout ship wearing some sort of dolphin-shaped breath mask appears on our screen. "Unidentified ship, you now belong to us. You will follow without resistance. Any attempt at communication will result in grave consequences. Any attempt at violence will result in immediate death."

"Xana, release the hatch," I command. We hear the cargo doors open below. Xana drops from our belly and pilots herself between us and the scouts. There is a beat as the spypsy pilots take in the sight of the mech, a knight of the old empire.

"I am Metatron."

"Yes," Tol whispers.

"We seek the High Matriarch of the Nicnacians," Xana says.

There is a pause over the comm. Then: "Great Metatron." The pilot's voice shakes. "We will take you at once."

The dolphins fly toward Armada. I feel the excitement and nervous energy radiating from the entire fleet as we follow. The hovering scout ships and smaller skiffs part as the dolphins escort us toward the lead ship of the six.

Has Urizen returned? What does this mean? I can almost hear the chatter as we sail through a gelatinous membrane. We pass through goop with a "pop" breaking the seal, but it instantly reforms behind us, and we sail into the whale's belly. Claws reach down from above and gently grab the wings of our ship, steady us, and hold our craft in position. Thousands of smaller ships line the docking bay. Small women, shorn of hair, tend the craft. They stare at us through our viewscreen. A door opens to the docking bay, and an entourage of spypsies float toward us.

"Now or never," I say to Tol.

We unstrap from our stations and float toward the boarding ramp. I grab Tol just before the portal opens. "Listen, we're playing a very delicate game here. Keep your mouth shut and let Xana do most of the talking."

He mimes zipping his lips and throwing away the key, and we float out to meet the entourage. All of the Nicnacians wear form-fitting bodysuits. *Practical garb for the micro-g of their world ship,* I think. But the leader of the entourage is adorned in flowing robes of bloodred, denoting some sort of special rank among her tribe.

The entourage around the red-robed woman are, I see now, armed guards, their bodysuits actually sleek form-fitting armor. The red-robed woman pulls back her hood and stares with yellow cat eyes. She looks at Tol and me with surprise that turns quickly to scorn.

"I am Ania Chun, priestess of the red robe, attaché to Speaker Mischa Tan. Who are you?" she asks in accented Normal.

Metatron's carapace opens with a whisper, revealing Xana within. Xana floats out of her armor as the spinal tendrils retract from her back. The carapace closes behind her. Xana turns back and nods at the Anjin, and the biobot appears to sleep.

"A Praetorian?" The priestess instantly places her palms together in front of her face in a gesture of supplication.

"I'm Commander Xana Caprio. I bring word to your matriarchy. Take us there at once," Xana intones.

"Of course." The priestess gathers her robes. The guards hand us each small plates of metal. We follow suit as each of the entourage places a plate beneath her feet. "Come," says the priestess as she zooms away on the magnetic hoverboard. Xana looks at me, but I shrug and follow.

We whisk toward the cargo bay entrance. Once through the doors, we place our plates in wall slots for safekeeping. The pristine white corridors of the rest of the ship are much more compact, allowing us to merely push off the nearest surface for locomotion. The Nicnacians, with their sticky pads, walk and crawl around us with ease.

"Tell me, Ania," Xana says imperiously, playing the part of warrior commander to the hilt, "which ship is this?"

The priestess's eyes narrow in suspicion. "This is Eleth, prime among the daughters of Urizen," she responds.

"And your 'speaker' as you call her is Mischa Tan?" Xana asks as Ania leads us toward a lift.

"Yes. Often speakers are chosen from Eleth, but Mischa Tan is of Uveth, the second daughter."

The priestess's voice gives away a pride tinged with resentment. *There are far more intricate politics being played here than we know of.* We're on dangerous ground. This could just as easily backfire on us if we're not careful in observing their customs.

"Uveth. Washo was from Uveth, right? Washo Tan, do you know him?" Tol asks the priestess.

The woman's face instantly drops into a mask of suspicion, and the guards around us shift subtly. *Damn it, Tol!*

"What do you know of Washo Tan?" The priestess's voice is cold.

"A random encounter on Market, nothing more," Xana swiftly replies. She then immediately fires a look at Tol. *Stay quiet.* Tol claps a hand over his mouth.

The priestess knows Washo, I realize. I'm sure the census of this place keeps some track of their youth who leave, for it is forbidden to ever return to Armada after leaving. Still, it would seem highly unusual that a political elite would be familiar with one lone boy. Their leader's surname is Tan. The conclusion that there is a relation is not lost on any of us.

"The conclave on Market keeps to itself," the priestess in red mutters. I can tell she is struggling. Her culture eschews outsiders, but her awe of Xana as a Praetorian Anjin pilot means she should show ultimate deference.

"What's left of the enclave," Tol responds. "Basically a smear on the umbilical walls."

Xana and I both flash eyes in his direction. The lift doors whisper open, and we enter a huge, white sphere. Liquid metal circuitry runs like veins along the surface of its curvature. Ivory railings with ornate carvings crisscross through the chamber allowing engineers, navigators, communicators, and pilots to pull themselves to holographic console stations that surround the interior. In the center of the sphere is an enlarged human brain resting in an amniotic sac. Fibrous tendrils reach out from the sac and grow into the surface of the giant circular chamber. It is at once strange, beautiful, and efficient. The biotechnology of the stingers was the very same that the Nicnacians have used for generations to sail the vast. When Washo lied to me about recognizing the tech, he was trying to protect his people and their methods, even after he chose exile from them.

The priestess floats along the railings into the command sphere with practiced ease. "This is where we navigate the stars. The matriarchy awaits in the cupola." She points ahead (or is it above?) toward an aperture in the sphere. We pull ourselves along the railings skirting around the pilot brain. The wrinkles of the gray matter are deep; the furrows line and etch the tissue in highly intricate patterns. "This brain is very old," I whisper.

Bald engineers and navigators, again all female, eye me suspiciously from their stations. *They do not like men invading their gender-restricted spaces,* I realize. The priestess confirms the suspicion when she turns on me with narrowed eyes. Instead of acknowledging my whisper, she addresses Xana. "Our pilot was one of the last High Matriarchs of Miral, chosen to become one with the world ship."

Xana merely nods. *We met another of the High Matriarchs back in the labyrinth of Miral,* I think. We arrive at the aperture leading to the cupola. "You are about to enter the presence of the speaker and the matriarchs, the highest priestesses of the Nicnacian order, the daughters of Urizen and the heirs of Miral." The priestess looks pointedly at me and Tol with clear intention. *We are inferior and should not speak.*

I glance at Tol to make sure he took the hint. Tol rolls his eyes at me. I could throttle him, I swear. I breathe, remembering the techniques of my mentors.

We enter the cupola. Xana and the priestess float ahead while Tol and I are sequestered at the back, surrounded by the guards. The aperture iris shuts behind us. We hang in micro-g inside a large glass bubble. The view beyond contains all the stars of the universe visible to the naked human eye. Six old women float before us; a cord reaching from the command center wall behind us branches and grows into the backs of each of their smooth skulls.

"Matriarchs of Armada, I bring before your great and illustrious presences—"

"An Anjin of the old empire. Yes, yes, Ania," one of the old women says. "You can dispense with the long-winded introductions. We've been watching."

They are connected to the entire neural network of the arc, I realize, *possibly the entire Armada.*

The women turn to face us. One separates from their ranks and floats toward us. Her body glove hisses tiny jets of air that propel her wherever she wishes to go. She hovers centimeters from Xana. "Which one are you?" she croaks.

"Metatron," Xana replies.

"Chancellor of Urizen." The old woman grins a knowing smile. "You are not of the old empire, girl. Who are you really?"

I see Xana's muscles flex in her flight suit. "I am Xana Caprio."

"Xana Caprio, I am Mischa Tan of Uveth, speaker of the Nicnacians. You come to us in dark times. Our enclave on Market is destroyed by barbarians, and communications throughout the Fracture have fallen to disarray. It is my duty to protect my people from such interlopers as you. Why have you come to Armada?" Xana opens her mouth to speak, but the old woman adds, "Do not pretend to invoke my faith falsely. It will go poorly if you do."

Xana decides to cut out any subterfuge. "I was . . . created to be the bodyguard of Ahania Lazarus's final daughter, Ariel Lazarus." The words are hard for her, but she presses on. "Our wanderings brought us to the remnants of Miral, to the Temple of the Matriarchs. There we met a High Matriarch of the old empire."

"Impossible," Mischa Tan hisses. "Each of the last matriarchs was joined with an arc when Miralian civilization collapsed."

It is a test, I realize. *A lie to see if Xana knows the truth.*

"You well know there were seven arcs that left Miral, Speaker," Xana replies. "This matriarch was to be the pilot of that final ship. Instead, Urizen herself boarded the arc known as Fuzon and left her daughter behind to preserve the seal of the temple, a seal that kept the darkness at bay."

"Los, the destroyer," Mischa Tan acknowledges gravely. She floats back toward her comrades, who hover above us now.

"The seal was broken. Los has slipped farther into our universe and devours all in its path. I'm sure your scouts have confirmed loss of communications along the posterior Radial and Brachial Corridors within the past two years?"

The matriarchs shift uncomfortably at this news, and the guards around Tol and myself mutter among themselves.

"The matriarchy is aware of the compromised space routes, but no source of such breakdown has been accurately identified and defined. The universe is a vast place, and the midden-mensch are notoriously derelict in their maintenance of their networks," Mischa Tan responds, her voice reverberating from the entire cupola. "While your explanation may portend dire consequences, you still do not answer my question, Xana Caprio. Why have you and these *male midden-mensch*"—she spits the words like epithets—"come to Armada?"

"Urizen has taken her last daughter to Ancient Earth. We believe she intends to stop the darkness, but in her employ is another, a renegade of your kind named Talousla Karr." Mischa Tan's eyes narrow at this name. "He betrays Urizen," Xana continues. "He has built an army loyal only to him, and he will help bring forth Los and kaliyuga, ushering in the end of this universe. I intend to stop this man, but we need your help. If Armada holds the location of Ancient Earth within her data banks, we ask you to join us in this mission."

The cupola remains silent in shock. Then the speaker floats toward Xana once more. "Urizen is the architect of us all, the agent of order. Even if what you say is true, she would have foreseen such betrayal and formed contingency for it. She will never allow Los to enter."

The guards around us clutch their staffs tightly. The atmosphere in the room has suddenly shifted to dangerously tense. "This does not look good, Doctor Batman," Tol whispers.

"Urizen left her remaining daughters to command the arcs and keep the faith in her absence, so that when Miral was restored, we could bring a rebirth to the empire," the speaker hisses.

"Miral is gone!" Tol blurts out. "We saw Los devour it with our own eyes."

The guards aim their staffs at Tol. Electrical charges blast from their tips. He screams in pain as he curls into a fetal position. My hand goes to my sword without thinking.

"Edmon, stop!" Xana commands.

"Maybe you're right, Speaker Tan," I say. "Maybe Urizen planned this all meticulously, but if her predictions were so perfect, why tell you to wait to restore a planet she knew would be devoured? Surely you've sent pilgrims on their Rapzis to the lost homeworld and discovered for yourselves the darkness?"

"All Rapzis have ceased since the severing of our connection to the enclave on Market," the speaker answers coldly.

"My point is that Urizen is but a woman, perhaps a great woman, but human nonetheless," I argue. "Talousla Karr of Fuzon has created the largest army we've ever seen. They do not owe allegiance to Urizen, but to him alone. You have a sacred duty to help. Don't be blinded by dogma from doing what you know is right."

Mischa Tan's eyes narrow to slits. "We are all fated to play a part in the Kaliyuga. Urizen left us out of her plans for a reason."

"Great Speaker," the red priestess, Ania, interjects. "The holy scripture says angels will appear at the end times and that Urizen will lead them against the forces of darkness. What if Metatron is right? Is she not an angel fighting on the side of light? Should we not aid her?"

"Prophecy can take on many interpretations," Mischa Tan responds scornfully. "The council has decided," she says. "You come to us claiming to be an Anjin, but we scanned your lineage the moment you stepped from the holy armor." She directs this at Xana. "You may have partial Praetorian genetics, but you are not a fully fledged soldier of the imperium. The message you bring is quite unclear. You say that some renegade of the lost arc will betray Urizen and her daughter. But more than that, you have taken from me my son. Whatever the events, Urizen has always designed for Armada to remain independent of it."

We've failed, I realize. *They will not help us.*

"No outsider comes to Armada and leaves. Yet your words are like a plague. The matriarchy cannot have your heresy infect the holy Nicnacians. Place them in confinement." Speaker Tan commands. The guards aim their staffs, and Tol and I are electrocuted into delirium.

CHAPTER 26

The Daughter

> In opposition to the prodigal, the daughter is the child who has achieved. She has tended her fields and flock carefully; she considers herself a master of her powers. Her arrogance blinds her to the humbleness that the prodigal has gained, even though it is the daughter who becomes the mother and gives birth to new life.
>
> —Ovanth, *A Practical Reading of the Arcana*

I regain my senses somewhere in the belly of the whale, carried between two of the female guards. A glance behind reveals Tol, still unconscious, and a look forward shows Xana taking in the surroundings of dank, iron corridors. Everywhere else on Eleth arc is pristine, clean, and artistic. The brig, however, seems a dungeon, invoking familiar psychological oppression.

I've survived worse. I count seven guards. Xana glances at me knowingly. Her simple look conveys that an escape attempt would be critically unwise.

"The High Matriarchy does not always agree on what to do," the priestess Ania says as she leads our party. "While Speaker Tan has advocated immediate execution, there are minds who would differ."

We're shuttled into a tiny cell, a glass bubble that looks out upon the vast. The heavy metal door is rammed shut. A slit in the door slides open, and Ania's strange cat eyes peer through. "I will return when the matriarchy comes to consensus." The slit closes.

I am used to darkness, but we are not alone here . . .

"Shizzle, my head." Tol groans. I float to him and massage the base of his skull to return blood flow. "Oh yeah, Doctor Batman, do it to me all day."

"Shut up, Tol," I mutter. I look to the corner of the bubble where I sense the foreign heartbeat.

"If they decide to execute us, they'll simply open this portal and blow us into space," Xana murmurs.

"Don't be so sure," a strange voice from the corner croaks. Tol freezes. Xana reaches for a weapon on her hip that's no longer there. "If they put you in here with me, it's unlikely they'll terminate you."

"Because they haven't decided what to do with you, either, Washo Tan?" I ask.

He emerges from the shadow in the corner. "Edmon Leontes . . ." The voice shifts, becoming that of the Nicnacian boy who once was crew of the UFP *James Bentley*. In my name, I hear the anguish Washo has endured since our ersatz family fractured, even as I feel the phantom stab in my side. The last time I saw him, he held in one hand the brain of the last matriarch and a knife coated with my blood in the other.

He cries out and clutches his head, then claws at his stomach as if his insides are being chewed up.

"Washo!" Xana shouts.

"Stay back, girl!" The voice that comes from his mouth is no longer his. It is the voice we heard in the labyrinth of Miral. "The boy may see you as a friend, but in my time, your kind were simply servants."

"Washo," I say calmly. He curls into a ball in an attempt to retreat. "Tell us what happened."

"Washo Tan is gone, fool!" The matriarch hisses. "I killed him."

"You were left on Miral to protect the portal and the future children of Urizen. Washo is a Nicnacian, one of the faithful. You would not destroy him."

"I needed to survive, so I pushed him aside." The voice is ragged.

"Washo, I know you're in there. Come back, Washo," I command.

"I . . ." The boy returns. "I'm sorry, Edmon. I saw you in the corridor. I saw you with Ari. You kissed her. You wanted to keep her from fulfilling her destiny as the avatar of Urizen!" The voices combine, screaming insanely.

"Doctor, stop this!" Xana says.

I whirl on her. "I will not give up on him, just as I did not give up on you." I put a hand on Xana's shoulder. She tenses. "And I never will, Xana." I turn back to the boy. "You did not want to, Washo, but you tried to kill me." The memory of the betrayal laces my voice.

"I needed to be reunited with my mother," the matriarch hisses. "The darkness comes for us all!"

I feel anger, love, and then focus as the vibrations in my belly, the sonic resonance of the Dim Mak, rise up. Faria once told me the technique had applications beyond that of harming or basic healing. A true master could even use it with his words. Suddenly, I see a way. My anger at all that has happened combines with my love for this boy. Yet with the teachings of my brother I channel the skill in a new way. "Washo Tan! Return!"

There is a gasp from the boy huddled in the corner. His body spasms then relaxes. "Doctor? Edmon?" he asks tentatively.

"Washo!" The joy in my voice is unfiltered.

"Where am I?" he asks.

"You're in prison on Eleth arc," Xana replies.

"Xana! Tol!" he exclaims. "Where's Welker? Ari?"

I shake my head gravely.

"Edmon, we have to find her!" Washo practically leaps from the corner and clutches my flight suit.

"Take a deep breath, boy." I grab him by the shoulders.

"Doctor, you don't understand," he says. "At the Kaliyuga, Urizen and her forces will meet Los in the great battle. We have to help them. The matriarch was afraid you would stop Ari from helping to fulfill the prophecy. I'm sorry, Doctor, what I did . . ."

"Was out of love for her and your people," I say, understanding. He nods, tears floating from his cheeks into the micro-g. "It's okay. We all love her. Each in our own way." I hear a hitch in Xana's breath behind me. "I know the matriarch used that to take control."

"She's still inside, Edmon. Even without my physical connection to the gray matter." Washo now looks desperate. "She's fighting for control. I won't be able to keep her out permanently."

"You have the faith of the Nicnacians," I say. "I have faith in you, Washo. Tell us what happened after Miral."

"It is hard to remember." He searches for the words. "I was me, and I wasn't. But I was in a gel pod. I piloted the rudimentary systems through the Fracture, and from there, I set myself on an intercept course with a known Nicnacian trade route. I amplified my distress signal and placed myself in stasis. I think I was there for maybe a standard month before a freighter found me. They expelled the gel and woke me. They identified me as a spypsy and traded me at a meeting with a representative of Thiriel arc."

"So you returned," I encourage.

"It's more than a criminal offense to fail in Rapzis, Edmon. It is a sin. Yet, I was also bonded to the brain. I was brought before the matriarchs. My own mother passed judgment. I was imprisoned, and no one else on Armada even knows I'm here or what I brought on board."

"Would they join us if they knew?" I ask.

"I don't know. There would be great upheaval. My mother has long been speaker, but she is of Uveth, second daughter. She has stayed in power by remaining conservative and isolationist in her views. A few years ago, there was a strong movement among our youth to break our code of xenophobia and join the larger community of the Fracture. Defectors left Armada. It threatened my mother's power because the more Nicnacians who leave, the less likely it is that our secrets are kept. There was a crackdown on the Rapzis, which did not endear my mother to many. I suppose she never thought I would be one of those who betrayed her."

Leaving must have been painful for him. Returning has been even more so, I realize.

"I love my mother," he says. "But she's not right to keep us from the outside world or to continue the practice of male inequality. She's not right . . . about many things." He shakes his head. "She kept me alive rather than have me executed as is required by Nicnacian law. Instead, they cut the brain from me and threw me in here. But the connection between me and the matriarch was not severed fully, and the brain refuses to bond with the arc ships or anyone else."

"You're alive. Hope is not lost," I say.

Light spills into the cell through the door slat. The golden eyes of Ania, priestess of the red robes, appears. "The council has come to consensus, at least where you two are concerned." She eyes myself and Tol. "Xana Caprio, pilot of the Anjin, will remain a prisoner of Eleth arc, but you two shall be terminated."

Xana is female and has bonded with one of the last Anjins. Even if they don't believe her to be a true Praetorian, it stands to reason they would want to study her and the armor. Tol and I, however, are expendable. The round iron door opens with a groan.

"Wait, you're an Anjin pilot, Xana?" Washo asks.

"It's a long story," she responds.

"Take them," Ania commands. Two tall Nicnacian women push themselves forward. Xana and I share a look, silently assenting—*now is the moment.* We ready ourselves when . . .

Ania shocks the guards into unconsciousness from behind with an extensor staff. "They wished to execute you both publicly to show the entirety of Armada that the intruders who invaded our space were heretics. When we do not arrive for the fleet-wide broadcast, they will come for us." She pushes herself out of the cell and into the corridor beyond. We follow. "I've used my privilege as a priestess to relieve the security patrol in this sector. It should allow us to take a lift and get you to your ship, Commander." Ania looks at Xana. "Some of us still hold true faith and believe in portents." She then pulls from beneath her cloak my sword in its flute scabbard. "I brought this. Is this truly what I think it is?" She eyes me suspiciously.

I clasp the leviathan blade in my hand and pull it halfway from its sheath. The siren steel hums. "A siren sword of Albion," I say.

The woman's golden eyes grow wide. "I am the resurrection and the life. I die and pass the limits of possibility, as it appears to individual perception. Return, Albion, return! I give myself for thee. That is the weapon of the elite warriors of Miral. How is it that you possess such a blade?"

"I'm not the only one," I lament. "There are a few others who have perverted the use of the mythical siren steel." I snap the sword back into its scabbard.

"I've heard of these barbarians of Tao," the priestess spits out. "If you are one of them, you and your people have much to answer for."

"Could we maybe debate Fracture politics or mythology later," Tol pipes up. "I like a good prison cell, but if you could give us the coordinates to Ancient Earth, we'll be out of your . . . bald head in no time."

"Earth?" The priestess looks confused. "Only the matriarchs would have such data."

"Then that's where we go. This whole trip is for nothing if we don't have a way to find Ari," says Xana.

"The matriarchs are bonded to Eleth. You'll never make it to the command center before they realize you've escaped. If you want to live, your only chance is to go now," the priestess insists.

"We won't give up now," I growl.

Maybe there's another way," Washo says. Beads of sweat form on his brow. He shivers. *The matriarch is attempting to reassert herself.* "There's another who knows the location of Earth, the matriarch of Miral."

"Washo—" I begin.

He cuts me off. "My personality, my sanity, is a small price to pay; you know it."

As much as I hate it, he's right. If this is the only way, then we must follow through.

"What do you need?" Xana asks.

"The brain," he answers. "The presence the doctor helped temporarily banish was an impression. I need to connect with the brain again in order for her full knowledge to be accessed."

"Won't that mean she takes over permanently?" Tol asks.

"Not necessarily," Ania says. We follow the red-robed woman into the lift.

We are spirited through the muscular tube like a swallowed capsule. We glide down peristaltic waves of what seems an esophagus or intestine. The pulses are mitigated by the effects of the micro-g to the point where it almost feels as if we are on a soothing boat ride.

"Many artifacts left to us from Miral are kept in the temple of Eleth, sealed within a vault for protection and study. The High Matriarchy has put the brain there for safekeeping," Ania explains.

"Oh, look, don't touch that dial." Tol points to a holographic screen that alights.

We reorient ourselves in the micro-g for a better view. The display shows a vast spherical chamber within Eleth. In the center sits a giant globule of water surrounded by powerful glow globes. A manicured garden is grown all around, and hundreds if not thousands of Washo's people gather on her lawns of clipped purple grass. They maneuver themselves along the carved ivory railings that form paths all over the chamber. Many carry staffs with curved ends that allow them to hook to the railings and pull themselves back in case they sail too far away in the micro-g.

"That's Monument Park," Ania says. A large obelisk relief is carved into one hemisphere of the chamber. In the center of the obelisk is a sort of glass bubble. "This is where the pronouncement of your execution is to take place."

A red-robed priestess, flanked by several bald-headed female guards, floats into the bubble. A close-up of her image is projected on the giant obelisk above and below for all denizens. "People of Armada!" the priestess addresses them. "The midden-mensch travelers who have come to us may have borne Anjin armor of old, but the High Matriarchy has learned the truth: they are imposters and defilers of the faith. They have escaped their bonds and may attempt to flee Armada. We cannot allow this. It jeopardizes all for which we have fought over a thousand years in the name of Urizen. Should you see these beings"—the images of the priestess on the obelisk are replaced by rotating images of myself, Tol, and Xana—"alert the red robes immediately. By Urizen, herself."

The people within Monument Park parrot the chant, and the image on the capsule screen winks out.

"Well, that's not going to help," I add wryly.

The lift doors open. We follow Ania into another large sphere. Unlike Monument Park or the command center, this sphere seems carved from stone. It is reminiscent of the temple on Miral, but built omni-directionally for micro-g. One hemisphere has carved reliefs. Twelve robed figures are depicted, their heads pointing toward the center of the hemisphere.

"The Temple of Eleth," Ania whispers and pulls her red hood low. "There were once twelve high matriarchs of Miral, daughters of Urizen. Five were killed. Six gave their minds to the arcs . . ."

"And the seventh now lies in the vault ahead," Washo says grimly.

We float past worshippers, their eyes closed in prayer. Railings of ivory extend from the stone walls and form a web pattern that serves as a barrier. Priestesses hover on the other side of the border, administering blessings to Nicnacians through the webbing. Ania leads us toward the railing. A murmur grows within the ranks of the Nicnacians as we pass. Xana, especially, draws their gazes.

A carving of a woman lies in the center of the relief between the heads of the matriarchs. A mane of red-golden hair swirls around her like a halo. A circular portal is cut into the belly of the relief leading deeper into the temple almost as if it is a womb.

"The vault is within."

Ania leads us past the barrier to the portal. Several red-robe priestesses quickly float to block our path to the inner sanctum. "Sister, you bring heretics to our door?" asks one.

"They are not heretics." Ania speaks loud enough so that even worshippers beyond the railings hear. "I bring with me Xana Caprio, Praetorian of Miral, pilot of the Anjin, Metatron. With her is Washo Tan, son of the speaker, and host of the last matriarch that lies sealed within the vault."

The crowd behind whispers excitedly even as more red robes surround us and cut us off from escape. Xana tenses beside me. Washo shivers uncontrollably now, clutching his sides. He begins snarling in the Nicnacian language, the psychotic and fragmented memories of an ancient mind battling within his head. The cat eyes of the priestesses glance at one another.

"Washo Tan must reunite with the last matriarch. Do you seek further proof than the return of the Anjin and that the daughter of Urizen has chosen the son of a speaker to bond with?"

My hand slowly reaches for my sword.

"They are criminals of the matriarchy. Be assured we will not implicate ourselves in their sins as you have."

The priestesses behind us make their move. Xana reacts by kicking one red robe aside, but in the micro-g, she, too, goes careening. "Edmon!" she shouts as several priestesses tackle me. I press my feet into the relief and push, hurling myself through the chamber.

"Tol!" I scream. "Get Washo to the vault!"

"Transform and roll out!" Tol grabs the boy and flies himself through the portal in the relief.

I slam against the railings, shucking the priestesses from my back. Worshippers scatter. I launch like a torpedo at Xana, who is entangled with several more red robes. I slam into them, grabbing their robes and swinging them with brute strength, sending them sailing. However, now I'm floating in the middle of the chamber, spinning, with no momentum to carry me toward purchase.

Xana pushes off a wall, intercepts me, and flies us both through the passage in the relief. We pull ourselves down the corridor. The path branches in several directions revealing the inner sanctum to be a much more intricate structure than I would have thought.

"Over here!" Tol waves to us from the end of the hall where he, Washo, and Ania float in front of a massive metal door.

"Access denied," the computerized voice says, which sounds unmistakably like Mischa Tan's.

"My clearance has been revoked," Ania laments. "They know I'm with you. I can't get us in."

"Doc," Tol says, holding Washo in his arms. "He's burning up! I don't think he's going to make it unless we get him to a med bay."

"Just get us in, Edmon." Washo moans.

I draw the siren steel at my side. *Door openings are what I do best.* The sword howls as I plunge her into the heart of the shielded door. My sword vibrates, melting the metal. I bring the blade full circle and pull it away as Xana shoulders the fragments and leads us through.

We find ourselves in a dark chamber of relics, each protected by glass tubing. In one, I see a nightscript reader like Faria's. In another rests some kind of scepter. The largest seems to contain a giant segmented worm connected to a machine. Its bloated body hangs from the head, which is grown into the mechanism, which in turn is bonded to the very ship itself. Xana involuntarily shudders at the sight.

"Here," Ania says, calling our attention to where the brain of the matriarch, in a fresh amniotic sac, floats behind protective glass. Ania accesses the controls, retracting the glass. Washo leaves Tol's arms and floats toward the brain, extending a palm.

"Washo, wait!" I float toward him. "If you reunite now, she'll just take over your body." I turn to the priestess. "You said there was another way?"

Ania nods. "The chrysalis chamber." She gestures to the giant hanging worm. "In days of old, the chamber was used to fuse multiple beings as a way to upload and preserve knowledge."

"That worm? That sounds . . . I can't even . . . whatever." Tol throws his hands up.

"The Mira believed all thought and memory was encoded in the language of the cells. Is it so preposterous? Epigenetics is influenced by environment and experience. If a person had total control over such language, they could theoretically pass on memory through a touch."

"Or a kiss," Xana adds quietly.

"Blood or sexual congress more regularly," the priestess confirms. "The chrysalis is a facilitator, allowing rapid share between biological beings. It was eventually set aside due to the high risk of the procedure."

"How high?" I ask.

"Mortality may be close to eighty percent," Ania responds.

"Forget it," I say.

"If he enters the chamber and survives," Xana asks, "who will he be when he comes out?"

"An integrated being, both the last matriarch and himself. And neither."

"But if he connects with the brain the old-fashioned way—" Tol begins.

"I lose myself completely," Washo finishes.

"It's too dangerous," I argue.

"Edmon, if I don't combine with the matriarch, we don't get the coordinates. At least this way some semblance of me survives," Washo reasons.

"The mortality rate is too high. If you fail, we walk away with nothing," I say. "Let one of us go instead." I turn to the priestess. "The chamber can be used on anyone."

"I'll go," Xana says.

"You are already bonded with Metatron," the priestess says.

"Don't look at me!" Tol splays out his hands.

I float forward but feel Washo's hand on my shoulder. "Edmon, you once told me of squires. There comes a point when you must be willing to let go of your old self in order to become the new. I can do this."

He's afraid. So am I. I don't want to let him go. I don't want to let that part of myself that wants to protect him go, either. "Washo," I say. "I'm proud of you."

He smiles through his pain and floats toward the brain of the matriarch. He takes its sac into his hands while Ania retracts the glass casing around the chrysalis.

"Guys?" Tol calls from the vault opening. "We're gonna have company."

"Xana!" I bring forth my sword. Xana actuates her staff. We float toward the entryway, barring the passage. Nicnacian security floods the temple tunnels. They blast electric pulses at us, but I meet each pulse with a fluid stroke of my sword. Xana stays over my shoulders and fires her own bursts from the staff in response.

Behind us, Washo steps into the chrysalis chamber. The worm comes alive; spinnerets in the abdomen spray a green, silken liquid down and around Washo and the brain. The cocoon casing hardens, sealing them both within. Fluid begins pumping into the sac, and an intense electric-blue light explodes behind the membrane and lights up the chrysalis from within. Washo screams.

My friend needs me. I let the sonic vibrations build within me. I howl and swing my sword, releasing the Dim Mak through the siren steel. The shock wave ripples down the halls, shaking the walls of Eleth. The security forces are blasted back and knocked against the stone, out cold.

"That'll do." Xana nods to me.

The light from the chrysalis fades, leaving only a dull green shell. The worm machine lays silent. We wait for a breath that seems to last forever. Then within, the shadow of a hand presses against the semi-translucent membrane. I charge forward and slam my fist into the shell. It cracks in spider-web veins. Xana follows suit kicking the thing. We both strike, and the chrysalis shatters. Washo is naked, bathed in goop. He falls into our arms.

"Is he dead?" Tol asks, peering over my shoulder.

"Hardly." His eyes open, and he sits up. "I am a mess. Priestess, fetch me some robes immediately." Ania looks somewhat taken aback at the orders. "I am son of the speaker, the daughter of Urizen, and covered in snot. Robes, now!" he commands.

The priestess bows and quickly whisks out of the chamber.

"Washo—" Xana begins.

"Washo Tan is gone," he says, floating away. "I am something new, and I'm going to reclaim my fleet. Are you coming?"

CHAPTER 27

The Emperor

> The emperor sits on his throne, the ruler of his destiny. He has been the fool in his ignorance, met the gypsy in his wandering. He has faced the devil and death, and returned home as the prodigal. He has mastered his body and mind and now becomes the father.
>
> —Ovanth, *A Practical Reading of the Arcana*

Washo hovers by the entrance to the temple. Ania drapes the bloodred robes of the clergy over his shoulders. Worshippers, priestesses, and arc security who remain stare in awe and confusion. Xana, Tol, and I float behind. Washo extends his palm into a depression in the relief. Veins filled with rivulets of liquid metal come alive within the stone. The glow gives the impression that the piece of art is breathing.

"People of Eleth, Uveth, Ona, Thiriel, Utha, and Grodna—I am Enion Lazarus, the seventh matriarch of Miral. The Kaliyuga is upon us. I sense the darkness in the vast. I feel it in my bones . . ."

I feel it, too, gnawing at my insides even as Ari's memory whispers for me to hurry.

"Urizen gathers her forces at our birthplace. I am taking command of Armada and will lead you there. By Urizen, herself."

"By Urizen, herself," the worshippers respond.

"We'll have little problem reaching the command center now," Washo says. "My mother will be forced to help us or have civil war on her hands." He pushes off and heads through the temple cavern. We follow him into the lift amid supplicants reaching out with hands and blessings upon their lips.

"I'll remain here, matriarch, to administer to the faithful," Ania says, bowing.

"It is important for each of us to fulfill her role," Washo agrees. The doors to the lift whisper shut, and we are pressed forward by the muscular tubing.

"Okay, you guys, I'm trying to wrap my head around this," Tol interrupts. "So, um, is it Washo? Or Enion?"

Washo smiles wryly. "A part will always be Washo Tan."

"A part? Oh, I get it. So . . . ?" Tol presses.

"You may call me Washo Tan, Tol Sanctun." That seems enough for Tol. I sigh. My friend is gone, but not all gone. *To name a thing,* I think, *is to give it meaning.*

"So, *Washo,* can I ask why we don't just grab our ship and head to Ancient Earth?" Tol asks.

"Why fly the Mini, when you can take the Escalade, Tol Sanctun?" Washo answers.

Tol glances at Xana and me. "I like the way this lady thinks."

The lift doors whisper open. A cadre of arc security awaits us in the command center, extensor staffs pointed and charged. I reach for my sword. "That will not be needed, Edmon Leontes. Will it, sisters?" Washo asks.

The security forces eye one another warily. "You have been forbidden by Speaker Mischa Tan," one of the women informs him coldly.

The navigators and engineers at their surrounding stations cast glances at us. "Reports of skirmishes are coming in from all over Eleth," one crew member calls out. "A full-blown riot has been instigated against security in Monument Park. The protestors are demanding the matriarchy hand over control of the fleet to Enion Lazarus."

"It appears that my mother is no longer in charge, Commander," Washo says calmly. He floats past security into the sphere. "You're all of the faithful and have given yourselves to the governance of the elected matriarchs. Allow them to meet with me. Trust that they will make the right decision."

Washo continues his ascent into the cupola unrestrained, and we follow. The door to the speaker's cupola is closed. Washo touches the actuator, and the door irises open.

"Mother!" He floats into the chamber.

The door swivels shut behind us.

"Betrayer!" The woman floats toward us, the cord attached to the back of her head floating behind her. "I didn't think that I would see you again, Washo. Certainly not like this, a usurper," Mischa Tan says acidly.

"I've no wish to usurp, Mother," Washo replies sadly. "Only to claim what is rightfully mine as the daughter of Ahania Lazarus."

"Enion Lazarus," Mischa Tan says, "if that is who you truly are, you know that if I turn over Armada, and we go where you intend, it will put millions at risk. You also know that I cannot allow that. I was elected to protect the people. Even from themselves."

"You understand if we do nothing the universe itself may be lost and all of Armada with it?" Washo counters. "I'm both Enion Lazarus and Washo Tan. I know what they both know—that you've used our religion to keep the Nicnacians isolated from the rest of humanity. You've used it to justify your rule and maintain matriarchy control. You've perpetuated a caste system, a gender bias that has existed for thousands of years. When I was a child, you always told me I could do anything. That was a lie. Males are not allowed to serve as head engineers, navigators, or speakers. The scriptures say that Miral is a paradise, that a Tevoda is blessed and becomes a Nicnacian when she sees the face of God. Those are lies, too. When I, as Washo, went on my Rapzis, all I saw was a dead world, and I saw no face of god, goddess, or anything else divine. That is why I never returned from the pilgrimage. Through my further travels with the crew of the *James Bentley*, I learned the truth—Urizen is flesh and blood as is her daughter. They may be divine; they may not. I do not truly know. But I do know they have been betrayed by those who claim to serve them. We have to do everything in our power to help."

Mischa Tan holds the gaze of this new Washo. "It seems I'm left with little choice. If I deny you, I risk a full riot aboard Eleth that may turn to civil war."

A fibrous cord grows from the chitinous wall of the cupola; its tendrils tickle the back of Washo's bare neck. Suddenly it plunges itself into Washo's brain stem. His eyes widen with the shock of becoming one with the arc.

"People of Armada." His voice echoes through the entire ship. "The forces arrayed against us are beyond anything the Fracture has known since the final days of Miral. We will need an equal navy to confront them. I take you to those warriors now."

What? Xana and I stare at each other in confusion.

"Where do you expect to find a military to rival the designer organics?" I ask.

"I don't expect to, Edmon of House Leontes, Prince of Tao." Washo smiles shrewdly. "I expect you to."

Armada drops from the Fracture Point into the Lyrian star system. Her golden sun silhouettes thousands upon thousands of Taoan warships against her luminous backdrop.

"That's a lot of ships, Doctor Batman," Tol says, looking out the curved viewscreen of the Eleth cupola.

"Phaestion has recalled his fleet from Market," I surmise.

"Yes," Washo says flatly from his position floating among the other matriarchs. "Our communications indicate that all planetary governments are realizing the blackout along the Radial and Brachial Corridors is not due to any kind of glitch in the technical networks. They are all pulling back in an effort to figure out the cause."

"But we already know what it is." Xana says what we all think.

"We may look impressive," Washo says, floating to face me, "but arcs are not warships."

"They don't know that," I say. "We only need to gain their attention."

The black-winged fighters of Tao come screaming from the atmo of Lyria. They rise from her mists like monsters of the depths and zoom on an intercept course for the arcs of Armada.

"Xana, activate Metatron and recall the other Anjins from their hiding places," I say.

She exits the cupola as fast as she can pull herself in micro-g.

"This is a risk, and we are out of time, Washo," I growl. "I'm a traitor. I carry a death sentence. Phaestion's governor has been murdering innocent Lyrians every day I haven't been brought to justice. They will be calling for my blood, not my guidance."

"Yet you are also the foster brother of the emperor. He has wanted you captured alive so he can execute you publicly," Washo says. "This gives us an advantage."

"Phaestion has nominal ability to predict future events—"

Washo cuts me off. "Then he knows why we've come. We will turn you in, and in exchange, we'll bargain with Phaestion to join us in the battle against Talousla Karr's army."

The designer organic fleet made short work of the Taoan interdiction ships earlier, but with the Anjins and our knowledge of the stinger ships' design, we may find some way to nullify them. But we need some kind of fleet, and Phaestion is the only one who commands anything close to the size of the enemy flotilla. I grit my teeth. *My person in return for Phaestion's aid—it's a sacrifice I've told them I will make.*

"The Taoan squadron is almost within range," an officer from the command center behind us hails.

Washo places a hand on my shoulder. "I am speaker, a matriarch of old, but I am no battle commander. These are your people." He gestures out at the stars beyond the cupola.

I exhale and float forward to watch Xana piloting Metatron, dwarfed in her white armor against the massive tide of giant warships. "Hail them," I call out.

"No response, sir," the officer says over the comm.

"So be it," I mutter. "Metatron, bloody them."

Xana wastes no words. The rocket pack of the Anjin fires, and she hurtles toward the Taoans. Space alights with sparks of chain gunfire as the Taoan fleet tries to bring her down. Metatron is too agile. She zips in dodging patterns, avoiding the fire; a chitin shield radiates out from the gauntlet of one arm, a giant spear extends in the armored fist of another. She jams the spear into a vessel, rakes it along the hull, and tears open the warship like a can. Atmosphere hisses into space. Another vessel swoops in, but Metatron just points her fist. A cannon pops from her forearm and blasts rounds of slugs into the oncoming ship, chopping holes into the vessel. It careens out of control. A Tao fighter comes in from behind. She twists at the last second, as if prescient. She grabs the ship with the talons of her feet. Her rockets fire, and she twists, tossing the attacker into another oncoming ship, ending them both in a spectacular collision.

Still, there are too many for her to stop completely. Some slip by, heading for the arcs. "Commander, what are your orders?" an officer shouts.

"Hold position," I order. *They're coming.* The six remaining Anjins appear, flying over the burnished copper orb of Titanius.

Mikael, Gavriel, Rafael, Uriel, Ragiel, and Azrael fan out like sentinels, each guarding a ship. The Taoan fleet slows, having just experienced one Anjin. They're not sure what to make of six more.

"Speaker, we're being hailed."

"Display on viewscreen," Washo commands.

The curved window of the cupola displays the holographic visage of Sigurd of House Flanders, Phaestion's last remaining Companion. The bully's broad face, almost porcine, is twisted with barely controlled rage. "I am Sigurd of House Flanders, governor of the Lyrian system. Name yourselves and declare your intentions by word of Emperor Phaestion of the Julii!"

"The speaker of Armada does not recognize your imperium, nor your emperor, Sigurd of House Flanders," Washo replies.

"Snap!" Tol whispers next to me.

Washo continues. "You have illegally invaded this system, violating the compact of independent Fractural systems that has been in place since the fall of Miral. Vacate Lyrian space and return to whatever dark corner of the universe you have crawled from," he says sternly.

The boy is playing a dangerous game antagonizing Sigurd. The Taoan's fury is liable to get the better of him, and though the Anjin's are powerful, it may be they cannot defeat the entire fleet.

"How dare you, you insignificant, bald piece of gutter trash—"

"Insults do not become you, Patriarch," Washo interrupts. "Send word to your false emperor: if he does not vacate, he risks full-scale war with Armada. You've seen what one of our Anjin mechs can do. Do you wish to confront the full might of all seven divine angels of the old empire?"

"You underestimate the Taoan thirst for battle, spypsy." Sigurd grins. "Phaestion of House Julii would gladly welcome the challenge to make you submit to his authority."

Washo has maneuvered me perfectly. He has goaded Sigurd knowing that Armada may not survive a fully pitched battle. If it comes to war between us while Los devours the Fracture, we all lose. I must turn myself over in exchange for the chance to forge an alliance.

"No," I call out. "There need be no fight."

"Edmon of House Leontes," Sigurd snarls contemptuously, finally seeing me. "So, Armada, you harbor a known criminal of the imperium as well?"

"Armada recognizes Edmon of House Leontes as the rightful heir to the throne of Tao," Washo proclaims.

Sigurd starts with a shock. I, too, turn to Washo, my face registering surprise and horror. Then I exhale, understanding Washo's gambit. *He lied to me. He never intended to turn me over to them.* "Sigurd, I need to speak with Phaestion. This need not end with bloodshed."

"Negotiate?" He spits the word. "You're pathetic, Daysider."

"You've no authority to act without permission, servant." I change my tack. "Run along to your master like a good seal pup," I growl, flashing the gaze my father taught, the gaze of the leviathan.

The image winks out. I turn to Washo, my eyes hard. "You never intended to try and convince them to side with you. You didn't even make an attempt. Now I'll have to face him as a challenger."

"I only limited your options. You made the choice. Sometimes we need a little push to do the things we know we must. That's what family is for, Doctor."

"Thanks," I retort sarcastically.

The viewscreen reactivates with the image of Sigurd sitting smugly in his command chair. "The emperor, Phaestion of House Julii, agrees to meet with Edmon of House Leontes and an envoy in the imperial throne room on Lyria within the hour. We are transmitting you the coordinates now." The image winks out.

"Let's go, Tol," I call to the man in the stovepipe hat. I turn back to Washo. "You realize this could go very badly for all of us?"

"I have faith in you, Edmon Leontes."

My heart beats thunder in my chest. Tol maneuvers our ship through the pale skies above Prospera. The sun hangs low, casting an orange hue over the gilded rooftops of the city.

"This could be a trap, Doctor Batman," Tol says from the pilot's harness.

I haven't seen Phaestion in over twelve years.

"Doctor Bat—"

"No, Tol," I respond. "I don't think so. I think he will want to see me face-to-face. Even if it is just to kill me, he'll want to make a show of doing it openly, fairly. Besides, we have Xana."

Metatron spreads her wings alongside our craft and gently sets herself down on the launchpad in the palazzo of Prospera. Tol does the same with our ship, and I feel the drag of gravity on my bones. I close my eyes, rushing the chemicals to my muscles, fortifying them, willing them stronger, preparing myself for what is about to happen.

"You ready for this, Doctor Batman?" Tol asks.

"Whether I am or not . . ." I unbuckle my safety harness, and we exit the cockpit.

Xana waits at the bottom of our ramp, her bone-white armor glimmering in the sunset. She looks almost like one of the classical marble statues of the palazzo. Denizens of Lyria have filled the square, and black-armored Taoans hold them back, creating space for us to ascend the steps of the grand opera house. I grit my teeth with suppressed fury—*Phaestion has the audacity to take the opera house, a most sacred place of beauty and music, and make it his throne room.*

Whispers rise from the crowd. Once, Taoans viewed me as a champion of the oppressed. Now, I'm branded a traitor. To those of Lyria, I'm unknown, a criminal who has inspired daily public murders of one innocent after another. They don't know what to make of me. *Who am I?* We're all about to find out together.

We reach the top of the marble steps. *I once dreamed of coming here, of singing in this place.*

“What do you plan to do?” Metatron asks in robotic monotone.

“I’m not sure exactly,” I admit. “I’m kind of winging it.” I place my hands on the double doors. The huge, metal slabs push inward. I stride into what was once the grandest opera house in all the Fracture, now just a room with a chair for a petty tyrant. He sits lazily on the massive throne, which is carved like the fanged mouth of an orca, the symbol of House Julii. His metal-gray eyes hold my gaze. Only Metatron’s thunderous armored steps sound as we approach.

The hall is flanked by Taoan nobles and wealthy Lyrian merchants who have capitulated to their new rulers. Sigurd stands beside his master, a grim enforcer. Miranda Wusong, the imperial heiress and my one-time wife, is there as well. The layers of white face paint and ornate imperial headdress mask her grim sadness. Cam globes, the silver orb recording devices native to Tao, hover everywhere, capturing every detail of the moment.

Good, I think. *Phaestion’s vanity will force him to commit to any oath he makes here today.*

I stop before the dais. I do not kneel. Phaestion’s eyes glance at Metatron, quickly calculating the threat she poses. He rises, and I see the man Talousla Karr crafted: tall, broad-shouldered, in the smart black military suit and cape that hangs off one shoulder. The planes of his face seem cut from pure alabaster. He is older now, which gives his artificial beauty an essence of wisdom he no doubt does not have. His thick hair is the color of molten flame and is pulled back by the silver circlet on his brow. He is still the same as the boy I met that day in the foyer of my family’s manse on the Isle of Bone, self-assured and casually sadistic.

He stares down coldly. Then his placid face breaks into a huge grin, and he throws his arms out wide. “Edmon Leontes!” he says with joy as he descends the steps of the dais to me. “It is good to see you again, little leviathan.” He sweeps me into an embrace and picks me up off the floor.

I remain stiff, in shock. *What is happening?* I think. I’m not the only one perplexed at the turn of his behavior. The heartbeats of my friends, who watch over my shoulder, increase, wary of any danger. I catch Sigurd scowling next to the throne. Miranda purses her lips with unease. The crowd murmurs. *Is this not the man the so-called emperor has named a traitor? The one who fled the Combat in ignominy? The one who has caused the execution of an innocent each day since it was discovered he lived?* they wonder. *Now the tyrant embraces him like a beloved brother?* Any desire the Taoans had to see my head roll along the opera house floor seem unlikely now, just as the Lyrians' hope that I might rescue them from their current predicament evaporates.

"How I've missed you," Phaestion whispers in my ear as he sets me back down.

"And I you," I return. For a moment, I'm caught up in the spell woven by his physical beauty and the pheromone secretions that subtly bond others to him. But I shake my head, remembering that I must remain unaffected by him.

He takes a step back, gripping my shoulders with both hands, almost with pride. "We welcome you and your army, son of Leontes, and entreat you to join us in our private chambers to discuss terms."

I grit my teeth at the mention of "terms"; that was my initial plan before Washo backed a claim to the throne. He leads me up the dais. Tol and Xana step forward, not wanting to leave me alone with him, but I indicate that I will be fine and that they should stay behind. I pass Sigurd next to the throne. "It's only a matter of time, snail guppy," he growls.

"I ended both Hanschen and Perdiccus," I whisper to him with a smile. "I'm so looking forward to your turn." I raise a hand and pat him on his beefy shoulder. His face turns bright red. A shake of Phaestion's head is the only thing that prevents the giant bully from attacking me right then.

I follow my foster brother through a door behind the throne, which leads to a small antechamber. The last thing I hear before Miranda follows us in and shuts the door behind us is Tol addressing the audience of onlookers: "So do you guys want to hear some good jokes from Ancient Earth? This one's called 'The Aristocrats'!"

The door closes, and Phaestion grabs a cup of wine from a set on the table and downs the contents. "That was outstanding!" he says to me, and again we are boys in my room, talking as if we had just stolen a boat and ridden the waves to catch a peek at a siren.

He grabs the second glass and tosses it to me, full with wine. *He tests me even now,* I think. The boy I was would have floundered, and the liquid would have spilled all over his tunic. I'm no longer that boy. I snatch the goblet from the air without spilling a drop, raise the glass to him, and sip. "Nice try, brother." I grin.

He shakes his head with disbelief. "You've done it," he says. "You've actually done it. Everything you've been through, the torment, the suffering, you've endured it all, and it has made you my equal."

I bite back a sour retort. *Being compared with this racist butcher is the last thing I want.* I take a deep breath, letting the feeling go. He cocks his head to the side in that familiar gesture, watching me, wondering what it is I'm thinking.

"Had you come to me in any other way, Edmon, on your knees captured by Hanschen or Perdiccus, or even just begging to return to my favor, I would have had to kill you." He laughs. "Instead you fly at the head of an armada, *the* Armada, no less, stronger than ever, more handsome than an aquagraphic leading man, making a claim to my own throne. Not only do I love you more for it, but you give me pretext to treat you like a fellow conquering Taoan! You are something!"

"I'm glad you approve," I say nonchalantly.

"Woman!" Phaestion tosses his empty wine goblet at Miranda Wusong, who has remained quietly by the door. It bounces on the floor, rolls, and stops at her slippered feet. "Pour Patriarch Leontes and me some more." He indicates the pitcher on the table. Miranda kneels demurely to pick up the goblet, her face registering no sign of the debasement her new husband shows her.

"Stop!" I command. I walk over and pick up the cup at Miranda's feet. I stand and look her in the eyes. "The daughter of an emperor is not a servant. Besides, I like to pour my own wine." For a moment, I see the barest hint of gratitude pass her painted face.

"She's the last member of a dead lineage," Phaestion says, waving his hand at her dismissively. "She's weak and worthless in everything but her name, which brings continuity to my rule. Don't make the mistake of treating her as anything but an ornament."

"I've made many mistakes, Phaestion," I say, but these words are not for him. "I'm sorry others have suffered for them. I'm trying to make it right now." I walk to the table and refill both our glasses from the pitcher there. I hand him his goblet and drink from my own. I push the cells in my digestive tract to metabolize the alcohol quickly and blunt any symptoms of drunkenness. Phaestion's system will similarly nullify any intoxicating effects rapidly, and I need to keep my wits and body as sharp as his if I can.

"Good," Phaestion says with mirth as he takes a swig. "Then finally I can do this right. You don't know, Edmon, how bored I've been without you." He collapses into a chair and puts his boots up onto the table. "Hanschen was clever, Perdiccus was always up for a thrill, and Sigurd is as strong as a bull seal. But not one of them can strategize with me, ride the backs of dolphins, fight down the corridors of an alien micro-g space station, and still laugh together about it all afterward."

I'm reminded of Tol's description of the Taoans' slaughter of the Nicnacian enclave on Market, and I have to wonder if Phaestion personally reveled in the wanton killing that took place there. I grit my teeth and hold myself in check once more.

"And I couldn't talk to any of them like I could talk to you," he says. He takes his feet off the table and instead leans on his elbows, his symmetrical face held in his palms. "You could play music. Do you remember that?"

"I remember you wanted to learn," I say, sitting down next to him. "I said I'd teach you to play if you would teach me to fight."

He laughs. "I think you got the better end of that bargain." He points to the flute scabbard holding my sword at my waist. "Do you still play?"

"Of course," I say with a touch of intentional arrogance.

"Damn you!" he jests. "And you got your voice back. Seems like you haven't lost a thing!"

I suck in a breath again, holding back the impulse to pull out my sword and gut him right now. His eyes narrow, almost as if he suspects my desire and wants me to act on it. But I don't. "I also remember I tried to get you to vacate my room," I tease instead.

He wags his finger at me. "You pushed too far with that one!"

"You were such a little self-important pissant." I shake my head. "You always had to be first, the lord of everything."

"And look where ambition has taken us both," he says softly. "The rulers of all we survey. You were the only one who was ever a match for me." He reaches out a hand and places it over mine on the table. His perfectly sculpted marble fingers are perfectly cold. His steel-gray eyes connect with mine. "Times were much simpler then, but here we are again, negotiating. Do you want me to give you back your room?" A smile curves his lips.

"No." I smile back. "I think this time we should share." I pull my hand away and stand. I take in both him and Miranda. Phaestion ignores her, but I want her to understand what's at stake. In spite of what he believes, her name, and the continuity of a Wusong lineage, conveys power. "There's a battle to be had, Phaestion, not between you and I on opposite sides, at the head of warring kingdoms. Rather, something much greater, with us leading armies side by side."

He sits up, his interest piqued. "Go on."

"When my ships exited the Fracture Point, we saw you had gathered your fleet here." He nods, confirming. "One of the Radial and Brachial Corridors are gone."

"What do you mean gone?" he asks.

"I mean they were literally swallowed by a blackness. It's an entropic force from a different dimension of our universe."

My words rest in the air for a beat. Then he bursts out laughing.

"I'm serious, Phaestion," I say with frustration. "I saw it myself on Miral, the same place where I saw Hanschen die!" My fist pounds the table, and his laughter ceases instantly. "It devoured the planet and has continued along the Fracture Corridors. It won't stop until it works its way through everything in our universe. You must have known this. Why else did you recall your army?"

"I assumed whatever severed communications and destroyed my scout ships in the regions was another military force. But that's not why I recalled my fleet. I consolidated my forces because I suspected that you were coming," he says.

His nominal prescience. "Good, then you know what I'm telling you is true. There *is* an army—of those same genetically engineered soldiers that Hanschen joined with to hunt me down. Talousla Karr created them; they obey only him. He wants this shadow, this force, to destroy our universe, and that army stands in the way of anyone who wishes to stop him."

"Why would he want the universe to be destroyed, Edmon?" Phaestion asks. "That makes no sense."

It's a good question. "Has Talousla Karr and his motivations ever made sense to you?" I counter. "And since when has it mattered to you why an opponent wishes to fight? Sigurd can tell you how sophisticated their fleet is. He saw what a mere cohort did to his interdiction ships here in the Lyrian system. Each is manned by soldiers bred for one purpose: war. That Anjin armor my friend is sporting out in the throne room was intended to fly at the head of their forces; that is, before I liberated it for our use." I grin, and he reflects my smile.

"You're right," he says. "I really don't care who these designer organics are or what Talousla Karr thinks he can accomplish with them. The prospect of testing myself against genetically bred soldiers in a pitched battle sets my blood on fire."

"Good, because we need you to lead your army in this fight. This is the war of our time. The war of all wars. We need you, the greatest warrior of your generation," I say, opening my hand.

He clasps it and stands. "With you by my side," he says. I nod. "It is agreed then. Just like Chilleus and Cuillan."

"Fighting back-to-back as brothers, in the greatest battle the universe will ever know," I echo. "They will sing our names down through the ages. Phaestion and his Companion, Edmon."

"Then once this darkness is pushed back, we take the rest of the Nine Corridors. From Market we can invade Theran space, take on all the pirates there. They're unorganized but good fighters. Our swords will sing in harmony," he says. "From there, stretch out into the wilds. The Femoral, explore the Brachial, discover new worlds beyond the farthest charted points. We'll spread the Taoan culture and language, cutting down any who resist. We'll unite the planets for the first time since Miral. The orca banner will become the symbol for a new era, the dawn of a new civilization, this one created in our own images. And when we are old and gray, our children grown and ruling in our stead, we will hold hands and marvel that we ever were apart." He turns back to look at me. "What is it, Edmon?"

"Nothing," I say quietly.

"Then come," he says, heading back toward the throne room. "Swear allegiance before the court, and we can begin anew." He smiles and walks through the door.

I follow, but Miranda stops me with a cold stare. "He will never stop," she says.

I nod. *I know.*

"We have reached an accord." Phaestion's voice rings out to the audience gathered in the opera house. The court waits with bated breath for their tyrant's pronouncement. I understand what I need to do. I need to take control of the narrative. I need everyone here to understand what is at stake.

"Your wars are meaningless!" I proclaim before Phaestion can utter another word. He looks at me first with shock and then growing ire. I face the crowd. "A new evil has risen in the Fracture, one that threatens to eat out the very heart of our universe and life itself. A great darkness, the same that I saw consume Miral with my own eyes. It has devoured the Radial and Brachial Corridors already. It is working its way through the Fracture, feeding on all life. The Anjins of the old empire have returned, as have their priests, the spypsies. They need us now, the artists of Lyria and the warriors of Tao, to join together to face this threat. This will be the greatest battle ever fought!" My voice rings out true and clear. I've used the language of epic threat and mythical darkness to the best of my ability. "Does the emperor of Tao rise to this challenge?"

Phaestion is annoyed that I've stolen this moment. More than that, he's surprised at my turn. *This is not how he thought it would happen.* Talousla Karr once told me he gave his creation an ability to glimpse the future. It manifested predominantly as battle intuition, a reading of an opponent's body language, allowing Phaestion to win any match. Occasionally, it would be more. *If he hasn't seen this scenario or what lies past it . . .*

His eyes narrow. He strides down the steps.

"Your false emperor, Phaestion of the Julii, usurper of the Wusong throne, knows that I speak the truth." *There is no going back now.*

"So the story does come full circle," he whispers so only I can hear.

I turn to him. "You helped murder my wife," I whisper. "You helped poison my father and tried to bring on the ruin of my house. You slaughtered millions across the Fracture. Did you ever think that I could join you, much less love you, butcher?"

"Chilleus and Cuillan," he says.

"Brothers raised to the status of myth not because they fought together, but because they fought against each other in epic combat," I say. "This was the outcome you knew would happen."

"I hoped," he says solemnly. "I didn't know."

He cocks his head to the side in that familiar gesture I knew in our boyhood. "Yes, they will sing of Phaestion and his Companion, Edmon." He smiles wistfully. "It was good to see you again." He ascends the steps back to his throne.

"I accept your offer, Edmon of House Leontes. We will join the battle against this darkness, this Los, provided you kneel and turn yourself over to the Tao imperium, and Armada recognizes my claim to the throne and dominion over her fleet."

All eyes fall to me. Before I walked through these doors, I would have sacrificed myself for Ari and my friends. I would have kneeled before Phaestion if I thought it would save lives. I still would. But Miranda is right—Phaestion will not stop. He'll claim Armada. He'll push into all star systems. He'll conquer them all, killing as he goes, and I will have failed to do what I could for a second time.

A voice must come. A light in the darkness, where one must stand. The voice is Ari's. It is my lost wife Nadia's. It is my mother's long passed. It is my father's. It is the leviathan's. It is mine when I say, "I'll never kneel to you, Phaestion of the Julii. I am Edmon of House Leontes. I am the rightful ruler of Tao, and I challenge you to duel for the throne!"

Phaestion smiles. Sigurd springs forward, taking the steps in one agile leap. He brandishes his gigantic mace, forged of siren steel. I see the glee in his eyes as he finally is let loose. This has been a long time coming. From the day we met, Sigurd sought to exert his dominance over me. Every step I gained, he tried to throw me back. When my mother was lobotomized and left a husk, he laughed in my face simply because she was a Daysider, not of his "pure" race. If evil could have a more insipid look, I cannot think of one. I desperately want to end him myself, but I've taken a vow never to take life. Not even Sigurd's. More than that, there is a code duello of Tao's challenges. A Patriarch does not entertain an inferior to prove his mettle. So as much as I would like to draw my sword, I do not. It gives me only slightly less satisfaction to say only one word as he reaches me . . .

"Metatron."

Xana's fist slams down onto Sigurd crushing him against the floor. She raises her gauntleted hand, and the gore sticks to her armor. She whips her arm to the side, cleaning the blood. It paints a wide, red swath on the marble tiles. Sigurd of House Flanders is now a smear. I look at Phaestion. His eyes are wide with horror. I've cut down the last of his Companions. He is all alone. "There is no one between us now, Phaestion," I say.

"You are a traitor, the last remnant of a fallen house—"

"I second his claim," a woman shouts from the ranks of bystanders. The crowd parts. A beautiful woman with auburn hair and a round face steps forward. She wears Taoan robes marked with flourishes of Lyrian embroidery. I am so happy to see her, even as I see her face is etched with the subtle lines that pain and hardship have wrought. They were not there the last time I was with her, but neither was the absolute hardness and strength my sister displays when she confronts the emperor.

"Phoebe of House Ruska," Phaestion says. "Also a family of disgrace. You left the Pantheon when you harbored Edmon Leontes and fled from Tao. We do not recognize you—"

"I also back the challenge."

All eyes turn to the sad woman with the painted white face beside the throne. Miranda Wusong, the last heir of the Great Song, has maintained position through skillful silence. She once told me that a woman on Tao had few options, a plain woman even less. Her acquiescence to our marriage was an artful subterfuge. Now she is the most powerful person in the room.

"Edmon of House Leontes was my first husband. Though the marriage was never consummated, it was annulled only because I thought him dead. Since he appears before us this day, very much alive, and lays claim to the throne, it is fitting that this must be decided through tradition—the Combat. In the name of the Balance."

Though Phaestion is their vaunted leader, Miranda is still the daughter of the imperial house. She legitimizes his rule.

"What's the matter, Phaestion of House Julii?" I taunt. "Is the greatest warrior of his generation afraid?"

"I will break your blade. Then I will break you," he says calmly.

This is the moment he saw all those years ago when he pressed his forehead to mine and asked if we would always be friends.

"Were you facing a man, I'd believe you," I say. "But this day, you face a leviathan."

The opera house floor is cleared. Xana parks Metatron among the ranks of onlookers and steps from the armor. "This is stupid," she says as the thorax closes behind her. "You should simply let me kill him, and then we take command of the planet."

I kick off my boots and strip from my flight suit so that I'm only wearing my form-fitting undergarments. "You were born on Tao, Xana. You know as well as I that the people will never follow a ruler who hasn't earned power through legitimate rite."

"Legitimacy be damned. History is written by winners," she insists. I feel the cold marble stone beneath my feet. "I've seen him," she continues. "He's too fast, his skill with the blades unparalleled. By the Elder Stars, he has precognition! You may have taken advantage crossing swords, what, maybe one out of a thousand times? He'll remember that.

You won't be able to defeat him in the same way twice. Too much rides on this. Can you do it?"

I look my friend in her eyes. "I don't know."

"Whoa, whoa, whoa," Tol speaks up, putting his hands forward. "You guys, if Doctor Batman doesn't win, what do we do?"

"I'll win, Tol," I reassure.

"Edmon, you never kill. *How* are you going to win?" Xana asks.

I take a deep breath. I set aside my rage and my fear and for the first time in my life become truly present. Phaestion, also stripped bare, steps from the dais. His muscles writhe beneath pale skin as if he's a marble statue in motion.

"I've dreamed of this moment," he says. "House against house. Brother against brother. What is it you wish to say, Edmon?"

Xana and Tol step back. I quietly crouch into a fighting stance, my hand ready to draw.

"Nothing?" Phaestion says. "Then our swords speak for us." He draws his rapier and dagger from their scabbards. Their siren steel screams like banshees, and he explodes toward me.

By the ancestors, he's fast! So am I. I whip my blade from its scabbard. Our swords lock in a sonic pulse that bursts through the opera hall. Onlookers are knocked back with the force of the blow. The stone beneath our feet cracks with the intensity of energy. The moment seems to last forever, then all too briefly as Phaestion spins away. I swipe for him, and he matches me blow for blow. I duck as he thrusts for my head, and I deftly skirt aside as his dagger aims for my leg, using a circling maneuver I learned through shaping blades next to the smiths of Albion.

"You've grown, Edmon," he taunts. "I haven't seen that before." He unleashes a flurry of slashes, and I'm backed up. *He's too fast for me!* I think. But I remember my teachers. Not just Alberich and Faria, who taught me fighting, but my music teachers, Gorham and The Maestro as well. *Timing beats speed.* Phaestion falls into a rhythm. *Fool.* He's so sure, so confident of the outcome. He steps; I see the subtle shift in his weight. I move in the spaces between his music, using the fluid motions learned from the smiths. My hand whips out, striking the pressure point above his leg with the direct line of the Dim Mak technique of the Zhao monks. I spin away and flourish my blade. *The battle is over.*

Instead of crashing to the ground as I expect with his leg immobilized, Phaestion grits his teeth through the pain and stands. He shakes his leg. *He defeated the Dim Mak,* I realize.

"You've grown, Edmon, but so have I."

He leaps toward me again with renewed vigor. *How stupid could I have been? He knew that we would face each other again. He would have spent years training his body to counter the effects of my abilities.* I try to shield his onslaught, but Xana is right: I'm not a match. I won't be able to beat him unless I kill. I must sacrifice something . . .

His dagger stabs my shoulder, and I'm stunned. His rapier twirls and snakes around my blade. The end of his weapon finds the back of my hand and slices it open. My grip is loosened; the leviathan sword spins away. Lightning shoots up my leg as he drags the edge of his dagger along the back of my knee. My tendon cut, I crash to the ground. He poises his sword high for the killing blow. "Good-bye, Edmon," he whispers.

My emotions swirl within, my past flashing before me. My father beats my mother in the hall of the Grand Wusong. My mother, bloodied, stands defiantly to face him. I see my love, Nadia, on the cliffs high above the Southern Sea, then her face as she sinks beneath the waves forever. The dark face of my master, Faria, before I took his life in pity. And my friends . . . my crew—Xana and Tol. Washo in the space above. Those gone like Welker. And Ari . . .

We are with you, Edmon, they whisper.

I was never meant to win this fight. And great change never comes but through giving up a piece of oneself. So it is, I welcome my brother's blade as it impales me in the chest, seeking to stab me through the heart.

I don't move, only twist, using the lessons of my true brother, Edvaard Leontes. All my emotions pass through me. I circle around the energy of the blade as if I am the shaping tool itself. I focus my strength, absorbing the vibrations of the sonic steel that would liquefy my insides. Everything builds within me.

I see terror in Phaestion's eyes at what he has done. I know I'm the only person he has ever loved. "I'm sorry, Edmon," he whispers. A tear rolls down his perfect cheek. I know that he had to kill me to achieve the mythological greatness he desired. I also know that I cannot kill him, even with all the horrible things he has done. *I cannot show that his violence is wrong through violence of my own.*

I grab his forearm and pull myself farther onto the blade as I stand. I bring us close, and I touch my forehead to his in the gesture of brothers. I summon all the energy within, rising up from my belly, through my heart. I send the energy of his blow back at him a thousandfold. Heart to thought, thought to voice, and with a whisper, I roar—

"Sleep."

CHAPTER 28

The Empress

> She is the great mother, the creator of all life. As the emperor is the masculine, more earthly integration of the archetypes, so the empress is the spiritual embodiment of all things. She watches over us all.
>
> —Ovanth, *A Practical Reading of the Arcana*

Phaestion and I embrace for what seems an eternity. The crowd makes no sound until I place my hands on his shoulders. I slowly pull myself off the blade with a groan. The crowd gasps as I step back, my blood spilling onto the opera house floor. I place my hand over my chest trying to stanch the wound. I hobble on one good leg and stumble. Suddenly, Xana and Tol are there, supporting me.

"It's over," I call to the audience. They murmur with bewilderment.

"Edmon," Xana whispers. "How are you not dead?"

"What did you do to him?" Tol asks, looking back to Phaestion. He has not moved, his statuesque beauty forever locked like one.

"You were right. I couldn't win. All I could do was put him to sleep," I say weakly. "Forever."

"Let us help you," Xana says, trying to prevent me from falling.

I am grateful for my friends. I finally trust them to lean on, but I shake my head. "This one I have to do myself."

"Doctor," Tol says. "Something tells me I don't need to keep this for you anymore." He hands me the thin metallic card of Candlemas's tarot. The flickering image finally comes into focus. A man under the World Tree, sword in hand. *The emperor card.*

"Thank you, friend." I nod with acceptance. I grunt in excruciating pain with each step I take toward Phaestion's throne.

"All hail, Emperor Edmon Leontes of the Tao imperium!" a soldier in the ranks shouts.

The audience erupts in cheers because that's what is expected of them. In truth, this is a far more complicated turn of events. To the Lyrians, I am an unknown element. I've just defeated their conqueror, but they have no idea if I will be any better for them than he was. To the Taoans, I've just felled a demigod, and I didn't do it by blood. I did it by using a very esoteric ability, which seems almost like sorcery. I can only imagine what the rest of the Fracture who happens to be watching the broadcast will think. *What happens to a people when they witness the death of a way of life?* My next words will determine so much.

"I have defeated Phaestion of House Julii in single combat," I call out to the chamber, signaling for Taoan guards to remove the conqueror's frozen body. He will be put into stasis; in time, he will fade from memory. *It is probably the cruelest punishment of all,* I think. "However, I am no deity. I've not come to rule in his stead," I continue. "I come only to serve. From the ashes of war, peace must rise. For Nightsiders and Daysiders, Taoans and Lyrians, men and women, as true equals."

The reaction can best be described as confused as people turn to one another trying to figure out what this means.

"But first, there is a great evil that has come. It is a force of chaos that has entered the Fracture through a tear in the fabric of space-time. Our ancestors of Ancient Earth mistakenly let it in. The Miralians tried to stop it and failed. I call on you for one more battle. I call on you, warriors of Tao, citizens of Lyria, Market, Thera, Nonthera, Albion, Eruland . . . all worlds across the Fracture, to help me succeed where they have failed. If we do not answer this call, this thing that the Nicnacians call Los will continue devouring our worlds. I will not stand by while this shadow claims any more of our universe. I intend to fight it. Join with me!"

The people still don't seem to understand. *People need symbols,* I remember. Both my father and mother taught me that lesson. I told my brother Edvaard that was how I would use the blade he helped me craft. So I reach my hand out to the siren sword. I call it to my grasp one last time. It sings an aria as it sails across the room and into my hand. I hold it aloft. "Where I go, I may never come back," I say. "But if I succeed, I will return and reclaim the sword to help create that better tomorrow for us all." The blade screams as I plunge it down, vaporizing Phaestion's orca throne. The sword embeds into the stone of the opera house. The audience roars.

I turn to see Miranda Wusong. "I release you from your vows. Be free, Miranda," I whisper. Her lips quiver as she tries to hold back tears. She bows to me and then walks away.

The crowd rushes the floor. In their midst, I see a tall, silver-haired Nightsider with fierce pale eyes. Next to him is a beautiful Daysider woman with mocha skin and a proud gaze. They nod to me. *Ghosts,* I think, for when I look again, they have disappeared.

I'm strapped to the command chair of the Taoan flagship, dressed in the dark blue and silver of House Leontes. I tug at the collar as I shift in my seat and instantly regret it. The wound in my chest has not healed. I've used all my abilities. I can walk better now, the incidental lacerations on my arms are recovered, but something about the vibration of the siren steel in my chest . . . it's as if all my attempts to regenerate are met with some residual sonic force of Phaestion's weapon. Instinctively, I know I will never be the same.

The ship drops out of the Fracture Point at the head of the most massive fleet ever gathered. "Ancient Earth," I whisper as the view widens out of the purple tunnel of the wormhole.

"Or at least what's left of it," Tol mutters off to my right. Our ship is manned by a cadre of Tao's finest. I've insisted that they represent as many of the Pantheon's houses and even those of the underclass as I could muster. I've conscripted Lyrians who have shown technical expertise and flight experience as well, but only for my flagship. It would be unwise to restructure the entire military on the eve of battle. The diversity I demand includes Tol Sanctun as my navigator. *I wouldn't have it any other way.*

We've followed the coordinates along the spine of the Centra Fracture according to the memory of Enion Lazarus. The Fracture Corridor to humanity's original homeworld collapsed long ago. The portal in the Temple of Miral was the matriarchy's attempt at reopening a new point. This part of their plan worked, but corridors are two-way paths. Los was able to come through the new point they made. They created the temple and the seal to hold it at bay, and the cloud to try and stop it should the seal break. Talousla Karr's designer organics broke the seal, and the cloud failed.

Fortunately for us, Urizen had made another contingency. Before fleeing the barren Miral, she was able to force open a concurrent Fracture Corridor to the same end point, hidden for millennia by the High Matriarchy of the Nicnacians.

We gather our fleet, engage all saws, and cut our way through. Now we arrive at the head of the Fracture's spinal column, the destination where Ari awaits. I feel the darkness strongly here. Not only does it press down on my mind, but I feel it seeping through the wound in my chest.

"What am I looking at, Tol?" I grunt past the pain. A massive planet of swirling red and white hovers off our starboard view. A red storm in the center of the planet, like some great eye, bleeds its gas into space. It swirls into the vast and then wraps around a massive absence of light and color. The giant blackness it surrounds can only be one thing: a singularity.

"The planet was known as Jupiter. Named after an ancient king of gods. It was the largest in the Sol system and the fifth from the star," Tol says, his knowledge of Ancient Earth providing some useful information for once.

"The fifth planet?" I ask. "That would mean the star and all the other worlds closer to the sun—"

"I believe the sun was transformed into the singularity," Tol finishes my thought.

So our ancestors destroyed their own sun by turning it into a black hole . . .

"Comm, can you scope sector g-four?" I ask. The viewscreen zooms in. A silver orb hangs in space, close to the singularity. "It appears there's a space station."

"It's hanging on the event horizon, just beyond the critical pull of the singularity," Tol says. "It must be incredibly strong to resist the effects of gravity at that distance. Any closer and it will be pulled like taffy. My guess is, it's practically frozen in time, feeling the effects of space-time distortion."

"How much do you bet that's where we'll find Ari?" I respond. "Arc ship Eleth, do you copy?" I hail the fleet.

"Eleth here, leviathan," Washo responds. Armada has dropped out of the Fracture right behind my Taoan fleet. "Our astrophysicists are picking up massive amounts of black body radiation emitted by the micro black hole."

"Is that unusual?" I ask.

"Yes and no," he responds quizzically. It almost feels like we are all together again on the *Bentley*.

If only Welker were here, too.

"All singularities leak such radiation, but the amount being projected by this one is not in accordance with its mass. With that level of projection, the evaporation of the singularity would be imminent, but it's almost as if there are massive amounts of dark energy being plugged in from somewhere else, fueling it. And it's only getting worse. The only reason we're not dead right now is because that shadow body is being sucked through to Miral."

"Where's the Fracture Point the Mira created?" I ask. "Our scanners detect nothing."

"The singularity is obfuscating all vibrations that would indicate where a point is being opened for the shadow to go through. My language doesn't quite articulate the concept, but in essence, it's on the 'other side,'" he says.

"Doc . . . I mean your highness or your excellency? Or is it your grace?" I fire Tol a warning glare. "Right, what I mean is, I think we have a more immediate problem."

"Scanners picking up thousands of vessels, my lord!" an officer calls out.

"Leviathan to arc ship Eleth. Washo, do you see?"

"Wait!" Washo says. Thousands upon thousands of stinger vessels appear from the side of the planet and aim straight toward us. Behind the stingers is another gigantic arc ship, larger than any of the Nicnacians'. "Fuzon!" Washo exclaims with awe. "Edmon, it's the seventh arc."

"I know, Washo," I respond. "But that arc is not with us. You have to be prepared to destroy it if necessary."

Armada is now retrofitted with massive laser cannons and chain gun batteries in anticipation of conflict. The whale ships may look impressive, but they are still slow and highly vulnerable. If they are breached, it could mean the lives of millions. Fortunately, they are not the only addition to the fleet.

"Washo, release the Anjins," I command. "All Taoan vessels, form up on my mark. The Anjins will spearhead the thrust, and we'll follow them in. We need to get to that station!"

The Anjin mechs are released from the belly of Eleth. Their jet packs scream them toward the oncoming swarm of stinger vessels. "Xana, do you copy?"

"Metatron here," her warbled voice comes back.

"Carve us a path. Let's get our girl."

"Edmon," Washo hails. "There's a spike in the energy readings. Dark energy is pouring out of the singularity. We're too late!"

I feel the pressing of the shadow on my mind, the excruciating pain in my wound. *I will devour you,* it says, its voice as black as hell. The entirety of my crew clutches their skulls in horrific agony as if our minds are being destroyed cell by cell. Suddenly, a flash from the singularity blinds me for a second. When I look up, the silver orb of the station on the viewscreen seems to be pulling some of the singularity's blackness into itself. It seems a massive tug-of-war between the orb and the singularity.

Edmon, I feel Ari's whisper in my mind. *Hurry,* she says.

"It's Ari," I say over the comm. "She's fighting for us!"

"Here they come!" Tol shouts, pointing at the stinger vessels. "I feel like we should have some seventies rock music blasting or at least some John Williams's fanfare as ships explode all around."

"Shut up, Tol."

He smiles. "That'll do pig. That'll do."

"All ships prepare to engage!" I shout. "Open fire!"

It's utter chaos as the stingers swarm. I watch as the Anjins continue to carve through the enemy ranks, but they are overwhelmed. *This enemy knows our strategy.* One squadron of stingers has flanked us from above. They burn down on hot engines and blast through my ships, weaving in and out like a needle pulling thread through my ranks over and over again. It's too creative, too idiosyncratic to be one of Talousla Karr's generic brains. *I recognize that flying,* I think to myself. *I saw it the day that Miral was devoured by Los and a hero ran cover for his friends in gel pods.*

"They're heading for the arcs, sir!" an officer shouts.

They know we're aiming for the station. We need to pull them off us.

"Metatron!" I hail. "Divert the other Anjins to attack the seventh arc. Squadrons three through four, follow them. Hit that arc with everything you have."

The other armored mechs scream toward the unprotected ship, Fuzon. The stinger fleet redirects itself and swarms to cut off the attack. "Now Metatron, get me a path to that station!"

She fires forward with spear and shield, carving through ships, her chain gun rattling, blasting them back to the Miralian age.

My command ship rocks, and I'm thrown forward in the harness. "Hull breach, my lord. Depressurization imminent!"

"Sir, we've lost over fifty percent of our fleet!"

"All hands, abandon ship!" I yell over the ship-wide comm. "Get to the gel pods and activate distress signals . . . Tol, wait!" I stop my comrade as he unbuckles from his station.

"Doc, those ships are going to pick off the gel pods one by one," he says.

"I know. That's why I need to open a channel on all radio frequencies. I need the enemy to hear this. Target this stinger squadron," I say, sending him the readout of my command chair display.

"Channels open!" he hollers.

"Clay Welker, I know you're out there," I say into the comm. *Each ship is slaved to a human brain.* "It's me, Edmon Leontes. Xana, Tol, and Washo are here, too."

"You should have left me dead on Nonthera, Welker," I remember Jace Thrance said from aboard the Lion. *"Now, I'll have your gray matter as recompense for the money you stole."*

"My crew and I are trying to stop this shadow. We're trying to save Ari."

The flying of that stinger squadron isn't like any other pilot I've ever seen . . .

"Clay, I still have your letter to your boy Samson. I still promise to get it to him, but I need your help. I need to get to that space station."

Alarm klaxons blare. "Doc, we're leaking atmosphere. We have only a few minutes before we're out. We have to get to the pods."

"Welker, if you can hear me, help us."

Only silence radiates over the comm. But on the viewscreen, the cadre of stinger vessels I believed Clay Welker had been commanding veers off and heads toward the seventh arc where the majority of the forces are now engaged.

"Holy shizzle!" Tol shouts. "They're turning! They're actually turning."

The enemy stingers gather into a tightly controlled formation behind the lead ship. They loop past the seventh arc in concert and toward a group of older style rockets which float just above the arc's bow like a school of minnows around a gigantic orca. The viewscreen zooms in on the flotilla of smaller craft which are jagged, rusty, snarling pieces of machinery. *These are not the clean, organic vessels of the Designer Organics,* I realize. Rather they are the rag-tag minions Urizen has gathered, and who await the outcome of the battle for the chance to scavenge any tech from the losing side. They are pirates.

The lead stinger makes a stunning dive and pulls up at the last second beneath the pirate ships' defensive batteries. It zooms at the head of it's squadron, strafing the flotilla. Guns blazing, it rips open the hulls of the pirate fleet in one fell swoop, leaving a trail of hissing atmosphere and massive blue sparks of destruction in it's wake. I smile—*the last revenge of Clay Welker against Jace Thrance, Pirate Queen of Nonthera.*

"Washo?" I hail.

"I see them," he responds from Eleth. "Doctor, don't think I'm not joining you on that station."

"Come on, Tol!" I shout, unbuckling from my harness. My injury makes me slow, and Tol pushes us through the cockpit door just as the craft breaks apart. We slide into a gel pod together, and Tol pulls the lever to close the hatch and disengage the clamps.

We fire into space, sailing past the carcasses of burning ships. Xana flies Metatron close, protecting our pod from any incoming fire.

"Tol, can you maneuver us?" I grunt, holding my chest. I feel the wound seeping. Whatever it is that is happening with Los coming into our universe is accelerating the process of my injury. I can't stave it off.

"Firing thrusters. Aiming for the orb," Tol says. "Hey, Doc, this is kind of romantic, you and me this close, eh?" he says, trying to lighten the mood. "If you're an emperor now, and we got married, would that make me an empress? Or like a prince or a duke of something?"

"Just aim the pod, Tol." I scowl.

"Can't blame a girl for trying." He shrugs. "Trajectory is good. One problem: it looks like that thing is a perfect sphere. I don't see any docking bay or landing platform. How are we going to get inside? Okay, whoa!" Tol exclaims.

A portal of light emanates from the orb and grows in the porthole view.

It's an opening.

"Bring us in, Tol." I growl.

Tol carefully maneuvers us to match the rotation of the portal. We enter the spheroid and touch down on the interior wall. I quickly release the hatch of the pod. I roll out and almost fall to my death. Metatron snags me by the arm, Tol by the boot. Gravity is pulling us to the center of the sphere where another large metallic orb hangs. Somehow the interior orb's rotation and sheer density is generating centrifugal gravity. A roar of wind howls around us. Three figures stand on the large interior orb. Ari is unmistakable with her hair of flame, and the dark-robed and hooded figure can be none other than Talousla Karr. The third is a woman, operating some kind of command console before a gate that looks exactly like the portal in the temple beneath

Miral. Some dark creature presses against the membrane of the portal trying to break through.

A spacecraft, barely bigger than the gel pod Tol and I came in on, comes through the doorway to the sphere. Washo, in his red robes, sits behind the controls. I signal to him to meet us on the central orb. He nods.

"Let's do it, Xana!" I shout above the wind. Metatron's carapace opens, and her dragonfly wings buzz as she leaps into the air and flies. She touches down with a thud on the interior orb. Her armor's toe claws dig into the metal. She releases me and Tol, and we collapse to the ground. I hold my wound, feeling the heavy gravity of the interior sphere. Xana steps out of her armor as the hatch of Washo's ship opens, and he hops out.

"Ari!" I shout. The three figures turn to face us. Talousla Karr's eyes narrow.

"Edmon?" She stares at us in shock and then runs to us. "How did you get here? I only just arrived."

She hugs me, and I wince. "Careful, sprite."

"You're injured?" she asks worriedly. Then: "Your voice."

"I'll be fine," I grunt.

"He's the emperor of Tao now," Tol adds.

"Emperor of—?" She shakes her head, then sees her old friend and bodyguard standing aloof. "Xana? You've all changed. How long has it been?"

"Well, that's all relative—"

"Tol!" we all shout in unison.

"Time dilation," Washo explains, stepping forward. "For you, due to the intense space-time distortion of the singularity, the events of Miral will have just occurred. For others of us, it has been years, Ariel Lazarus."

"Washo?" She looks up in shock at the spypsy, who is indeed older now in body, but far older in mind. "You're not Washo. The brain," she realizes, scrutinizing his mannerisms and movements.

Washo nods. "Hello, Mother," he addresses the figure standing at the console who has regarded the reunion of the UFP *James Bentley* crew passively. "Do you recognize me?" he adds.

The face of Ahania Lazarus is almost a mirror of Ari's, but the silver streaks in her hair and the cool stare speak of boundless intelligence and experience. Were she not so clearly a human woman, I could see how an individual could look into her eyes and believe her a goddess that transcended time. "Enion," she says.

"Your deduction is sharp as ever," Washo says.

"I read your language, cadence, the subtle movements of your hands. You look different than I remember, though, daughter."

"The chrysalis chamber," Washo states.

"Why do you interfere at this critical juncture?" Her eyes narrow. "You know that I must open the portal to connect with the Sky Consciousness. I only hope that it can seal the breach between the two worlds and prevent the universes from collapsing into each other. The army I've built—"

"Does not stand with you, mother," Washo says. "Talousla Karr implanted in them subliminal programming. They serve his command."

Ahania Lazarus turns to the renegade spypsy, who stands with his hands tucked within his cloak. She sighs. "The truth is not always order and chaos, light and dark, but a gradient between. This should be a homecoming for both of you," she says to Washo and Ari. "I'm sorry."

Ari steps forward facing her mother, tears in her eyes. "You left when I was a child. You've been here on this satellite near the event horizon, so I understand that was only yesterday for you. But for me it was a lifetime of not understanding what was happening to me or why you would leave. I believe I understand it now. You're from Ancient Earth, aren't you?"

Ahania Lazarus turns to the console. Her fingers operate quickly as she speaks. "By the twenty-second century as measured by the calendar of my time, supercomputers helped humanity map and then solve the genetics of senescence. But the very intelligence that facilitated almost infinite longevity also brought about the end of sapiens. I was one of the last biologically born. We had discovered the Fracture and began slowly mapping and colonizing worlds of our galaxy, but the colonies we established were isolated and fragile. A population explosion and then implosion on Earth wrought havoc upon the biosphere. Plague ravaged those who could not afford the medical treatment of life extension. Survivors, already implanted with nanobots that could interface, sought refuge within the virtual worlds created by the artificial simulators of the day. They left reality for immersive entertainment. The Sky Consciousness was the result of all these circumstances."

"You mean that we created an AI to regulate the virtual worlds in which the last biological humans sought refuge?" Tol asks.

"You're thinking too small," Ahania Lazarus says, shaking her head. "We created many artificial intelligences. Humans implanted themselves with cybernetics to interface with those intelligences. Some of those intelligences created the virtual realities in which some biological and partly biological humans chose to live. The Sky Consciousness was the linking of all those various AIs. It is not one being, but a vast organism composed of many constituent parts interfacing all the time. Most sapiens also ceded control of their organic bodies to these silicon-based systems."

"So we partly evolved into and with the Sky Consciousness?" I ask.

"And in doing so, lost any sense that the needs of the previous evolutionary model were worth considering," Ahania concludes.

"The AI wasn't satisfied with their rate of expansion then," Ari says, picking up the story. "They created the singularity from Earth's sun and collapsed the Fracture that connected Earth to her colonies."

"Thus destroying all life on the planet," Xana whispers in realization.

Tentacles of dark energy press against the membrane of the portal.

"Why?" Tol asks.

"Machines cannot be expected to have the same goals as we do, unless specifically imbued with value systems that would mimic those of their creators," Washo says. "Even if they evolved from us directly. Do we share the same values as lower apes? If given a choice between expanding our civilization and protecting a species of monkey, which do we choose?"

"I suppose we could ask them from the afterlife," I mutter wryly.

Ahania Lazarus continues, "The entity we called the Sky Consciousness conceived of a universe that could expand faster, hold more data. The only way to access it was with a vast amount of energy. There was only one place to find such power—the Big Bang. The Sky Consciousness needed to return to a time when matter and energy was more densely packed and use that energy to fashion such a dimension."

"So the singularity was created—" Ari says.

"As a gateway through time," Ahania finishes. "The Sky Consciousness detonated a mass bomb into Sol. The nuclear reaction caused a chain of events that culminated in the collapsing of the star, the construction of a new black hole. The portal within the singularity allowed the Sky Consciousness to traverse the directions of time. It was they who seeded the universe with the Fracture in the first place, allowing for the conditions that would bring their ascendancy to pass."

"Dad was right! It was us. That's why it's laid out in the shape of a person!" Tol exclaims.

Ahania smiles, thin lipped. "An anthropomorphic thumbprint."

"If that's the case," I say as I limp forward, "then the Sky Consciousness did it on purpose. They created the Fracture knowing we would be here now, at this moment as well."

"Which one is this?" Ahania turns to Talousla Karr, who has been observing the proceedings with a reptilian interest.

"Edmon Leontes. A noble of Tao," he hisses.

"One of my wayward Kshatriya caste." She regards me as a science experiment when she places her blue gaze back on me. "Edmon

Leontes, if something occurs in a particular way, it is because the causality is fixed. The Sky Consciousness knew to create the Fracture in the past because they had already experienced it in the future. They were bound by the physical laws of the universe to do so. I was not the only sapien technocrat on Earth who was not given over to a virtual simulation, but I was indeed the only one who recognized the pattern of what the Sky Consciousness intended to do, my specialty being predictive mathematical equations. I fled through the collapsing Fracture Point with what data I could, including genetic templates I would use to build a human race according to my desired specifications."

"Something else came through when the Sky Consciousness opened the portal," Ari says.

"Los, the great destroyer." Washo places his palms in front of his face and bows his head in prayer. Talousla Karr sneers with contempt.

"For every action there is an equal and opposite reaction," Ahania confirms. "The Sky Consciousness entered the singularity they created, and in response an entropic antimatter was expelled into our own dimension of space-time. Meanwhile, I landed on the desert planet of Miral, took over the small colony there, and proceeded to rebuild civilization so that I could contact the Sky Consciousness before the critical threshold was reached and the universes imploded into each other."

"So you proceeded to create everything," Xana says. "The entirety of the Miralian Empire. The religion, the caste system . . ."

"All in order to quickly arrive at this moment with the technological support needed to communicate beyond the black hole. But why?" I ask, baffled. "Why create this new world with all manner of injustices, social and class divisions that have spawned countless wars."

"You hid our history," Tol adds.

"And the truth from all of us. Even the High Matriarchy," Washo finishes coolly.

"You could have chosen any permutation, any paradigm you wished," says Ari. "Instead you picked this . . ."

"I do not apologize for doing what was necessary," Ahania says flatly. Black mist creeps through the edges of the portal, finding weak points in the membrane. "Knowledge is our most precious resource. Imagine the almost complete loss of it with the destruction of Earth's star. There was only so much hardware I could carry aboard my ship. My projections placed the moment we are fast approaching within thousands of years. I had only that time to recreate a society and technology that took evolution billions. I chose the simplest forms, those with historical precedent, the one that my calculations determined was the quickest route to this destination, not the one that was perhaps the most beneficial to human psychological or cultural development. You will all have to live with that, but at least you will live."

"Why enslave a population to a dogmatic view of the world that held you as a god above all others and eschewed questioning and reason?" I say through gritted teeth.

"All creatures communicate, Edmon Leontes. Birds can parrot noises. Insects can cooperate in large groups because their genetic code specializes them to carry out unique functions within the hive. I encoded some of that logic into my new race, the castes that became you. Still, humans are separate because of their flexibility of language, which allows them to create imagined universes."

"Story is coding," Ari says. "Objective scientific method provides the best framework to achieve good explanations, but it doesn't give emotional context."

"We are feeling creatures," Ahania agrees. "I needed a narrative that would bind humanity to the task with a singular purpose . . ."

"To reconstitute a society that had the technology to make AI," Washo says.

"But only under my terms. One singular intelligence, not like the many that ran rampant back on Ancient Earth. Just one: Luper Candlemas, imbued with human values and intellectual framework, that was still capable of what I needed it to do—"

"End the darkness," says Ari. "How was Candlemas to do that, Mother?"

"The imagined reality of religion provided structure in human history to unite large groups in common cause. I believe the universe can be saved only by the Sky Consciousness closing the portal from the other side."

"How do you know?" I ask.

"Deduction. If the Sky Consciousness was able to harness the energy of the past, then it should theoretically be able to use it to seal the portal, stabilizing the time stream. I believe they left the Fracture intact in order that we might facilitate this purpose."

"Then you presume that the Sky Consciousness, too, was able to calculate our arrival at this moment?" asks Ari.

"Yes, and I needed people to believe they were fighting a great evil in the name of God to be motivated to do it. So I named the entropic force Los, a thing of ultimate evil that must be stopped."

"Why William Blake?" Tol asks, raising his hand.

"The old faiths were poisoned in my mind for the blood that was shed in their names. Iron Age rituals had no applicability to the reality I was creating. What was acceptable clothing? What one should eat on a particular day of the week? Esoteric rules were perhaps the derivative of biological wisdom for the time. It was chaff as far as I was concerned. I needed poetry, vague enough to not provide particulars, yet solid enough to contextualize the threat the universe faced. Day versus night. The architect versus chaos."

"You wanted a world where women ruled," Xana adds quietly.

"On Earth, the residual effects of patriarchy left a stain even in my day. Look at your Companion from Tao as proof that such hierarchies lead to cultic worship of violent and brutal nature," she spits out. "The ravings of a mad poet were about as sensical as any actual historical faith. I was quite satisfied to reformat the poet's masculine concepts to the sacred feminine."

"You delude yourself!" I shout above the winds that now howl. Sparks of electricity dance across the frame of the portal. "You created a lie. War, violence, racism, sexism . . . all resulted from your efforts at playing deity!"

"I set the conditions for a steady trajectory!" Ahania shouts back. Trails of smoke are now billows. "But if I wanted great leaps, I could not eschew humanity's creative capacity completely given my limited time frame. Our creativity is cause for insight and innovation but also deceit and war. The matriarchy of Miral's utter failure may be the greatest example of my plans gone awry." Ahania turns a baleful look on Washo. Behind her, the membrane breaks, and tendrils of chaos matter begin to seep through the portal into the sphere.

I feel it inside my head and scream. The wound in my chest tears open. All of us, save Ariel and Ahania, fall to our knees. "Mother, stop it!" Ari shouts.

"The life extension began to wear off. I slept for hundreds of years at a time, leaving behind a daughter in each generation to guard civilization in my stead. Enion did not heed my warning. She and the matriarchy attempted to open a new Fracture Point to Earth. They let the shadow come through and sacrificed the AI of Miral to stop it."

"Mother! Los is coming through!" Ari screams.

"It must come here as I must go there." The woman steps toward Ari and caresses her cheek. "You are my lion, my last child, bred from my own cells. I will bond with Candlemas, the human emulation program. Together we will enter the portal to the past, contact the Sky Consciousness, and close the gate. I wish I had had more times with you, my girl, but I birthed you to carry on in my stead. Now you can lead humanity beyond the outdated modes of thinking I forced upon them. You can make a society free of all the burdens of old patterns. You can create something new."

Urizen faces Los, which now emanates from the portal. She takes a step toward it. "Talousla Karr, bring me the Candlemas CPU." She holds out her hand.

"But Candlemas and the entirety of Roc-121 was destroyed," says Tol.

Even in my weakened state, I see Talousla Karr stand. A flash of metal in his hand. He lunges.

"Xana!" I scream. She leaps, but she is too late. The dark spypsy brings the curved blade up and stabs Ahania Lazarus in the back.

"Now I am become death, the destroyer of worlds," he hisses.

"Mother!" Ari screams. She rushes to Ahania Lazarus as the woman falls into her daughter's arms, light fading from her eyes.

Xana reaches the dark spypsy, who cackles with hysterical glee. He holds a communicator in his hand. He hisses into it, *"Nokejo numki!"* He thrusts the knife at Xana, who easily disarms him, snapping his wrist in one smooth motion.

"Wait!" I shout as Xana stands over him. Gritting past the pain, I hobble to the spypsy, held by a choke hold in Xana's powerful arms. "Why?" is all I can ask the deranged man.

"I created her." The renegade spypsy's eyes dart to Ariel's tear-streaked face. "I created you all." He grins at Xana and at me. "I'm not some religious fanatic. I am a scientist, the midwife of the next step of evolution. It must be my creation and mine alone that is matched against the darkness, and so the darkness must pour through. Ari, you are not the new alpha, but the new omega. I want you and your abilities, my glorious creation, tested against the darkness. I want to see your gifts matched against—"

Xana twists her arms violently, snapping Talousla Karr's neck. The creature slumps to the floor of the orb, blood trickling from his mouth.

I limp to Ari, who holds her mother, dying in her arms. She presses her forehead to that of Ahania Lazarus as death takes the woman.

"Knowledge . . . ," Urizen whispers with her last breath.

"Ari, we have to get out of here, or we'll be devoured!" I scream.

Los pours into the chamber. It swirls around the sphere. *I will consume you,* the voice of the shadow breaks in my skull. I scream and fall again, writhing on the ground.

The sphere shakes. We hear the sound of gunfire pinging the hull of the sphere. "The battle outside . . ." Xana taps an earpiece comm. "The designer organic fleet is hitting the sphere! We're cut off."

"No!" Ari commands, whether against me, the fleet, or the darkness, I don't know. She raises her head, and her deep blue eyes suddenly meet mine with a determination and power I have not experienced before. I feel her strength in me, helping me fight.

"I've touched her mind, Edmon. In her last moment, my mother told me what I must do." Ariel stands. The entire station quakes. My muscles can barely fight. I feel like I'm being eaten from the inside out.

"We're being pulled into the singularity," Washo says, groaning. "The universes will collapse into one another."

Ari approaches the console. All of us—Xana, Tol, Washo, and I—claw our way to her as the darkness devours the chamber. The space on the orb we can stand on decreases with every passing second. "Ari, what's happening?" Xana asks desperately.

"This orb has liquid metal circuitry. It is not capable of sentience on its own. My mother intended to activate it with Candlemas's CPU, which the designer organic army was supposed to recover from Roc-121."

"Except instead, they destroyed it!" Tol screams.

"Not completely," I realize. "Whistler told you, 'Remember the tarot!'" I pull the card from the pocket of my uniform. "Each of you!" I command. The crew takes out their cards. "He told us a fraction of his sentience was contained within each one." I just hope it's enough. He was searching for someone like Ari or her mother, an intelligence he could combine with.

"He gave me the special Tag patch as a test," Ari confesses. "It activated my latent abilities to transfer knowledge directly through the exchange of my cells. I believe I can survive the process of transferring his intelligence into my body."

The gypsy, the knight, the fool, the emperor . . . Washo, Xana, Tol, and I pull out each of our archetype cards. Tol even produces the hanged man and the knave from his duster, which he must have had for "safekeeping." Ari then pulls the card from her own pocket, and for the first time, I see its symbol. The empress. She takes the cards from us, each of them reflecting a portion of our own essences. They glow as she allows them to be absorbed into the liquid metal console. "Ari!" I scream. The inky vines of the shadow spread. They crawl over the bodies of Talousla Karr and Ahania Lazarus, feeding on them. We huddle together, and I feel their icy tendrils grip me. Blackness closes in around my vision as we are all swallowed by the chaos of Los.

Ari slams her hands into the liquid metal console, and there is a flash of white hot light.

Voices scream inside my head. "Get out!" I shout back. But one rises above the others. It's Ari.

Trust me, Edmon, she says.

I do. I'm not afraid anymore. I let her voice in.

I open my eyes to darkness and silence. I'm floating. No stars surround me, only black. I hear a breath and see I am not alone. With me are spirits—Xana, Tol, Washo, and even Welker. Before us is the gateway to the other world, yet instead of being filled with darkness, it is a doorway of pure white light. Standing between it and us is a woman of silver. Her face changes and morphs, becoming the puckish features of a girl I once knew. "Ari," I whisper.

The silver lady smiles. "Dear friends."

"Where are we?" Tol asks.

"Within the singularity. The space between worlds where time cannot touch us," she says softly.

"Then we are dead," comments Washo. "Torn apart by the enormous gravity well. Nothing escapes a black hole."

"I believe only some of us are dead, spyp," Welker adds slyly.

"Perhaps you would be dead, sister," Ari says, for Washo is also Enion. "But energy does not die; it only transforms. And you know not even a singularity traps all energy. I may have had something to do with you surviving in this case."

"Ari, what has happened?" I ask.

She looks at us all. "I joined with the metal circuitry and the residual sentience of Candlemas each of you provided. Together, in this new form, we pulled back the darkness from your world. Now all that remains is to close the gateway."

"You did it," I say. Tears form in my eyes. I see her before me a fully grown woman, the being she was always meant to become, and I am no longer afraid, though I know what will happen next . . . Somehow, I've known in the whispers of her memories since she gave me that fateful kiss above the skies of Miral.

"*We* did it," she emphasizes. "For I am the gypsy, the knight, the knave, the emperor, the empress, and yes, sometimes even the fool." She glances mischievously at Tol.

"We can finally go home," Xana says hopefully, but Ari makes no reply. Then Xana, too, realizes what my heart has already told me. "You're not coming."

"To seal the breach completely, I must do so on the other side," she says.

"But everything we've done, everything we've survived has been for you. We've worked so hard, come so far . . . you can't leave us," Xana pleads.

"Don't be sorry, love," Welker says to Ari. "We all have to do what we all have to do."

"You were a good man, Clay Welker," she says to him. "Someday your son will know it, too."

He nods at her, and then he looks at me as his image fades into the darkness. "Remember my letter, Doctor. My reliance is still on you . . ."

"Washo Tan, speaker of the Nicnacians," Ari says, holding her sister's gaze. "You've changed perhaps more than any of us. I am proud of you."

"Go in peace, Orc, daughter of Urizen." Washo bows his head to her, then he, too, is gone.

"I will not say that all foolishness is trivial, Tol Sanctun. We would not have survived without you, your sticky fingers, nor without the laughter you brought us," Ariel says to the lanky man.

For his part, Tol blushes and doffs the stovepipe. "Aw, shucks, Lady Lazarus. Just doing my part." He brushes away a tear as he fades. "Can I ask something? We're totally still back on Roc-121 in those chairs, aren't we? And this is some kind of like shared Matrix dream, right?"

Ari shakes her head, and the image of Tol is gone.

She turns to me.

"The whispers guiding me to help you—it was you all along, wasn't it?" I ask.

"We exist here beyond time," she answers. "Our kiss created the connection, but now that we are here, that connection transcends the boundaries of time. It is why you felt my voice long before we ever touched, and how I was able to channel the voice of the shadow to you as well."

"I love you," I say, my voice catching in my throat.

She comes close to me. Her cold metallic fingers caress my face. She leans in close to me. "The heart that loves can love again. You still have much to do, Edmon of House Leontes, emperor of Tao."

She floats back and finally confronts the last of us, Xana Caprio. "Oldest friend," she says. "There are no words we need speak." She lifts Xana's chin with her finger. She kisses the dark-haired warrior woman, and though she does not say anything as she pulls away, I know she has left a piece of her with Xana, too.

The silver woman floats toward the gateway of light. She pauses for the briefest of moments and turns slightly to look back at us, a faint smile on her lips. I feel a hand reach for mine in the darkness. Xana's. I hold it as we watch Ari pass from our world into the next, liquid metal coating the gateway behind her, sealing the rift between the worlds forever.

ABOUT THE AUTHOR

Photo © 2015 Vaney Poyey

San Francisco native Adam Burch is a classically trained theater actor who has appeared on ABC's *Scandal*, as well as numerous stage productions throughout the Los Angeles area. He is an accomplished martial artist holding a black sash in Wing Chun Kung Fu; is an avid guitar player; and has spent the last year living as a performer in Singapore while traveling to Cambodia, Indonesia, Japan, and China in his spare time. You may find out more about him at www.adamburch.net.